LANDOR'S
TOWER

Also by Iain Sinclair

LANDOR'S TOWER

or

The Imaginary Conversations

Iain Sinclair

Granta Books
London · New York

Granta Publications, 2/3 Hanover Yard, London N1 8BE

First published in Great Britain by Granta Books 2001

A CIP catalogue record for this book
is available from the British Library.

1 3 5 7 9 10 8 6 4 2

ISBN 1 86207 018 0

Typeset by M Rules

Printed and bound in Great Britain by Mackays of Chatham plc

In homage to the (film)maker of *The Blue Summer*
and the poet of *The Magic Door*

mighty, sinner's tower,

side-piercing spear,

world transposing in an hour

G.H.

Torn corner of paper, used as bookmark
in a copy of *Studies On The Legend Of
The Holy Grail (With Especial Reference
To The Hypothesis Of Its Celtic Origin)* by
Alfred Nutt. London: David Nutt. 1888.
Purchased as part of a job lot at a general
auction in Mid-Wales.

Book One

CREEPING WESTWARD

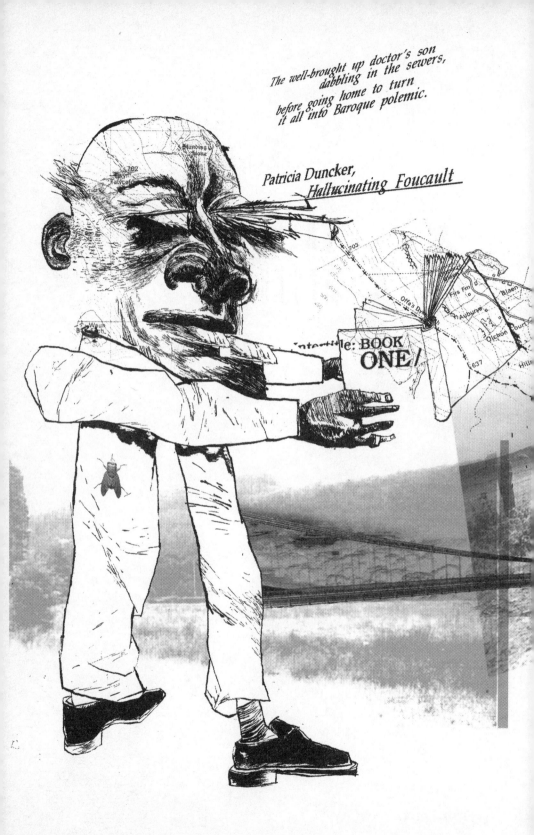

The well-brought up doctor's son
dabbling in the sewers,
before going home to turn
it all into Baroque polemic.

Patricia Duncker,
Hallucinating Foucault

*The well-brought up doctor's son dabbling in the sewers,
before going home to turn it all into Baroque polemic.*
Patricia Duncker, *Hallucinating Foucault*

1

No flies, no flies on Billy Silverfish.

Wide sky. A long straight road shifting and simmering in meridian sunstrobe. Borderland landscape censored by ragged hedges.

Clammy hands squeezed the piecrust indentations of the slippery wheel. Silverfish stamped on the brakes, skidded, wrestled the rented car, thumpthump, onto a low grass verge. What kind of car? A silver one: when their journey started, back in the heat of London, several lives ago.

Silverfish tore the upside-down map from Dryfeld's grip. He was melting inside his undervest, white shirt, leather waistcoat, sports jacket, corduroy car coat. His vest was sweating, his waistcoat was sweating. Tarry fingers slipped and slithered. When he locked his arm around Dryfeld's bullish neck, the dealer gagged.

'Brilliant. I entrust the map to a guy who's colour blind. That blue thing is a river, you asshole, not a road. That's the fucking Wye.'

'If you insist on dragging me away from civilisation, you deserve everything you get. You see a forest, I see ranks of future books.'

Dryfeld was enjoying this, feeding on Silverfish's rage. The pumping of the driver's agitated heart rattled the pens in his pocket.

'Forest? What forest?' he screamed. 'I come from Canada. Watched any airline commercials lately? Canada is one big forest in which three nebbishes buy books and one sells them. That's me. Numero uno.'

'You want to be a map fetishist, help yourself. I'm gone.'

Dryfeld wrestled his bulging book sacks from the back seat, leaving the door wide open, while he strode off between scraggy hawthorn hedges down an undeviating road.

Silverfish beat his head against the horn, crows lifted from stone fields. Now, in the midsummer heat, the flies were on him. They liked him, they loved this crazy Jewish diabetic. They described him, ravished him with tender, frenzied tongues. They bit and burrowed among the black hairs and salty craters of Silverfish's wrist. They danced in his sweet blood, extending and retracting a multiplicity of jointed legs. Recognising a member of their tribe, a future ancestor, they paid their respects, shitting into his invisible wounds. He was as fast as they were. He lived on bug time: burning, ranting, forcing. Silverfish chewed Benzedrine wool as a tranquilliser.

Suddenly, it was too much. The puff went out of the man. His sugars had been stolen, converted into alcohol. He oozed syrup. The broiled cabbalist pressed his cheek against the merciful chill of the windscreen; he rolled his beard, a coating of honey and fly-knots, between glass and bone. Leaning back, he fumbled in his breastpocket for a loose cigarette; demolished it in three deep drags, lit another from the stub.

Dryfeld, in a shimmer of distance, crossing between dark bars of shadow, printed by irregularly spaced trees, onto the pink road, was a squat, toadlike excrescence, burdened with two sagging pouches. A hunchback striding towards oblivion. The vanishing dot on a TV screen in a prairie motel. Silverfish smoked and watched. At the very last instant, before his fellow dealer was absorbed into that secret cleft of darkness where the hedges met, he cupped his hands, shouted.

'I don't need a map. I'll track us to Hay. You can smell the fear twenty miles off. I'm part Native American.'

When Dryfeld, back in Reading, had asked him *which* part, he'd ripped open the buttons of his shirt to expose the lettering on his undervest: *Seattle Indians*. 'My heart, bonzo, pure Kwakiutl. We walked over the Bering Strait in the first pogrom when your great-granddaddy was figuring out a way to barbecue his Diplodocus.'

Shivering in mirage distance, Dryfeld held fast to his occulted puddle. Veins pulsed in his throat. His tongue was too thick for his mouth. He chewed his lips for moisture. His cropped skull wavered with leaf-fish, a hairnet of cool foliage.

It was a standoff. Silverfish wouldn't fire the engine, Dryfeld wouldn't take one step down the road. Shadows lengthened. This is how they advanced through England, over the Severn Bridge, up the Golden Valley – along the border country, dipping, without consideration, in and out of Wales. Between bookshops they argued and fought, stopping frequently to go toe-to-toe under motorway bridges, in service stations, with the car jammed across a pedestrian precinct. They ate (slept when they could) on the move. The car was ankledeep in burger cartons and jerk chicken wrappers, insulin syrettes, Moose Head lager caps (Silverfish); silver foil dishes with bean curds and threads of sprouting stuff (Dryfeld). It was an ashtray, a depository for ravaged newsprint.

Dryfeld headbutted Silverfish in a Happy Eater outside Swindon; split his nose, cracked his spectacles, which were now held together with Elastoplast. Silverfish stamped on Dryfeld's ankle and kneed him in the folds of his kilt. In Middlesbrough they'd been stoned in the street. In Bath they'd been taken into custody for kicking down the door of a bookshop that was still closed for lunch at five o'clock. In Margate they fisted sand down the throat of a runner who propounded, at inordinate length, insane theories about T.S. Eliot's breakdown and the strategic impact of Margate on *The Waste Land* – instead of delivering the receipted bill he'd promised for the poet's stay at the Albermarle Hotel in Cliftonville.

Zero on zero. Nothing connected to nothing. In millennial Margate the only connections left were for smalltime pill-poppers, Balkan exiles trading charity chits, the officially disabled, hole-in-the-wall businesses that doubled hairdressing with the cashing of dubious cheques. Pawnbrokers fencing electrical goods to punters who couldn't afford electricity.

'The shelter overlooking the beach, the pier, the sands, that's the moment of fracture in twentieth-century consciousness, the birth of modernism,' the runner spluttered, spitting rock diamonds, as he lifted his face from the gritty poultice. 'Read it yourself, lads, on that wall. The Eliot anagram: TOILETS.'

Dryfeld and Silverfish were gone, on the road out, Canterbury,

Rochester and points west. The only books in Margate were hooky rent books and pseudo books, porn videos in plastic overcoats.

I watched them. Didn't I tell you? I was there in Wales; making up the numbers, taking my turn at the wheel. But it was too late, I'd lost it, the old fever. Disqualified. I'd turned grass, written up a previous trip, very much like this one; book dealing is cyclical, you visit the same places and the same people on a seasonal basis until one or other of you hands in the endpapers. That's how the pragmatist Dryfeld called it. Keep moving, accumulate, fill as many houses as you can with stock; undisclosed addresses, garages, back rooms, rented lofts. Take words out of circulation. Then vanish, disappear, die. Achieve immortality through rumour. Plot your suicide like a novel. That's right, I thought: the suicide novel. The unrepeatable confession. I'd opted out of my proper sphere of activity, gone public. I was banished from the freemasonry of the disaffected, the chronically peevish. Book dealers identified the wound, their sorry lives were dedicated to picking the scab, keeping it wet.

Dryfeld and Silverfish were manacled together by the exigencies of plot. One standing beside a filthy, mud-spattered car, elbow on the horn, smoking and coughing, and the other, balanced by two heavy canvas bags which he will not put on the ground, keeps his back to the man who is shouting his name, his *nom de guerre*: alibi, a.k.a., inhabited lie. A blood-red sun dropping, more slowly today than any other day, into the west. All of this is so theatrical. It doesn't have the nervous inevitability of proper fiction. I believe it, but I don't care about it. That's the problem. *One* of the problems: like the shooting pains in my left arm, trapped nerve or a failing heart, arteries silted up with motorway breakfasts; or the wrecked knees, the final demands, stalled imagination, tendency to repeat myself, short-term memory loss, tendency to repeat myself. Night sweats. Death fears. The commission to write a book on Walter Savage Landor and his gloriously misconceived utopian experiment in the Ewyas Valley.

What had Landor said? 'Intricacy, called plot, *undermines* the solid structure of well-ordered poetry.' Poetry for Landor, as fiction for the rest of us, was 'a sort of ventriloquism'. I could have Silverfish say anything I fancied, but I would still be talking to myself. Dryfeld could live or die. Or so, squatting beside Arthur's Quoit, I tried to convince myself. Not true. Such plot as there was, they owned it. I was lost without them. I couldn't write another word until they were back in the car, freewheeling into Hay. Cranking up another dialogue, another argument, a final reconciliation.

Silverfish was a dead man, cancer of the tongue, but I didn't know it. Not then. I couldn't do a Dickens and play for sympathy. Dryfeld was finished. As a name. He would abandon this way of life before I did, before I was aware of his decision. Of how that decision would be taken for him.

In this strange golden light, fossil forms in the stones of the megalithic cromlech came to life; constellations of mould gleamed like nicotine patches. The burial place with its balanced capstone was a petrified gun carriage, a folly. I remembered something I'd read, broken phrases, an early attempt to get this book moving. 'Big sky. Long straight road. Leading nowhere. Notches in the hillcrest: gun sites.' My pen was in my hand, my red notebook open on my lap. That was now. This is then. Trying to isolate details that might, at some unspecified future date, initiate a narrative. A set of photographs. A film. A poem.

The thing was that neither Dryfeld nor Silverfish, pressganged into contiguous but untouching autobiographies, realised that I had gone, that I had ever been there. Ungrateful clowns. They were rapidly and selectively transcribing their own diaries of this day. Dryfeld, blinded by sweat, unsuitably dressed for life on the road (in a four-piece yellow tweed outfit), saw himself as the hero in a fiction. I was eliminated and Silverfish was recast as a Vietnam vet (to excuse the psychosis): the Chopper Jock. That was Dryfeld's running gag: Silverfish, who could pilot a Chinook, napalm any jungle co-ordinate, fry flesh, was incapable of parking the hire car on the pavement outside a bookshop without tipping over rubbish bins, jamming traffic cones in the undercarriage and breaking the feet of unwary pedestrians. Low comedy masked despair. The silent shriek. This book business, the never-ending quest – paranoia, double-dealing, bounced cheques, gratuitous and long-premeditated insults – was a way of holding off the darkness, converting hell into a lurid cartoon. If it was funny it couldn't

hurt. The palms of Dryfeld's hands were black with blisters;
broken, bitten nails scored tramlines into the innocent meat of his
balled fists.

Silverfish was all undertext. Dryfeld, blustering against this mis-
guided odyssey, the lost hours when we couldn't be in bookshops,
had him all wrong. As I did. Silverfish, blocked autobiographer,
knew himself to be incapable of describing the events, actions and
reactions of a mundane life. What he was composing, as he waited
for Dryfeld to return (which that stubborn man would never do),
was a premature memorial notice in an antiquarian book journal.
His own obit. Honour among his peers. What else should he aspire
to? '. . . after a long and painful illness, stoically borne. William
Everard Silverfish, well-known to British dealers for his scholarship,
especially in areas of minor Eastern European fiction in translation,
will be sorely missed.' (What other sucker can we find for those
unsaleable dogs? *Missed*? I'll drink to that. One less bounty hunter
out in the territory. More stock to fight over. Here's to you, Billy
boy. Wherever you are.)

Our accidental parking spot in the Welsh borders was a place of
revelation, off-piste, but sited at a notable conflux of energies. All
my narratives begin here. You have to make a proper entrance,
arrive by the most propitious route. This I had arranged. I was at
the wheel when we left Clifton (two shops and eight junk pits
gutted in two and a half hours, a sluggish start). I guided them over
the old Severn Bridge into Chepstow, an estuarine hamlet living on
its memory rind, shuddering from the loss of status when a bypass
carried traffic away from the steep descent to the quayside. Here,
under red cliffs, were the ghosts of transported Chartists from
Newport. Here, against the black castle walls, perish all republicans
and freethinkers. Here begins the cussedness of the forelock-
tugging, piss-in-your-boots Welsh, border folk bred into playing
one side off against the other, trimming to a shifting wind. The
sense, standing on the battlements, staring upstream, of exile; dense
woodland, reaching to the water's edge, hinting at malarial scenarios, parallel world jungles.

There was nothing in the Wye Valley to hold us. Silverfish had
no taste for the picturesque. Dryfeld loathed the countryside;

between bookshops he would bury his head in catalogues. His sense of geography was functional and perverse: Chinese take-aways (the only places where he watched television), newsagents, grease caffs, charity shops (for ties, jackets, shoes), barbers (Trumper's of Jermyn Street), swimming pools, railway stations, massage parlours, morticians. The rest was invisible. Tintern Abbey, he judged, very reasonably, to be retail landfill: adequate parking facilities, easy access to the M4, M5, M50, decent stone left by the Cistercians, culture chaff scratched in the sand by pre-vious tourists. One man's sublime is another man's heritage wrapping paper. Poem-things for honey pots, J.M.W. Turner's lightshows revamped for wine labels.

We were agreed (try York, Winchester, Lincoln, Durham), it was a waste of time to hit bookshops within bell range of some notable hunk of ecclesiastical architecture. They thought they were doing you a favour. Locked glass-fronted bookcases with stock displayed like holy relics, unwanted desiderata, near-first editions in tattered wrappers unimproved by a glassine makeover. We were in and out of the Tintern shops in seconds, a yawn of country stuff (chewed up and bloody with squashed insects), a pederasty of kiddie colours, dormitory romps, strict discipline in alpine chalet schools, yakking bunny rabbits. Dryfeld bought nothing. Silverfish refused to look at such horrors. 'Do you have any *real* books?' he asked the snivelling proprietor. (These come in two sorts: the kind who ask what you're interested in, then deny they've ever heard of it, and the ones who force stock into your pockets, pour lukewarm coffee down your throat, beg you to abuse them.) To the scorn of the others, I made a small purchase: a well-weathered copy in black cloth of Eric Gill's *Beauty Looks after Herself*. I had no special interest in the old goat, but vaguely recalled that, like Landor, he had tried to set up some sort of community at the neck of the Ewyas Valley at Capel-y-ffin. 'The art of the spider is the art of God,' Gill wrote. This was a mistake, buying a book that could never be resold. I consoled myself by studying the shape of the stains on the endpapers, the subtle gra-dations of decay, chemical compromises between nicotine pulp and the damp of some riverside cottage: bruised greys and blues, the pink of wild thyme breaking from the hinges. An aerial map of a landscape still to be penetrated. Gill's abbey in a fug of vaporous conjecture.

They had gone, or it was too dark to make them out. Too dark to complete my tour of the megalithic stones. I was marooned by my own design. The sweep and rush of the energies of this place had been enough to hotwire those hairtrigger psychotics, and they were right. The carefully chosen burial site aligned – using creases in the surface of the igneous rock as a sighting device – with the topography of the hills, with other notable features (including the monolithic Dryfeld). That's why Alfred Watkins, author of *The Old Straight Track*, apologist for ley lines, man of business, haunted this country. It had been the locus for his original revelation: everything connects and, in making those connections, streams of energy are activated. You learn to see. You forget to forget, to inhibit conditioned reflexes. You access the drift. Watkins was an outrider, a brewer's rep. If he were still in the game he'd be jockeying a Ford Mondeo around the motorway system, stumbling on the karma of the M25, speculating on London's orbital road as a prayer wheel, a dream-generator on which the psychic health of the city depended.

Watkins was a photographer, an inventor, a champion of the pin-hole camera. The stalling (or recomposition) of time seemed to complement the transcription of the ley lines, when, in fact, it was creating relationships that would not otherwise have acquired any significance. Photography is a fiction, a partial reading of landscape, a remodelling of the flaws and contours of the human face. Riding west out of Hereford, over these hills, auditioning future photographs, Watkins suffered his moment of inspiration. His grey images, fated to bleach in reproduction, are stupendous in their dullness and quiet obscurity. Better to have built himself a chamber of transformation, a cloud chamber, a room-sized version of his pinhole camera. But he was fated to burden himself with box after box of static scenes: dim arrangements, green pathways bleeding to grey, chlorophyll light repressed and silenced. Watkins's photographs of mounds and steeples and solitary stones did not chart the lost culture of a people in sympathy with the planetary circuits; they fixed their own time, the twenties. Outdoor coves in sturdy boots smoking stiff pipes as they rest on a gentle tump. Long-striding chaps with cod-scientific gubbins in their capacious pockets. Measuring devices. Stout twine and a thingummy for taking stones from horses' hooves. Drill that brain pan, let in Babylonian starlight.

What happened, so I believed, staring at Watkins's photographs, was that the ley hunter was seduced into making journeys. It wasn't the alignments that mattered, or any of the individual stones, it was movement. *Track Sighted on Notch, Llanthony*: that was the frontispiece of Watkins's 1925 publication. Movement fires the imagination, carrying us back across suppressed landscapes we remember but have not yet located. There is something in this borderland, the transition between shale, greywacke and Old Red Sandstone, that haunts me. Watkins refers to the occultist and imperial geographer Dr John Dee, and his excavations among the Longmynds. A great treasure remains undiscovered (or undisclosed). Watkins repeatedly photographed the area around the ruins of the Augustinian priory at Llanthony. His prints become doors swinging half-open or half-shut, according to taste. One page in *The Old Straight Track* confronted me with a triptych, panels for a pagan altarpiece. They summarised the novel I couldn't write.

These narrow photographic strips had everything my Landor book would never achieve. Better to cut my losses, pull out before it's too late. I can't hold it together. I haven't begun to plot the moves, build up the characters, and already there's too much narrative, too many digressions. All I wanted, and I'd engineered it quite successfully, was a knockabout scene with two bookdealers on a long straight road. Midsummer's Day. The privilege of being out in the air, on the gentle slope of a hillside above Bredwardine. With the prospect of great finds in the town of books still to come.

I was frozen, mesmerised by Watkins's arrangement. In his left-hand panel was 'The Dodman', a horned snail crawling across the pages of a book (which might, in fact, be a table). Dodman or deadman. Dod was, Watkins suggested, another name for a wand or stave, used in measuring distances, confirming alignments. Quite right. I had seen these priapic fellows before, gathered from east London cemeteries, set to work on maps, laying down silvery, alchemical tracks. Death as a snail. ('I'm a regular Dodman, I am,' said Mr Peggotty, by which he meant snail, being an allusion to his being slow to go.) Slow to launch. The snail crawls (we assume) towards Watkins's central panel, which reveals *Llanthony-Ley Sighted through the Abbey to a Steep Track*. Sited, as I suspected, from the place where Walter Landor tried to erect his senatorial manor house. The right-hand panel used staves to carry the ley on towards a notch in the hill, the notch that provided Watkins's frontispiece.

Time was thin here. I couldn't breathe. It was like the account my great-grandfather left of crossing the Andes, blacking out, falling from his mule, remounting, falling again; until they descended into the mist, a landscape that was to haunt him for the rest of his life.

Arthur's Quoit. Which Arthur? Arthur Llewelyn Jones who became Arthur Machen? Tennyson's King Arthur? The bearded laureate was here, he stayed at Caerleon. They all did, they passed through, leaving their tracks, snail trails. They must be acknowledged. My great-grandfather, it was his Christian name: Arthur Norton, Fellow of the Royal Colonial Society, Member of the Aberdeen Philosophical Society. Etc., Etc.

They took a skull away, to reflesh it with laser beam scans at the National Museum of Wales in Cardiff; a poor facsimile. Five thousand years old, they said. Bright as a waxwork. A being, wrenched out of deep time, infecting the perpetrators of the deed. Padding the bone map with borrowed skin. Projecting a feeble narrative on an object placed in the ground with circumspection and awe. These are stories to be discovered, not told.

I would drop down into Bredwardine, follow the ley towards the hillock known as the Knapp. I would search out the grave of the local diarist Francis Kilvert, another hill wanderer, another unfulfilled man.

The publisher Longman declined to take on, even at the author's expense, a slim volume of parsonical verses. This courteous refusal came a few months before Kilvert's death. In the late nineteenth century, with a swifter and more efficient postal service, Kilvert received the bad news only four days after he sent off his manuscript.

At the end of his story, the story of the journals that were to grant him posthumous fame, he begins to fulfil modest ambitions. He is appointed vicar of a small rural parish and he marries Elizabeth Anne Rowland (who outlives him by thirty-two years).

His death grants a book he had no expectation of publishing a nice conclusion and an unintended poignancy. Worldly success, even in a small way, had already undone the quiet melancholy, the barely disguised pleasure Kilvert took in his encounters with dark-eyed schoolgirls, farmers' daughters. They spoiled the fireside conversations (unachieved Henry James novellas) with Mrs Venables, his superior's wife at Clyro. Kilvert's afternoon walks, his long tramps over hard country, anecdotes of past wars, confessions of peasant violence, granted him a privileged status as conduit for the spirit of place. Then, as the diary comes to its close, he achieves a moment of clarity and self-consciousness. The pitch of the prose loosens up as the writer accesses (he has earned it) a prevision of death. The hypochondriac is justified at last: a white stone cross, honours noted, title and degree. 'He Being Dead Yet Speaketh.' He is separated from his wife of five weeks who is buried in the southwest corner of the new churchyard, on the far side of the lane.

As I walked in the Churchyard this morning the fresh sweet sunny air was full of the singing of the birds and the brightness and the gladness of Spring. Some of the graves were white as snow with snowdrops. The southern side of the Churchyard was crowded with a multitude of tombstones. They stood thick together, some taller, some shorter, some looking over the shoulders of others, and as they stood up all looking one way and facing the morning sun they looked like a crowd of men, and it seemed as if the morning of the Resurrection had come and the sleepers had arisen from their graves and were standing upon their feet silent and solemn, all looking towards the East to meet the Rising of the Sun. The whole air was melodious with the distant indefinite sound of sweet bells that seemed to be ringing from every quarter by turns, now from the hill, now from the valley, now from the deer forest, now from the river. The chimes rose and fell, swelled and grew faint again.

2

Coming up Barnet Way into Stirling Corner roundabout, no problem. Then, poor sod, he can't get out. Clocked on tape. I saw the tape, a degraded copy. Traffic helicopter, one of the digital channels. You'd love their stuff: 24-hour motorways and suburbs. Overpasses, underpasses. Giant hoardings with photographs of desert resorts, monumental bosoms. More like a surrealist travelogue than somewhere humans would choose to live. Halal butchers, Killarney Motors. Welsh Harp reservoir. Where do they get these names? A stone circle, I'm not kidding you, laid out on a traffic island.

Round and round he spins. Not quite long enough for the mobile noddies to take an interest. He should, like every other day, have come off onto the A1 and into Borehamwood. To GEC. Punch his card. Never late in seven years. Company man. I thought he'd been in an accident, bandage around his head. Must be confused, I decided. Doesn't know where he is. Then I discover he's a proper north London boy, a Sikh. Kenton. Ever risked it? Sounds more like a band leader than an excuse to take out a second mortgage. 'Harrow's back passage,' they call it. Cancer of the colon with mock-Tudor trimmings.

Next thing we hear, guy's in Bristol. Never been west of Legoland in his life. Kenton/Denham, Denham/Kenton, that's it. The occasional run up to Birmingham, where there's family. A Sunday whizz around the North Circular. Sikhs aren't supposed to cop for religious pilgrimages. North Circular must be the exception. They've got IKEA while the Hindus paddle barefoot through their ice-cream temple in Neasden.

Balder Singh played squash, bit of DIY. New semi. Married. Wife expecting. They kept to themselves. Nothing known. Nothing suspected.

The spooks are floating rumours about a millennial cult, fire-worshippers in Harlesden. I don't buy it.

Never been one for holidays. Back to India twice, no other breaks. PC at home if they wouldn't let him into the office. And here he is, splashed across the pavement under the Clifton Suspension Bridge, burst fruit. 'Just another jumper,' say the local fuzz, 'trousers round his ankles.' Car unlocked, key in ignition. If I was going to take my first-and-last unsupported flying lesson, I'd make damn sure I was far enough onto the bridge to land in the water.

That's all I've got at the moment. Balder had been working on underwater guidance systems with Marconi. Ran some kind of simulator. The booklet called it 'a computer suite which embodies operational software and control hardware identical to that being used in the weapons being developed'. There were whispers that he was about to quit. Liquidity, more readies. Having talks about a new job, financial consultancy in the City.

Didn't get anything from the wife. She's in shock. But Kenton is something else, one of those places you visit for a funeral. Houses built for the bringing of bad news. Right opposite where they lived, I filmed it, there's a topiary cross growing out of a hedge. You'd think the Klan were moving in. I pitched it to the Sundays. Didn't want to know.

Send the cheque, c/o Mrs Franks at the White Hart in Portishead.

I listened yet again to Kaporal's tape. There was something addictive about it. Fantastic as seventies television, *The Avengers*; too much plot, too little time. My unease began with the voice, an educated drone in which humour apologised for itself, intelligence cupped a hand across its mouth and coughed. It didn't help that it sounded as if he was making the recording while on the receiving end of an amateur, but enthusiastic, blow job. You could hear the bed springs, sink-plunger gobblings and, further off, coarse golfers, seagulls swooping on sewage outflow.

Kaporal had been institutionalised, unmanned by too many years rummaging in closed files on behalf of defunct production companies. East End lags, getting their pension from turning up at funerals, reckon twelve years inside will do it, break you beyond the point of repair. Twelve months in Shepherd's Bush, the White City gulag (travel, health and social life taken care of), beavering anonymously for the BBC, on left-field projects that will never see the light of day, permanently disables the spirit. Kaporal was spooked, washed up; on the case. A few bad relationships in which he had made too heavy an investment took their toll. Now he'd gone to ground.

I got his address (there was no phone) from the film-maker Jamie Lalage. Lalage tossed Kaporal a crust whenever he could; as a researcher. That's what the man did best, lose himself in libraries everybody else believed to be closed down. He was good, he had a rare feel for 'post-contemporary ruins': nuclear silos, the prophetic debris from experimental aircraft, bunkers hidden beneath farmhouses in the Essex countryside. The Aztec West Business Park, a few miles outside Bristol, was his major inspiration. A site, he claimed, of enormous significance: the design of the traffic islands, incorporating stepped pyramids and serpentine motifs, linked a necklace of ancient holy wells with the hungry spirit of enterprise culture. J.G. Ballard praised a booklet of Kaporal's photographs, vanity-published: 'A disturbing and equivocal record of the covert architecture of our era. In the canted floors of these multistorey car parks, rephotographed from surveillance tape, we recover the black box flight-recorder from which the occult narrative of an expiring century will be assembled. Jos Kaporal's impersonal images have a chilling beauty to which traditional artists can no longer aspire. Their inevitability is such that they appear to lack an authorial signature. I can offer no higher praise than to recognise this elegant, matte-black file as unmediated evidence.'

Kaporal had perfect pitch, lips that didn't move. The voice of a statue. His tapes were retrospective. He spoke like a man clearing his throat of congenital hairballs. Listening to his reports brought about my current lethargy.

The light was weak. Autumn in my mean-windowed cottage on the edge of the Black Mountains was like winter in the Outer Hebrides. Hebrideans, I remembered, signalled the hour of the wolf by starting the day's drinking; postmen appeared, a bottle in each pocket, to share the old hippies' weak, homegrown dope.

In the Welsh borders there was no such happy arrangement; the farmers and grim, chapel-going bourgeoisie (for whom the poisoner Herbert Armstrong was the role model) plotted ways to expel the sorry rump of travellers who huddled in threadbare tepees, shacks made from sections of corrugated fencing, on the slopes below Hay Bluff. Self-important local politicians (rival bookdealers) fought for office on promises of zero tolerance.

'I'll hire vigilantes to bulldoze the camp site and crucify every last man, woman and child,' announced the *faux*-aristo inbreed, rentier of a gin-distilling dynasty who made their fortune on the wreckage of the London poor. This bumbling writ-dodger, infamous throughout the booktrade for his rubber cheques, had been forced to order, sight unseen, containerloads of books-as-ballast from fleeing African despots, then pad out the rest of his shelves with ex-lib fodder, Robert Maxwell's remaindered hagiographies of Balkan warlords. The castle-squatter's rival, a shadowy metropolitan businessman with rumoured Sicilian connections, who was trying to lose enough paper wealth to make divorce viable, was more direct: 'I'll nuke the scum. I don't pay a retainer to Hereford for nothing. Trust me. The regiment won't let you down, they're the most reliable beaters in the county. They scare up birds with thunder-flashes, then strafe the lot.'

Contacting Kaporal was like running a screen test through John Dee's crystal, it was a way of reading my own future, the next chapter of my never-to-be-completed Welsh novel. Kaporal was crazier than I was, knew more, had better contacts. He was the obvious fall guy, the surrogate. Studying Kaporal's baggy face in an article I'd clipped from one of the broadsheets, a provisional account of a film, his current work in progress, convinced me that he was the man for the job. Existential terror was palpable: he stared out of the frame, spreading his hand on the interrogator's table, gripping the pen with white knuckles. (The Swiss-American photographer Robert Frank reckoned that hands were the most important element in a portrait. 'Always show the hands.')

On good days, Kaporal was a fatality in remission; when the light was too harsh, you noticed the stitches, ears attached wrong end up. A thick, bulb nose. Recidivist's hair, basin-cut in the dark with a pair of nail clippers. Kaporal, nothing like me in temperament and background, was the wilted Polaroid of what I might become. If I didn't get out of Wales, fast.

Who else would touch this gig? Something had gone wrong in the city, in London. Hackney was a hive in which none of the bees spoke the same language: squatters in tower blocks could read in bed by the beams from police helicopters. Every morning new jumpers were scraped off the tarmac. From the suburbs, the drift was west. Anything beyond Heathrow was a suicide note. Travel further than you could walk in a day and you were dead. But the lemmings still queued for their exit visas. All roads led to Bristol. What was going on?

I'd snacked the usual conspiracy brews, spent hours poring over maps that listed heavy clusters of defence industry establishments in the Thames Valley corridor. Asian technicians were making metaphors literal. They had discovered something ahead of the rest of us, tapped into the Big One: riding into the sunset. Crossing the bar. Treading air. Dancing in the empyrean.

An accredited technician from Walthamstow finished work for the day, got in his motor, straight down the M4, left swerve to the M5, through leafy suburbs and the dramatic pink-grey limestone of the Gorge, to park overnight on Clifton Downs. By the water tower. Next morning he turned off the road, bumped over wet grass towards a circle of trees known as the Seven Sisters on Durdham Down. Pines growing on the site of a supposed Bronze Age barrow. He attached a newly purchased rope to the trunk of one of the trees, looped it around his neck; put the car in forward gear and took off. Messy. Over-elaborate.

Kaporal's tape was very thorough. The researcher was beginning to enjoy himself. The weird details of this case conformed so precisely with his view of the world: random surrealism speeding towards that pinpoint of white radiance where everything fuses in a flash of enlightenment and annihilation.

There were three 'partially smoked' Hamlets in the car. That's what the report said. As if anyone would want to do more than get a quick burn from a Hamlet, a carcinogenic preview, before chucking it. Point is, Dipmal had a THANK YOU FOR NOT SMOKING notice on the dash. He was fanatical about it, keen hockey player. Didn't drink, religious.

He stops off at a service station on the way down, buys cassettes and leaves a long rambling message for his father. They're trying to suggest he knew Bristol, worked at Filton, sweetheart contracts with British Aerospace, surface-to-air guided missiles. Difficult to crack those files. There's talk of a thing with his supposed landlady. Doesn't play. I stayed there. A knocking shop, whites only. The woman's out all afternoon, servicing shift workers in Avonmouth. But she's home by the time her kid's back from school.

Someone's writing this one up ahead of us. Nothing fits. No condoms in the car. A junk script crying out for a lazy hack. A pb original in the raw.

Could you make the cheque out to 'Lalage/Evil Eye Films'? He'll put it through his company, save me from VAT.

I'd gone looking for Kaporal on my way to Wales, the final recce before I got stuck into the Landor novel. My car was freighted with emergency provisions, bedding, books, charts, photographs: 'research materials' as they might flatteringly be described. When I said Lalage had given me an address, I was exaggerating. It was more of a map reference, one of his throwaways at the end of a dawdling monologue about something entirely other.

'Kaporal's slacker generation, grafts when he has to. Once you've pressed his switch, that's it. Family have been trading down for generations: land, military – picture dealers calling in favours, second-rank stringers in former outposts of Empire, chemmy greeters, pimps, the Beeb. The addresses have got skidmarks: Highgate, Fulham, Battersea, Herne Hill. No way back once you cross the river. Couldn't tell you *exactly* where to find him. A church in West Drayton, St Mark's, St Martin's, something like that, you'll pick up the Green Way. Over the footbridge, skirt the pond, there's a farm thing abutting the burial ground of another church. He's there somewhere. I ring the pub, leave a message for him to contact me. He knows I don't go out much these days. Harmondsworth, that's what it's called. The graveyard gate has a pernicious sound. More of a scream than a squeak.'

I'd sold him the odd book but I scarcely knew Lalage, and here I was setting off on a fool's errand on his say-so. His voice had that effect on civilians. Authoritative, world-weary, a little impatient. Impressionable young women found its wounded melancholy devastating, but resistible. The precision, the pacing, were quintessentially English, which is to say quintessentially fraudulent; disguising, in Lalage's case, a family of lunatic keepers in Galway (where a French-sounding surname hinted at the old alliance).

Kaporal had worked on Lalage's only *succès d'estime*, a festival makeweight called *Amber Lights*. I now considered this forgotten film, shot in the year of Margaret Thatcher's accession to power, to be a prevision of the nightmare that was to come, a poetic meditation on collective inertia. Spiritual paralysis, in Lalage's case the loss of faith, was countered by a somnambulist's drive to the west.

Kaporal travelled the back roads to Bristol relentlessly. He interviewed petrol-pump attendants who claimed to have been working on the night of the Eddie Cochran crash. He talked to crop circle freaks mooning around the environs of Silbury Hill. He monitored military transports to the camps on Salisbury Plain. He visited a West Country GP who wrote extensively about Albigensian reincarnation. Cathars for courses. He picked up pub yarns about a disgraced Liberal politician's adventures, high and low, in the dockside meat racks of Bristol and the Georgian terraces of Bath. He kept pushing until he convinced himself that he had a personal watcher, an extra shadow. *They* were after him. He was being lined up for a wet job. Or so he hoped. Most of the white suicide victims from the defence industry were listed as 'auto-erotic fatalities', botched mummifications; yards of clingfilm around a screaming mouth, plugged with an oversize Jaffa. That was the only satisfaction Kaporal was likely to achieve: justified paranoia. State-funded sex. A library of porn tapes downloaded at the expense of Special Branch. His existence, his significance, acknowledged in his extinction. If they eased out the deep drawer in the freezer compartment, Kaporal's eyes would still be open.

The fields alongside the motorway were planted with golden cereals, too bright for their own good. Poppy haemorrhages. I was happy to have postponed, if only for a few hours, my expedition to the border country. This was more country than I could cope with, country with a function (it screened the incoming procession of planes). Furled poplars baffled the susurrus of heavy tyres on a hot road. Dark shapes drifted at two-minute intervals above an indeterminate horizon of low-level storage units and double-glazed Alamo hotels. The Stars and Stripes were so well starched that they stood stiffly out from white flagpoles. Butterflies insinuated. Startlingly blue dragonflies, translucent and without content, hovered at the verges of the Green Way, confirming its validity. Kaporal could have feasted on blackberries. I smeared my face, crammed in a fistful, licking the varnish of crop sprays, sucking juice from sweet purple warts.

The gate creaked, as Lalage said it would. I tried it several times, relishing the tonal range of the unoiled hinges. Then realised, hearing the slam of a metal door, that the creak acted as a warning system for a broken-down caravan lodged in the hedge at the corner of the burial ground like a piece of agro-industrial debris.

Tartan curtains twitched. There was no response to my knock. I was happy to bide my time. Sunlight polished the gravestones. I filled a green plastic bucket from a high-pressure tap. That was another good sound, the spit and rush: a drench of deadheads, marigolds, string bundles rotting on granite slabs. I floated on this suspension from the forward momentum of my life; the view across the scrubby fields to the distant and remorseless agitation of the motorway, the road west. How often can we take time out to assess our mortality – without nightsweats, those luminous green digits that always read 3.33? Three sleepless hours before another grey dawn.

I trudged back to the caravan. It was cruel to keep Kaporal trapped in his sweatbox on a day like this. He'd be much happier in the saloon of the local. Cigarette fug, idiot rattle of fruit machine, old boys yawning and farting. Fat-lipped slatterns, blotting up lurid syrups, past hope of worthwhile action: franchised torpor. That's where Kaporal belonged. Lalage had debriefed him over plenty of shapeless afternoons, one anecdote carrying just enough heft to justify another trip to the bar. 'Make mine a double and I'll give you the SP on the BCCI warehouse fires.'

'Lalage,' I shouted, between thumps on the flabby panels. 'Lalage said you might be interested in some work, a paying gig.'

No response. I counted rusty rivets. The door swung open, a large boot looming out of the darkness to stop it closing again. Kaporal was a big man, big but soft, invertebrate; his leg could reach daylight without its owner having to move from the bunk. The interior of the caravan, even on such a bright day, was shady; fixtures and fittings unsure of their outlines. A table decorated with a waxy orchard of gutted candles.

'Got a straight?' Kaporal's hands were shaking too much to finesse a roll-up; he spilled tobacco shreds into his lap.

'Sorry, don't smoke.'

That took care of conversation. Without advancing from the doorway, I logged the chaos of Kaporal's immobile home. I kept very still. Any sudden move had the drum rocking wildly on its slack-wheeled cradle. It was like being out in the Channel, this sur-vivalist set. Unwashed mugs in a bowl, cans without labels. Cheap lavatory paper, the waxy kind (liberated from the pub toilet), scrolled out and covered with a tiny and rather elegant script. Photographs that might have been borrowed from police files, or intended as publicity stills for one of Lalage's TV films. (Lalage had drifted into the outer reaches of the digital networks. He no longer shot original material, he assembled 'found' footage over which he could lay down, in his own voice, a doleful commentary.)

'What's the pitch?'

'There's no commission. We're on a promise, between depart-ments at Channel 4, waiting for an editor who's been shafted and who wants to stiff his successor by signing a cheque for a career-threatening fuck-up. That's our speciality. We're the virus in the system, a corporate time bomb. You'll get your percentage, cash-money.'

'Right. The usual. Zilch. Lalage involved?'

'Peripherally.'

Kaporal liked the word. That was were he lived. Where we all lived. On the ledge of the peripheral. He held out a hand. 'What's the story?'

Hard ones first, I thought. Keep talking. That's the first rule of the script conference. Don't force them to ask questions. They don't like it. Hit your pitch, any pitch, stop short before you've said anything for which they can hold you responsible. Talk fast, but not too fast. Watch the eyes. The eyes under that wrinkled brow, that freshly barbered hairline. You've got to cut out one *nanosecond* before they go dead; that air-conditioned caffeine high, the institutional glaze. Filtered light in white rooms. Boredom. You find yourself staring at the only object on the minimalist shelf: the Bafta or the tribal mask, the book with a title too long to fit on its spine.

'It's about the west,' I improvised. 'Journeys, heresies, grail quests, utopian communities. You know the turf. Bristol, Coleridge, nitrous oxide, Humphrey Davy, Pantisocracy. Suicides in the defence industry. There's a lot of narrative out there, but no editor. The strapline will say: Memory, exile . . .'

'. . . Madness.' He grinned, a gold incisor hinting at better times known. Kaporal was ahead of me. 'Book or film?' he said, knowing that it didn't matter, those nice distinctions no longer had any currency. Truth, fiction. Sports report, road kill statistic. All part of the spectacle. The Spectacle.

Kaporal's library, leaving aside a few culpable promo packs for BritArt (catalogues for eye candy that had already been sold and now had to be explained), consisted entirely of conspiracy dreck: the suicide option in Dallas, revelations of Fatima, cancers so intelligent they had degrees from MIT. I memory-flashed as many titles as I could: *Secret and Suppressed: Banned Ideas & Hidden History* / *GCHQ: The Secret Wireless War* / *The Templar Revelation* / *Rinkagate, The Rise & Fall of Jeremy Thorpe* / *Busted! The Sensational Life-Story of an Undercover Cop* / *Alleged Assassination Plots Involving Foreign Leaders, An Interim Report* / *Investigation of the B-36 Bomber Programme* / *Mind Invaders* / *Thatcher's Gold* / *The Jew of Linz*. And Julie Burchill's *I Knew I Was Right*.

A predictably orthodox bibliography for a man who lurched between binge reading and total abstinence, textual bulimia and the purge of silence. Kaporal had sunk through lithium deeps to a resolved catatonia. He needed nothing except a dripping tap, rooks in the churchyard, a gate with a squeaky hinge, the mantra of motorway transit.

'Starts,' he said, sounding as if he'd been here many times before. 'You're looking for starts, Fortean incidents from which we can deduce a pattern. Let me tell you right now, you're pissing against the wrong tree. It's all pattern, one vast, pulsing, interconnected, bio-electronic web. No coincidences, fusions. No outside, no inside. Yeats's egg flattened by a juggernaut.'

'What I want,' I told him, 'is facts, dates, snapshots. Filler material to add conviction to an already written story. Documentary evidence confirming an impossible fiction.'

'Try this,' said Kaporal, passing me a time-coded auto-disaster photograph. 'From a fast-food joint on the A4, the old road west. Near Chippenham. An Asian man with a personally valeted Vauxhall Cavalier, old gold, fills his boot with cans of petrol. He drives straight into the wall of a boarded-up Little Chef. Result? A fireball you could see from Salisbury Cathedral. Turns out he worked for Marconi, facing a transfer to Portsmouth. He'd never left London before. Not without his family.'

There were more pictures, monochrome abstractions. I found myself studying the granular texture of the road surface, while avoiding black scorch marks on the brick wall. Kaporal's genealogy was obvious: he played straight back to Lalage, a necrophile aesthete determined to replace the dripping-heart martyrology of the saints, scourges and silk underwear, with a cold-turkey programme of post-religious icons. Lalage constructed image shrines to business parks, airport travelators, pylon forests, anvils of cloud reflected in the sliding glass doors of Holiday Inns at the edge of the desert. Cold fusion. Kaporal fed on Lalage as Lalage fed on J.G. Ballard. As Ballard paid his dues to Burroughs. This vampiric chain led to the spirit at the root of white world capitalism; the winged helmet a sweat-lodge shaman conjured from Burroughs's arthritic shoulder. A spirit that manifested itself in the shooting of his wife, Joan Vollmer. The spirit that damned him to write.

I passed Kaporal a brown envelope, he was on the payroll. A trick I learnt in the booktrade. A fast payment, however small, *before* the first invoice, builds up substantial future credit. Kaporal, in reduced circs, was still a gent; he dropped the envelope unopened into a pocket in his unstructured, French blue jacket. My publisher's advance was disappearing fast; if the West Country project remained uncompleted, somebody in New York was going to close the book. My credit had long since run out. I bored critics who once patronised me as a rough-trade novelty act, a dirty walker. I had the potential, so they said, to become a W.H. Davies supertramp with a diploma in psychogeography; now I was damned for sticking too long to the same midden, riverine London. The next stage, I knew all too well, was oblivion. I'd be lucky to have my name misspelt in a *Time Out* round-up.

So Kaporal would feed me tapes, sound tapes. There was no VCR in the Welsh cottage I'd rented sight unseen. No TV, no radio, just newspapers from another century. Kaporal would keep me informed. He'd talk. His monologues would be my only entertainment. I'd have to write. I'd have time, finally, to plough through those Landor biographies, the verse epics that had dropped out of the syllabus. Landor's *Imaginary Conversations* were a great idea, but unreadable. 'To others when ourselves are dust / We leave behind this sacred trust.' He was a passionate classicist, a shaper of frozen monuments. The mask of formal language disguised rage; domestic dramas, restless migrations. Landor was on the move before his trunks were lifted from the carriage; expelled from Rugby, rusticated from Oxford. That was to be the pattern of his life: the drive to solitude, remote places. I identified with the ideal and bought a condemned property in Hackney. The green lung of Victoria Park stood in for the Welsh Marches.

I sat in a sylvan grove, watching the joggers, the dog commanders, while I leafed through the pocket-sized, blue cloth Camelot Classics edition of *Imaginary Conversations* put out by Walter Scott in 1886. Crazy stuff. Landor was a perverse matchmaker: George Barrow locks horns with Isaac Newton, Alfieri with Salomon the Florentine Jew, Southey with Porson. 'Imaginary conversation' is shorthand for fiction. Landor's book was proto-sf; voices travelling across time, chat lines opened between the living and the dead. Walter Landor in a one-to-one with the Abbé Delille.

LANDOR. *He stuck to them as a woodpecker to an old forest-tree, only for the purpose of picking out what was rotten: he has made the holes deeper than he found them, and, after all his cries and chatter, has brought home but scanty sustenance to his starveling nest.*

Kaporal extended his leg to reopen the caravan door. With my small wad in his pocket, there was no point in hanging around. Get them in, Jos. Cruise the craic.

I took the hint, but as I walked away I saw Kaporal point something at me. There was no shelter, nowhere to hide. He had me bang to rights on Hi-8. He didn't have to lift the viewfinder to his eye. It was one of those fancy silver jobs, the size of a cigarette lighter (probably a Lalage cast-off). Kaporal's thick, sausage finger whipped across a small screen, revising reality, bleeding the flush from my cheek, whacking focus. Camera on wrist, he described a showy pan across the graveyard, overexposed middle ground, hazy distance. Camcorder pastoral. You couldn't call it a pan. It was a Jamesian paragraph; it meandered, hesitated, swooped back on itself. Light values went wild. Here, at last, was a valid poetic for the expiring century. Intentionless narrative: flow, colour, accident. Alchemy lite.

I couldn't be sure if I'd made the worst decision of my life bringing Kaporal into this. I'd been shafted. I was paying a stranger to allow me to act in his film. His paranoia was more powerful, better managed than my own. Coming west, telling you about it, made me a minor character in whatever gonzo thesis Kaporal was constructing.

I presumed that he would behave in this way. If he let me down I would have to strike the episode from my novel. But I would be condemned to perform my cameo in Kaporal's unedited video. 'Never embark,' Kaporal told me, 'on a story for which you can provide a conclusion. Endlessness is immortality.'

I was trapped on a small flat screen. I went into noise. Somebody, some time, would have to activate that creaking gate. Warn Kaporal. Launch him on my travels.

3

His silence silenced her.

'His silence silenced her.' I was struggling with a Ruth Rendell novel that wasn't a Ruth Rendell, a Barbara Vine, and thinking about names; names that weren't punning allusions to real people or lifted from books. The struggle wasn't of Rendell's making. She was well up to form, the consummate professional; sleek, aerodynamic, unforgiving. My struggle was physical, the light. I couldn't organise enough of it to find a box of matches. Reading was an exercise in masochism, more guesswork than the opening of myself to another voice. By necessity, I was as much author as reader. I helped Rendell out. I filled in those blank half-pages at the ends of chapters. I should have received a share in her royalties.

The Hay cottage didn't use standard electricity, it exploited some antiquarian substitute, part bovine flatus, part recycled spark plug. An intensely local episode of burnt air cranked from a spiteful generator. Light flickered, teased, faded. I sat on the cold slate of a wide window ledge, set low to the ground, and tried to hang on to what was left of the day, a moping residue of water droplets on sodden grass, fungoid luminescence. The garden behind the cottage was prolapsed, washed in septic light, a candle in the darkness.

A black box in the cupboard under the stairs devoured my coins and gave up the ghost. It was better without this teasing half-dark, the nicotine interference. Now I could chase the text through diminishing circles of torchlight. Barbara Vine was all that was keeping me from getting into the car and heading straight back to

London. My pleasure in the deftness of her performance was double-edged: I relished the parallel world to which I had been granted access, but I was unnerved by the way she did it. This was how fiction intended for an audience should be assembled; the tiny detail in Chapter 3 that will be resolved in Chapter 21; past events remembered in present time, teases, hooks, cross-cuts far slicker than the standard soap opera. And, always, beneath the nicely managed surface, cruelty and pain. The impossibility of human relationships. Karma. Ancient crimes, insignificant acts that blight future ease. A man deciding, out of character, to walk down an icy path. A woman who doesn't pick up a ringing phone. Nothing is here that doesn't belong here. Even the literary references are user-friendly. The line from Shelley will be tagged and identified. The Latin epigram given in translation. The reader is nurtured, humoured, without the condescension of the *grandes dames* of the Golden Age of mystery fiction.

If I wasn't careful, I would be well on the way to knocking out a critique, an unpaid review. I couldn't switch off. Three times in the night I scrabbled through the dark for my notebook. Rendell/Vine had some of Simenon's ice, that sense of being a spy, a watcher behind the curtains of a small hotel. There was an exigent sexuality, a liaison between tailored elegance and up-against-the-wall primitivism. Armpits sweating in a Chanel suit. Silk stockings running through the dog shit of Leytonstone. Pearl earrings of spit left dangling against a powdered cheek after an incident in a pub car park. A glass decorated with sticky finger marks picked up with yellow rubber gloves. Vine did slow-burning resentment, secret bruises, disguised identities, the minutiae of shifts in social identity; she did spoilt bitches. And made them attractive. She saw time as all of a piece, a seamless construct. And she nailed, which was how I justified the hours I spent in her company, place. North Devon, near Barnstaple. I felt that there was something I needed to tease out from that side of the channel. Views of Lundy Island, Exmoor, steep cliff roads. Vine didn't bog you down in redundant detail, flashy stuff, overdressed paragraphs of topography. I was sick with envy. She'd killed my Welsh book before I'd written a line. I left Landor in his box, crushed by an excess of Vaughans, Machens, Gills, Joneses, by maps and guides, geology, meteorology, picturesque excursions, rambles down the Wye. All of it to be digested, absorbed, fed into the Great Work. Wasn't that the essence of the modernist contract? Multi-voiced, lyric seizures countered by drifts of unadorned fact, naked source material spliced into domesticated trivia, anecdotes, borrowings, found footage. Redundant. As much use as a whale carved from margarine, unless there is intervention by that other; unless some unpredicted element takes control, overrides the pre-planned structure, tells you what you don't know. Willed possession.

Barbara Vine skewered authorship, the price it took to produce, year after year, books filled with lies, twisted facts, coded confessions. A life to create life. The price was too high. *Keep going, going on, call that going, call that on.* Vine was beginning to sound like Samuel Beckett. In the novel I was reading she introduces, as the mature lover, a Bloomsbury bookseller called Sam. He is even said to resemble the late, lightning-struck philosopher. All bone. Hair as sharp as bone. Drawn into her world, that world possesses you: the sound of the words, your breath intoning sentences, succumbing to flow, going under. Everything that is to be known about these black-edged phantoms is on the page: no subtext, no detail of their histories that is not properly back-referenced.

By now, holding the book (dust jacket carefully set aside) up to my face, I could clarify the forward momentum, a line at a time. 'You can do the explaining,' he said. 'I don't understand what this is about.' It's about itself, not metaphor, not equivalent reality. If I give this universe my trust then I have no choice but to stay there, an invisible intruder, a bump behind the shower curtain. I could never pull it off, I wouldn't have the nerve. The creatures in my books have lives of their own outside my text. I borrow (and distort) a few rags and tags. No real damage. Or so I persuade myself. With Vine it's absolute. This is their only shot. This is all there is.

But what if I were to meet one of Vine's fabulous beings, out in the territory, in a location that I know? In which I am comfortable, minding my own business. Because that's what happened. That's why I couldn't sleep in this cottage, why I moved my sleeping bag to the ground-floor room, why I walled myself in behind boxes of books, unopened comestibles. Back in London, taking my afternoon circuit of Victoria Park (the only thing that kept me sane), I saw a man who looked exactly like Samuel Beckett. Like a stroller with a

black-and-white photograph of Beckett strapped across his face – a
photograph that broke into a smile! He had a woman, nicely turned
out, dove-grey slacks, long jacket in complementary shades, hanging
on his arm. They had trespassed into the wrong novel, the wrong set.
They'd never make it back to west London.

I don't think any of the other park regulars noticed them.
Zoophiles gabbed while their beasts were at stool, or sniffing the
steaming residue of that operation, or snapping at cyclists; steroidal
hoods kicked the shit out of the harmless air; cloud-watchers com-
peted for ribbed furniture clear of pigeon droppings. And here,
sauntering down the long avenue, under the plane trees, was this
written couple, seeing another park, emerald-green grass, a chain of
glittering ponds, a fountain plume bowed by a warm wind. I saw
myself reflected in the mirror glass of the woman's extravagant
shades. These were the Barbara Vine characters I would recognise,
years later, by torchlight in a clammy cottage on the outskirts of
Hay-on-Wye.

Mornings, as ever, were more tolerable. Shaggy monsters lowing in
the fields, unseen behind tall, unkept hedges. Diaphanous mem-
branes of cuckoo-spit trapping weak light. A grey road, gently
cambered, slicked by overnight rain. And behind me, in or out of
the mist, the unfamiliar (but remembered) hills. In the past, I'd
arrive at Hay, having driven to Oxford and across the Cotswolds,
through Cheltenham (head down to avoid the school and the
GCHQ huts), before the 9 a.m. opening time. I was hot to plunge
in among the stacks of the Cinema Bookshop. Enthusiasm wilted
with every yard of alphabetically arranged fodder; only by exhibit-
ing so many books that nobody wanted would you disguise the
magical sleepers. Or so the scouts told themselves, for the first
couple of hours, as they hacked their way through shelf after shelf
of titles that never make it out of used book pits, the wrong Waughs
(Alec and Auberon instead of Evelyn), R.H. Tomlinson, Howard
Spring, Thomas Armstrong, the second edition of Andrew
Sinclair's *The Breaking of Bumbo* that was there three years ago.

I'd drudge through the town, shop to shop, finding it harder as the
years went by to get my hands on anything that proved my journey
was necessary. A few gaudy paperback shockers, makeweights in

containerloads of US remainders, dug out of a cellar: junkies, axe murderers, teenage hoods, bikers, beatniks, tame outlaws. The occasional fantasy classic that slipped the net. Some deservedly forgotten Whitechapel hack waiting to be reinvented, reassessed, talked up. By lunchtime the books smelt like waterlogged peat. One of the wide boys who ran the town even promoted them as winter fuel, fill your car for a fiver. They wouldn't burn. I tried it in the cottage. Coal wouldn't burn. Petrol-soaked rags sputtered and coughed black smoke. Firelighters didn't fire if you left them overnight in a microwave.

In the early afternoon, the first swift circuit completed, I'd call on Becky in his private office, where he stored a few semi-respectable items raked from the overwhelming tide of dross. The cream of course went into his own collection, that was the only reason he hung on to his virtually unpaid employment as manager of this open asylum. Becky's giggly vivacity and his despair were co-tenants of an eccentric form: a gentleman farmer, a back-woodsman with a taste for Baron Corvo and Father Ignatius, posh crime, bisexual travel, *belles-lettres*, spookcraft by bent toffs. Becky's eyes were alarming: one held you (it was made of Venetian glass), while the other roamed the shelves to find the single item that might amuse (if not delight). Lady Penelope Betjeman was a chum. So was poor dear Bruce Chatwin who had knocked off his Black Hill thing in borrowed properties in the neighbourhood. Becky, in his baggy fisherman's sweater and gumboots, clapped his hands at the sight of an old friend; all his punters were friends, but his friends were not necessarily punters.

'Yes! Wonderful! Don't ask. *Utter* disaster. Joy to see you. When was it? Nothing here of course. Her in the castle is worse than ever. Menopausal. Gaga. You haven't been out to Becky's new pit, have you? *Do* come for a meal. Yes! George left me a pike. Do you know the Mellys? Such fun. You game? Marvellous!'

Becky's double life was by all accounts hair-raising, the scars gave character to an otherwise near-handsome profile, a choir school juvenile who was ageing incrementally, recklessly. There weren't many free days in the Evil Empire of Hay, but Becky put them to good use, cruising the Cardiff waterfront, adding to his cicatrix portfolio, before limping back to the books and catalogues

and the phone that was his lifeline. Reporting to base after an
extended tryst with a sass lad from Hereford, Becky found that his
office, his typewriter, his reference books, his spare wellies (and the
entire bookshop that went with them), had been sold off to Hay's
alternative warlord. 'Sorry, Becky. Bit of a cash flow problem,' the
King mumbled, bells jingling in his jester's cap. Becky was resilient,
unsinkable, bruised but never bitter. He started again. It was Becky
who found me the whitewashed outhouse in which to begin work
on my Landor book.

'Great lark! Let me make a couple of calls. You easy with bible-
bashers? Very decent, *very*. Enchanting family, rock solid. Known
them from the cradle. Charming place with a view across Highgate.
You'll adore them. Marvellous!'

So it was that I was interrogated, given various scraps of paper
with names and numbers, impenetrable instructions, well-meant
advice. 'Don't worry about noises from the boiler. If it works.
Rather temperamental. Do you get on with Taffies? Wonderful
storytellers, once you let them in. Count the spoons when they've
gone. Don't try and cross the farmyard at night. Or in the morning,
come to that. Before ten o'clock. Stroke of luck, the place coming
free. For you I mean.'

The cottage was fine. The atmosphere was the problem. I put it
down to the location, the Hay effect, but it was more than that.
One night upstairs had been enough. I heard the sound of rain, but
that didn't bother me. It was when the sound stopped that I worried, rain was a comforting constant. This was like rain but it wasn't
rain. Torrential indoor precipitation. As if a tap was running in the
bathroom, if there had been a bathroom. Torch in hand, I went
through every room in the place, two up, one down, outside privy,
bumping my head on all the beams. No leaks, no drips, nothing to
explain that sound. So I got back into my grandfather's coat, my
sleeping bag, under the feathery quilt and sniffled through another
night. I couldn't be sure that I fell asleep, but the dreams were vivid.
They were there, playing against the damp walls whether I inhabited them or not.

Heat. A black road near the airport shimmering with pools of
imagined water. Noise. Wailing on transistors. Strangely compelling
asexual voices, power women or drama queens in full travesty. The

metal of the car too hot to touch. Dead flies on the windscreen. The windows don't work. They won't open. Banners slung across the road; fierce turbans, weaponry. Slogans I can't read. Breeze-block, flat-roof buildings. Ballard says that roads from the airport are the same everywhere.

Harsh light off the sea. The wrecked pleasure beach of the Corniche. Hackney tower blocks transported to the seaside. Bright washing hanging from balconies, potted plants. Bougainvillaea. Heady scents: palm trees, cheap cigarettes, petrol, mutton sweat, animal shit on the road, human shit against the walls of white buildings. A city on fire. A burnt-out Art Deco cinema.

I took the path across the fields. Hay looked at its best from this distance. I hummed. I carried a guide to wild flowers, ready to check plants that curled in on themselves, playing dead against the promise of an early winter. My boots squelched, my socks soaked up brackish water left in shallow indentations in the heavy, red earth. I was chirpy enough to persuade myself that I knew how the curate, Francis Kilvert, felt when he walked over the fields from Clyro to Hay. Did he compose his journals on the hoof? Did he make notes? Or did he leave it all to the hazard of memory, so that his days were translated (censored, colour-enhanced) into fiction? One sentence begetting another. It goes wrong from the first word. You're always struggling to recover from that initial mistake, the accident of language.

Bearded Kilvert, seated for ever in a single pose, constructing his novel of provincial life, a fable worked from documentary fragments; underwritten by love of place, this place, the lanes, ruins, stone bridges from which to watch animals swept away in a flood. Kilvert's walks were his sentences, the anticipation of society. The stories he teased from old soldiers, Welsh aboriginals. Drunk peasants, wife-beaters swaying down untrafficked roads. The mutual embarrassment when he arrived at the farm owned by Rev. Vaughan of Newchurch to find Vaughan's agreeable young daughters castrating lambs. Kilvert was a truth-teller, a dangerous man whose confessions couldn't disguise the ache of exile, the unfulfilled passion for girl-children in village schools, sweet-scented daughters of landowners, anyone, anything who could scratch that itch.

I had the satisfaction of managing to walk from Hay to Clyro by the fields without meeting a single person, always a great triumph to me and a subject for warm self congratulation for I have a peculiar dislike to meeting people, and a peculiar liking for a deserted road.

I wouldn't do the Hay shops. I wouldn't call on Becky. I needed Kilvert's deserted road. I needed time to exorcise the sound of the rain in the house, the strobing images of that drive from the airport, the suspicion that a door closing was closing for the last time. I'd buy a bottle of whisky, a few cheap cigars and take an afternoon off, get to the end of the Barbara Vine. That felt like a good idea, a rare example (for me) of forward planning. Pleasure postponed. But I didn't want to know how the story turned out. That was my problem with Vine. The opening, the introduction to a world for which I had no responsibility, was so seductive. A trip into the mirror. Then, as the mystery unravelled, as all the pieces fitted together, and the engine clicked, cog by cog, towards revelation, I lost interest. The various narrators were, it turned out, servicing the same tale. I love beginnings, everything that happens before the crime. The rest is procedural tedium. The crunch with this book – the point at which I decided to drop it into the first bookshop I had never previously visited – came when the novelist anti-hero, a man with whom I was reluctantly beginning to identify (dissatisfied grafter, nice wife, beautiful daughters, working out his traumas by exploiting everybody he'd ever met in the name of fiction), agreed, on his last legs, to take part in the Hay-on-Wye literary festival. That blew it. Anybody stupid enough to make the vainglorious trek to the great tent in the cabbage patch deserved everything he had coming to him. 'When his publishers wanted him to accept the invitation to attend the literary festival at Hay-on-Wye he agreed happily.' Agreed happily? What a family! Then the masochistic, black-clad daughter, spoilt but not quite rotten, the one in whom I felt a compelling interest, compounded the error. She actually expected to be able to wander down to a shopping-centre bookshop in Plymouth and pick up a copy of one of her father's novels. If you know how this one turns out, don't bother to write.

The streets of the town were deserted, the tourists had not yet arrived, and the transsexuals were still in rehab. What was the attraction for gender jumpers? Dull grey buildings, a lull between weather systems, a river in spate, rushing to be elsewhere. Tijuana of the Welsh Marches. A border town without a border. Narrow streets, a market perch for cheeses, charity caves and a clock tower. A small, steep hill running up to the ruin of a castle, which was surrounded by barrows of dead books, future kindling. Hay was bereaved, mourning past glories, resigned to its present shame. 'The town,' said the poet Anne Stevenson, 'is full of people who have limped this far and don't have the strength to limp any further.'

The morning declined as rain leaked and dripped, spattering slimy pavements. This was not the place in which to start work on a book. Who needs another trumpeting volume to chuck on the pyre, another dreary effusion to bulk out the melancholy mound? Hay was aversion therapy for bibliophiles. The old shops, the grocers and butchers with their gloating displays of bloody flesh and matted feathers, decapitated rabbits, garrotted hares, demonstrated a bracing contempt for the wimpish vegans and New Age riff-raff who had been conned into making a final fresh start in this penal colony. (Interested in the etymology of the expression 'riff-raff', I checked out Jonathon Green's excellent *Dictionary of Slang*. Raff, Taff. Rhyming slang meaning 'a Welsh person'.) The chaff that fetched up against the walls of Hay Castle were honorary Welsh folk, whatever their origins. That is to say, they were paranoid, gabby, boastful, and rancid with self-deception. They had a proper sense of the apocalyptic. And they blamed someone else for this mess, God the Cleanshaven. That's why Kilvert and all the evangelical despots, the heretical clerisy, wore thick black beards. To dissociate themselves from their Founder.

If the day had been bad enough and I wanted to make it positively suicidal, I dropped in at the Poetry Bookshop. The proprietor was the real thing, a poet. This was alarming enough, with no other action required, to scare off casual visitors. The shop was peaceful. The poet could get on with his work uninterrupted. He would stand, in his official poet's union smock and sandals, grooming a spare beard and rolling a thin cigarette while he stared out in satisfied repugnance at the bleak street, the straggle of unwashed, dole-bandit travellers dragging themselves into the only pub in town that would tolerate their sullen, rusted presence. When the cash was gone, the deals done, they would shuffle back into the hills.

The poet, if you had the time, if you could bear to see all those mint-condition (unread), self-published, anorexic small press volumes properly ordered on clean pine shelves, was a good source of local gossip. A wintry smile played on his lips as, coughing consumptively, he outlined the latest atrocity, another venal scam worked by the nabobs. Every few months some scribbler, down for a reading, or hopelessly lost, would wander in and make a barter. Tweezer an unsaleable book from the shelves and leave a couple of his own. There was a freemasonry of despair, a threadbare fellowship. Poets didn't have conversations, they grunted in sympathy, dissed rivals who had achieved any sort of success, however illusory; they picked up on a contagion of rumours, nodded in gleeful sympathy at natural cullings, kindly cancers that had carried off a few more anthology space-fillers. 'I'll be an incomer all my life,' said the shop's owner, shortly before he took up with a visiting performance poet and left Hay forever.

A visit to the Poetry Bookshop would be too much fun. I wanted to know if there had been any sightings of Dryfeld and Silverfish, but that could wait. There was a place I hadn't previously noticed, a light at the end of an alley, down the side of the castle, near the car park. A painted board, BOOKS, wept in the rain on the pavement, the two fat os like a pair of misted spectacles. That would do me, a convenient spot to get shot of my Barbara Vine.

The shop was lit by a paraffin lamp. Even by Hay's standards that was pushing it. Seeing the soft flare of the lamp in the bowed window, I thought for a moment that I'd blundered into a rustic massage parlour. If I left the Vine on the green baize card table by the door and walked out, I'd be doubling their stock. This was a pre-charity pitch, undecided as to which great cause it would attach itself. The owners were still waiting on the boxes of dross that other failing enterprises of the town would unload with the hope of burying a rival in enough damaged and untradable ballast to keep them tied up through the winter. Old hands were always willing to offer a newcomer good advice. Such as: 'Don't bother opening at weekends, the town's full of time-wasting grockles.' Or: 'Never turn a customer away. Buy anything they bring you, however

wretched. They might come back with a Gutenberg Bible.' Or:
'Always look your best before welcoming your first customer. We
have a reputation to preserve. Keep a smile on your face.'

My smile of complacency, at the cynical one-liners I was composing, vanished. The vim knocked out of me by the woman
lounging in the doorway of the back room. That she should appear
like a resolution of darkness, a gathering of intelligent shadows,
increased her impact. She was assured, unflashy. Inevitable. I felt the
shock of recognition that something unique always delivers.
Memory stalls as you search frantically for an equivalent. There isn't
one. You gape like a fish. You develop a fish's memory. In five seconds you've forgotten what she looked like, what it would do to
stare into those eyes.

I stared. I couldn't be sure, spectacles abandoned after the rain,
that I wasn't embellishing my pitch. She had the arrogance loafing
about in the better class of bookshop gives you. Bookshops that
don't behave like bookshops: discreetly carpeted premises with too
many bindings in locked glass-fronted cupboards. Young gentlemen
in suits they obviously can't afford. A smell of leather polish and
unopened chequebooks.

She smoked, flicked ash with a thin finger. She was professionally bored. It was a vocation. Her lips were pouting, inky threads;
there wasn't enough oxygen for her in this pit. She was very pale,
with bright spots in her cheeks. Her hair was long, dirty gold; it
tangled down her neck, pulled back to reveal freakishly small and
delicate ears.

'We don't,' she said, turning her back on me, 'buy. Books.' She
spoke slowly. She was too weary to complete her sentences.

'I'm not selling. It's free, a gift. I'm finished with it.'

'Then. Drop it in. The. Bin. And close the door on your. Way.
Out.'

It was hard to judge her age. I was increasingly vague about my
own. She'd been around, but she had a clear, luminescent skin; the
glow of well-being that comes from a cancer in remission. One
transfusion too many. There was something orchidaceous about
her complexion, the set of the slender neck above strong masculine
shoulders. My god, was she one of *those*, one of the Aprils, a
Casablanca snip job? The aristocratic hauteur (fuck off, peasant),

the shrug and smothered yawn, might be inherited or acquired. Some of the Hay transsexuals were exotic, others were dumpy, twin-set and sensible-shoes matrons who thought that changing gender allowed them to reinvent their ancestry and come out as thoroughbred Welsh cobs.

Not this young woman, she was kosher. The rolled-down wellies, boy's cricket sweater, muddy tarpaulin mac: she contradicted them, shone out of their drab camouflage. 'Glistening as the saturated fields,' David Jones wrote. And he was right.

I couldn't do this. I never had. Didn't know how. Voluntary socialisation with a member of the booktrade.

'Why don't you close up, officially?' I said. 'We could go for a drink?'

4

Getting comprehensively lost in a car with a full tank of petrol, at someone else's expense, you can't beat it.

As he nosed along, following whatever came, whatever the road offered, fat hedges brushed against the dark blue paintwork of Kaporal's motor. Unsheared, thorny: the lid closed over him and he welcomed it. He was advancing, if he cared to think about it, at walking pace. Pure, trouser-swelling pleasure. Being and not being. Being so far *in* that he was out of it, system crashed, watching himself watching; tipsy with the drag and slur of movement. Resigned to this abdication of velocity. In sync with diurnal rhythms, moving west as the sun moved. His windscreen crusted with limey droppings from the green tunnel that enclosed him. Shadow bars across a pink road, honey stones crushed on a griddle of grit.

Kaporal took his hands off the wheel, found a cigarette and lit up. From outside, a smeary flare in the slick black window.

The English jungle swallowed him, that was good. Uncharted lanes, narrower and narrower, until the blue Ford Mondeo had to nudge the branches aside. With Kaporal, mind-travelling, slouched and upright, comfortably uncomfortable, drifting a couple of feet over the roadskin of north Devon.

What he wanted, in justification of this near-erotic sense of vegetable entombment, hedges growing together in fairytale inevitability, was to record it *as he experienced it*. To sample the flickering leaf dance, the lanes that ran into other lanes, *while* he drove. He would activate the camcorder by thought alone, without taking his hands from the wheel and going through all that tedious fiddle, the battery stuff. He didn't, god forbid, want to see what he shot, he was seeing it now. He wanted to erase it. Denarrate that which had no narrative beyond the racing digits of the time code. These lanes were no longer asphalt: drovers' routes, mudslips to slaughter sheds. There hadn't been a signpost for miles. Not since the promise of the tank museum. A tank museum in the middle of this featureless, overgrown nothingness? There was only one reason to come here, to disappear.

If I disappear as he did I might find myself, Kaporal improvised. Day Two, Somewhere off the M5: *The Case of the Lost Leader*.

Kaporal's people had been Liberals when that meant something (something to fill the eternity between luncheon and dinner, something to talk about between port, cigars and the impossibility of finding the same bedroom twice). Jeremy Thorpe was a throwback, a saturnine Edwardian bounder who could (adequately rehearsed) do the chat, off-the-cuff witticisms. Famous one-liners recalled in a late hagiography, *In My Own Time*, ghosted by its subject. A feeble old man ventriloquising the tailor's dummy that had been his youth.

Kaporal reckoned there was still juice in the Thorpe story. If it played, he'd be back in the game. If it was no go, he could charge it to Norton. Serve the bugger right for invading his caravan, involving him with this idiotic trawl to Bristol and the coast, raking over events that made no sense first time around. Hold a straight trial in Minehead? Forget it. What Kaporal liked was being on the road, out of reach; seeing how it fitted together, defence industry suicides, sado-masochistic loners from the Secret State, dragon lines of earth energy, the Thorpe conspiracy. What if *there was no conspiracy*? Unmediated chaos. Heat prints on an endless road. Thorpe is alive if I think he's alive, if I can – no mean feat – work him into Norton's fiction. A good researcher secures his alibi before he hands over the bullets.

Kaporal could present himself, if he had to, as borderline schizo; a metropolitan media-hawk dressed down with the same fussy care his mentor, Jamie Lalage, took in deciding what length of black leather coat to sport for a Q&A session at a film festival. The director had been known to cancel an appearance rather than take a decision about whether to appear part-shaved or unshaved. Influenced by Lalage's concept of styleless style, Kaporal was decisively non-socked in clean white daps; putting a break on his first speech of the day (the week), no subclauses, no speed rush, vodka-splash gratitude at having an audience, a face in the screen of his Hi-8. Asking directions from a rural cyclist, he submitted his victim to a forty-minute rant on Baudrillard. When he found an audience, he made the best of it.

He had scammed the royal blue (it gave him confidence to say that, use those words) Mondeo from the BBC car pool in White City. The motor and the cellphone. He had a production number and he had a production office, so he said, in Bristol. They were doing a piece on out-of-town shopping malls, dome cities, car parks with retail facilities attached. He gave them, in triplicate, Lalage's signature – which he had long since (with the owner's bored compliance) perfected. The Mondeo was his office and his bivouac.

Cribbs Causeway, with its mounds and water features, its omnipresent press of weather systems hitching their skirts over the distant Mendips, was paradise prefigured. Kaporal was boosted by surveillance, his power-pack booted into a swifter register. If this Neo-Marrakesh (commodity porn) gutted the centre of the old town, so much the better; the complacent slave port deserved everything that was coming to it. Bristol was in thrall to the Serpent, so Kaporal believed. The inhabitants, for the most part, couldn't work up the energy to yawn. As his old mucker Nik Cohn said: 'From time to time, a stray dog takes a dump. That passes for a commotion.'

The Avon was a two-headed Mayan god, chopping through estuarine marshes, demonstrating the classic head-to-head of Old Red Sandstone and Dolomitic Conglomerate. Clifton Gorge carved its way into Kaporal's throat like a tracheotomy. He gasped. What amazed him was not why the Sikhs jumped from the bridge, but what took them so long.

Sour milk splashed Kaporal's incipient beard. The lips of the waxed carton, splayed in a duck pout, coughed gouts of warm white slop. How do you *drink* this muck? It explodes in his face, then stops to a mean trickle. He wolfs nuts and raisins and dark chocolate. His strong but unbuffed English teeth are mushed with shell and sugar varnish, shitty sweet. A couple of cigarettes burn out the taste. He revisits the complex of malls and glass-walled walkways to find strong black coffee, coffee which is always too hot or too cold. Bladder-irritating beakers of fluid he would rather not touch, but which he needs to keep up the buzz, the imminent headache, the taste before (and after) the next Camel.

During morning hours, Kaporal skulked around the parking lot. He photographed yellow lines, empty grids. He tried to repli-cate the autistic pans of the CCTV. He eavesdropped (sound-dipped) girls sitting outside the revolving glass doors in the sunshine. Their stories were better than his (more content); towns visited, drinks taken, clothes exchanged, men admired, men shafted, films seen, jobs walked out on. The overlapping double narrative, Suffolk accented, made no reference to where they were or how long they would stay. Tight vests, jeans and boots, struck Kaporal, struck at him. Bosoms supported by the natural elasticity of youth. The way they smoked so much faster than he did, small hungry drags; flicked ash, tossed hair, firm bottoms wriggling on stone flags. They paid no attention to the families shuffling grimly into the debt-enhancement facilities, no attention to lurking secu-rity operatives; or the suited woman who perched, cross-legged, on a low wall, passionately engrossed in a one-sided mobile mouthfuck.

You respond. You go to places that respond to you. You log what you find. And you wait. That was Kaporal's script, the interstices. That was the difference between TV and cinema: TV was preor-dained, highpoint following highpoint, cut cut cut. The car. The petrol station forecourt. Three lines of significant chat. Bang bang, slap. A woman faking a phone conversation as a man joins a group of strangers sitting in a canteen. Television allowed no space for the hole in which Kaporal lived.

Nothing happening outside Bristol. The delicate, soul-shredding mu-mu-murr of motorway flow, centrifugal and centripetal impulses. Out here on the edge of Filton Airport, where one of the dead Indians was supposed to have put in time. Let it run without

intervention. Then push on, go west until you stick. Until someone stops you.

Kaporal took the Thorpe route into Devon by way of Taunton and
the Quantocks. (He was working a cold trail, memory traces of
Coleridge and Southey on the hoof, utopian fantasies withering in
the bud. Wordsworth and his party spied on by a government
agent. Opium dreams. Wedding guests. Ghost ships with the stink
of rotting sea bird.) If he pulled in, as he did, beside a village green,
wondering if he had seen it before, childhood, he would watch
glossy, avariciously-beaked crows bouncing on coarse thick grass;
the size of them, cats on springs. One word in his mouth: death.

In Combe Florey he tracked rumours floated by a mischievous
journalist to their point of origin. Auberon Waugh, a lifelong hack,
made a career of spite, despoiling his small gift to force some
response from an unreachable parent. 'See what you've made me
do.'

Jeremy Thorpe, with his supposed sexual inclinations, his charm,
became something of an obsession for the cadet Waugh. Like so
much of English culture the feud emanated in prep school; mucky
boys and their little triumphs. Different schools, different strokes: a
West Country backwater, hag-ridden by priests, looks across at
Eton.

Thorpe was a Flashman figure in a preposterous waistcoat, a
Flashman who got away with it. Waugh was awkward, unloved.
Thorpe jumped fences, cultivated the beaks, flogged spotty youths
caught, trousers around ankles, bungling acts he had perfected in
secret. Behind the closed doors of privilege. Then he was grassed,
betrayed, sold down the river. The Establishment, who knew him
as one of their own, saw to it that his punishment was subtle, not
public. Exile rather than execution. Waugh was left with a bowd-
lerised account of the trial, a scissors-and-paste number delivered
with a certain venomous flair.

There was something profoundly unnatural, Kaporal decided,
about Thorpe's hair, that flat sweep across the scalp, plastered down
with water or linseed oil. His barnet looked as if it had been kept
overnight in a salad bowl. On the hustings, Thorpe favoured a
brown derby, tilted at an upbeat angle. Quizzical eyebrows (curls of

unlit gunpowder) and a mock-sulky mouth. An immutable *moue* miming – yuk – the anchovy aftertaste of cold semen. Was Thorpe the last person in public life to turn up at the Bailey in a felt-collared topcoat? The vessels of wrath were into him by that time, he couldn't decide if the gesture was ironic or confessional. Did he want to be broken on the treadmill or returned, fatally damaged, to the ugly realities of political life? His rivals would hang him out to dry with their carefully worded letters of support. They wished cancers on the man, heart-hurt, spine-eating bugs. They willed his internment in the green hell of Devon. They wanted to see thorns grow from his fingernails, snails crawling out of empty eye sockets.

The West Country was a zone of disappearances. If you took London as the norm, the place where the battle was fought. What did he remember about the Jeremy Thorpe story? Another era. Kaporal lurched through puberty in one of those short periods of contemporary history when it was possible to shirk a good war; he avoided conscription or national service (that had been a very near thing). His good fortune was compounded by his relationship to the Pentonville Rubber Company monopoly. His first (other-sex) relationship came at a time when women took care of contraception and felt obliged, in some cases, to celebrate their newly acquired freedom by putting it about. (Celibacy, revenge, litigation would arrive years later as the reminiscences of bat-crazy divas began to roll off the presses. There wasn't much point, Kaporal reckoned, in giving up underwear when nobody wanted to do anything about it, except pretend not to notice.)

Later there had been a series of theoretically monogamous bondings (feasible through prolonged absence and the safe sex of the video-letter – which was his preferred art form). Kaporal avoided rubber technology, its ribs and flavours, and was glad of it.

Thorpe, he believed, although a generation or two older, came into his pomp at that same golden moment, the mid-sixties, the summer of the hypocrite. He floated across the surface of the city, disguised as a sardonic dandy; performing, clowning, delivering the good word. *Liberal.* Which was not then a crime, an obscenity. He was sound on Africa, in tune with the spirit of the times on social reform. If his shoes weren't suede you could see your face in them. He was taking over a party with a glorious past and he was poised to lead it into an exciting future. He cruised London in his dark-blue Sunbeam Rapier – himself a sunbeam, a quality of light; you could hear the swish of the swordstick as he strode through the lobbies, bounded across studio floors, worked embassy parties – doing the voices, Macmillan, Wilson (who was fascinated by him), Hailsham, the TUC dinosaurs. (Not Witold Grossman. The great fixer was sacrosanct. His skin always looked as if it was under a barber's towel. He was carved from suet, clever tailoring disguising simian body hair. But they feared him like a rabid Pope.)

Thorpe had the style of Disraeli, over-tailored, over-prepared, with none of the substance. He drove along the Embankment, under plane trees, sun-splinters on a cresting flood, to the House; interviews on College Green, gladhanding the terrace. He motored to Draycott Place in Chelsea, a room he had rented for Norman Scott, his timid catamite. Echoes of Wilde. Between the barracks and the river. There might be time for an urgent penetrative episode, then on to a dinner party in Holland Park. Or, if Thorpe didn't want to get out of the car, he tooted the horn – this was King's Road, a Michael Winner flick with Oliver Reed – and Scott would come scampering down from the child's narrow cot on which he dossed.

And they'd roar off, partners of convenience, Scott in one of the oyster-blue shirts Thorpe bought him at Thresher and Glenny, strategically unbuttoned. Along Chelsea Embankment and over Battersea Bridge, ghosts of the Festival of Britain. Risk was everything, otherwise it was too easy. Pockmarked businessmen, offshore financiers, charity mafiosi: the chancers and fixers and blackballed clubmen who wanted a back door into political life. Resurrect the mummified corpse of Liberalism as a third force; green earth, no bombs, brotherhood of man. They'll clean up the litter too and make the streets fit for cyclists.

There was a white handkerchief in Thorpe's breast pocket, flopping over the brim, priapic in its coded signal. Kaporal recalled the photograph taken at Westminster Abbey, a memorial service, 1970: Thorpe flanked by two prime ministers, Heath and Wilson, in their morning suits. Thorpe is showing too much cuff, his handkerchief a stiff snout. Heath favours a widow's peak, a different message. Wilson could be muttering something from the corner of his mouth. Heath has twisted his head to disguise the weight of jowl. Thorpe is caught, arms folded, swallowing his lips. Eyes down. One wing of hair breaking loose over his right ear. A gold chain looped across his waistcoat, kidney to kidney.

Pulling the handkerchief, generous quantities of lawn, free – thin knobbled wrist – Thorpe presented the thing to Scott. He unbuttoned his flies, fumbling, fingers thick with excitement. Then he turned away from the event, this mechanical process of orgasm inducement: dappled light, the breeze from the river. Though he pulsed, twisted in his seat, the repetitive snake-strangling was tedious, unaffecting. It was authorship, the power over Scott's life that provoked him. To keep a man in a kennel, to use him like a dog.

The car door slammed. Thorpe was away. Scott recalled it, when Kaporal tracked him down in his 'eleventh-century long house' on the edge of Dartmoor, as the 'most miserable' of walks home. Poor Norman. 'Poor Norman,' he muttered. 'Not a night passes without dreams of that man's ghastly horseface. I don't feel safe until morning comes. He wants to cut a piece from the back of my neck. He wants to stitch up my mouth.'

Kaporal looped around the territory, picking up survivors, taping contradictory reminiscences (if memory men would work on a promise). He kept the tapes to himself. He played them back with the volume down. In silence, the sweating untrustworthy faces of occidental England endured their instant of fame. A dog-killing conspiracy. The players were defunct, disgraced, dying in rural seclusion. Let the story go with them, that was the decent thing to do.

Passing through Porlock, the pub where Scott had spent an evening getting drunk with the bungler who had been hired to shoot him, Kaporal picked up rumours of a second man, another stableboy and putative model, who had been paid, and paid well, to stay out of it, to settle in Amsterdam. Now he was back, up there on Exmoor, skint and willing to talk. But it was too late, nobody wanted to know. There is no percentage in outing those who are already posthumous. Nobody other than Kaporal, with his perverse and puritanical sense of history – how everything will one day be revised, all secrets revealed – cared. He reeled out of the Castle and executed a swooping tracking shot across the ornamental tiles on the other side of the street, the Moorish pavement, spikes and diamonds, where the amateur hitman parked his car.

First he would see Thorpe, the man was ill. Kaporal gambled that there might still be some residual germ of vanity, the desire to put the record straight, have the last word. Like fuck. The veteran politico wasn't stupid. Kaporal would settle for a decent, long-held close-up. But he didn't know where Thorpe was hiding; somewhere in the neighbourhood of his power base, Barnstaple, somewhere quiet and retired in the back country.

He started his Porlock investigations in the town library, which had rack upon rack of leaflets – flower gardens, steam trains, sharks in tanks – but no books. The librarian was very helpful. Kaporal didn't want to come out with it: 'Can you give me the address of the old shirtlifter, Thorpe?' In Bristol he'd leafed through a couple of the biographies and found the name of the village where Thorpe had settled with his second wife, the one with musical connections. Higher Chuggaton. That had to be phony. The librarian called it up on her computer: no such settlement known. Kaporal resigned himself to weasling his way in among the Barnstaple Liberals, feeding them bullshit about researching a *Secret History* documentary. Provincials would sell their grandmother to get on TV.

It had taken most of the afternoon session to loosen up the broken-veined soaks in the Castle. By the finish, bar aslop with beer puddles, sticky with chasers, one of Kaporal's temporary lifelong buddies crooked an arm around his neck. 'Tell me, Jos boy, London. You toddle down one of them posh knocking shops and there's this young bird, right? Mask on 'er face, like. You don' know 'er and she don' know you. Not a stitch coverin' 'er particulars an' you can try whatsoever you fancy. Right then, Jos. What you do?'

Kaporal let him wait on the answer till the rest of the sots quieted down, intrigued to know: what perversion could a sophisticate such as Kaporal invent?

'Only one thing to do,' Kaporal said, pushing back his chair. 'Ask her where she keeps her smokes.'

Coming off the A361, out of Barnstaple, heading towards Tiverton, Kaporal nudged and wheedled, followed hunches, talked to

hedgers, women with dogs. Higher Chuggaton was unmapped and
if the agro-industrial peasantry had ever heard of Thorpe they
weren't letting on. He was respected as one of the dead, a necessary
sacrifice. In his disgrace he outflanked his rivals. That's all that can
be asked of a redundant politician, to vanish. Wilson pulled it off,
the abrupt and final resignation: Alzheimer's, silence. Thatcher
didn't understand the system, power followed by ritual strangulation; she became a spectre at the feast, the hell-harridan in the iron
mask. Duck out, Madame, let time grind you to dust.

Caught in these green tunnels, there was no time. Grass broke
through asphalt. Dead elms, oak ancestors choked in ivy, made
grotesque shapes as they marked out the ancient trackway. The
dark blue Mondeo drifted at its own volition. Kaporal had pulled it
off, become the video. He was experiencing perception. He saw
with his skin. The slower he moved, the more the past closed in on
him, hedges thickened and scratched. If, at a twist in the road, he
glimpsed the sky, there was uniform darkness, grey-green infection.
He became a kind of Cretan mountain man, measuring distance in
cigarettes. One mile on the signpost might take an hour. The same
destination never appeared twice. He was looking for Cobbaton,
the Combat Collection, redundant military hardware. He'd work
his way out from that.

It would have been easier to crawl backwards up the birth canal.
There was a horrible triangle of submerged country between South
Molton, Barnstaple and Umberleigh. That was where Kaporal lost
himself, lost it, the thread of conspiracy he was expected to uncover.
Thorpe had pleaded necessary ignorance. He didn't care about the
details, the offshore bank accounts, fat men with carpet warehouses,
strip-club boasts, hired muscle. He was folded too tightly around the
grub in his gut, the fear of (and desire for) exposure; having Scott
down on his knees, gobbling and gagging, as the Whips march
along the corridor, stride for stride, towards his office. Nothing, no
tabloid revelation, no electoral disaster, could stop him behaving like
a chorus boy, highkicking over fences and bridges, swinging from
trees. He was innocent. *Jeremy Thorpe is Innocent, OK*. Kaporal
would assure him of that. He understood. The conspiracy was elsewhere, everywhere. In the landscape. The second man, the potential
whistle-blower in the Exmoor cottage, would confirm it.

On a roll, guided by the liberated spirit of the man he would defend, resurrect, Kaporal motored into the heart of the maze. There it was, Chuggaton. One farm and an immodestly thatched cottage. The silence was awesome. The absence of motorway whisper unnerved Kaporal. 'Camcorder pastoral' was all very well when you were assembling it in a borrowed editing suite in Dean Street (sleeping bag rolled under your chair, chainsmoking through the night). But here? Raw, unmediated? Kaporal strode in at the open gate, with no notion of what he would do next.

One car in a two-car parking space. With luck the wife – hatted and Burberry'd, tight-mouthed, lurking loyally in the vicinity of the stumpmeister's triumphantly exposed armpits, the yards of white cuff – would be out, dealing with the world. In town. Kaporal could stride up to the door, which would be one of those knotty wood numbers with no obvious bell or knocker, make his presence known. He'd yell, kick, stomp, scream. Rouse the bugger. The red burglar alarm tucked under the lip of the thatch worried him. There were probably other, blinking, surveillance eyes. The cottage would be monitored. How could he cross this beach of tiny golden stones *silently*?

'Mr Thorpe. Sir. Jeremy,' Kaporal wheedled, pressing his face to windows that peeped out from a trellis of yellow roses. Lemon-painted frames. Was that the Liberal colour? Funk? 'Mr Thorpe.'

They say his voice is a gravel whisper, a mummy croak. Journalists, from time to time, wake sweating to the nuisance of an answerphone message in the middle of the night. Even on enhanced playback they can't make it out. Psycho-acoustic feedback. How did Thorpe get their private numbers *before* they started work on the story?

I don't like it, Kaporal thought, that open gate. You don't have a rusticated portcullis unless you intend to use it. A double bluff. You don't leave a door unlatched unless you have something to hide. *Unless it's already too late.* He tried to work his way around to the back of the cottage. He was blocked by a converted barn, a garage–studio. The cottage was a Thomas Hardy quotation at the centre of a sinister and complex rural masquerade. Merrie England as it might be set-designed by the Politburo. Trying to get at the rear of the house, Kaporal came up against the museum-quality gravitas of the barn. Sanded floors too bright for human footfall. Glass art. A piano, a concert grand, cryogenically dustsheeted: a jaw-defying quadrant of iced cake. He'd have to backtrack, out into the lane and over the wall.

He perched, fell. It was a longer drop than he'd expected. Into a secret English garden. Musk rose and iris, narcissi and heavy-headed foxgloves: the sudden drench of scent, the ordered chaos of a disciplined wilderness, stopped Kaporal. He couldn't tramp through this soft–tough enclosure, mashing grass stems, ripping out tendrils of flowering stuff, tipping bees from flower heads. The garden neutered him. He wasn't there, not really. To tiptoe across the ribbed lawn to the french windows would be to stamp soot into a wedding dress. He stayed in the shadows, among the trees and the tangle. He went for extreme magnification, telescopic invasion of the space behind the glass doors. Video-truth doesn't come out of life. It reduces three-dimensional objects to a kind of nervy varnish. He wanted to blow the focus, jump the exposure.

Checking if anything had been captured in the nozzle of the viewfinder was like keyholing a burial chamber; watching a film that hadn't happened, not yet. As he cranked up the light values, he saw, or imagined, the outline of a man. A skull with staring sockets, a man 'stripped of flesh', as one of the late biographers reported. Thorpe was arranged in a chair, all bones and sticks, dressed loud as a Fauve mannikin. Cranberry-red leisure slacks! A bruise-blue shirt with a yellow cravat! He'd been placed and he'd stay in position until someone moved him. But the lips – Kaporal went in tight – the lips were self-cannibalising, a hollow mouth gumming words that wouldn't come. Thorpe was a thing in a bowl, an experiment in air pressure. His tongue was out. He was biting glass.

'Excuse me. Excuse *me*, but would you care to explain yourself?' Kaporal's heart jumped, breath in a hot ball. The woman with the big, concert-hall hair, the tan, the sensible too-bright shoes had put down her bags, thrown open the french windows, and was advancing faster towards him than he could zoom out. Her head was lion-sized, the mane black as polish. Cuttlefish ink. 'Excuse me. Excuse me. *Excuse* me.'

Kaporal slammed into close-up, ice-picked by glacial politeness, the threat in that voice, stronger than any man, firmer in purpose;

a voice thrown, so it seemed, from the stringy lips of the skull in the chair.

Thorpe laughed. On the tiny screen Kaporal watched in fascinated horror. Eyebrows arched like crows' wings, an open toothless mouth. Shuddering shoulders. He laughed, eyes tight shut, in a terrible bone-scream of blackness and mania. He knew, Thorpe knew. Nothing mattered. Nothing to be done. He had looked into the pit. There was nothing there.

What Thorpe's lips had been trying to form, what he throat-breathed down the wires of late-night telephones, was always the same. The sentence that his wife Marion had to translate for him: 'Why should I write your book for you?'

Kaporal ran. Through thorns that tore flesh. This was his vision of Thorpe, the lost leader, the English conspiracy: a nervous breakdown in a suit. A faked suicide. A long-jawed skull cackling with rictal laughter. Reggie Perrin. The late Leonard Rossiter as Reggie Perrin. A situation comedy doomed to repeat itself until it turned into something by Strindberg.

5

I love watching women eat. How they manage this awkward business of cutting up insufficiently dead matter, spiking it, carrying it towards an open mouth. Talking all the time, as if it wasn't happening, the cousin-cannibalism. They have such a gift, women, for doing what has to be done without moral recrimination, with free-floating minds that run, simultaneously, over yesterday's perceived insult, the organisation of tomorrow's affairs, the meal that is still a list of ingredients. They know just what you are going to say before you say it. They smile, swallow. You don't hear them chomp or grind. They have already kicked off one shoe and decided that, although their earrings are beginning to pinch, the mild discomfort can be borne, and is in fact rather pleasurable. Having decided it, your companion turns a fleshy lobe towards you while she unclips the slightly warmed silver shields, slips them into your hand, challenging you to know how to behave. She massages the indentations, going on about the theatre tickets she tried to book on your credit card and what the official said.

You don't want to speak. You want to be allowed to sit in contented silence, watching the performance, babbling compliments. Knowing that, should the phone ring, she'd launch into a quite different version of the tale, a more detailed account, with audible exclamation marks and laughter; a version appropriate to whichever friend is on the other end of the line.

Why, I wondered, is it that women fall asleep with open books, firmly clasped, the story just where it was three days ago? The book is an excuse, a comforter to lay across their bellies while they think about something else. And why is it that the first thing I do is read the title, hoping, fearing, it might be one of mine? Grateful that it never is.

The over-polished bulb of glass slipped from her gesticulating hand. Red wine spilled, soaking into the pink paper cloth, splashing over the plate, an awkward oval shape; no room for tumblers, self-important condiments, side plates so thin they'd crack if you dropped a bread roll. One sad yellow rose in a thin vase with a twisted green stem. A drugged caterpillar staggering along a droopy petal.

'Sorry,' she yelped. 'My choice. Absolutely filthy tucker. So sorry. Shall we? Another bottle? Told you. *Did* I tell you? Disseminated sclerosis.'

I wasn't quite as drunk as she was, I frowned concern.

'Don't worry, chum, I'll walk your legs off.'

Prudence.

Her name. I had to drag it out of her. I couldn't bring myself to use the diminutive. She'd been christened BT, before television, when parents recycled the birth certificates of those they looked to for future patronage. Or branded mewling infants with a moral virtue, a charm that would act as its own antidote. She talked and I listened, she came from somewhere outside my experience. Her stories were about parties, gatherings, big houses. She would be cooking a pan of sausages, steak and eggs, in the early hours of the morning, after a wild night. There were attendant beasts, dogs that ran off with Uncle Harry's false teeth embedded in a hunk of venison. Processions of guests, behaving badly or inappropriately, not knowing the form; climbing into the wrong bed (which was the one they'd been shown to on arrival). So that Prudence, at the critical point, leaving the sausages to disintegrate in the pan, would walk out. Into the woods, down to the lake. She'd fall asleep in the gazebo or ha-ha. Bright as paint, the members of the house party who could still stand up would march into the darkness and blast a few more animals. Or knock the heads off statues. Or piss in fountains. Singing hymns to a gibbous moon that floated like a birthmark on placid waters in which somebody's cousin had been drowned.

Prudence gushed, checked herself, ran on, peppering her monologue with strange, outdated slang she'd picked up from her vast
family, in Australia or Argentina. Lapsed monarchists, Franco sym-
pathisers, favoured those destinations, she said – while Lefties, Jews,
and slippery Surrealists took off for Mexico. I could never transcribe
her scatter-gun anecdotes. She'd been mixed up with Catholics and
Communists. Now she was babysitting a bookshop in Hay-on-
Wye, without stock or cash float. Or expectation of being anything
other than a visible tax loss, a scarlet smudge on the balance sheet.
Someone, a lover (I assumed), had left her there, hoping the shop
could nurse her through whatever it was that was killing her.

Her pillow talk had exactly the same rhythm and velocity. As she
undressed, back to the bed, she wittered on: how they'd visited, in
fancy dress, as a kind of jape, an art gallery in Birmingham; she
really couldn't see what these new painters, the Pre-Raphaelites,
were on about. She might, she would, fall silent, gesture that she
wanted help in pulling off her boots; she'd freeze. 'That *shit* Annie.
I need those drawers, haven't had a clean pair since Easter, starting
to scratch. She's always doing it she was the one who . . .'

She'd walk, barelegged, wearing a grey schoolgirl vest, over to
the window. Limping, toppling, one boot on and one boot off.
'Why do these places always smell the same? What is it, disinfectant,
carpet gunge? Tomcats? Awful bloody lavender, bog spray.
Windows don't open properly and if you try . . .'

She saw red light bulbs screwed into the giant o of HOT (the TEL
masked by the angle of the wall). A small, flower-patterned back
room with a sliver of view, the car park. Doors clunking, heels on
gravel. The sound of the main Talgarth to Brecon road.

She started again, head in vest, over to the bed, the ridged can-
dlewick bedspread, as she was; climbing in beside me. 'Dai would
watch the sea for hours. And I would watch him. Check on him
really. Still crocked. I made him come away. Quiet place with
rocks, toy harbour and railway, full of melancholics. Great empty
sitting rooms more like a hospital enough to make the cheeriest
soul want to stick his head in a noose, ghastly nosh. Dai didn't
notice of course old sweat, sitting safe on the right side of the picture window, horseblanket over thin knees. Snout tin. Nose in
Dickens. *Bleak House* for the umpteenth time.'

It was hard to tell if this Dai was rough trade from the valleys or a Kensington waster, border Welsh; naff Taff or society pimp trading on his Tudor connections. He dressed well, apparently, in so far as she'd noticed. Gieves and Hawkes indoors and an old trenchcoat which he tied like a potato sack if she coaxed him out for a stroll to the end of the jetty (distant glimmer of Welsh coastline, low hills behind Swansea, brought tears to his eyes). 'Got a gasper, mate? What a sod of a place?' She remembered the way he spoke, as if he had never left the trenches.

She was very sweet and stopped talking, finally, to make strange small noises, to nip at my shoulder with mustardy serrated teeth. To stroke my back, pick at some flaw in the skin, thinking about – who knows? – the sea, a pet sheep they'd barbecued in Scotland? The thing was easy and unimportant, quiet, light and sudden. I think she'd learnt generosity by surviving her large mad family and their guests, the constant flux, the cold; impossible houses on rundown estates. She made love so readily because it allowed her, for a short time, to let up. To forget, by going somewhere else, what was happening to her body.

For me, the proposition was much more urgent. I liked her. I enjoyed her company. I could sit for hours listening to that lazy, low-pitched voice. Even the dry cough was tolerable. Anything to keep me from the cottage. It was manageable – but there was also, chemically, a zone that was compulsive and crazy in our coupling. The smell, the heat she gave off, not exactly unwashed, but foxy, pungent, harsh. The first sight of her in the doorway of the shop, self-contained, indifferent. Dressed for the fields, the boots and matte-black coat with muddy traces. I wanted it. As most men do, many times a day, part of the baggage, the human contract.

What I felt guilty about was the meal. Sitting here, even with the terrible food, plates heaped with steaming green compost, was a subversive pleasure. Bed didn't matter. I wouldn't speak of it and it didn't impinge on anything that affected my other life. But the meal, that was different. Relationships are built around these leisurely conversations, time out, confession and gossip and the indolent deprogramming of frenzy.

Getting hold of food that didn't put you straight on an intravenous drip wasn't easy in the border country, that was part of the challenge. 'Sound advice from a chum,' Prudence said, 'what to do about food in Wales. Fast. Copy the bloody monks and fast. Or catch your own.' But there were places, written up by celebrity foodies, packed to the gunnels. You had to book six months ahead to be shoe-horned into a bar loud with weekenders and detoured film crews. There were good chefs who might condescend to service one of the country manor hotels for a season. There were even publicans who knew their way around a microwave. But, taken at random, you'd probably find yourself chipping a crust of napalmed pastry to release the icy mess beneath. Quantity was everything. Factory farm fish, gelatinous and pink, were dished up in chainmail skins that blinked like neon on a bed of limp lettuce, the colour of geriatric laundry. Chips drooped on the fork, saturated with sump oil that leaked and spread as you tried to break the skin. Steak squeaked. Rabbit shrivelled into rat droppings under fierce radiation. Lamb bled into ridges of purple-grey mash, potatoes with the life beaten out of them.

'Coal,' Prudence announced, bending her knife on something walnutty and black. 'They used to mine it, now they serve it with a hollandaise sauce.'

The worse the grub, the more lavishly it was presented. Descriptions of gourmet dishes were giddy with unpunctuated foreplay: *lapin* love-crushed on a bed of diced seaweed, crab smothered in a gush of colitic chocolate, antelope placenta sieved through a mesh of smoky fishnet. You'd sit for an hour pondering a sheet of vellum in the bar while waiting to be summoned to your table in a blind corner by the kitchen. (The eccentricity of Prudence's eveningwear might have had something to do with it. She didn't go along with the suburban nonsense of changing for dinner, but she wanted a rest from her wellies. And came up with a shapeless, anklelength, black velour shift, borrowed or inherited from a relative who had been twice her size, and probably male. The pearls were genuine. Her face was powdered like Halloween; the lips vampiric, sharp cheekbones emphasised with crimson bruises. I'd seen such things in Ireland, where confused ladies who retained an appetite for five-course dinners were let out of their asylums at the weekend, in the company of some waif of a minder.)

'Where are you living?'

'Oh well,' she said, 'you know. One of Becky's spare book rooms, anywhere actually.'

She didn't ask why I hadn't brought her back to the cottage. Other people's motives didn't interest her. There was the ever-present narrative of her past and there was disease, the viral invasion that promised a punchline.

We risked a couple of glasses of toffee-coloured Muscat to round off the evening. I sipped steadily, listening and half-listening to her description of another dining room, in Lynton, her friend Dai telling her that he had, all things considered, 'a soft spot for Hitler', a complicated kind of softness. There were positive cultural ideas in what the little Austrian was spouting, but his sense of colour was deficient and he couldn't draw a line. His lines were like road markings; they didn't breathe and tremble. Dai was evidently a painter. Or had once been. Before the breakdown. Which Prudence said was a breakdown in the consciousness of Europe. Forest darkness had fallen over our cities. But this wasn't altogether a bad business. Ruins and Romans, mythical swords and lances. And of course the grail thing.

She swallowed her Muscat at a rush as the shape of the story she was telling began to come apart. 'Mmm, yah.' A sharp pink tongue (flint arrowhead) cat-licked the corners of her mouth, trickle-syrup from her lips.

'I won't do another haul to Hereford, piss in a bottle, shit in a test tube. Blood in a syringe. They could clone me from the samples they keep in that place. It's the best there is, for the lads back from wherever, deserts, fiords. Absolutely fine. *Christ*, I hate, I bloody hate hospitals. Waxy linoleum and flower-painting tosh along the corridors. So tomorrow let's walk over the Bluff, Gospel Pass, to Capel. I won't open the shop and you won't do whatever and we'll get sodden. It's time it really is time lazy sod you saw the abbey.'

I couldn't help myself, on the creaking stairs, no idea if we'd find the right room, knowing it didn't matter. Not to her. This didn't touch her. It was part of the fever; my arm around her waist, the pelvic bones. She was too thin, too brittle. She wanted me to rest my hand on a spot at the base of her spine, propel her forward. Like pushing air. She subverted gravity. She had another coughing fit.

She was talking when I dropped the keys and went down and couldn't get them into the lock and had to take out the long key and try again and fell into the room. Fell on her. Tried to nuzzle the slope of her shoulder, unable to get at it through the rucked dress, high on her neck and no easy way to slip it down.

Prudence didn't help, she let me struggle to lift the heavy slippery material above her waist. To touch her was to bruise her. Thighs and arms, the next morning, as if she'd been brutalised; not taken up, carried gently to bed.

The dress came over her head, I couldn't do anything with the pearls. I lay beside her for a long time. I could see the glowing red o through the partly drawn curtains, one of the bulbs on the blink. And I could hear the faulty plumbing. Voices from the bar. Old timber stretching and contracting. Squeaking boards. Television. Lovers in other rooms.

She let me watch her, on her side. Tasting declivities. My fingers searching out tiny imperfections, rough spots, tufts in the pits of her arms. The sniffing and comparing of skin scents, the testing of textures and moistnesses, folds and thickening ridges and hair that was coarse or downy. She was complaisant, well-mannered, obliging but tired, not talking, talking faster in shorter sentences; then responding and not wanting me to stop, to take off my clothes, my jacket, my shoes even. She weighed nothing. She climbed up on me and came away from herself, swearing and biting. And I encouraged her, I wanted the sharpness of it. Then later she locked her legs around me and I found myself yelling while she shushed and laughed.

And sometime after that, the lights from the hotel sign were off, there was moonlight in the window. She had her dress on, nothing else, standing up, looking out; watching the film of it in the long mirror. I went back to her, where I had been and she moved and we made love again, without urgency, until we were, each in our own way, satisfied, exhausted, able to retreat to the soggy, too-short bed where we shared a dreamless sleep. A sleep in which dreams and bodies and identities were exchanged, expunged. The sleep of that country.

The nice thing about Hay, it was a good town to leave behind. I'd taken my time, followed hedged lanes from the cottage onto the open hillside; a steep climb up the main road, passing beyond the viewing point where, on good days, you could scroll a panorama that was difficult to absorb. Landscape stretched the bones of your head. Your eyes were too dim to facilitate the detail – woods, copses, small farms – the glint of the twisting Wye, the hills beyond Kilvert's Clyro. Most days were not good. Most days turned cloth into blotting paper. Drovers' Texan dustcoats, extravagantly shoulder-flapped and panelled, pockets big enough to carry slaughtered hares or middleweight badgers, looked cute in catalogues, and might keep the damp out of an open-windowed Range Rover, but in the Black Mountains they did nothing except direct the spill towards uncomfortable areas of the trousers. You sweated inside rubberised bivouacs; sleeve-tubes worked like run-off pipes, hosing underwear, filling up your boots. Rain from the west was solid, a scowling revenge out of Cardiganshire and Powys; a cloud of unknowing saturated with the red dust of the Margam steelworks, the black grit of the valleys, anthracite and consumptive sputum. Spirochetes and cancer triggers and particles of asbestos frisked in a protein soup that stung like sea salt. Walking into Welsh rain was like setting off for Ireland on foot.

Every morning I'd leave the cottage early and come back when the light went (a couple of hours later). I'd make more notes and settle in for another long night trying to convince myself that there wasn't something seriously wrong with this place. No human entity was coughing the night away under my bed. Nobody was running a phantom shower in the kitchen. Nothing was forcing me to wall myself into a narrower and narrower space.

The poet from the Poetry Bookshop had given me a tip before he left for the north. He tried quite discreetly to steer me away from the Ewyas Valley and its mythological overload – Landor, Eric Gill, Father Ignatius, J.M.W. Turner and the rest. Not catching my eye, absorbed in his tobacco tin and the thin white cigarette he was rolling, he said he felt it might be worth my while to visit Craswell Priory, out on the high ridge, the road between the Olchon Valley and the Golden Valley. He floated the suggestion with such tact, it was as if he hesitated to revise another man's poem. Write it any way you want, mate, but this is what I'd do; come in at a more oblique angle, work through analogy. Simile not metaphor.

And he was right. What he was getting me to do was take my time, acclimatise myself to the quiddity of this pluralist landscape. I wanted in any case to postpone my visit to Capel-y-ffin and Llanthony, too much rode on it. Craswell still had its integrity, it hadn't been worked over by literary snoops and predatory academics.

I arrived, coming off the moorland road, down a farmtrack. There was a lull between storms and the sky had the unreal brightness of a bulb that's about to blow. It pulsed, particle-charged and ecliptic, offering an unnatural clarity, a clarity nobody wants. It was like the moment before the barrage. Every stone was visible, delineated with its own crisp shadow. Fields hummed with earthed lightning. Voices sang in the droop of the single electrical cable slung between poles that leant away from the narrowing road.

The ruins of Craswell, a priory of the obscure Order of Grandmont, were part of a working farm. If the poet hadn't alerted me to the place, I would never have found it. This was the proper location, I decided, for Robert Graves's druidic Battle of the Trees. Trees swallowed walls. Gnarled stumps took the form of petrified animals, sheep carved from fossilised timber. Brick courses collapsed to reveal earthworks. A low altar of unbonded stone slabs stood at the east end of a sunken grass enclosure. Some of the oaks were so deformed by age, so twisted, it was impossible to separate wood and stone; trees became architectural follies, towers of thorn and ivy.

I mapped arrangements of birch and rowan, ash and hawthorn. Craswell, because it had been left alone, because successive inhabitants had recognised the validity of the site, its alignment with other sites, retained a ferocious sense of stillness, immanence. The wind didn't bluster, it was generated by the movement of the leaves. A proper response to this place would release Graves's poetic daimons: delirious vision, prophecy, erotic power. The beginning of language is ecstasy. This disregarded amphitheatre with its weathered cup marks, broken columns, triumphant vegetation, was the gatehouse, the lodge that had to be visited before any assault could be launched on the Celtic heaven.

I was a trudger, steady, grim, lurching to favour whichever knee or calf or Achilles tendon was currently out of commission. Moderate pain was as comfortable as it was going to get. Throw in rain that wasn't rain, saturated air, and you have a proper sense of a walk in the Black Mountains. Jets screamed out of the half-mist, aborting lambs, making windows rattle in dark cottages. This, they reckoned, was as close at it comes to the Falklands.

We stuck to the road, there wasn't much traffic. Prudence in her rolled-down wellingtons, her black coat slick with slithering runlets, set the pace: long-striding, light across the ground, swivelling strong, square shoulders. I'd lose her, gasp at her heels, come alongside at the very moment when she'd lean over to launch another anecdote, another torn snapshot from her never-ending childhood.

'. . . a hunk on the grill, absolutely smothered in garlic which he abominates and I adore, nothing mimsy. Pa vanished into the cellar, oh, a couple of hours, two or three other chaps ravenous booze gone Pa gone candles guttering to stubs. I wandered into the woods feeling shitty and pissed actually the steak I think it might have been horse just beginning to burn. Wasn't hungry couldn't face food thrown up three or four times gold-brown colour like that barrel wine we had in where was it nothing no substance and Pa . . .'

We came off the road above Pennant, a severe climb, hands and knees, coarse mountain grass, to Lord Hereford's Knob; no view. The edge of the world with the world slipping away from us.

'Dai. Your Dai. What does he do? Did you really know a person called Dai?' I asked, hoping to slow her down.

'He was at Capel. For years. Lovely hands. Nice hair, quite clean. Smoked like a chimney, kept his tobacco in a little tin with a picture of a pyramid, a sphinx. *Hated* outdoors.'

'Was he religious?'

She'd moved ahead again, out of earshot, found the path. I shouldn't climb hills with women I like. It's too distracting, tautologous. There was no way in this weather, the wind winging Prudence's coat, hair wild, to interest her in premeditated spontaneous embraces; leaning against the gale, a kneetrembler was out of the question. A four-hour walk still ahead of us. Women were always more realistic about this, about everything, more practical. They wanted to check the ground for ants, to make sure there was a car waiting on the other side of the hill, a room with a hot bath, the prospect of a good dinner. Women, when they weren't reprocessing the past, were co-directing little upcoming screenplays.

Where did Mary Gill, Gill's wife, get the strength to cope with this walk – over the Bluff, in winter, six or seven miles between the abbey and Hay, a basket of provisions, letters to post, Gill's shag? Enduring – or did she relish having her husband to herself? – his incessant, self-defining blitz of asterisk sex. In the journals all those columns of recorded fucks, wanks, guzzles, gropes. Hailstorms of come. Jism blizzards. There she sits in the pencil drawings, brandishing her knitting needles; the tight bun, the round spectacles. Eyes shut in justified exhaustion. Not a tramp over the hills without the attentions of her hairy, sweating husband, the fuss and the mess of it. Sacramental, he might call it. Pagan with stains, crusts of the previous knotted into her pubic thatch.

Rock cliffs dropped abruptly away to the east; grey grit with quartz pebbles, waterworn sluices, slithering runs of unsecured stone. The rain had moved on. Light levels changed with disorientating speed: near-night to weak sunshafts edging from cover. Cloud-race sweeping across the ridges on the far side of the valley.

Lust and spiritual discipline. Woven together in a critical mass. The high secrecy of Ewyas, snow-blanketed or lamby and lush, encouraged the formation of cults, mad utopian schemes, New Republics, communities of sexually obliging seekers, damaged gurus. Prudence, I considered, taking my revenge on her for not dropping to her knees in the spirit of Gill's family harem, belonged on the fringes of one of these millennial knocking shops; convalescent, compliant, and out of her tree. I could still feel the necklace of rabbit-sized marks that she had left in the skin of my shoulder and across my chest.

Walking the ridge at the head of the Ewyas Valley, I felt the presence of other walkers; Eric Gill's impatience, the exuberance of the young Victorian curate Francis Kilvert. Gill couldn't kick free of London: machines, machine-built temples of commerce, commissioners, priests, and the fat white wives of patrons. The stone here was wrong. It crumbled or splintered under his hammer. He locked himself in a dank coal cellar and ran a pencil around the outline of his engorged member. He slid away sheets of drawings, cocks in rows, catalogued in their diversity; circumcised, bent, biased, hooded and beaded. Skin candles in the chill of this mistaken retreat.

Kilvert was heretical and ecstatic, modest in his openness to the rush of sensory input, mornings when he set out on some pleasure quest that could never be repeated; because it was written.

Gorse that glowed and flamed fiery gold down the edge of the hill contrasted sharp and splendid with the blue world of mountain and valley which it touched.

Spring and summer lived in the folded hermaphroditic spike of yellow-rattle, white and mauve badges in the coarse grass; a bare path above the line of ferns, above the woods.

Kilvert, enjoying whatever society he could, those who came from outside with news of civilisation, novels and scents and complicated dresses. He took tea with the mother and the sister of Joseph Leycester Lyne, the so-called Father Ignatius. (Ignatius presented himself, with a weary smile, as 'The Anachronism'.) It was Ignatius who conceived of this community on the lip of nowhere, a Tibet with a train service (half a day's ride down the valley) to take him out of it when it became too much for his nerves. Incense and the flogging block.

She waited. You miss the right descent and you don't get a second chance. I kissed her and she returned my kiss, in affection. A mild replay of mushrooms, bacon. Saliva brushed off with a sleeve. The mouth that doesn't quite part. And then we went down, slithering, through the spidery trees. Prudence, nimbler, not slowing to tug at branches, brake her momentum, ahead of me again; her black coat disappearing into the darkness. Footfalls muffled in piney mould.

By the time I caught sight of her she was out of the wood, hurdling stiles, away on a newly asphalted farmroad that was more like a stream, a rivulet that rushed from a fissure in the mountainside. I tried to work out which building might be Father Ignatius's abbey. There were several possibilities, set back from the road, glimpsed over hedges or through gates.

Prudence called to me, before being lost in a clattering, clopping, tail-tossing line of horses. Every rider, from the woman in charge to the smallest girl, had to mime some form of greeting. The horses, sweated up, were returning to base, filling the narrow lane with their delicate-legged movements, nervy and unpredictable, tugging towards a twig that took their fancy or standing firm to drop hot dollops of grassy shit.

'Any books?'

One of the horses spoke. A voice from the field. A voice filled with grievances.

'*Books*? What else? It's a monastery, dumbo. Monasteries have libraries, libraries have books.'

'What kind of monastery? Protestants don't do books. No market – outside Belfast.'

'How should I know? Freaks who don't take baths and creep around in shit-stained dressing gowns and no underwear. They let you sleep here.'

The voices sounded exactly like Dryfeld and Billy Silverfish.

The horses stayed, the voices moved away towards the distant white buildings. The odd couple got louder as debate escalated towards the point where physical insults would have to be exchanged; knockdown, boot in, kidney-stomp. One man would dust himself off and hurry to catch the other, squeeze an elbow – before his rival could ring the sanctuary bell and claim first crack at the bookshelves.

'We drive to the door or you can forget it.'

'Great. I'll stay here while you trot back four miles to fetch a car with a flat battery.'

'And let you clean out anything worth having? If you had the fucking wit to recognise it.'

I climbed the slippery bank, trying to see over the thorn-thatch, the nettle forest, into the field. Nightsmoke wiped the frame. Mist rumours crept from the conifers, ameliorating a green twilight. The buildings at the top of the field made a single block with a pointed roof, a cubist Monopoly piece on the wrong board. Over a single strand of barbed wire, a brown donkey with a white nose turned its head in my direction. Of the phantom bookdealers there was no trace.

The buildings went, the donkey went; I tumbled back to the road while I could still find it. Damp air followed me in a slipstream. I set off in the direction Prudence had taken. A naked Christ had been crucified in a diamond-shaped shelter that looked, against the green tump on the far side of the valley, like a Tyrolean shrine.

There was no time to appreciate the skill of the carver's chisel, I was mud-drenched by a white van that came fast out of nowhere, bucking through puddles as wheels fought for purchase in the drowned lane. It brushed against me and I saw rolls of carpet swing from side to side. Here was an optimist who reckoned he could sell fitted shagpile to a monastery.

Kilvert had come the other way, through Gospel Pass, on an early spring morning: *The old chapel short stout and boxy with its little bell turret (the whole building reminded one of an owl), the quiet peaceful chapel yard shaded by the seven great solemn yews.*

The diarist begins by responding to the spirit of place, this enclosure with its still-to-be-defined atmosphere. Visitors must start their explorations in the hamlet of Capel-y-ffin, where the Honddu rushes under the bridge, where the valley narrows and steep paths carry you back into the mountains. Abbeys and follies and communities and detox writers come and go, they scatter, but the whitewashed church with its haphazard turret, its plain windows, outlives them all.

Prudence drifted among the gravestones. The churchyard sat in a hollowed bowl of earth, overlooked by a ring of mature yews. Who *was* this woman? The shock of hearing Dryfeld and Silverfish twitched me into another mode. Prudence was a false memory, a fantasy from another life. The sight of her, half-turned, stooping to read inscriptions on the erased stone slabs, was something I couldn't process. A mortality Polaroid. If my blood was to make one final charge on the brain, I'd freeze a single frame: Prudence in the bookshop, the blue flicker of a paraffin lamp. Face in shadow. Leaning, bored or tired or ill, one hand in the pocket of her jeans; huddled in the black tarpaulin coat. The first sight of her gave me access, so I hoped, to her past, her childhood, her lovers; access to experiences that were still to come. I wanted, from that one instant, to take possession of the woman, forcing her to invent the fiction of a life.

'Gill carved some of these inscriptions. Haven't been back in years. Not since Dai.'

She was kneeling, trying to decipher blackface letters on weathered stone. Cultures of decay, slate poxes: the broad-shouldered tablet was a decapitated figure buried up to its waist in leaf mould, limed by crows, fed by maggoty gases. Earth meat. *William Leycester Lyne, Adopted Son of Father Ignatius.*

I'd read about this boy, one of the priest's flock who became a
mad shepherd. A hill wanderer driven out of his wits by something
he had seen, some revelation, an accident of the light.

As you might expect, there were a number of Davids in this
community of the dead. Evening thickened to absorb the hill-fret,
the gravestones became a scatter of shields planted after a battle.
Shale envelopes with deleted addresses.

'What was the name of your David, your Dai? Is he still alive?
His other name, what was it?'

'Jones. David Jones.'

'Like the painter? The poet?'

'Carver, writer, affectionate friend. Of course. Absolutely. Blaeu
Bwch, up there, that little anvil-shaped hill. David drew it all the
time. With the spotted horses. In his dreadful old coat. Shivering in
the top field.'

'Hold on. David Jones died in, what, '73, '74?'

The woman was mad. Prudence would have been about eight or
nine years old when Jones died, troubled, agoraphobic, wasted on
a cocktail of anti-depressants: Nembutal, Drinaryl, Trofanil,
Librium. He had been told by his doctor that he should 'accept
incapacity' and count himself lucky if he felt no pain. The spectres
of childhood came back with a sharpness he could taste; rooms,
smells, a south London street seen by a sick child from an upstairs
window. A dancing bear becomes the spirit of Arthur.

He watched his aunt and his mother overtaken by senility, shadows. Trapped inside a tight mantle of skin, white sheets, a cramped
room with a shifting, darkening view. Nuns. Residential homes.
The torment of healthy afternoons in exposed gardens. Harrow and
Brockley were easily confused, suburban ridges; a boyhood walk,
uphill to a park, a glimpse of the Thames. A boat marooned in a
playground becomes a set of playing fields witnessed from a tall
house. Loud stripes on the shirts of these fine young men.
Remember the drop to the west from the bench by the grave of
Byron's friend in St Mary's? Keep it at a safe distance, a petrol
mirage; circling aircraft over Buckinghamshire and Berkshire.

I wanted to hit her, do her damage. Kill her. The business with
David Jones, that whole narrative of self-immolation, anxious
visions invading layered hillsides until they shivered and cracked

with nervous indecision, was too painful. Wrenching, brain-tearing breakdowns. Drug voices, the voices of the dead and the inhuman silence of this valley. I wanted to grip her by the shoulders, shake her, keep shaking until she let the fantasy go. Until she accepted my version of what she was, how she should tell her story.

In the floating island of the little churchyard at Capel-y-ffin confusion was manufactured. It seeped from the earth, from the strong roots of the yew trees, from stalled lives. The burial place was dense with silent figures, none of them moved. I'd lost Prudence. It was too cold for her. I couldn't hold the image, the bookshop in Hay, the doorway. She was gone. I whispered her name, too shamed to call it aloud. She walked into the night. I couldn't write what I couldn't see.

6

A vixen, rough-collared, hard-travelled, broke cover with what appeared to be a length of white stick in her mouth. Foxes were not much seen in the hill country. The Hereford sass boys, with their grenades and rapid-fire weaponry, had taken care of that. A few jokers were hitting poachers' pubs and toll-bridge taverns in Davy Crockett caps with dangling ginger tails, playing the spread-finger game with bowie knives on polished teak bars. That's where Conor had miscalculated. Conor Kwilt, gardener, handyman and potential artist. He collected animal parts – beaks, claws, ribs, pelts, anything that he could scavenge or slaughter. Road kill, agro-industrial casualty, crow-pecked lamb case, he wasn't fussy. If the body count dipped, he was quite prepared to do his bit; a walk through the woods, crossbow slung low on the hips, to visit snares in which panicked creatures twisted and tore.

Of course Kwilt was not his name. Nor was Nievidonski (another a.k.a.), although he did have, in a bad light, a Slavic glint. A border guard wearing an ex-Gestapo coat in a Cold War programmer by Ken Russell. Kwilt experimented with alternative identities, but the core never changed. Rebirthing. Processing the dead. Shaping caskets that would incubate the spectral radiance of decomposing cormorants, gannets or rooks. He facilitated pain. He would have been shocked, had he known of it, by BritArt exposures of sectioned cattle in tanks. He laboured, with twine and thread and carved whalebone, to construct receptacles that might do honour to the multitudes he had offed.

A couple of punters had turned up at the abbey, without luggage, in outfits that had enough of the animal still twitching in them to have Kwilt reaching for his twelve-bore. They'd hoped for charity, a free billet for the night, but offered cash when confronted by Kwilt's manic Jack Nicholson leer. Kwilt had too many teeth, mouth like a mantrap, flush with ironware. He could never take a plane without setting off alarm bells and calling out SWAT teams.

Dryfeld had a thing about teeth, teeth in fiction. He was putting together – in his head – an anthology of oral inscapes, with particular reference to American hardboiled crime novels, Charles Willeford and the like. Kwilt's riveted incisors and spot-welded overbite had him gobsmacked. Silverfish was unimpressed, he'd lived all these weeks on the road with the sorry aftermath of British dentistry (leave well alone or go in mobhanded with chisel and brace). No wonder bookdealers preferred to keep it buttoned, never uttering until they were forced to mumble: 'Got a man for that.'

Two other men, unconnected so it seemed, were present in the stone-flagged kitchen as the paying guests shuffled through, steeling themselves to risk a little food, a bit of social give and take – before they made a dash for the books. The dude at the table had a busby of Eel Pie Island hair, early Stones, Twickenham R&B, ostensibly unwashed but, close up, quite considered; layered, cut on account by one of those double Christian names. The shirt was discount, wide-collared. He had a three-bar grin, underwritten by a flaring spliff. Skin tone you don't find in the Welsh Marches: woodstain that was going off. Genial to a fault, he offered the affronted Dryfeld a toke. 'Howard. Howard Marks. Get you fifty per cent off anything you fancy in wool and nylon, foam-backed. Pick a card.'

Howard didn't do jackets; in some later incarnation, Dryfeld fitted him with a money belt, a Portobello Road silver buyer, ethnic art pimp, holding sagging belly muscles in check with a corset of multinational bills. Fishing into a slightly camp shoulder bag, leather so recent it made the vegan Dryfeld's nostrils flare, Marks unearthed another resinous block; another set of fiddly rituals to hobble time. The card, when it had served its purpose, read:

Norrie ('Piles of Style') Dikkon DISCOUNT CARPETS PYLE.
Largest Stock of Remnants in South Wales. Visit our
warehouses in Pyle & Treforest.
Accredited Rep. J. Howard Marks, BA (Oxon).

'We carry weaves so fine you could wear 'em to a dance.'
Silverfish bummed a light from Marks's heavy-tipped spliff.

'You guys keep a pool table?' Pool was his weakness. It was how he psyched himself up after a day on the road, a session or two smashing coloured balls around the green baize; watching them *plop* as they slid from sight sharpened the hurt he needed to rip books from shelves. 'Pure and applied math,' he said, calculating the angles, whipping his cane like Heifetz. Pow. Pow. Pow.

The other kitchen squatter was coming to the end of his cycle, he slowed his spin to a gentle St Vitus's dance. Arms spread wide, Manson hair on the horizontal, a yard from the scalp. Fast feet in winklepickers curling at the toes like Turkish slippers, he had a dervish delicacy that stopped all conversation and made the lowlife clap.

'Nick's into Sufi this week,' Kwilt said. 'He's doing it to fuck up his band, a bunch of sarf London scrotes, pillheads.' Nicholas Lane was the subtlest English blues guitarist of his generation, so the mad critic Doc Hinton had written. But who wants subtle? So Lane brokered deals in the music underworld and let the light of the universe flow from his eyes.

'Now watch this.' Kwilt smacked his left hand on the table, hard. 'Slicker than the *I Ching*. Each finger is a ridge, the Black Mountains. You're looking south. Little finger, Hatterall Hill. Ring finger, Bwlch Bach. Middle finger, Waun Fach. Forefinger, Pen Alt Mawr. And the stubby thumb, that seems to lack a joint, is Mynydd Troed.'

He unsheathed, with a swish, an ugly blade. More hieratic than the bowie knife, this was a bone-cleaving butcher's tool; innocent of previous fat. Diamond dustings danced on its hungry edge. Even Silverfish paused midway through an imaginary pot.

Thwap!

Kwilt wrenched the tip from the wood, found his range; an itchy pickpickpick teasing the surface, gathering momentum, veins on the back of his hand a relief map of mountains he alone saw.

'Where will the plane crash? Hatterall, Bwlch Bach, Waun Fach, Pen Alt Mawr?'

Thwap!

'Mynydd Troed?'

Movement a blur. Faster and faster. 'Where will the next one come down?'

Kwilt was a cargo-culting wrecker, waiting on fate's bounty, Perspex and alloy, metals lighter than breath. He saw fantastic possibilities for his art if he could marry ex-hedgehogs with tyre tracks and the alchemised essence of the newest death-machines from British Aerospace. He'd already picked over the mangled carcasses of Second War transports and Wellingtons with faltering Hercules XVI starboard engines that had gone down in bad weather on Offa's Dyke. At a distance, breaching the ridge above Llanthony, coming through the springy gorse, Kwilt found a mess that looked like a sheep's afterbirth, picked over by crows. Lumps and strings and long brown tears in the earth.

'Shit.'

Blood gushed. The blade had taken off the top of his thumb. 'Shitshitshit.' He had justified his misgivings about the abbreviation of Mynydd Troed.

Kwilt addressed pain by picking up the amputated thing, striding to the door and flinging it out into the night. It was warm in his hand, the still-pink nail like a blind eye from which colour had started to drain. The soft sound of recently bereaved flesh falling into the long grass of the lower meadow alerted predators; owls, slick scampering nervous nocturnal mammals, a fox on the prowl. Kwilt's thumb tip was borne away like a surrogate mouse. A trophy for Renard.

It had been quite a performance. Lane blew a slow wow, Marks passed him the draw. They nodded in unison like toy woodpeckers dipping a glass of water. Kwilt gave the broth a stir, then went away to fetch needle and thread. Pouring himself a heavy glass of something homebrewed, he set to work to stitch the flap. Disgusted by the baroque turns of events, appetites repressed, Dryfeld and Silverfish decided to turn in. It was the first time since they'd left London that they found anything on which they could agree.

'End of the corridor, down the steps, first door. Only one bed but you'll manage. If you need a piss in the night, force the window. Stick a couple of books on the chair, you'll reach it. No moaning and don't tear the pillows. You pay for any lubricants you use.'

All things considered, Kwilt was pleased with the evening's show. He had another parallel-world past life to call up: the Yakuza Years.

Part-Native American (Northern Shoshone/Mohawk with Kwakiutl traces), part-Ashkenazim, all Canadian (Pacific Rim), Billy Silverfish lay on his back, arms folded, a chrysalis withdrawn into its corduroy coat. He stared at a circle of thin light as it illuminated a portion of the tall, whitewashed ceiling. A pattern of flakes, flaps of desiccated emulsion. What the fuck was he doing, sharing a monk's narrow bed with a wired skinhead – in a decommissioned High Anglican monastery?

'The light I can live with, but the radio?' Silverfish moaned.

Dryfeld licked a stubby finger, using spittle which had the consistency of cowgum, to wrench open another page. He raped text.

'You'd think, given the number of institutions he's been thrown out of, one of them could have taught the bastard to read without grinding his teeth,' Silverfish kvetched. 'You sound like a climaxing dyke, Dryf. Hoovering seaweed through a rubber straw.'

'We're as thick and thin now as two tubular jawballs.' Dryfeld had to bellow to hear his own voice above the yammer of the radio. *Finnegans Wake*. The perfect book at bedtime, the begin-everywhere cyclic fable; pick it up again tomorrow, lost as you ever were. The punster's bible. 'Clean and easy, be the hooker!' Dryfeld the binge-eating vegan gurgled, sour wind in his pipes. He leaked bad air in a puff that lifted the sheets.

Dryfeld couldn't sleep. Silverfish *chose* not to shut his eyes, to lose control, waste precious hours of darkness when he could be recalibrating the culture, seeing east as west and west as east. Moscow was the coming hot spot for an alert bookman. There were as yet no books, so he had a clear field. The Krogers had been the forerunners. Heroes of the suburbs, bookdealers *and* spooks. The first of a moonlighting generation, multiple career,

double-identity invisibles. Respectable agents of a foreign power –
with a disreputable second life peddling antiquarian literature.

Meanwhile, the Cossacks were thundering into Bloomsbury for
the monthly book fairs (car boot sales under cover). The Royal
National Hotel was like Moscow Centre; surveillance corridors,
cardboard walls, Hawaiian muzak bars with red plastic banquettes,
bamboo screens and lethal, sharp-edged glass ashtrays. Sinister and
silent beer drinkers pretending to play with miniature chess sets.
Sturdy tarts with p.m. moustaches and trowel-applied slap staggering from bar to lift with Mediterranean businessmen and an armful
of Jiffy bags. Kremlin mafiosi copping for blow jobs in bugged
bathrooms, two open suitcases on the twin beds; first editions of
Virginia Woolf with spidery purple inscriptions traded against
condom-wrapped fingers of skag.

Smoke. Sweat. Dirty money. Bowels lurching between superglued constipation and saffron-yellow squitters.

The National was Silverfish's kind of gig. The only set in which
he was anonymous, one of the crowd. A Grand Canyon growl:
argumentative, shocked, delighted to be shocked. On the buzz,
steaming between stalls, stuffing business cards into unpurchased
stock, deflating reputations, puffing his own eccentric but genuine
expertise.

Weather stats, names of Atlantic rocks, temperature charts recited
in a monotone that franchised tedium, wolf-hour whispers. 'I have
to read aloud,' Dryfeld snarled, 'to hear myself above the financial
reports. I need the radio to drown the voices, bad stuff that gathers
in bedrooms. Psychic condensation, colonel. To drown you, your
incessant yap. You're all noise and no signal.'

Beneath the barbed-wire beard, Silverfish smirked. He'd initiated
a dialogue, an audience for his next riff. Silverfish had only to talk
Dryfeld down, bore him into a sleep-snack, twenty winks, and
he'd be out of the bed, through the door into Gill's chapel and
among the books. What was left of them. The problem was the
scale of this room, a monkish dormitory with windows so far from
the ground you'd have to stand on someone's shoulders to see out.
Into what? Velvet darkness. This gothic revival folly teetered on the
edge of an infinite William Hope Hodgson chasm, a cosmological
anomaly where time gurgled and 'abyss' was another word for

extinction. Extinction of individual identity. Of Silverfish. And
that was altogether too individual.

Silverfish had to choke a scream; light a cigarette, pay his dues to
the yellow cancer gods to get himself off the hook, trade a small
tarry death against the death of the planet, the solar system, the
Kosmos.

Abiosis. How could he locate a single word in the lexicological
forests of the dictionary? Especially when he started at the back. He
scrolled frantically against the blank white screen of the soft ceiling,
columns of words photographically recalled. He wanted the worst
one in the book. He wanted to speak, out loud, his greatest fear.

'Abiosis!'

Dryfeld hit him with the bedside lamp, a brass altar candle pastiche. The bulb exploded. Silverfish, bleeding, blacked out,
tumbling head over heels into the pit of his fears, while his bed-
mate, in vest and longjohns, rolled from beneath the coarse blanket
and stretched one leg in the direction of the floor. An uncannily
long reach. The bed had been built for giants. Cold feet slithered
on tiles as treacherous as a shower stall. He skated, lost his balance,
grabbed for the edge of the bed, ripping the covers off Silverfish,
waking him.

'You bastard.'

'I'm answering a call of nature. Necessary micturation.'

'Micturate in my ear, slaphead. You were going to scam the
books.'

'What books? Come with me if you're frit of the dark, take my
sturdy member for your compass.'

To add conviction, as he thought, to his cover story, Dryfeld
groped his way across the long chamber towards the sink, where he
pissed like a horse. It was too late, Silverfish was already shoulder-
ing aside the tottering pile of scrap metal, ancient cookers, tumble
dryers, that blocked access to a heavy wooden door – the back way
into the chapel.

Soon, by flares of matchlight, with curses and the odd blow,
Dryfeld and Silverfish scavenged the muniments, the last relics of
the monastery at Capel-y-ffin. The papers of the founder, Father
Ignatius, the household accounts of Mary Gill, incomplete inscriptions by David Jones. Or so they imagined. Not knowing that the

entire archive had been immaculately and precisely evaluated by
Nicholas Lane; sorted, creamed, bagged and passed on, via Becky,
to the vaults of the castle at Hay. All that was left was a fraudulent
journal by one of the brothers, a drunk with shoe-blacked tonsure,
an ex-journo called Jonah.

Brother Jonah's scatological improvisations, purporting to be a
true account of Ignatius's ministry, lived up to the standard of the
reports he had once filed for the *Guardian*: bile and wind in equal
portions, character assassination with what he considered passed for
stuttering charm. Jonah was poison in a brown sack. But his trash,
along with a few hymn sheets, charity appeals and prices of live-
stock, was crammed into a pillowcase by Dryfeld, as he and
Silverfish prepared to flit.

Was it morning? Shapes without firm outline loomed out of the
sepulchral darkness; sheeted chair-lumps, a massive oak table like a
pathologist's slab. The heavy drip of a leaking tap that left a rusty
fern-tongue on the slippery wall of the basin. Everything was out
of scale. You needed siege ladders to climb into bed. Silverfish's
journey in search of the bog was longer than the tramp from Hay.
His bowels, costive for weeks, tight as a condom packed with pebbles, groaned and lurched. Pulling himself up on his elbows, he got
his head into the basin, sucked the ancient spigot. Sharp splinters of
tin, dead spiders, dust balls: he inflated his cheeks with slow-
flowing, mud-red water. Then the whole head, white skin and
greying horsehair, was plunged under the stagnant trickle. Owwsh!

That's what turned his spine to tapioca, freed his compacted
gut: the view. There wasn't one. The monastery set, so Silverfish
believed, in a circle of hills – lift up your eyes – had no exterior
windows. Through the constricted, diamond panes of the leaded
slit above the basin, Silverfish contemplated a withered tree in a
prison yard. Gill's beloved 'garth'. The windows on the far side of
this barren patch were dirty and impenetrable. Here was everything
Silverfish wanted. What an extraordinary notion! How inspired, to
pitch your retreat on a sacred piece of ground – and then to cover
its eyes. Capel-y-ffin was a metaphor for Silverfish's most cherished
fantasy: the blindfolded man in the perfumed harem. Damp walls,
the musty afterbreath of incense, dried-out palm leaf crucifixes,

blankets steaming under Dryfeld's troubled sleep. His seal-bark snores excited the Canadian bookman to a pitch that had him rushing, wool-footed, across red tiles in search of the communal lavatory.

Dryfeld groaned. His radio hissed, droned fatstock prices. Silverfish gushed into his fist. Then in a blur – timorous beams from the east hauling themselves over the monastery's high walls – the dealers were up, dressed, out. Comforted by panic, returned to their corporeal uniforms; alert, alive, on the burn. The word was: move! Swag over shoulder, cartoon-style, Dryfeld waddled past the kitchen door, ready to pretend, if challenged, that he was removing a pillowcase of rubbish that represented one night's kip.

If Silverfish, scholar despite himself, hadn't paused to check an inscription, they might have made it. Free and clear. Salvaged early work by Gill, the sign said, commemorating in stone something wholly forgotten; carved letters linked in a fetish, twigs breaking out of cracks.

'Hey, hold up,' Silverfish commanded, wondering if there was any way he could work the tablet free with his fruit knife.

ERIC GILL LIVED AND

WORKED HERE 1924–1928

ALSO HIS ELDEST

DAUGHTER ELIZABETH

ANGELA – BETTY – 1924–1956

my work is my leisure · my leisure is my work

'Dig it. Eric Gill Lived And. Beat that for an obit.'

Silverfish had just begun to scratch at the surface with his knife, teasing out the undertext, when Howard Marks, eyes like blood blisters, drifted up on them, a voice in the cloud.

Gill's disapproving portrait, a man weighed down by his beard and then asked to remove his spectacles for added gravitas, peered out myopically – an enlarged postage stamp waiting to be franked.

'Nice timing, boys,' said Mr Affable, the carpet rep, from whose lips there never emerged a sour note. Howard was all puff and twinkle; coal-measure chuckles, rib-rattling coughs. 'Give us a hand loading the van and I'll run you down town. Right, bach?'

Which town he didn't say. They were pressganged members of the Taffia, honorary boyos without the flat caps and mufflers, the dining rights (chips from the *Pink 'Un*, chips with chips). Howard, the dope smokers' Roy Jenkins, was already well on his way to charming the Saeson. Cleverly, without apparent premeditation, he was reinventing his past: he wanted to be more Welsh than a temporary residence on the coastal strip, the road to Swansea, justified. The valleys were a mysterious hinterland. He knew the times of all the Paddington trains. Unlike Roy, he was trading down, doing a Tony-Hopkins-as-Lecter, training his voice to acquire a melancholy roll of sentiment and roguery that fooled the toffs. He was a future politician in a one-man party, with a libertarian manifesto, licensed not to offend. When they shared an Oxford scratch-pad, Howard taught Bill Clinton how to smoke without inhaling (breathe with the belly like Allen Ginsberg). How to keep talking on the phone, with an even modulation, while enjoying a Somerville blow job.

'I'm down Blackwood to check out a likely band. They're ugly, loud and too clever by half, the time's right. They'll go all the way, these ones. So get a shift on, there's good lads.'

Dryfeld was reluctant and Silverfish horrified and ashamed. He had no experience of manual labour. Marks would evidently turn a blind eye to the sack of swag. Or anything else where he could work an angle. So they packed the hideous carpet rolls with bales of dried leaf, the product of the monastery garden, the greenhouses.

Kwilt the salaried horticulturalist was nowhere to be seen. Lane was poking about the paddock, splitting poppy heads with a sharp blade, dripping thick juice into a tobacco tin. He chanted as he worked. He heard the rhythm, the faint heartbeat of the wakening land. Jewelled dewdrops. Drunken bees. Bright streams. The overfull Honddu surging against the low stone bridge. Wood pigeons. Creaking planks in the rickety tower of Kilvert's owl church.

Nick was himself a plant (mushroom-chalk), feeding on starlight, uncurling as the sun lifted over the boundary fence. He possessed the secret of time travel: stay still, shut down all systems, take air through complaisant pores. Let those long fingers twitch and run with the natural pulse of whatever is. And was. And will be. Early-nineteenth-century chapbooks were more present to him than yesterday's newspapers. He knew this ground as it had been *before* Ignatius attempted his revival of monastic life.

As Howard's white van, loaded until it sparked, slid down the flooded lane, they saw Kwilt marching towards them with a brace of bloody hares slung over his shoulder, a crossbow dangling from his left hand. The Condor Legion William Tell: hot life-spill snaking down the oiled slope of his leather coat. The van free-wheeled, fired, leaked steam as it began its tortuous climb up Gospel Pass. One tractor, a dozen sheep, a postman cycling the wrong way, would finish them. The engine would never fire a second time.

Howard was bombing, red eyes hidden behind aviator glasses, his own roadie. A space cadet who laughed until he shook, shook until he coughed, spat green and left it dangling from the hedge. He didn't feel the chill that had Silverfish hugging himself inside his corduroy coat. For Howard it was always summer, white jeans, thong sandals, Super Furry Animals T-shirt. He never left the beach. Tacky Welsh tarmac became the black sands of Lanzarote. The curved windscreen with its splattered flies looked out on some fabulous harbour, white pleasure boats dancing at anchor against a sparkling blue curtain.

Howard wouldn't have seen the lurching giant if Silverfish hadn't screamed. Dryfeld *had* noticed the lunatic in the middle of the road, but didn't care; it was none of his business. He was, as ever, writing up the previous day's events in a ring-bind folder. Heavy letters cut through layers of cheap paper. SIX OTL. ONE FYAF. SILVERFISH READY TO CARPETBOMB HAY.

Marks was more interested in codes than apparitions, road spooks that lay ahead. Reality, over the last few years, had warped. 'What's OTL? FYAF?' Was he missing something?

'Out to Lunch. Follows You Around Farting. Bookshop cat-egories,' Silverfish growled his interpretation, wrenching the wheel from Howard's one-handed, tapping-along-with-the-beat grip. The hiker, copiously suited (with a mud respray), hefting a Gladstone bag, wasn't going to budge. He had the air of an abortionist fleeing from a house call that had gone badly wrong. Silverfish didn't want to look into those eyes. They were colourless, with a faint bias towards pink, melting ice cubes rescued from a Campari and soda.

'Wa wa wa ka ka ka . . .'

'Drive over the bugger,' Dryfeld ordered.

'Wo wo woo wa . . .'

A night on the road hadn't unthawed this huge man's capacity for language. He dressed like a tenured academic and had the hands, now clenched, of a man who killed cattle for fun – by punching them between the eyes. He was near the edge. Silverfish knew his psychotics; Marine Corps gook-butchers with rivets in the skull, leg-breaking Italians with too many rings. He could read the signs: the way, for example, the man had hooked his arm around Howard and hauled him, neck and crop, out of the van. The way he knotted his fist in a skein of Howard's hair and was banging his head against the dented side-panel.

'Wa wa www where's ka ka Capel-y-ffff fff fucking fin?'

Easy ones first. They pointed back down the road.

'Wa wa www where's ka ka ka Kwilt?

The same response. In triplicate. Three thumbs jerking in one direction. This unfortunate, it appeared, was an associate of Kwilt, casually offered a country weekend. Name of Joblard, an aboriginal from south of the river, somewhere back of the Elephant. The man had spent the night on the mountain, in and out of ditches, after a day at the mercy of local buses, shuttling between Hereford and Brecon. Dropped off at a remote public house, he had been given a traditional Welsh welcome: gaped at by the toothless mouths of feral inbreeds, hit on for rounds of drinks, assured of the inferiority of his status as an outsider, an Englishman, a dirty Cockney. Treated to yarns of the heroism of Glendower and Gareth Edwards, Graham Henry and Llywelyn Fawr. Embraced, sung at until the tears ran down their craggy, weatherbeaten faces – then tipped into the dark with a set of incomprehensible and contradictory directions – 'up by 'ere, down by there and back, isn't it?' – that left him two or three miles shy of where he'd started.

Howard couldn't turn the van, the lane was too narrow, tall hedges, overhanging trees. They ran backwards, Joblard next to Marks; the others fending for themselves in among the herb-smelling carpets. They freewheeled blind, jolting in potholes, bumping against earthbanks, skidding on mudslicks, down to the little church of St Mary's, in its enclosure of ancient yews, beside the fast-flowing Honddu.

There was, as there had always been, a woman working in the kitchen. Kwilt's woman, his wife. That was one of his peculiarities, a long, even-tempered monogamous relationship that couldn't (and didn't need to) explain itself. Dryfeld and Silverfish failed to notice Mrs Kwilt's presence. She flitted and stared. She wasn't, of course, allowed near the stove, but she did her bit in skinning and gutting the various beasts that the preternaturally morose Kwilt dropped on the table.

'What's your wife's name?' a cheeky young acolyte of Kwilt once asked. A person from Coventry working on an open-ended interview, a few words to soften the shock of Kwilt's necrophile sculptures, photographed for an overfunded magazine. This youth, feet under the table, unknown and unpublished, swilling Kwilt's whisky, smoking his grass, majored in arrogance. He saw nothing that was going on around him, knew nothing beyond the prompts in his notebook (there were columns of these). He didn't want to waste time looking at the work, it was cold in the shed. It smelt of formaldehyde and rotting shark. 'What's your wife's name?' She was standing close behind him, peeling potatoes for his dinner. As invisible as the youth's mother. He gobbled the food on the plate she passed him, but her hand was carved from ectoplasm.

'My wife's name is Mrs Kwilt,' said the sculptor, as he frog-marched the whimpering freak to the door. Before booting him into the night. The attentions of the yard dogs.

Mrs Kwilt and Joblard were old adversaries. Mrs K had stubbed out a cigarette in an unstable mound of couscous that Joblard was trying to tease into life by the addition of random herbs, anchovies, cockroaches. The cigarette went unnoticed until Joblard's latest jailbait-crumpet spat out a cork tip. In revenge he'd managed to switch Mrs Kwilt's medication, with alarming Tourette's syndrome consequences.

They knew where the respective bodies were buried and had grown fond of each other in the way of old friends who make sure they have no good reason for an in-the-flesh rendezvous. Joblard went back far enough to remember Mrs Kwilt's Christian name.

But he was too canny to use it. Mrs Kwilt had a shoebox of photographs from the Maidstone house that Kwilt and Joblard had shared with a twenty-stone S/M dominatrix and her hydrocephalic dwarf lover. Kwilt kept them fed on road kill and Joblard spent his days in a dowdy Kentish museum, sketching delicate Egyptian *ushabti* figures and reading H.P. Lovecraft paperbacks.

Joblard accepted the proffered mug of tea and sat mute in a chair by the stove, waiting for Kwilt. Mrs Kwilt continued her skin-wrenching, slippery, gut-spilling operations, her eye never leaving Joblard as she kept pace with a fantasy ruralist saga on the radio.

Nicholas Lane appeared, twirled a couple of times to exorcise the spectre in Kwilt's chair, and left again. His soft feet making no sound on the tiles.

Joblard ate, dozed, smoked a pipe. Mrs Kwilt unknotted short lengths of parcel string before knotting them once more and winding them around a spindle.

There was another meal in progress, another ladling from the stewpot, when Kwilt finally took his place at the head of the table. They ate in silence. Mrs Kwilt carried the plates to the sink. Kwilt rolled a joint. Joblard stretched out his glass for a refill, before reaching into his Gladstone bag.

With a sweep of the hand that was parodic in its fastidiousness, Joblard set a large black revolver down on the table. Oil leaked into the indentations in the planks of pale wood.

'They wa wa want us to ka ka ka kill a dog. As a wa wa warning. For ka ka cash. You game, Kw wwwww ilt?'

1

Woken by a rasping cough that didn't belong to me, I heard the shower running. There was a man with his face pressed against the glass who seemed to be crying. Several things were wrong. The man's height, the droop and sag of him as he tried to keep his head from disappearing into the low ceiling. That a human of this size could be reduced to such helplessness. Then there was the fact that the shower was in my kitchen. The cottage didn't have a shower. And not much of a kitchen.

The man was large and soft and emaciated. Thin arms, sunken chest; a vulnerable, childlike pot of belly. You could see the ribs like a toast-rack poking through a crust of white dough. His hair was long, matted, his beard grey. Uncut fingernails left red weals in the flesh where he tried to scratch a persistent itch. His lower back was covered with bites. His nakedness gave off just enough glow to shine through the earthed darkness of that small Welsh room.

> The Chief Defect of Henry King
> Was chewing little bits of String.

So he intoned in a sanctimonious pulpit baritone. And the heavy shoulders heaved. He sobbed. Sobbed until he coughed. Looked out from wherever he was and saw me looking back at him.

I'd had enough. Night after night of water sounds and nothing to be found next morning but the usual misted-over shaving mirror, the toothbrush frozen in its beaker. Now this. Television ghosts.

Monochrome newsreel spooks escaped from a satellite propaganda channel. Borderland ghosts spoke in nonsense verse. They quoted Belloc. There was something deeply sinister about nursery rhymes written by Jew-baiting Catholic trenchermen.

Henry will very soon be dead.

Still in my sleeping bag, I rolled out of my stockade in front of the embers of the fire and across the floor towards the kitchen. I lurched upright, pulling the downy wrap to my chin. I hopped. The man was gone. Pale moonlight on a dirty towel.

Henry will very soon be dead.

I placed myself where the man in my dream had stood and saw what he had seen. Blinding whiteness. A chin-on-the-sill slice of dazzling light. I fell back. Clear sky, hard outlines, blue hills; a Mediterranean city in its afternoon death. I closed my eyes but that didn't help. The road was still there, the perimeter fence of the airport, the gun towers and refugee camps. Banners slung across the road. Roadblocks. Military men in red caps, bandits. Oleander, hibiscus, bougainvillaea. Human and animal shit. The imagined shimmer of the sea.

I thought of Prudence, what had happened to her, where she had gone; the Kaporal tape I hadn't yet played, the Landor book which would never now be written. Ruin, poverty, divorce and, much worse, a return to bookdealing. If I stayed awake, I tapped directly into the hallucinatory pool that lay beneath this dank cottage. If I slept, I dreamt the dreams of the man in the shower. I didn't dream *of* him, that would be too easy. I dreamt what he dreamt. Endless shelves of books, a library of the world. His trembling hand reaching out, fondling spine after spine: Golden Age mystery novels, theology, *Swallows and Amazons*, and absolutely nothing with naughty bits. No politics, please.

Books were squeezed so tightly against each other they couldn't be withdrawn. Leather squeaked at the touch. Bindings groaned. Fine, pale pages of India paper waited to be cut. Perfumes of Morocco, vellum, glue. Slithery jackets. Wobbly spines. Hinges cracked. Bruised fore edges. Top edges in gilt. Mint. Very good. Nice. A reading copy. With all faults.

Overloaded shelves lifted into a tent. A hammerbeam roof of austere volumes in the original cloth that might drop and crush me.

Book-walls weighed against my chest. I couldn't breathe for the
dust and fear. A bibliothèque of yellow-tobacco spines that lacked
a Nicholas Lane, in beret and cigarette, to pick out the books that
mattered. My ghostly incubus, by holding so determinedly to this
cottage set, was forcing me to share his claustrophobic nightmare.
He was dreaming me. I was a walk-on in his narrative, an interloper
on his turf. By invading his cottage, I besmirched the purity of the
memory-place that was keeping him sane. If he *was* sane. If the
horror of what was happening to him hadn't already uncorseted his
libido and released a plague of slithering, sucking, oozing, shriek-
ing grues.

Henry will very soon be dead.

I was out of there. In the morning I would return the keys to
Becky. Leave Wales to the incomers, exiled illiterati, weekenders.
The hills were loud with the sound of Wesker. Poor Arnold, pride
of Spitalfields, bemoaning past glories and present neglect. And
those other urbanites the Mellys: a fine stretch of the Usk for
George to fish and somewhere for Lady Diana to entertain. I
thought of her guiding Bruce Chatwin to the poet Henry
Vaughan's grave in the little roadside church at Llansantffraed,
telling him how Vaughan's mother had once lived in the Scethrog
tower the Mellys now owned. The emblem of the alchemical
twins, curled together in soixante-neuf intimacy, floated between
Vaughan's flat tombstone and Chatwin's incipient novel of the Black
Hill. This border landscape was ripe with markers that became
hinges, marrying the mental worlds of disparate writers; the living-
dead questing for confirmation. Mischievous predecessors not quite
ready to let go.

Allen Ginsberg, I knew, was one of a number of writers who
had visited the publisher Tom Maschler's retreat, above the abbey at
Capel-y-ffin. By curious coincidence I had been shooting a documentary film with Ginsberg at that time. As we sat on Primrose
Hill, he questioned me about the building that fascinated him
most in the bright spread of London: the Post Office Tower. It was
a symbol, seen from this druidic eminence, of thrusting sixties'
phallicism: paranoia. Barnacled listening dishes processed, as the
poet saw it, all the secret voices of the western world into a single
band.

The gentle ascent from Regent's Park, from the white mansion where he was camping with his small entourage, doubled for the climb from Landor's Llanthony. Ginsberg's break in filming – he didn't reveal his destination – was to Maschler's bungalow. The book of that trip, the LSD-fuelled hill walk, was there to be read in the Hay Poetry Bookshop. This earth-brown pamphlet differed from the edition Cape Goliard put out, *hors commerce*, in 1967. The text had been revised and there were photographs that hadn't been seen before: the poet in his gumboots communing with a chunk of glacial debris.

> *Remember 160 miles from London's symmetrical thorned tower*
> *& network of TV pictures flashing bearded your Self*
> *the lambs on the tree-nooked hillside this day bleating*
> *heard in Blake's old ear, & the silent thought of Wordsworth in*
> *eld Stillness*

Long-breath Blakean invocations. Ginsberg's scribbled journals bring the cycle around; bring back my longing for London. There could be no nostalgia for hills that never left me alone. The landscape of childhood was the only true recipe for sleep: streets that followed a river along a valley floor, steep terraces, industrial dereliction. Railway lines leading to collieries, slag heaps, winding gear. Hill farms and dustbin-scavenging sheep. An interior landscape which doesn't fade, even when I let it go.

Packing was easy, I hadn't taken any of my research books out of their cardboard box. I'd read two-thirds of a novel by Barbara Vine and a poem by Ginsberg. I scribbled a card for Prudence to be left with Becky. I marched three times around the cottage, widdershins, exorcising malign influences. And I stalked for the last time over the fields to Hay.

Becky was on his lunch break. He hadn't seen or heard anything of Prudence, but he knew that, from time to time, she retreated into the woods as Lady Penelope Betjeman's helpmate; mucking out, chopping wood, casting spells, whatever was needed. His own place was in much the same direction. Would I care to join him for a tin of sardines and a splash of Chablis? I could whistle at his collection: Beckford, Corvo, Firbank and others of the Fellowship. There might be the odd duplicate for sale. Becky was dressed in his usual mustard-coloured cords, wellington boots.

What was it about rubber footwear? The town was like something out of John Wyndham: a gathering of defence industry accidents creeping about in anti-radiation drag. Wellingtons for booksellers, hippies, Notting Hill colons. Judy Garland slippers with six-inch heels for the rest, the gender-reassignment mob. Twilight in Hay, at the change of the watch: book folk to their fox-holes, transsexuals on parade. The twisted streets of the narcoleptic market town were dressed for a Chelsea Arts Club ball: Farmers and Fairies. What I would never understand is why changing sex meant changing nationality. New women seemed to be created with a compulsory Welshness, a leek in the gob.

I helped Becky with four or five boxes of books that had just come in; he wanted to sort through them in the privacy of his retreat – 'Becky's Bunker' – before putting the dross, his employer's tithe, on display in the Abattoir. Buildings that might once have offered form and function to Hay had now been taken over for bibliographic internment: Castle, Cinema, Co-Op, Cow Sheds. Even – Becky's operational base – the old slaughterhouse. There was, he asserted, something reassuring about books-as-furniture, leather bindings being brought back to their place of dispatch. He swore that, on winter evenings when the shop was shut, he could hear the shelves lowing, as milk-calves called for their mothers.

We picked our way across a stone-flagged floor (which still featured the gully where the blood of butchered beasts had been flushed away), dodging marble-eyed invertebrates who refused to accept that there was anywhere else to go. Becky didn't bother to lock up for lunch, the Abattoir had nothing worth stealing. Most of the punters were only here to confess. They would travel miles to earwig a captive bookman. Hay was the cheapest psychiatric clinic in the Marches. Lugubrious out-patients and unfrocked Presbyterian ministers would corner Becky in his private office and treat him to an account of their fall (the long version with detours into childhood abuse, broken marriages and failed suicide attempts).

Revived, the perkier among them would then pick their way along the shelves explaining to Becky, book by book, how they had

once owned those *very* titles, before losing them in a divorce settlement or having them stolen by their only friend. Seeing old
favourites on display was enough to trigger another and probably
terminal collapse.

Becky ended the day, battling through the rain to a station wagon
with a flat battery, under a double cloud: the miasma of whinge and
moan to which he had been subjected – with its inevitable corollary,
an area of low pressure creeping in from the west.

Parking privileges at the back of the castle marked Becky out as
the King's man, courtier to the Great Salvationist. This nickname
had attached itself to the predator who had bought the town on
tick (then sold most of it to keep his creditors at arm's length). The
Salvationist was a master of publicity, understanding that to shift a
dull wet book mountain he had first to sell himself, to come out as
a woofing and gibbering public idiot. He was of the bell-ringing,
jumping-in-the-river tendency; books were fun, books were an
event, books were more eco-friendly than fossil fuel. Play with
them, let the kids build them into pyramids, burn them to keep
yourself warm. Masochists from the surrounding countryside
turned out in droves to confirm their sense of millennial doom; the
mortal danger inherent in literacy, freedom of access to alien ways
of thought, novels by Marie Corelli, Berta Ruck or Nat Gould.
Hay was a day tripper's Sodom for Primitive Methodists: the prices!
Two pounds for a *book*! They drove home, after a day returning
product to the shelves, with a proper sense of satisfaction; that
Satan had been stared in the eye – and conquered. Next weekend
they'd be back as usual at Poliakoff's, at the Heads of the Valleys,
sorting through stretchwaisted polyester in salmon pink, nicotine-
friendly cardigans racked in a warehouse that represented the Welsh
equivalent of the Wal-Mart experience in an off-highway Texas
town.

Becky was a better talker than driver. Sunlight splintered on the
blue curve of his glass eye. (The functioning orb was slate-grey.) He
had the nervous habit, when the road twisted back to the west, of
closing the working eye against the dazzling beams and relying on
his replica. It generally worked. Becky knew the road so well.

'What news of the Corvines of Highbury? Any scandal from the
rooms? We're utterly *starved* of gossip.'

He was too modest. Becky lived on the Salvationist's phone (he didn't keep one in the Bunker). He had a multitude of intimate friendships that stretched across the social spectrum from country house to dockside dive. You might, as easily, find him chatting to a mystery-writing dowager, Hereford squaddie, or chapel elder. He knew Mormons, Modernists, Neo-Georgians, well-connected ley-line brokers – and the man who dyed Lord Berners's favourite poodle.

In his opinion, conversation took precedence over keeping the car on the highway. Leaving Hay in the general direction of Cusop, tracking the Dulas Brook, any notion of 'road' was soon forgotten. These were farm tracks that became tributaries of the brook. Agricultural vehicles claimed any surface on which they could get a purchase. Private citizens, drunk, drugged, deranged, let Land Rovers and station wagons find their own way home.

'Dryfeld – you know Dryf? – called in this morning. *Farouche*, no? Jacket so loud I took my eye out and left it in the drawer until he'd gone. Travelling with a Eskimo. Anything in that? You never know with Dryf. Is he one of the Fellowship? Very hirsute the Canadian. But extremely bright. Musky as a game dog.'

A man with outstretched arms (like a Polish nun being exorcised) lay in the middle of the road. Any motorist with a conscience would have stamped on the brakes. I was getting used to these hallucinations. Things, when you didn't walk, were always odd. These empty lanes were crowded with spectres: frustrated anecdotalists, hedge-priests, characters too baroque to be of much use beyond the outer limits of genre fiction. Let Becky run straight over the idiot.

He leant an elbow on the horn, but didn't slow down. The man, beetle-browed, thick-fleshed, Asiatic as Grock the Clown, rolled aside with consummate timing, catching the draught from the skidding wheels. Noticing Becky, he bowed in ironic acknowledgement and raised a hand. His straining trousers, cricket off-whites, were held up with a regimental tie, backed by scarlet braces.

'That's Cap'n Bob, Robert Maxwell's double,' Becky said. 'Lives on the road, cadging lifts from unwary strangers. The Salvationist found him outside Tewkesbury years ago and took him in. Acts as a kind of comic butler at the castle, insulting guests as part of the entertainment. Crack shot, plays a decent hand of bridge. We're all convinced he *is* Maxwell. Appeared soon after the bouncing Czech took his midnight dip. And then, of course, there were all those biographies – Ceausescu, Honecker, Pol Pot – turning up on the Abattoir shelves.'

Becky helped himself to three sardines, scooping them onto a cut of farmhouse loaf that had the colour of peat and the texture of pumice stone. He passed me the tin and a white plastic fork. The wine, so far as I could judge, was rather good. (It didn't have that telltale aftershave kick.) The cottage was an advert for the picturesque, knocked off by Thomas Jones, or J.S. Prout on a bad day. Mumpy garden, with oversized rhododendron clumps, declining to a mill stream. The roof was so low you risked decapitation by ducking through the door. The property agents had done a great job: Becky's bunker was whitewashed and neat on the outside, with late yellow roses, ivy and wisteria. Inside was a different story: the contents of a country house sale decanted into a gamekeeper's cottage. Oils in ornate frames, cases of *premier cru*, portfolios of steel engravings interleaved with tissue, odd volumes in stacks, and as much dark furniture as the dim and sunken room would hold. Water came from a pump in the garden. Candles in Georgian silver holders were the only source of light.

Before I could get at the books for sale, I was given the full tour of Becky's mouthwatering holdings: rare pamphlets of Uranian verse, a pearl button from Horace Walpole's waistcoat. I used the time to pump Becky for what he knew of Prudence and where she might have gone when she disappeared into the mist at the little church in Capel-y-ffin.

'Pru? Lovely chap. Been around forever, but she comes and goes. Hasn't a bean. Could be Chelsea for a jolly or Exmoor after stags. She'll turn up, always does.'

I started to rummage through the boxes Becky had set aside. I wanted to get back to London. There was no way I'd sleep another night in Hay. Most of these books were straight roast beef, spies and spinsters and Greek Island romps with Larry and Paddy and Xan. But at the bottom of the pile was a mass of scruffy paper that looked promising, amateur drawings of stone heads from Abbey

Dore in the Golden Valley and zoomorphic carvings from the corbels of Kilpeck Church. Bizarre frames of a primitive Romanesque kind: Sheelah-na-gig with vulva stretched to accommodate all comers. Hares and hawks and fiddlers, dogs with beards. All the sins were on parade: Lust, Pride, Anger, Gluttony, Envy, Sloth. And Avarice. A sermon you could walk around.

Beneath these savage cartoons was a tattered ledger, which proved to be a journal. I caught the name of Father Ignatius, references to events in Norwich and London, and I decided that I'd better take it away for further study. I was just making up a pile of decoys, a jacketless William Faulkner, a late John Cowper Powys, and a Michael Moorcock with an unbelievable inscription (it was genuine), when we were interrupted by a thunderous pounding on the door.

Cap'n Bob rolled in and reached for the Chablis. He rinsed and spat. 'Battery acid cut with athlete's foot. It'll do for now. I don't know why you persist with this French muck, Becky, when I could get you a couple of cases of best Albanian Riesling at knock-off prices. I've got the run of the Salvationist's cellar. He's pissed most nights.'

Bob was followed by a squat and powerful man, bald as Emmental, smocked and very particular where he set his feet – which were bare. 'Marc Pyratt of Corby,' the traveller announced. 'I ran over Bob. He told me where I could find you. Not much damage. Garage will sort it out. I'm liquid and hot to trot.'

'Marvellous!' said Becky, toeing my box under the table. 'I'll welcome you at the Abattoir anytime. A friend of Bob's is . . . Well, really, this is my luncheon break – which I'm foolish enough to enjoy in the privacy of my own home.'

'Stop that Wodehouse bollocks, you old queen,' shouted Bob. 'Marc's kosher. His own transport and he's packing a Coutts chequebook that doesn't let out moths.'

Pyratt, who seemed to be perpetually backlit, tracked by his own nimbus (like Arnold Schwarzenegger bursting through a plywood wall to splatter the lowlife), was appraising the goods with a canny eye. The force was with him, so he said. He glowed, he glistened. Books leapt from their stack like amorous doves returning to the cote. 'Amazing times. I only have to step through a door to feel the flow, the current. The way the scattered library of the world yearns to be reunited, under my care.' He lifted a finger to his lip. 'Don't say it. Virgo. Ambitions to work with clay. Schooled by the monks.'

'Actually, no. I can't stand *gemütlich* tosh. I was educated at home and I've lived here since . . .'

'Stop. Stop right there.' Pyratt smiled indulgently and held up an open-palmed hand. 'I'm getting the heat of your aura. You're confused now, but you'll be deep into *Siddhartha* before I've loaded the first case of books into the van. Trust me. That's a promise. Here's what we do. You deliver a lorryload of the Salvationist's least-favoured remainders. My boys stack it in the Corby warehouse. The schnorrer, the one with the Sicilian connections, the Salvationist's deadly rival, pulls in as arranged and takes the selfsame books *back* to Hay. Within twenty-four hours they're in the window of the Don's shop, fifty yards from where they started. I cop my fee as middleman, you're in for a nice little drink, and Bob's your uncle.'

'Like fuck he is,' growled the Cap'n, tipping out the cutlery drawer in search of a corkscrew.

The cottage suited Pyratt. Sizewise. If they did ballets for weightlifters, he'd be your man. He had the hands-on-hips stance of Mussolini performing t'ai chi: delicately sturdy, swivelling on the balls of the feet. Fingers, tanned to the colour of wartime newsprint, reached out to push back a spinning ball of invisible energy. That's what happens, I thought, when you abandon a sixty Rothmans Royals a day habit. And switch off the intravenous caffeine drip. That's a lot of karmic energy to reroute. All the fizz he'd dredged up to fight these poisons had been elbowed. Carcinogens and heart-twittering rushes converted into pathological calm. There was no hair left on Pyratt's head to earth the jolts of hungry magnetism. The force was in his eyes, the pain. The calculation. The residual melancholy of Europe, of a dying world. Book deals were a game he didn't need. As was life, that sorry rehearsal; the drudgery of plodding around a circuit he'd covered so many times before.

'I'm losing it. Your magenta's fading to pink.' Pyratt spun and then he wasn't there. He knew, as he used them, what words did. How. Every. Particle of Breath. *Counted.* He spoke slowly, with rabbinical deliberation, cultivating an air of oracular wisdom. He accepted that each word spent was a portion of mortality. It hurt to watch.

'Sorry about the tradesmen.' Becky was visibly relieved to see them go.

The Corby magus, after treating Becky's doorstep, in some weird ritual of his own, to a couple of passes from a can of sea-salt, strode off; he made straight for the passenger seat of the Jag – before remembering who his chauffeur was. Cap'n Bob, who had liberated a couple of bottles, slipped on his dark glasses and swivelled his massive head in search of the last green rays of sunlight. Vampire-wary, he wanted to make it to the castle before nightfall. They disappeared with an anachronistic roar, churning up a small cloud of dust that hung in the air for longer than we cared to watch.

We sat on a bench by the stream and sipped our wine. In that sound, water over stones, was the antidote to folly. Agoraphobic by conviction, Pyratt was rarely happy away from his own patch. The world, he was convinced, would beat a path to his door – if he learnt how to stay still, shut out distractions, deal with his duties *in one flash of enlightened consciousness*. But the only way to sustain this illusion of permanence was to escape: retreats, monasteries, artists on the edge. The good thing about being on the road was that you were closer to the time of coming home.

And he was right. I hadn't left London in thirty years – until now. What a mistake! If life had the time-in-remission quality of Becky's garden, if I could sit forever in the twilight watching the landscape fade, the magical moment of the shift in the light, I wouldn't want it. Keep your owls and orchards. I wouldn't subscribe if you could order pastoral bliss on a digital channel. The cost is too high. I was going home to a place where I'd always be a stranger. Stuff Wales. Far better to stay in Hackney and make it up, pad out the story with characters from the Mediadrome (preferably dead). No fiction could equal the reality benders of the mainstream press.

Becky was happy to let the box go. I overpaid for the novels and took the Capel-y-ffin journals as a makeweight; maybe I could work those up, steal enough material to get the Landor book started. I fumbled for the keys to my Hay cottage and handed them back with an enormous sense of release.

'When's the other tenant moving in? God knows how he manages to live in that place, it's haunted.'

'Hard to say, actually,' Becky muttered, shading his good eye. 'Frightfully nice man, buys the odd romance from the cheap bins. But he does bang on a bit if he catches one on one's own. Wanted me to drop to my knees. Hello, I thought. Then he clasped his great hands in prayer. Tricky situation.'

'What's his name?'

'Name? Didn't I say? That's why it's been so hard to . . . The cottage *had* been let out, originally, to a fellow who'd gone abroad. Terry Waite, in fact. The hostage chap.'

8

This is going to cost you. I think, I know, they're out to get me. And it's all connected. To do with the dog. The dog in the cottage on the edge of Exmoor. It sounds crazy but there's absolutely no doubt about it. There's a contract on that dog.

Oh god. Another good man blown. Kaporal had been on the road, in his own company, far too long. Mondeo fever. I couldn't listen to any more of this garbage. I ejected the tape and went back to the Beefheart bootlegs (received in lieu of payment from Filthy McNasty's): good sensible stuff from the desert in a smoke-voice conjured out of trout masks and molasses. *Dachau Blues.* All the roads that night, the A40 on its swing through Monmouthshire, the A449 running south towards Machen's fabulous Caerleon and the even more fabulous M4, back to civilisation, to London, were so smooth, so clear, that driving became dreaming; the pilot was the passenger. Bitumen blacktop floated through my windscreen like a strip of film feeding into the camera, erasing its image bank, returning to pristine darkness.

I was leaving – not running away from – the land of ghosts, my dead fathers. There would be too much to go through, too many tedious histories, before I could approach the truth. Whatever realms of wonder David Jones and Vaughan the Silurist monitored from the passage of light over these hills, whatever mystical enlightenment was attainable through meditation and silence, it was not for me. Not now, not ever.

I was with Kaporal, irredeemably corrupted (informed) by life in the city. I liked this night drive, when tarmac became a jetty running into a featureless sea. Nothing to read, nothing to explain. Kaporal was creeping about the south shore of the Bristol Channel, while I, his sponsor, inventor of his narrative, escaped from Wales. If he drove down to the beach at Portishead and flashed his lights, I might pick them up. I could signal back to him from Goldcliff. Then we could go our own ways: Kaporal deeper into the nest of conspirators, the suicide cultists of Somerset and north Devon and I, sabbatical over, to my work and family. To bookdealing.

I relented. Having to concentrate on the urgent flow of the M4, the fairy lights of the twin Severn bridges ahead of me, I gave Kaporal another spin. I wouldn't be taking that right-hander towards Bristol, but it was the appropriate place, the last of Wales, to hear the rest of his report. I might even send the man a few quid, to keep him out there, out of harm's way.

. . . Barnstaple. You might wonder what I'm doing here. But this story is both more complicated than we anticipated and much simpler. It's all of a piece, that's what you have to understand. I'm not moonlighting, it goes far beyond defence industry flakes topping themselves in imaginative ways around scenic locations in Bristol. It goes beyond cancer victims tuning in to their Cathar pasts, the pain of being burnt alive in Languedoc somehow making chemotherapy bearable. It gives pain a context. Heresy, I mean. That's what it's all about, locating and defining the heresy appropriate to this diminishing era.

Look. Let me run the tape back a bit. Barnstaple. You've read in the linens about Michael Jackson? He did a half-hour set, unannounced, at the local theatre. What the fuck was that about? A sick, shivering man, a blacked-up albino in a white mask arrives in a black limo. Wearing a white leather suit of lights and black leather gloves. He performs, vanishes. They say he wanted to buy the Beast of Bodmin.

But how did I get here? How did I find myself renting a room above a dry cleaning shop in one of those anonymous English streets that slope towards a covered market. The Pannier Market, they call it. I took the room despite, or because of, the aura of doom and decay. The terminal inertia. Acrid fumes from the cleaners. Saturated fats of the Chinese takeaway. Eastern Delight: *perfect!*

I was trying to wire myself to the backstory, entering that diseased mindset. Norman Scott, Jeremy Thorpe's boyfriend, had been banged up here. Waiting for the man who wasn't going to come.

Yes, I know. Thorpe. You didn't ask me to check him out. He's not part of your research. But all the lesser characters seem to have some link to Thorpe and Liberalism and the Money Tree. Did I explain? Donations filtered from the Bahamas, through the Channel Islands, in the general direction of a Great Cause. That's what they kept telling me.

My contact has a stall, books, in the market. Hippie type. Looks like he's up in the clouds, Kerouac paperbacks, Buddhism, self-help – and then you check his prices. On the button with Bloomsbury. There aren't any provinces left, no sticks, no backwaters. They've got the reference book, the yellow price guide. They all subscribe.

This guy's definitely got Marxist leanings, Howard Marks. A kind of Legalise Marijuana Liberal. Been to the meetings. Knows the story. The businesses funded by party donations. The bribes. The conduits. How you could launder anything if you had proper Houses of Parliament notepaper. Jesus, man, look at Archer! Don't you understand yet? All the undercurrents of English life, the dark secrets of the Mediadrome, begin in Weston-super-Mare. Archer, Cleese, Jill Dando. Lalage had it spot on, all those years ago. Amber Lights. *That fucking film, man!*

Hold up. Wait. I've got to break off. I had this amazing stroke of luck, coming back from the market, one of those old-fashioned tobacconist shops. My all-time favourites, they had them in stock. Petit! *'Small cigars' in the yellow packet with the decorative diamond border. 'Dominican.' Petit Dominican produced by E. Nobel. Dynamite smokes, man! With the added Catholic guilt trip, like small sin. I fumigated my room with that first packet, thinking about Jamie Lalage.*

That's what I've been doing, night after night, neutralising the stink of sweet and sour, and replaying Lalage's VHS. The true alignment of English culture is this: Margate to Weston-super-Mare, Bristol to Newcastle. Swords crossed on a green cloth. Every twitch, every symptom fits that pattern. Lalage understood – if only the first chapter – so they killed his career. What happened?

Who knows? Lalage won't talk or he's forgotten. No two viewers could describe the same plot for Amber Lights. A man, burdened with self-doubt to the point of catatonia, mopes about his Camden flat. There's been a death, a brother or double or alternative version of himself. He's a stiff before he starts. Probably on the payroll at Marconi or GEC, a defence industry copywriter. Or peddling black propaganda as film critic for Time Out.

Not important. Get on the road with the tapes. Road therapy. Weather psychosis. The Westway's as grim as he is. Good Friday, riding westward. Get going. Pick up a squaddie. News from Belfast. In transit to Hereford. He's going to write a blockbuster, bend the truth – define the heresy! Silbury Hill. Road kill rock cults on the cusp of punk. Bristol. Women from East Germany in sinister raincoats.

My sixth night in Barnstaple, I ran the bit where they arrive in Bristol, over and over, the way the headlights burn and blur. Drowned light, man. And I began to see it. God knows why I was so dim. I'd researched every inch of that trip for him. Found the hotel and booked the rooms. Lalage was programming the suicides! *He was testdriving a dark future. Pouring mood syrup over black emulsion, nice songs, nice tracks from Berlin. Cabaret tarts and turned agents, ring-kissing bankers and heresy brokers from the inner cabal at the Vatican. Nazi gold. Falcons as currency.*

Every plot has to have a believable landscape, a map you can trust: Heathrow, Silbury, Bristol. Sites of megalithic ritual, earth stars, mounds, energy-generating alignments. So where does Lalage lead them? Where else? Weston-super-Mare. The Bristol Channel. He makes it feel like Finland. The final commission, the ultimate debriefing.

So he thought. So it might have been, back then. Now the plot has moved on, down the coast. Porlock, Lynton, Barnstaple.

The Money Tree, man. Dan Farson. Know him? Old Soho soak, great purple-faced gargoyle. Exiled down here, Appledore. Knew Scott, knew Thorpe, knew everybody. Trunks of photographs. Drinks at a pub called the Royal George. Met him at Derek Raymond's wake. 'Drop in anytime you're passing, old boy. Everybody does. Open house. Gilbert and George, Ted Heath. Bring a bottle.'

Dan says there's been a culture shift, tectonic plates, the cream of Wapping, all the faces from Limehouse, down to the seaside. Exile. Giving their livers a rest while they punt their memoirs. He's going to introduce me to a publican from Tilbury, Bobby Younger. Younger understands about Thorpe and Bristol and Weston and the Cathars and the Sikhs and who shot Jill Dando. But the main thing is the dog. The dog they want killed.

He's a runaway from a hushhush experimental project, outside Glastonbury. This friend of Thorpe's, the lab technician with the Exmoor cottage, smuggled him out. Bobby swears they've been doing grafts on the vocal cords, sessions of trans-species interfacing, implants. This animal

*knows all the secrets. And it can talk! They've hired a couple of heavies to
kill the fucking dog. If I don't get there first.*

The Aust Services had improved since they opened the new
bridge. As a location, I mean. The entire zone, this Hitchcock retrospective, had settled with an audible sigh into its preordained
obscurity. A low glass-fronted citadel perched, like something out
of *North By Northwest,* on the edge of steep red cliffs. An almost
deserted parking area, more air terminal than motorway service station, was bordered by curved, half-covered walkways. The asphalt
was potholed; springy grass clumps breaking through the cracks,
struggling to return this outdated set to an estuarine wilderness.
There was one other vehicle in a space built to service hundreds,
a mucky white van, its rear doors roped to accommodate an over-
spill of rolled carpets.

I was visiting Aust at the optimum moment, when it was drifting between function and fantasy. A pleasure palace from the early
days of motorway utopianism had been reimagined as a zone of disappearances. Once upon a time citizens had driven over the old
bridge, from Newport, Cardiff and the valleys, in search of a good
night out. A fish supper with a view of the river and some subcu-
taneous muzak. Aust was a destination, rather than a comfort
facility. Now I had my pick of the parking spots.

GRANADA. That's what it said above the entrance. A cream-
coloured Spanish airport with a flat roof and a mess of outdated
electronic gizmos. A frontier post. A convalescent hotel in which to
recover from the trauma of Wales. That must be why they charge
you a whopping toll to leave England but let you back in, sadder
and wiser, for nothing.

Rows of telephones in hooded Perspex booths, bullet-deflecting
shields modelled on the Eichmann trial. The phones were hooked
a few feet from the ground, in deference to the average height of
bus passengers on tour with Evans Evans of Clydach or Bevan
Bevan of Ammanford. The rest of us could stoop and like it. They
had no use for cellphones here. The only person I'd ever seen
using one, an aluminium-suited rep, had blathered, from car park to
escalator to restaurant, in the coffee queue, down the escalator,
into the shop and out to the Gents. Where a disgruntled Taff

nudged his elbow, causing him to drop the device, still whistling, into the blue chemical wash of the piss trough.

One of the phones was ringing as I dived through faulty automatic doors. Lack of custom had ruined their timing mechanism: with an evil hiss they tried to squeeze the breath from anyone stupid enough to enter the building. I was tired. It had been a long day and I still faced a couple of hours on the road before I reached London. I was in that state when it's too much effort to process new faces. Everyone I met had to be on file, a retread; a pale fax of friend or foe.

Coming into the air, his reflection mingling for an instant with mine, as we tried to dart through the same small gap: a Howard Marks impersonator. He had the genetic profile: the all-for-the-best-in-the-best-of-all-possible-worlds laughter lines common to all great con men. He believed his own lies.

This guy, stepping into the night, was a rubber mask. He slouched, soft-shouldered, hands in pockets. Smiled and nodded. The tan went too deep. He'd been microwaved. He was waiting for a battery of flash-bulbs to bring life to weary eyes.

A telephone was ringing in the empty gallery. A line of rectangular light blocks, in low relief against the sound-baffled ceiling, threw a distorted geometric pattern onto the tiled floor. There were probably cameras, fish-eye lenses, hidden in those lights. The watchers, if they were on duty, would see me. But I couldn't help myself, I moved down the line, picking up dead phone after dead phone. I made contact with the Voice. The stranger who was out there, doing his or her bit to keep my quest on the boil.

'Sorry about the delay, boy. Problems our end. Glad you waited. Quality's fine, the man said. You can double the consignment next month. Usual package waiting for you in the third cubicle. *Nos da.*'

This is preposterous, I thought, as I searched for those emblematic figures that advertise the division of the sexes. What if the voice on the telephone had been mechanically distorted? Nobody who has watched television could fall for so obvious a trap. They're tracking me. That's why this building is empty. They don't want civilians killed when the SAS, DEA and ARU let rip. Strafing innocent bystanders with initials.

A heavily built man with too much hair was swabbing the floor of the Gents. His grey eyes followed me as I tried the doors. Third cubicle from *which* end? My hesitation was captured in the thick lenses of the cleaner's rimless spectacles. He could have understudied my old Whitechapel drinking partner, S.L. Joblard. There was something about the way he abused his mop that reminded me of a photograph I'd taken of Joblard, sweeping rubbish from the grass outside Hawksmoor's St George-in-the-East. Joblard was more lowlife than the snapshot demanded. He pushed his role to the point of absurdity. Unsure of his identity, he could become anything he wanted, open himself to any form of possession, keeping nothing back – beyond that steely sense of self-control. Joblard was a man obsessed by Chinese whispers, initiated and then forgotten.

I turned my back on the cleaner, washed my hands. Everything was back to front. Who washes *before* voiding their bowels? Soap-spill glooped reluctantly into my cupped paws. There was no water. The Joblard lookalike was leaning on his mop, watching me. The last I'd heard Joblard was an Oxford professor, an 'internationally respected' sculptor. I knew that academic salaries were mean, and that he had a tribe of barefoot kids to support, but this was ridiculous, even in an age of multiple career strategies.

The soap dispenser worked in one basin, the tap worked – if you cracked its secret – in another. The problem was that you couldn't reach the water before the soap oozed between your fingers. Water, when you accessed it, burst forth under enormous pressure, for just enough time to splash your shirt and trousers. My lightweight, foreign-correspondent suit had been a big mistake. I looked like an incontinent boozehound, with trails of gummy slop slithering down my inside leg. The air machine blew a Los Alamos scorch straight into my face, fluffing thin hair into wild horizontal wings. I was the last panel of an explosion-in-the-mad-doc's-lab cartoon.

The cleaner shuffled off, pantomiming disgust with a loud Oliver Hardy, bucket-and-mop routine. I darted into the third cubicle from the door and locked myself in. *Who is Eggman?* The only graffito was still wet. I stood on the seat to check the cistern. That's all I need, one slip, foot down the toilet, and Joblard's doppelgänger returning with the cops. My arm, jacket soaked to the elbow, went down into the tank. I felt for – and found – the package. Foil-wrapped, crossbound with tape. I sat down, took out my knife, slashed through the waterproof layers.

A severed finger. Diskettes. Pornographic Polaroids, featuring my tryst with Prudence. The proof copy of a novel I had never seen: *Landor's Tower*. Banknote-sized bricks of newspaper. These were a few of the stock surprises I rehearsed. But not this: clean, crisp cash. Plenty of it. In fifties. Too much to think of using, or leaving behind, or taking with me. This kind of loot carried a health warning. It was too fresh to be imprinted with cocaine traces, the sweat of hands and the darkness of a thousand cheap wallets. The money boasted: covert political acts, death and retribution.

The shop was closed. I found a copy of the *Financial Times* in a wastebin. I rewrapped the package and took it straight out to the car. I left it in the boot under the mat, in the hole that should have contained a spare wheel. It could stay there until I got back to Hackney. Park the car somewhere near the Holly Street estate and my problem would be taken care of, the buck passed. Let the cash karma be inherited by an unselective booster. A pre-teen who didn't mind dissing himself in an antique BMW without three-spoke alloys.

If the exterior of this building was out of *North By Northwest*, and the grassy knolls that surrounded it from *Torn Curtain*, then the second-floor cafeteria was a compromise between *Vertigo* and *Marnie*. The room was on two levels. The suspension bridge, in that red night, was a painted backdrop.

I was hungry. I piled my tray with slithery cartons of juice, with tiny bowls spilling over with an excess of fruit chunks, distinguishable only by the virulence of their dye. Soup and yogurt had the same texture, the same absence of taste. There was no cod to be found at the chilled core of a coat of electrocuted batter. Baked beans squeaked when you bit them. Chips, the colour of corn-plasters, bounced from the plate. The coffee wasn't too bad. In flavour. But the glass pot was so cold it might have been recovered from the mud of the estuary.

With a sufficiency of this industrial muck inside me, and the rest pushed aside, I felt as good as I'd felt since I left London. I rinsed coffee grains and stared out into the darkness.

It was happening again.

As I carried my tray to the lower level, opting for a window seat, I saw her. True, she didn't look anything like my mental picture, the way I remembered her. The hair was different, combed back, with loose side strands and a knotty tangle at the nape of her long neck. Her clothes were resolutely retro; loose, chiffon, all of a piece – with a bit of a ruff at the neck. I couldn't tell if this garment was under-wear, shower curtain, hunt ball or Hoxton. Subtle colour washes, saffrons and high-sky blues, pulsed under subterranean lights. A red fur jacket was thrown around her shoulders. She nursed a glass of wine, tapping its rim with an empty one-shot whisky bottle. Smoking, she was condemned to the outcasts' corner: the yellow mist on the river. I caught the B-movie smell of – what? – *L'Heure Bleue*.

Prudence.

I'd have said, if questioned next day, down at the station, it was Prudence. But she didn't catch my eye. She was absorbed in her meditation, the sound the bottle made against the glass, the anti-taste of smoke in her mouth; bright nails pinching the cork tip. I was hopeless with faces. I had long since decided that there were no new people to meet. All strangers were reprints of previously published identities, avatars. This woman was a Prudence type and so was Prudence. Faces dissolve. The shapes of faces form and re-form. Making contact, initiating a conversation, is a major step. Let it go.

How should I know if it is indeed the same person beside me in the bed? Catching an unexpected glimpse of my own face in the shaving mirror there is no shock of recognition. 'My Father, / my age, still alive,' as Robert Lowell wrote. (Why did he capitalise *that* word?) Allen Ginsberg in a city-wandering nightmare met his dead mother, as much herself as ever. More so. They are always with us, mother and father conjoined; finding each other, as all couples do, finding themselves. Dead ringers. Eyes tired, drilled into the skull. Tributaries of small folds. Bruised pouches. Marble breath.

It wasn't that I couldn't accept this woman as Prudence – who-ever *she* was in the film of memory – but I couldn't accept the definition of myself, if Prudence acknowledged me. Hay had worked its malefic magic. If I spoke to the smoker in the window seat, I would be speaking to a character who was already a wraith: a presentation of myself as a woman. Alfred Hitchcock remade as James Stewart, the thin man who got out; remade as Kim Novak, remade again. In Edith Head drag. Seeing Prudence and believing that I saw her would be an act of gender transgression.

No writer I knew had peeled off so many versions of himself, his living spirit (male, female, old, young, Muslim, Jew), as Michael Moorcock. Moorcock's concept of the multiverse, in which alternate selves lived different lives, simultaneously, was the truest model for the fix I was in. Characters appeared in many novels, retelling fragmentary autobiographies, experimenting with identity and sexual orientation. The myth of history was remade on a daily basis. But when I sat with the writer in one of his favourite Viennese-style tearooms in Marylebone High Street, he frowned, shook his head and asked: 'Is that my daughter? I *ought* to know. Could be. The eyes aren't quite right.'

It was that sort of place. A man sitting behind Moorcock, an interestingly wasted presence, turned out to be (or claimed to be) one of his oldest friends, a lost collaborator. The man looked up when I was called back to the table. 'I think we've met. Do I owe you money? I know the face.'

I didn't. Didn't want to know that ghost outside the window. The serial killer staring in at me.

I was gazing back in the direction of Wales, watching the Prudence clone, when I noticed a couple of drunks lurching in my direction. Night people who live in service stations. The insufficiently deceased. It was too late to get out. They settled themselves without a word at my table. One, the worse, began to rummage through a plastic carrier bag. The other, purposefully bespectacled, blunt in gesture, dived on the remains of my tray, tweezering up cold beans with spiky fingers. Both were smoking, coughing, in my non-smoker's privileged zone. With a twitch of civilisation left, the bean thief chased his snot across the Formica, before mopping it with my paper napkin, and shoving the result into his jacket pocket.

'He's Mutton,' said the gourmet. 'From Birmingham. He wants you to put him in one of your books.'

'Bad News. Bad News Mutton, that's me,' said the Brummie brown suit. 'I'm a mate of Nicholas Lane.'

Plenty of provincial accents have their charm. Geordie, for example, on the radio, or the other end of a very long telephone cable. But native Bull Ring Birmingham is like gargling with glass, all the lithium flatness of Leicester with added gravy browning.

Language is mangled, gobbed into an uncut string of consonants –
like sausagemeat.

Mutton sneezed speech. His riffs were reverse cocaine. A spark
of white light from deep inside the thalamus expelled as a shower of
wet mud. The conceptual brownness of this pair was hard to take.
Shirts missing buttons, visible vests, raincoats so stiff with grease
they were freestanding. Mutton's sports jacket had only witnessed
one sport, the indoor kind that preceded a vodka binge. The dandruff he shook from his collar looked like rust.

'Hold on, Humpp,' Mutton cavilled, 'you've got that back to
front. I'm *in* the books. I'm the one with the hour-glass stomach
and I can prove it. Cop a feel. I'm a posthumous-modernist, barred
from every Poly between Wolverhampton and Woolwich. What
happens is that we identify the authors who have *already* sketched
our autobiographies and we put them right.'

Humpp washed down a fistful of tablets with the dregs of my
coffee. He struck me as the saner of the pair, although at this level
who needs to split hairs? Davy Humpp was in employment. That
was the first shock. He'd worked for twelve years in a Bristol hospital, as an operating theatre technician – which gave him access to
the laughing gas. Nitrous oxide was his buzz of choice.

Responding to the spirit of place, the communalists and Romantic
poets who wandered the Downs snorting from brown paper bags,
Humpp took his hits straight from the mask. 'Unbidden bliss, the
gold-white light.' Out of a fingerless rubber hand that enclosed his
face, he tumbled, rolled through chasms, lost himself. The experience
was, he admitted, 'de-centring'. He dis-identified. He found himself
(non-self) unanchored in a formal garden. The rush was like inhaling mentholated slate. He bungee-jumped with his own entrails.

The mind-at-large shut down in favour of a roller-coaster ride
around the nervous system. The 'dialectic interplay of identity'
was where Humpp frolicked. News channels announced cease-
fires. Dead princesses swam out of Parisian underpasses, garlanded
in myrtle. The Light he saw was Love.

Then one of the surgeons walked in, wrenched the mask from
his face, gave him his cards. Reliving the experience, Humpp was
eloquent and resigned. The man was possessed of the kind of
experimental courage that sticks wet fingers into light sockets.

Mutton, glugging caffeine-adulterated vodka from my cup, had heard it all before. This double act had been on the road for years. They'd been run out of Hay (which is where Mutton had found one of my books in a remaindered stack) for barracking Baroness James and bumming fags from Beryl Bainbridge in the middle of a public anecdote. Mutton played his guitar in the street and sold membership cards to the Society for the Ontologically Challenged. Until they had enough change to move on to Bristol, for rumoured readings and unannounced guest appearances at the Arnolfini, down on the docks.

3 a.m. in a motorway service station is where you'll find them. Mutton and Humpp were the Equal Opportunities version of music hall undercards who almost made it into television. Egg and chips from a plastic plate. Drained faces. Driving back from a gig in Swansea, a one-night stand at Butlin's, Minehead; a personal appearance at the Jersey Beach Hotel, Aberavon, or The Talk of the Town, Splott. They all washed up here, the double acts. A wannabe Little and Large. Mike and Bernie Winters ghosting as themselves. Spectres of the night with their too-bright overcoats and chipshop skins: layers of slap, blue eyeliner, the juice squeezed out. Mutton and Humpp were of this company. Dryfeld and Silverfish too. Infesting the M-numbers, partnerships of disgruntled straightmen. Dependent rivals. Asexual, quarrelling lovers. On their way to the bridge. To Aust. Neutral territory between worlds.

One of the saddest sights I remember from my years on the road was the comedian Dick Emery, unrecognised in camelhair, pulling into a petrol station near Ross-on-Wye. Alone. In the middle of the night. Trying, as he handed over his credit card, to come back on. Wanting to be invisible and wanting to be acclaimed. Left with nothing but anger. An unjustified outburst that meant zilch to the bored attendant.

'Listen, man,' said Mutton, leaning forward, 'you've got to acknowledge your responsibility. You invented me. The condition of my stomach, the nature of the damage inflicted on my psyche by my life as a peripatetic bluesman. Bar of the Birds, Nice. Mazet in Paris. All the buskers' bars, man, you laid it out. Payback time. You've got to share the blame.'

'Turn it off, B.N.,' Humpp groaned. 'You're talking bollocks. Coincidences, writing influencing reality in non-rational ways,

Derrida, synchronicity: it's crap. You're a pisshead. There's not a spark of originality in you. Undone by cheap vodka you've boosted from the Paki minimart, you see the world in its essential chaos. You spew it down the phone to some poor sod who's trying to get a few hours' kip before going off to work. You don't have a life, so you try to insinuate your non-being into works of fiction.'

'I *am* fucking fiction,' Mutton shouted.

Humpp turned his back in disgust and sampled the remains of a tuna sandwich from an adjacent table.

'Man, you gotta read this. My six-year, psychogeographical investigation of the Birmingham Triangle,' Bad News slurred. The Smirnoff mouthwash was running from his nose.

One piece of good advice Moorcock gave me in the tearoom with the painted wall was this: '*Never* read anything this side of a proof copy. Refuse, on sight, all typescripts and bundles of word-processed genius stuff. If lunatic fans persist, then I feed the whole lot into my printer and go to work on the clean side. Which explains some of the stranger prose published under my name. Involuntary cut-ups, that's how *New Worlds* made its reputation at the cutting edge.'

He was right. I chucked all manuscripts, including my own, into a black rubbish sack. Some survived (and might one day be sold off), but most went the way of tea bags, tax forms, charity bites, newsprint and foil trays of cold pilau rice. Accepting the contents of Mutton's bag might be a good exit line. I could use the loose sheets as packing around the dope dealer's cash in the boot of my car. Nobody would ever get beyond the first paragraph of Mutton's navel-fluff ramblings.

Humpp, coming up to speed, tore open his shirt to reveal the letters printed on his vest: KK. 'You'll know us next time. The Ketamine Kreeps. Bad News is going to get together with Nicky Lane to produce a cassette, swamp music with a swing. Something to flog at readings. I'm finishing a paper called *Ketamine Konfessions*. K is the final frontier, the best near-death experience on the market. If it's good enough to tranquillise animals on their way to the slaughterhouse, it's good enough for me. What K does is convert energy fields beyond the human brain . . .' He pointed dramatically out of the window at whatever floated on the broad reaches of the Severn. '. . . into material suitable for fusion, TV implants.'

I pushed back my chair. There was a nasty glint in Humpp's eye. He was ready to induct me by way of a giant needle.

'Ketamine turns material reality into a soap opera. You become a part of whatever you're watching. You interface with *EastEnders*. You can actually affect the plot. You access the inaccessible. Through the Brotherhood of K I've made contact with a Bristol-based group of DMT researchers who are investigating recorded links between tryptamines and alien abduction.'

There was something hypnotic about this pair. I found myself writing down my phone number on the palm of Mutton's hand. It seemed a fair price to pay for my escape. Humpp was refuelling on downers. He had to be back on the job by 8 o'clock the next morning. It hadn't taken him, with his scholarly interests, long to get fixed up after the debacle in the operating theatre. Now he was a signalman on a privatised railway.

'I've got to tell you, man,' Mutton yelled at my retreating back, 'you're copping out. My character has shifted from a Jungian fetch in your first novel, in *White Chappell*, to a shorthand cipher in *Slow Chocolate Autopsy*. Your prose is getting really slack, all those one-word sentences, the reliance on a narrow band of imprecise adjectives. Neglect the armature of grammar and the world loses definition. I have to say it, man, I'm sliding into caricature. Some days I don't know if it's worth crawling out of bed to enact myself in such a shoddy cartoon. Where's your subtext? The authentic pain of childhood? The Polish part of my story? I go along with Terry Eagleton when he talks about the literature of a subject people taking refuge in linguistic showmanship, neologisms, farcical excess. I'll ring you soon to let you know how you're getting along. I'm working on a new chapter. You're plagiarising my existence, man.'

The Severn smelt good, under the slithering cliff from which panicked sheep scratched Rhaetic fossils; it smelt heavy, oily and old. I needed a walk to clear my head after my encounter with the Ketamine Kreeps. I needed a last look across the bridge before I drove back to London. In this light it was difficult to appreciate the red and green Triassic marls, the black shales and pale grey clays that made Aust Cliff a favourite field trip for geologists. And solitary stalkers. There was always a squeaky carpet of condoms in the

watchtower at the end of the field beyond the Services. It was a
great viewing platform to spy on the river, on the site where all the
pylons began: a lost landscape of listening posts and concrete
bunkers buried in bracken.

The lights of the bridge swayed on a fast-flowing tide. Now, as
always, there was the pom-pom-pom of traffic speeding out of
Wales. Thin grass ran to mud at the water's edge. Headlights swept
the ambivalent air, reminding me that this was a place owing its
allegiance neither to sea nor to land. I tried to climb up under the
bridge. I'd done it before, in daylight, scrambling onto a railed-off
promenade and sitting, under that stream of sound, waiting for the
tide to turn. Tonight was different. Some other lost soul had beaten
me to it. I could see a hunched shape – male or female, old or
young – at the water's edge, unmoving, head tipped forward, fishing for shadows.

To come from the beach, meant clawing, hand over hand, up the
stones. I lost sight of the figure. I had to feel my way along the
rough slabs that ran beneath the bridge.

A man. Definitely a man – pale, with a wispy moustache. He
looked like a younger Nicholas Lane. He had that Chattertonian air
of unforced recklessness. A posturing suicide who would carry out
his adolescent threats. 'Come off it, son,' you wanted to shout.
'There's money in my car. Blow it any way you want. But *please* don't
tell me about it, your problems and the books you hope to write.'

My elongated other, my double, stretched by a lamp on the
overhead gantry, crept away from me, along the wet pier. I would
have to approach with caution. I didn't want a jumper on my conscience. What was it with bridges and suicide? The poet Weldon
Kees leaving his car on the approach to the Golden Gate Bridge in
San Francisco (a marker for Kim Novak). John Berryman leaving
his imprint in the road. It might have been the soundtrack, those
plops and pings, wind whistling through hawsers, foghorns and
distant sirens from Oldbury power station. The end of things, a
fresh start across the water. A broad river running into the oceans of
the west.

The man was gone. He'd vanished. There was nowhere to hide.
No other path for him to choose. In the twenty paces it took me to
reach the point where he'd been sitting, the youth had written

himself out. I'd heard the whispers, but I'd discounted them: how Richey Edwards, the missing musician and lyricist, the Manic Street Preacher whose car, batteries run down, had been found at Aust, could sometimes, under peculiar meteorological conditions, be seen. Rumour creates its own circuits. A searcher can easily persuade himself that he believes a projection cast on fog. We can all, if we delude ourselves, play Hamlet for an hour. Suicidal sons willing dead fathers to push us over the edge.

Aust was a Futurist Elsinore of steepling walkways, ladders, cages. From the promenade, climbing through the levels towards the road, was a rush of small terrors, handholds, grazed knees. I didn't wait to enjoy the warm air and the taste of petrol, the headlights of the cars. I climbed over a mesh fence and ran around the path that led from the observation area to the car park.

Mine was the only car. A woman was leaning against it, huddled into a fur jacket. Prudence. Her lips were blue with cold. The wispy, diaphanous thing she was wearing wouldn't have wrapped a bracelet from Asprey's.

'Not going up the Wye, are you? I have to get to Hay. A job in a bookshop. Might be fun.'

'Sorry, I'm heading back to London. With no detours.'

I was close enough to be almost sure, the special scent of Prudence: saddle soap, none too fastidious underwear, chilled heat. My hand, reaching out to touch, and meeting no gesture of acknowledgment, finished with an awkward grab that crushed her thin fingers. We introduced ourselves. It was Prudence, but we'd never met. She was returning to where I'd seen her for the first time. Somehow I'd flipped too many pages. She'd fished the Usk, visited friends in the Ewyas Valley, but had never been to Hay. So she swore.

Over her shoulder I saw the Ketamine Kreeps, holding each other up like a pair of inward-leaning bookends, advancing rapidly towards us. There was no time to sort this out.

'Good luck. Maybe I'll see you again. The Severn seems to be the kind of river everybody steps out of twice.'

She took a light and kept my matches. In the flare, I saw that mouth, those lips. Then I was away, clear. Aust deleted. London in my sights.

9

The city was sick; Chinese 'flu, money-grafts from renegade Russian labs. The city sneezed and spat, played host to showers of viral particles, the infamous 'wind from the east'. Whitechapel dust infected the high gloss of Bishopsgate's glass cliffs.

They bandaged buildings, dressed them in bridal lace for a punk wedding. They excavated plague pits, scratched bones from heavy clay, uncovering shallow ditches into which hundreds of the poor had been shovelled. They labelled cabinets of yellow skulls. They placed open coffins on display in museums and ran real-time tapes, detailing the painstaking processes of exhumation, on monitors in public galleries.

Close-packed underground trains stalled, waiting to pick up a jolt of electricity from reservoirs of undispersed pain, blind tunnels in which Blitz victims and crash victims, and the faceless dead with their smoke-blackened lungs, were stored; bricked up, awaiting the summons.

Every citizen sponsored a family of rats. Cold noses, watchful eyes, scrabbling paws. Flesh-eating, indestructible vermin are never more than a few inches from your resting hands. Silent tribes scavenging waste, breeding, thriving on bait. Watching, waiting. Awful in their discretion.

Waiting and busy, the flies. Late-season buzzers. A noise in the head, a sugary thickness on the lung. Ears throbbed, retained their wax. Teeth worked loose in the gum. The city couldn't breathe, couldn't hawk this blockage. Raw throats. Oozing eyes. Sneeze allergies.

A shuffle of black coats. Pavement-hugging processions of revenants knuckling tired faces, shaking bacteria from grey hand-kerchiefs; hugging bottles of dead water. Smoking in doorways. Smoking in granite-rinse porches. Dripping in lunch clubs. Always too many clothes: wet Prada raincoats, lightweight jackets, tight shirt collars with a body-print shine. A black umbrella-cosh left under a tall stool and forgotten.

Air cooked by central heating. Sea-damp of clammy buildings. Sweating concrete. Paroled workers enter the furnace of the pub, the sandwich bar, the sushi kiosk. They return to their cubicles, hungrier than ever, stomachs growling, through a corridor of near-rain. It's not fierce enough to unfurl your weapon. Contact lenses mist, moisture infiltrates creased tailoring.

Sandals and slippers, and thin shiny shoes that let in puddles, are stubbing and twisting on raised setts. Get back, get on, get out from the hating and hurting; tolerated fevers, necks stiff from cradling cellphones.

Voices.

Complaining, begrudging, discussing symptoms. Taking it personally: the weather, the economic climate, the fix we're in. Turning discomfort into disease. Turning the body-case on a stiff axis. Suffering as a response to civic corruption. Corruption of the flesh: an antidote to grandiose architectural follies, domes and wheels and wobbly bridges (ruined by pedestrians).

'I object, therefore I am sick.'

On good days, London mornings, the light is graded and delicate, dull stone gleams like coral and you walk out in a state of disbelief, elation. For a few privileged hours, the sickness is in remission. On stolen afternoons, you feel the energy-rush when it's all possible: books will be written, images stream at you unbidden. The body electric is preparing itself for the next wave of infection. By evening you'll be hugging radiators, sucking lemons. This interlude is a defence mechanism, you'd better grab it.

I came down, through Shoreditch and Hoxton, Clerkenwell and Smithfield, to the Fleet and the sequestered Temple. It was a walk that never quite bored me, but which, before my brief Welsh exile, was becoming routine; an autopilot ramble to Blackfriars and the river. Now it is sheer indulgence: the shadow-path through Bunhill

Fields burial ground, the peeling mask of Bunyan, the obelisk of De-Foe. The grey stone tongue of William and Catherine Blake. The passageways around the old meat market.

There were Belgian bars with mussels and Trappist beers, breakfast cellars; bands of coffee fragrance, windows of exotic sausages. Magazines, cigars, foreign newspapers. Florists, bakers, picture framers. Holy wells, sections of the Roman Wall; St John's Gate (where the grubbing antiquarians of the *Gentleman's Magazine* once flourished). There were jewellers, Hasids, Rastas, cellars of gold and silver, secret Orinocos to set beside the Fleet. Con men, thieves, hustlers. Prostitutes, working wives, slappers, totty, lap-dancers; office managers, PR girls cradling hot telephones. Gallery owners staging their nineteenth nervous breakdown. Lawyers, grafters, bankers. Builders, cabbies, road drillers, cable-layers, cone-setters. Holborn hacks, comic-strip inkers, serial composers of Westerns and Tarzan adventures, layout jockeys from *Dazed & Confused*. SWP Lefties and BNP polemicists. Waiters and wasters and walkers. Suicides brushing against congenital optimists. Surgeons, women in childbirth. Sick men letting go of the pain on the last morning of their last life.

I could expect to encounter the unexpected: Peter Ackroyd returning from the gym with a brown leather bag. Stewart Home pushing a blue-eyed Nordic infant in a buggy towards Victoria Park, where a pregnant Rachel Lichtenstein is sitting on a bench, watching her son, David, as he skitters over the grass. Keggie Carew, in trousers, is striding purposefully towards Redchurch Street. The man in the Clerk's House bookshop rolls a stick-thin cigarette and taps titles onto a screen.

I swallowed all of them. I was high on the pleasure of not writing, setting aside my Landor novel, sneaking back to the city like a trusty on parole from purgatory.

There was, there had to be, another scheme, another lunatic project: I was searching for a man who took pictures of invisible people. A friend, the poet Gwain Tunstall, working in the Temple as a law clerk, had picked up a story originally floated by Heathcote Williams in his book *The Speakers*. A veteran photographer, with all his conjuror's paraphernalia, his self-published pamphlets, was hiding out as a freelance caretaker in a Smithfield basement.

Tunstall had been to see him. And was impressed. The system worked. Men in curious costumes coming out of basements, captured on misty photographic plates.

I didn't want to prick his enthusiasm, but St John Street on a Sunday morning had all too many of these, moustached gentlemen with eye-shadow, play-executioners in leather hoods, wasted boys with parodic upper-body musculature; popped veins in bare arms, chopped T-shirts. There were also, Tunstall insisted, cloud portraits in which angelic forms were clearly visible. The old man fixed images of folk who were no longer there. Which is, of course, a simple definition of photography.

If there was anything in this gizmo, I was keen to give it a try. I'd start with the backstory, a return to Deptford, the scene of the Christopher Marlowe hit. Then De Quincey's Ratcliffe Highway. Certain gangland pubs and back rooms. I'd keep well clear of the Ripper trail, which had been bled dry by video bandits, but I'd probably visit the garret of the Spitalfields hermit David Rodinsky. I might, if the results justified it, have another attempt at the Ewyas Valley, planting my tripod on the vantage point above Llanthony Priory, where Landor laid out the foundations of his manor house. The flaw in using this device was that, as with fiction, you opened yourself to a form of possession. Got more than you expected: prophecies of death, lizard faces that winked back at you, crying, 'Come on in, boy, the water's fine.'

The print is solid ectoplasm. It requires *you* to make the push, supply it with a modicum of life force. You see what you fear. Those who were safely invisible were provoked into movement. They behaved like Bad News Mutton and Humpp. They sat down uninvited at your table, cursing you for creating them, dragging them into the narrative. The gig was risky, but it was a good excuse to share a drink with Tunstall, pick up on the gossip.

Tunstall wrote in purple ink in a clear, childlike hand. His notebook, a legal pad, looked like a negative blackboard. Tasks for the day. He was intelligent, but functionally educated. The sheet he was working on was blocked out with primitive sketches and tentative genealogical tables: *Llud – Bladud (?) – LEAR*. He spoke hesitantly, honouring the wit and gravity of language. He took great care to say what he meant, to be sure his words carried a proper freight of meaning. Pedantry laced with passion. Given his employment, he'd learnt the value of keeping it buttoned, biding his time. Four or five spliffs into a session he might let rip: the mythological accretions that gave this quarter of London, the banks of the Fleet, the Inns of Court, its pluralist ambience. Solitary habits and a background in the southern suburbs had schooled him in Jesuitical caution. Tunstall was a gentle fanatic.

We met, at his suggestion, in the Old King Lud, at the foot of Ludgate Hill. The drag was that the pub was now the New King Lud, its façade preserved, the rest gutted: 'Smart Dress, No Muddy Boots', fizz-from-a-hose, muzak and aquarium light. Banging on about real ale and beef carved from the living flank, windows that hadn't been cleared of soot since the Great Fire of London, made you sound like some pain in the arse from a novel by Kingsley Amis. What had gone was gone, good riddance. Remember? Bread rolls that had to be carbon dated. Warm slop recycled from the ullage tank. Fleet Street drunks – in coats and ties – chucking it back to stoke their small prejudices in the only forum to which they were admitted. Doors that wouldn't shut, allowing killer fogs to add body to an impenetrable cloud of pipe reek, lung tar, and perfectly executed smoke rings.

Tunstall was a pub romantic. He was a poet and a Neverd ('never 'eard of'). There were plenty of them about. The best writers of their time, dismissed for being unknown, because the world at large was too lazy to search them out. Verse commissioners wanted it on a plate, noises from Ireland they could borrow in lieu of hard thought. Copywriting that behaved like sponsored graffiti, ruining your tube trip. Recitations to the TUC. Prison visits. Buffing corporate egos in the City like tolerated boot-blacks. Tunstall was unexploitable. He got his start with readings in rooms above pubs in Carshalton, poetry and jazz. *The Diary of an Hashishim*: sampled journals, extracts from letters that were never sent, lyric seizures – and always that dark teak, brass rail background. The pub on the South Circular was San Francisco for the beatniks of the Surrey fringe.

1962: Man slowly unfolds a Telegraph *in a Victorian public house lounge tawdry with Christmas decorations – cigar smoke hangs in the air –*

mist at sunset over lowlying fields – I hold the girl's hand: we listen to an
early drunk at the bar unreeling his life to a bored, patient barmaid. 'I bin
on television you know.'

Post-Rimbaud (post-Kerouac's response to Rimbaud), they were
all assassins, these Catholic-Buddhist legal clerks. Wage-earning
second-generation Beats, weekend ravers. It was a period of innocence. The suburbs, leafy and repressed, were protected by an
outer ring of golf courses, catteries, asylums; colonies of urban cra-
zies gathered around Italianate water towers. City Lights
pocketbooks invaded net-curtained bedrooms. Tunstall proclaimed,
'Mingus is God.' He was currently reading, on the journey to
work, Jack Kerouac's *Lonesome Traveller* (as a preliminary to travels
of his own). Kerouac, so he informed me, had once drunk in the
King Lud.

Outskirts of the city in late afternoon like the old dream of sun rays
through afternoon trees – Pack on back, excited, I started walking in the
gathering dusk down Buckingham Palace Road seeing for the first time long
deserted streets – fumes and shabby English crowds going out to movies,
Trafalgar Square, on to Fleet Street where there was less traffic and dimmer
pubs and sad side alleys, almost clear to St Paul's Cathedral where it got too
Johnsonianly sad – So I turned back, tired, and went into the King Lud
pub for a sixpenny Welsh rarebit and a stout.

Tunstall nursed his stout, rarebit was off the menu. (He should
have got together with Michael Moorcock who never, by choice,
ate anything else.) He was teaching himself to notice everything,
using his notebook as he swooped across the city: pediments,
drinking troughs filled with dry leaves. He'd just discovered, scampering, late for our appointment, in an obscure porch alongside St
Dunstan in the West, close to where Temple Bar had once stood,
three statues. Figures, so he decided, from Lud Gate. The founders
of the city: Llud, a builder and sacred architect; Bladud, the English
Icarus, who flew from Bath to crash into the Temple of Apollo on
the summit of Ludgate Hill; and Lear, shamanic visionary, dreamer
and sacrificer of daughters.

I was up for it, sucking the black stuff through a ruff of creamy
froth, letting him run. But we only had an hour before he was due
back in his cubbyhole in the Middle Temple. He had to make the
introduction to Frank, the man who took photographs of invisible

people. We could scoot up to Smithfield and he'd still have time, he was spare-fleshed and springy, to sign in before they docked his wages.

As we walked, Tunstall, nervous of traffic, crushed by the lowering bulk of the buildings, flicking sidelong glances in the hope of identifying a few threads of black-bindweed, began to pour out the story of his morning's adventures. An episode that had shaken him. He wasn't sure if he'd imagined it, or if he was now in possession of a terrible secret. Hence the rotating head. The poetic assassin might himself be assassinated in a most unpoetic way. Poison darts fired from an umbrella as he crossed Blackfriars Bridge. A swerving car. A swim off the foreshore with pebbles in his pocket.

He had overheard a conversation he wanted to forget. He would tell me about it and pass the burden of guilt.

Tunstall worked for Sebag Sewell Plantain in a set of offices lit by fluorescent tubes, at the end of a cloister, in a collegiate labyrinth off Fleet Street. He'd hoped to be entering the world of *Bleak House*; candles, lamb chops, jugs of porter, fusty documents, eccentricity. Disputed inheritances that took generations to untangle. Instead of which he was a pre-fax casualty waiting to be found out, a delivery boy for documents; an inky-cuffed scrivener who was cheaper to run than a Colour-Xerox machine. Sebag Sewell Plantain lived on generous crumbs swept in their direction by Grossman Derry. These backwater functionaries (facilitators of marital severance, apologists for District Line exhibitionists) lived in awe of the Alpha Chimp, the Blessed Witold Grossman. Grossman had only to belch to have them signing up for high-risk insurance policies.

Tunstall arrived early that morning. He sat on a bench in Fountain Court, listening to the plashing water, watching the ripples; weak sunlight firing the heraldic windows of the Middle Temple. He opened his notebook, but there was nothing to report.

Cervix.

Could he legitimately use that word for the lip of this pool? He wanted to say *something*, but was overwhelmed by place and light; the way this liquid dish became a device for centring consciousness. He thought of that other, tighter, grubbier Fountain Court, down the Strand, the high room in which Blake died, died singing. He thought of that song and the machinery of the river. This was the best of it. As good as it gets. Nothing to be said. Nothing to be taken down. Pens still capped in his breastpocket: the purple (for prose), the green (for verse), the red (for notes to himself, facts to be remembered).

He felt the urge then to walk to the office, type out his resignation, call the lab where Jean worked, board the first train. They would take off together for somewhere unlikely, the Channel Islands. Because it was never going to get any better than this. Why carry on? *Carpe diem.*

He wandered, as he often did, along the cloistered walk to the circular Temple Church. Sitting on a stone bench, in the shadows against the wall, masked by a black pillar, observing and unobserved, he tuned in to the voices of the stone knights. They gave out a repetitive, monotonous chant; a humming and throbbing that brought heat to cold blue lips. The noble dead on their marble pallets. Swords, shields, chainmail: petrified, pulsing. A dormitory of unactivated sleepers. A mock hospice.

Tunstall felt the cold enter his veins. Sound *moved* from knight to knight, Templar to Templar, until the circular church began to revolve and spin. Behind these effigies were other voices: two men. Voices he didn't know – like television heard from the next room in a cheap hotel. It was the hour between communion and tourism. Two men, keyholders, were strolling through the apparently deserted church.

'I see myself as the big fat spider in the corner of the room. Sometimes I speak when I'm asleep. You should listen. Occasionally when we meet I might tell you to go to the Charing Cross Road and kick a blind man standing on the corner. The blind man might tell you something, lead you somewhere.'

The second man, the listener, gurgled. 'Priceless. Oh very very good, Jeremy. On the button. But surely it hasn't gone that far?'

'Further. Much further. That's the version Harold reserves for gullible members of the fourth estate.'

Tunstall was quieter than the horizontal heretics, the statues, less well informed. Even on trains he avoided newspapers. But the television voice, travelling around that sacred space, pillar to pillar, was Wilson. Harold Wilson. Wasn't he dead, victim of an MI5 plot? Or had he simply lost his marbles, brain stem reduced to honeycomb? Tunstall didn't partake, but even he registered elements of the myth; how the citizens voted Harold in because he wasn't Sir Alec Douglas-Home, the satirist's friend. Now Wilson was a conspiracy freak like all the rest, spinning plot from selective revisions of the truth; tapes and diaries in a private drawer.

'Face it, Jeremy, we can no longer rely on Harold. There's been a subtle . . . shift in the wind. If we still used radio, we could do what they did with Winston, bring in an actor. You carry Harold off better than the man himself. Unfortunately, it won't wash on television.'

The voice was deep, dark-tawny, clubbable: lungs, lights and vintage port. This second man had the 'trust me' pitch of Robert Maxwell announcing his latest scam. Trust me or I'll shake the foundations of the temple with my roar. The bigger the liar the growlier the tone.

The pair were now in plain view, standing like mourners over a Templar tomb. 'Seriously, Witold, what are my chances?'

Tunstall knew them as client and employer (at one remove): Jeremy Thorpe and Witold Grossman. Thorpe could do the voices; in his pomp he'd been a famous mimic, Eton and Trinity College, Oxford. Green room, smoking room and members' bar. He did Harold Wilson better than Mike Yarwood. Jeremy's *bons mots* were legendary. Who could forget his one-liner when Princess Margaret announced her engagement to little Jones? 'Damn. Two of my ambitions dashed at a single stroke. I planned to marry one and sodomise the other.'

'The thing. The thing, Witold. It has to be the thing we discussed. Funds are in place, secondary banking ventures. The channels are operative. We've got the support of Goldsmith and his gang – who loathe those satiric rags and all their foul rumour-mongering. We can have this creature sectioned, leucotomised. It's no worse than shooting a dog.'

Grossman winced, pulled out a yard of linen, mopped his brow. His face was creased like a haemorrhoid cushion left too long in the bath. A pouch of rubber on which to raise a crop of warts. He had the saddest, most bereaved, pug-dog eyes in the universe. But behind his back, dining privately at the Slug & Slipper, with Bessell or David Holmes, Jeremy would take his revenge on Witold for this enforced subservience. 'Why can't that fat Jew get his jowls ironed?' The risk was awful and the others never responded, mute-smiling, so that the gay waiters wouldn't overhear.

Thorpe dived into a soup bowl of steak tartare, vigorously mixed with olive oil. He ate like a starving man, dribbling spine-splinters and mashed tail. Risk was what it had always been about, dancing on snakes' eggs. Laughing at lobby fodder. He was a brighter Faust, a son of the morning who would never plunge to earth.

People who knew Grossman knew how to read the signs: the rumbling belly, when the first breakfast dissolved and the mid-morning refuelling, devilled kidneys and a necklace of poached eggs, was still an hour away; tubby finger pressed against wet lips in a gesture of reluctant benediction. They knew the news was bad. Witold was offering damage limitation, a decent wedge when the story was sold to *The People*.

'In my opinion, Jeremy, for what it's worth, and please feel free to seek advice elsewhere, it's rapidly becoming a situation in which I am powerless to intervene. We won't meet before the trial. I'm off to the Med, quack's orders, incommunicado for at least a month – half-rations on a Greek boat. Dry bread, retsina. The occasional filleted sardine. Purgatory, old fellow. Leave you in capable hands.'

'No, Witold. I insist. How can I make a move without your good word?'

'Dear boy, you know what a hypochondriac I am. Heart of oak in a sawdust frame. It's very simple, Jeremy. Say nothing. Do nothing. Deny everything. And absolutely no talk of evidence or they'll want to examine it.'

Thorpe stood for some time, fiddling with his watchchain, after Grossman had gone. Grossman sick? The man could eat for England. The only exercise he took was folding his hands over his belly and balancing a teacup on the ledge. They say he courted wealthy widows, but without success. He was a prized partner at the opera – and could make the draughtiest box appear full. But when the clothes came off, when he was stripped to his combinations, it took a stout-hearted woman not to blanch.

If Witold was making a strategic withdrawal, the game was up. Grossman was privy to all the secrets. Information and patronage passed through his system like a salt-water drench. Gossip scoured the tubes faster than colonic irrigation. Whatever happened, Witold anticipated it. Tory, Labour, Liberal: he was their fixer, their moral conscience, their confessor. It was his burden to atone for their sins, to swallow them and lick his lips.

Thorpe slumped, leant against a pillar. Tubercular glands ached in his stomach. His tongue filled his mouth. He could do the speeches with the best, ad libs that took hours to rehearse – but silence? That was too hard a call. He spasmed, rushed from the church.

Now Tunstall was left to the echoes, the replays. He had to convince himself this eavesdropping-on-courtiers-to-advance-the-plot wasn't the false memory of a history play by David Hare, or one of the other socialist plutocrats. He knew he could never go back to the fountain. He was alone in the Temple Church with the crusading knights. *They* hadn't moved. They picked up colour from the strengthening light. The heresies of which they'd been accused were still unproven. Tongue rimming fundament. Baphomet. The head on a dish.

If Tunstall rewound the tape, he could enjoy once more his envelope of meditative calm. Water puckering water. Bliss on the never-never. Unknowing knowingness. Like fuck he could. In telling me, he confirmed the tale. His fantasy was grounded and likely to be further distorted in my inevitable exploitation of it. Meanwhile, my advice to Tunstall was to skip. And pronto.

He was quite ready, he assured me, to treat the episode as an auditory hallucination, a Ketamine flashback to a TV thriller, seen silent in a bar: a bad trip. Then, coming out of the heady gloom of the church, into the bright morning air, he tripped over a brown bowler. Thorpe's hat. Filled to its brim with sick. Stomach heave. Red-yellow grains of minced cow in a liquor mash.

We passed under Holborn Viaduct, silver dragons with scarlet tongues, and into Smithfield. Tunstall had to vanish, that much was certain, but he needed reassurance, the confidence to risk everything on becoming what he already was, a poet. Fatty carcasses stunk in the aisles. Wafts of bacon and blood sausage rose from underground restaurants, mirrored bars where aproned slaughtermen and bummarees made their arrangements with steroid-brokers, off-duty bouncers and cousins from Dagenham and Bow.

'Try this,' I said. 'I've got an explanation of sorts. Wilson's dead. Grossman's dead. And Thorpe won't be winning any salsa competitions. What you saw was like the Marie Antoinette vision the two Oxford bluestockings conjured up in Versailles. We're not talking about anything that actually happened. You were in a suggestible state, looking for an excuse to quit your job. You saw what you wanted to see: something heavy enough to make you run. This scene had nothing whatsoever to do with Thorpe, the sorry human, and everything to do with mythological projection.'

Tunstall was satisfied. He'd got it both ways. His resignation was justified and he had something unexplained to think about when he took the Jersey ferry. He could, if he was ever tempted to write a book for cash, creep back along the branches of the Money Tree: examine the way Thorpe's campaign chest was topped up by Jack Hayward in the Bahamas, laundered by the unsuspecting Nadir Dinshaw in the Channel Islands. Tunstall recast himself as a gumshoe, with Jean as his faithful Velma, his ever-obliging secretary and helpmate.

An art effusion was defacing the walls of the Slaughterhouse, the upper deck. A gibbering ninny with bootblacked hair and a congenital Prozac grin tried to bar our access to the rattling cellars in which Frank the photographer hid out. He said his name was Jones and that he'd been a monk. Guarding empty galleries and trashing shows put on by rivals in other (pre-development) holes between Shoreditch and Mile End Road was all he was fit for after being elbowed by the Dominicans. Who wouldn't take him back at any price, even as a Tertiary. Jones licked your paw, while working out the best way to exploit its flavour, trace elements of other hands that you had gripped. Laughing nervously, his head rocked loosely on its base, anticipating jokes that would never come. You felt like asking the creature, 'Have you been exorcised?'

He didn't want us to attempt the basement ladder. A drunken lesbian who had fallen over the parapet at some recent rout was suing the absentee landlord – who, in his turn, threatened to have Jones skinned and nailed to the door. The art geek couldn't decide

if he liked the idea. Meanwhile, he was fated to promote unwatch-
able video-interference. The pictures came with natural sound:
amplified traffic, stone-breaking drills, police sirens, cooing pigeons,
humming invalid carriages, the tap and drag of an army of gimps.
The film didn't require a title. I recognised those streets, a circuit of
the damned, inland from the Ford factory. The whiteman's East
End, Cockney London, shunted into the wilderness. The video
was Jamie Lalage's attempt at conning his way into the art racket by
running real-time loops of street life. *The Dagenham Purgatory*, he
called it. Sudden flares and burn-outs bringing spurious excitement
to mechanical footage. Cars parked on broad pavements. Every
walker with a stick.

The show was on a loop. It ran for ever – and began again. Jones,
despising every frame – dreaming of a return to the period when,
damp behind the ears, he'd been invited to talk up Turner Prize
contenders, or explain Duchamp – had found a purgatory of his
own. We were the first visitors of the week. He had started to
unspool his own confessions and was considering bringing in a tape
recorder. He might remember who he'd been.

A big part of what I liked about Frank, before meeting him, was his
name. Tunstall and I were agreed that Robert Frank, the Swiss-
American, whose book of back roads, 'hydrogen jukeboxes', flags,
signs, bikers, faggots, politicians on the stump (introduced by Jack
Kerouac), was our favourite photographer. Which betrayed our
literary bias, a romantic/poetic sensibility leaning towards narrative;
mist on the bayou announcing an obscure voodoo ceremony, not
an aesthetic frisson. Everything in Frank was about loss. Everything
was predicated on mortality. Human meat in its fragile dignity,
scuttling towards extinction, meeting the swift lens with jaunty
seriousness.

And there was another thing, I found out much later. How all
the separate compartments of our lives, our secret enthusiasms,
the friends we keep apart, are linked, part of one field of force.
Robert Frank, shooting *Pull My Daisy*, belonged to the myth of
New York, the Beat Generation, Greenwich Village; café poets,
painters arguing in the Cedar Tavern. But Frank also had a house,
or shack, in Nova Scotia – worse than Wales, bleaker than

Ireland: on the edge of things. He made films, serious home movies, with Rudolph Wurlitzer. Who wrote *Pat Garrett and Billy the Kid* for Sam Peckinpah. And who was the subject of a TV profile by Jamie Lalage. So all my interests, Beats, Hollywood, utopian communities, the austere European cinema of Lalage, knew each other, interacted, paid their dues. I was the one excluded, through ignorance and self-conceit, from my own party.

Like a Dog.

There was a period when Frank wanted to rough up the purity of his prints, draw closer to painting and script. Over an affectionate, rather slapdash photograph of some yellow flowers, he had written: *Like a Dog.* Then he photographed *that.* Making reference to Kafka, the death of K. A knife thrust into the heart and turned twice. *'Like a dog!' he said: it was as if he meant the shame of it to outlive him.*

In the early fifties, on a commission, Robert Frank visited Wales. In the mid-nineties, flicking idly through his book *Moving Out*, I'm struck by a print entitled 'Caerau, Wales, 1953.' Caerau is at the head of the Llynfi Valley where I grew up, the harsher, bottle-necked end of town; penal estates, worked-out mines, before the road snakes on towards the Rhondda.

When Frank arrived, the mines were still active, the landscape was scarred. Tough grass over slag. Black-gashed dunes. North's Navigation Collieries had converted an area of hill farms into a war zone. There was always a cold wind. Railway lines spread out from the Mayan ruins of the ironworks. Loose timber, pit props from which we used to build cabins, lay around like the relics of a dynamited settlement. Housing was thrown up fast to shelter long-term labourers, or the tent Irish who stayed on after the pits were dug. Slate-roofed terraces were interspersed with every shade of chapel, invisible points of doctrine divided families. Three-storey pubs on corners belonged in the Klondike.

I can't remember.

I was allowed, with a small gang of friends, to make local expeditions to the park, to Sychbant, Garn Wen; tin-coloured streams, rubbish dumps, secret culverts, conifer plantations. We'd heard so many warnings about strange men that any pensioner with silicosis, gobbing on a bench, was a potential serial killer. What these men *did* was unclear, but the hills were full of them. Damaged walkers. Monologuists in fawn gabardine, caps and mufflers. The war-wounded and the casualties of peace. Anyone with a camera would have been reported to the police.

But there it was, a lucid dream, brought back by Robert Frank's photograph. One afternoon, going further than we'd gone before, higher, above the colliery, narrow tracks zigzagging at random: a man with a camera. Who pulls a face at the gang of kids, promises to show them what he has taken. And now, after all those years, that promise is kept.

The child I never was, barely visible behind another, taller boy. Buttoned jackets and wellington boots.

Frank, successfully photographing an invisible person, my dead self, undid everything I knew of the workings of culture and memory. From that moment, my story was misaligned; revising a singular instant meant seeing myself from another angle, cancelling all the intervening lies.

The Slaughterhouse basement, through which reverberated the sound of underground trains, was divided into three unequal caverns. Two were arched and generous, the third was a hole in the wall. We relied on torches. Frank's paraphernalia was spread about him. The cellars were loud with undispersed backdraughts: cattle and slaughtermen, funky sculptors, acid casuals who never made it home from the party. Tunstall, who knew the layout, pulled up a hinged metal door to reveal a black drop which, by its smell, led directly into the sewage system.

'Convenient, ain't it?' chuckled Frank. 'All me facilities close at hand.' He was chipper for a man who lived in darkness, a tolerated mole. 'Sit down, sit down, lads. I'll reveal you my system. How it works.'

Frank's hands were fast-moving; long wrists poking from grubby celluloid cuffs. His head swivelled busily. When his eyes met yours they didn't focus. They shone in deep sockets like splashes of solder. Frank was unsighted. Tunstall had landed us with a blind photographer. Who better?

We could hear the recurrent skids and wails of Lalage's

Dagenham circuit above us, tube trains beneath our feet. We perched on our conceptual raft and listened while the blind vagrant pitched his philosophy of light.

'Frith Street's where it began. Had my own little Soho gaff. Working nights at the Windmill Cinema. Started out, didn't I, with a pinhole camera? Through the karsy window? Immense. The sky trapped between those buildings. Never saw such colour. Silver-white. So I put out my first book, in two parts, *The Spectrum and Polarised Light.*'

Tunstall was leaning forward, nodding, wanting to run his fingers over Frank's lips. He'd heard it before and it got better every time. Observation as the precursor to inspiration, that was Tunstall's bag. Thickets of purple and red prompts in his notebook, clearing the path for an explosion of green, the inevitable harvest of verse. Science and poetry as equal elements, seamlessly blended.

'With my Polariscope strapped to my head, I voyaged all over London. Covent Garden, the Embankment, Vauxhall. Over one bridge, back by the next. When polarised light is projected into the colours of the spectrum, it brings into view the presence of invisible people, the ones who have been here before us. Marvellous beings. Wise folk from other worlds. Men and women, old ones and kiddies, *stitched from light*. We are born from light, to light we return.'

'Can we see one of your prints?' It had to be asked and I was crass enough to do it. Frank was describing a process I had been struggling with all my life. To reduce the essential mystery to a strip of card held in the hand.

'There ain't no prints, son. All in here.' He tapped his smooth forehead. And he laughed. 'You learn the hard way. I made my prisms from tourmaline and Icelandic spar. Periscopes and dark-lanthorns. Walked the town with black boxes strapped to my head. Now I know better.'

There was one last throw. I suggested it: as much to indulge Tunstall as in expectation of a result. What if Frank could be persuaded to come with us to the Temple Church? There was still time. Frank's time. The time he factored from expired light. We would tell him nothing of what Tunstall had seen or heard that day and we would ask him to give us a reading.

Bribed with a late breakfast, bubble and squeak in the Cock

Tavern, a couple of stouts, Frank was up for it. With Tunstall
steadying his arm, we made our eccentric progress back down the
Valley of the Fleet. In my green canvas rucksack was the Polariscope
that Frank had sold me.

I was late home, traces of dinner were still on the table, and a plate
that was too hot to handle was waiting for me in the oven. The
builders were in. Or rather they weren't. They *should* have been.
They had been. They'd decamped to another job in Shepherd's
Bush. They'd be back if it started to rain.

We had no sink. The bath was filled with dirty dishes. My dried-
out food was peppered with brick dust. I washed it down with a
vinegary claret, which had probably been uncorked for a week. It
was great to be back, back with my family, back in London.

I realised, seeing how difficult it was to find my mouth with my
fork, how tired I was. The drive back from Wales, the incident with
Prudence in the car park at Aust, the mad day with Tunstall.
Another glass, an early night. Let it settle. Then reserve a slot at the
book fair. Give up the nonsense of authorship and get on with peddling the countless millions of books that were already out there,
jostling for precedence. I could hear the phone ringing somewhere
in the distance, but I ignored it.

'It's for you,' my wife called. 'From Wales.'

I walked out of the kitchen. My throat was dry. I was shivering
slightly, otherwise calm, ready for what I knew was coming.

'Mr Norton? Oh hello, you don't know me.' A Welsh lowland
voice, lilting and careful. As if I might not understand the language.
Respectful. A voice talking to another voice, in another land. 'It's
your father, Mr Norton. He's passed away. Heart attack it was.
Very sudden. He didn't suffer. And just back from Tesco's with all
the shopping. Can you come down tonight? Your mother, see,
she's very confused. Neighbours we are, next door but one. Sorry.
We're all very, very sorry.'

Book Two

SIARPAL

intertitle:
BOOK TWO

SIARPAL

Authentic tidings of *invisible*

things

Authentic tidings of invisible things
Henry Vaughan

1

Burne off my rusts.

Walter Landor quoted Donne, tested him. Sounded the poet against the urgent brook.

Rotating his heel, he made a mark in the soft ground. In his conceit, it became a mason's signature. Landor, his own architect, was signing the portrait before it was completed. Signing an empty canvas. The gesture was typical of the man. He knelt to erase it, to brush out the gibbous moonshape with his hand, to feel – in dread – for the worm he had bruised.

So much was green and fresh and wide.

He saw the avenues of his planting, pastureland and parkland declining to the ruined priory. Here is my place. *Siarpal.* A mansion, commodious but plain, facing the warm south, respecting the nature of the chosen site; a fervent spirit responsive to method, the laws of proportion, simple husbandry. The Roman model. Senatorial retirement from the fuss of society. Estates, well-managed, conversing quietly with the original rudeness of this remote valley; withdrawn from the vanity and pomp of the careless world, its princes and popes. Here Landor declared his republic. Here would he bring his young bride.

He fetched from his pocket the flat red stone he had picked out as he forded the stream. Drove it into the mud; damaged it with the force of his boot, chose another. Stone upon stone: my tower. The dog Giallo, his current Pomeranian hairball, yelping at his heels. Dickens would declare that dog and man were one. Giallo spoke for his master, they agreed on every topic. The dog shared Landor's prejudices, snappy and shrill where the man was strong and simmering. Colour rising, before he gave way to passion. A summer storm rattling the windows in their casements.

'Ignorance is in their blood,' he declared. The dog yapped. 'These Brythonic peasants wallow in ancient vices, tugging forelocks to parson and magistrate – "Yes, your honour. No, your honour. Certainly, your honour" – while they bury their ground rents under the flagstones and serve every abomination upon innocent daughters. A lawless couple in these hills will engender, in a single generation, an entire tribe of Israel; imbeciles and thieves getting bastards upon their slatternly siblings.'

The dog was snarling, boxing the air, when Landor kicked at the heap of loose stones, sending them flying in every direction. Here it begins. I am the architect of my ruin.

I looked at this first sheet, words scribbled confidently in black Biro on a lined pad. My attempt at making contact with the spirit of Landor. Disaster. I couldn't do the language or locate the period. The pad of paper, with its grey-mauve rules, was all wrong. It was intended for meaningful work, figures, calculations, notes that made sense of gabby meetings: salient points isolated from the gush of acoustic froth. This paper belonged on a clipboard, not being defaced by dud literature. If the words took fire, they could be punted as 'holograph material', filed as a 'work in progress'. But if, as in this case, they lay down and died, the act of composition was exposed as a time-wasting indulgence, ecological irresponsibility.

You'd think, wouldn't you, that a country house hotel in the process of rebranding itself as a suitable venue for breakfast meetings and gung-ho seminars for peripatetic evangelists (the God franchise) would provide a better class of notepaper in their de-luxe (en suite and complimentary fruit bowl), river view bedrooms?

I'm not a complainer. I'll lay my head on a dented pillow, pick curly hairs from a cake of rubber soap. I'll suffer the room above the country-and-western bar, the plumbing that clanks and surges through the night. I'll put up with TV sets you can't put on and sets you can't turn off. I'll swish the lumpy evidence of salmonella replays from the bath, then toss down a breakfast brandy and hand over my credit card, chiming 'Fine' to the reflex smirk: 'How was your stay?' But this pulp paper, it disturbed me. How was I supposed to do justice to Walter Savage Landor (1775–1864) on see-through sheets of crushed rag and bone? He was a classicist, a disenfranchised gent; one of nature's exiles.

Landor walked for hours in Welsh weather, exposing himself to voices in the stream, the bleating of his Spanish merino sheep, pheasants breaking cover. He walked the woods, tearing his flesh on thorn and bramble and branches that whipped back on him; zigzagging through bracken and flint, on rough paths, up the hillside above Llanthony; pausing, settling, hand on hip, dog beside him, to evaluate the swift transit of light, a golden hour for the Golden Valley.

The solitude. The expanse of underexploited, unwritten land.

His argument was with himself: frustration at his awkwardness, his inability to find the terms, the *precise* words for what was happening. Shifts in pressure, amorous susceptibilities. Out of human fallibility – he couldn't prevent it – came disconnected rhythms, near rhymes, columns and cantos and discriminations of language: to be controlled, shaped, muzzled. Made fit for public consumption. These were not, God forbid, the spontaneous effusions of a mad boy.

He must lock himself away in the tower of the priory, until hurt was healed, written out; ecstasy made intelligible. With a decent pen. On Egyptian paper. In a waterproof journal. On a walnut desk. At a west-facing window. In *Cwm Siarpal*. His future mansion, his retreat; his tower.

The natives, muttering into their smocks, knew the rill, the spit of storm water that chased the Honddu. They had a name for that which he left unchristened. They knew the site he had chosen and called it ill-favoured, haunted by goblins. With feeble-minded reliance on fairy stories, self-aggrandising mythology, they saw his tower, undesigned, as a ruin.

The Sharples. Sharpil or Sharpll: so they cursed it. Sharp Hill, something of that sort. The Welsh had a flair for stating the obvious and making it portentous by speaking in an awe-struck whisper; saying everything twice, arsey-versy.

My pad lay on the window ledge. I wouldn't write another word. Why should I collude in this absurdity? 'In your own time,' the suits

said, 'as you remember it.' What a strange bargain: rustic hospital-
ity in exchange for a work of fiction. 'Get it down, get it out. Keep
nothing back.' Like an irritable bowel movement, a small sour fart.

Coming here, up the long drive, slowing for the bumps, admiring parallel mower-strips on damp lawns, I had a moment of panic.
It could have been the smell of wild garlic. Or the monumental
clumps of gunnera (like over-mulched rhubarb). Prolix nature taken
in hand, colonised. Rhododendron bushes, colour bombs you'd
never get away with in Kew.

It was like going back to school. The red brick of the campanile,
the Italianate tower; an *ad hoc* collection of slate roofs, gambrel and
mansard. Blue-grey walls quilted in ivy, wisteria and honeysuckle.
Architectural quotations, improvisations. Late additions with mad
angles. Chimneys that were decorative rather than functional.

The garden, so the driver told me, misinterpreting my horrified
scanning of the grounds, had been laid out in the early nineteenth
century by W.H. West. 'Notice the gravel paths, the herbaceous
borders, the way the eye is led, hither and thither, by colour and
texture; senses lulled by subtle perfumes; mind soothed by the constant babble and chatter of the Usk.' Swallows, swifts, and house
martins swooped deliriously on the early-evening midge cloud.
The sun hung on the lip of the hill.

I've never felt so helpless. I passed through the necessary for-
malities, and on up a broad staircase to the room that had been
allocated to me. It was happening to someone else. The woman at
the desk, the pattern on the carpet, the skewed corridors: generic
elements. Clinic. Funny farm. Ritzy Bedlam. A gold card cure.
More sleep than you have material to deprogramme.

The steps were so far apart, you were always stretching out. You
played for time by pausing to appreciate the view from a long
window, a bush woven from purple shadows. When you moved,
searching for the right door, you couldn't hear your own footfall:
carpets with heavy rubber underlay, boards that screamed in resentment.

Thinking back, I might well have imagined all this: the
Ordnance Survey map on the wall, the pike in the glass case, walking sticks and muddy boots in the porch. Everywhere, all through
that house with its gleaming furniture and high plaster ceilings,

light from the river intruded, provocative and unstable. River sounds, so soothing they drove you into a frenzy: turn it off, can't you? Water torture. Compulsory bliss. It affected me in a way for which I was not prepared, recalling days making a pedestrian circuit of London's orbital motorway; winter afternoons when bare trees baffled the rumble of wheels on the cold road.

There was, so they told me, a maple, more than a hundred years old, on the East Lawn, *Acer palmatum septumlobum saguinium.* A tree that in autumn was as lurid as a wine-soaked dowager. A presence, a being, you might stare at for hours out of a schoolroom window.

Too much fecundity, too much privilege. These places were a penance, for which guests paid a premium; the country house weekend for the lower orders (metropolitan sportsmen, decayed gentlefolk whose incessant bridge-playing turned drawing rooms into geriatric day-care units). They limped, stumbled, drooled, or sat smooth as pillows and were fed with spoons. The morbid silence of the breakfast table interrupted by choice extracts, sex crimes or massacres in foreign places, read aloud from the *Telegraph.*

Why, I wondered, did I see the same couple every time I stayed a night in one of these hotels – Crickhowell, Southwold, Blakeney, Ullswater? They were walking across the lawn, on the diagonal, as we came up the drive: city-smart, a short man in a too-bright, yellow suede jacket and his taller wife in a white raincoat. He was a face you couldn't put a name to, an actor, television. The wife, she must have been in the business, in black and white: she knew how to move.

When we passed close enough for me to read the detail, the managed but thinning hair, heavy eyebrows and tight, vulpine mouth, I recognised him as an interrogator, a quick-tempered copper, Special Branch, Sweeney; a paid-off professional. They weren't making those programmes anymore: out of Birmingham or Manchester or the riverine suburbs. Cheap offices in which this man could shout. He was wearing soft, tasselled loafers and his tread was dainty. They had strolled too far from the path, then realised the lawn had been a mistake, evening dew soaking their stockings.

The man touched his wife, with a gesture that was almost religious. I superimposed an embroidered black skullcap on the crown of his head. He had a rich graveside voice, prostituted for too many years in trash. Now he could dedicate himself to following me from watering hole to watering hole, sharing an unresolved retirement. When, later that evening, sitting apart, we nursed our iced brandies on the terrace, we both, I think, dreamt of a comeback.

I watched the shadows lengthen. If I could manage one good night's sleep, without the pills, I might produce a few clean Landor pages; I might still broker my way out of here. There was a tap at the door. The lights went out. I stayed where I was, looking down towards the river, waiting for the Jewish actor to step out into the moonlight. To dance.

His eyes stretched wide, but he didn't see me. It wasn't a penetrative gaze. I could feel him looking through my glass skin at the hills to the south of the valley – as they would one day become: metatemporal. They stood for themselves, though he wanted to shape them, break them into stanzas; compose them, make them serve. If he could prevent his tenants, those villains, from cutting down his trees. 'The whole of human life,' he roared, 'can never replace one bough.'

Squire Landor. In my dream: lying on the grass, alongside the River Usk, letting my thoughts and fantasies drift, in their hypnagogic state, down to Crickhowell and over the layered hills to Ewyas and Llanthony.

Landor should have adopted a second 'l' for his new persona as Celtic landlord: Llandor. Landlord Llandor. Llan d'Or. Church of Gold. Landor: a muzzled savage, a dog man. A man whose name sounded so much like London.

Should he fit his wife to the estate or the estate to his wife? Never take a woman who rhymes to your bed: Julia Thuillier. Julie Julie, be mine truly. The banker's daughter, a provincial princess from Banbury, given to this driven man. Given to be driven. She would drive and he would learn to love the yoke. The difference between society and the marriage bed. Julia had been schooled to defer and Landor, over-mothered, to have his way (knowing there was a higher power). The battle could never be resolved; a strong, reckless son having to submit, to delight in his weakness, his lack of practical sense. No time for bankers and guardians, office-holders, money lenders, those who took their small portion and made it grow. An impossible conjunction: her youth, her expectations, his folly (blind trust in the eternal verities of truth and honour). Creatures from separate species locked together in this remote wilderness. You might as well ask a Pekinese to mate with a bison. She was ready to occupy her role as mistress of the household, arbitrator of rustic society. But there was no house, a few Parian stones fetched out of the mud; they squatted like starveling crows in the ruins of the priory, in the rude bitterness of one of the towers Colonel Wood of Brecon had fitted out for the grouse season. The stench of rotten flesh, spilled claret, mutton fat; barrackroom outrages, tuppenny whores. Mrs Landor lived in the penultimate panel of a set of Hogarth engravings. With a debauched fop incapable of satisfying her curiosity or providing her with suitable company on which to practise the domestic arts. It was an hermetical enslavement. She would rather have been pressed into a Turk's harem than married into this irreligious monastery.

Mrs Landor, craving attention, admiration, her glance quick to delineate hierarchies of style and fashion, a singer without an accompanist, was forced to endure the humiliation of a boorish husband, who aspired to no company better than his dog, or some stuttering Bristol verse-maker. Landor, who insisted on long hours of solitude, hill wandering, scribbling late into the night, would have his own way in all the arrangements of their life. In bed, the sentimentalist, he yielded. But that didn't suit her. The bulk of him. Heavy eyebrows like the tracing of muddy thumbs on clean Irish linen. High forehead with its halo of gummy jute. Was there miscegenation in his blood stock? His hair was wool, side whiskers leaking like tar juice from flabby ears. The ghost of a moustache. Protuberant lower lip. Then the folds, dewlaps, wattles.

Walter Landor was cattle. He fathered bastards with cockle-women from Swansea – but with his wife he had no way of encouraging her, schooling her in what he expected, or desired. What *did* he want? He stood, his engorged member in his hand like a pheasant's neck presented for strangulation.

It was so cold, wind howling through the crumbling masonry; days of unforgiving rain, the swollen Honddu breaking its banks,

flooding the low fields. Cattle sharing their quarters. Not a penny
of rent collected. She longed for sunlight through a shuttered
window. She aspired to elegance, Mr Landor remade as a Tuscan
princeling: straw-coloured suit, linen that was fit to be seen, shoes
that didn't carry half the slop of the byre into her parlour.

Wearied, exhausted by inaction, she sank into a Tyrrhenian
romance. She wanted to lie, exposed to his gaze, her hand over her
bosom; the noise of the stirring street beneath them, all the time in
the world. A woman singing to her child in the kitchen, baking
bread, flowers on the sill, bougainvillaea. He took her hand and
pressed it to his lips. He was a medical man, a gentleman practi-
tioner. He admired the slenderness of her figure, the languor of her
abandonment; one leg raised. 'Madame has exquisite ankles.' His
touch. Golden down on the inner thigh. Delta of tight curls
between her legs. He is struck dumb by her beauty, unable to
breathe; holding his breath in case he should disturb her, bring her
out of her reverie. He can master his impulses no longer; he turns
from the window, kneels before her – and he is not Mr Landor,
Landor transformed; he is another, a suitor. She submits to his
admiration, but he must take care not to crease the perfect line of
his trousers, to damage a pearl button on his waistcoat. Black thread
in her teeth. Red tongue.

Bovine Landor, skelping breath, groaning, doesn't see this
woman, the scandalous heroine. Eyes cold, grey as a herring,
fetched from the sea. Clothes like an accident in a Chinese laundry;
shapeless, snuff-coloured, choked at the neck, loose at the waist, ill-
shod in apple-pie boots.

'Up at Oxford,' Landor said, misinterpreting her hot glare for
one of admiration, 'I was the first man at Trinity to wear my hair
without powder. "They'll stone you as a republican," Southey
warned me. And he was right, as ever. Noble fellow.'

She could smell the sweat of his body on the old blue necktie, a
rag he used for bandaging his dog's paw when it was caught in a
poacher's snare. She flinched from adding the print of her hand to
other stains, the sauce residues that besmirched his unstarched
cotton shirt.

Landor fired a gun from the college window. He was rusticated,
banished. Rustication was the metaphor his life required: to be

made over as a countryman, a man willing to be always in the wrong place.

We were standing above the tumbledown bridge over the mountain stream, open hillside behind us and, in front, a glorious avenue of beech, chestnut, larch, the Cedars of Lebanon running down towards the distant priory. Landor's villa with its haphazard courses of local stone, grouted with mud, had a pinkish glow in the evening light. He saw something half-built, incomplete, resonant with potential. I saw a sheep shelter soliciting ruin. A squatter's cabin from a range war that had been lost, a dirt shack from New Mexico.

'Notice the strength in those beams. My own timber,' Landor said, relighting his cheroot. 'I drove them to it, every yard of the way. But we have come through. In the end. We have come through.'

The house, on two levels, was both classical and primitive. There was nothing fussy in the detail. Bald stone, unevenly set; bricks that might have been picked from a beach. Ruddy against the deep green masses of woodland. The doorways were broad and noble, their eyebrows nicely finished with vertical trim. A crude fascia. Why shouldn't it work? The villa was a restoration of something that had never existed. Too well made to fall down. Too ill-judged to survive. An instant relic.

Landor, a film of distance in his eye, looked down on olive groves, the sparkle of a blue sea, square white block-buildings, gilded domes: an approving and respectful peasantry. As he brooded on the gentle contours of the land, he reclaimed that first moment before the Augustinian monks recognised this valley as a nave dedicated by God to perpetual cycles of prayer and worship. With his instinct for savage solitude, Landor aligned himself with the hermit saints who paused here, dug into the ground like moles, to contemplate their mortality. This was one of the sacred places of the earth.

The movement of Landor's mind, his dreams, led him, alive or dead, from his stone platform on the edge of a wood to the priory, the Honddu; the visionary instant recognised and improved by J.M.W. Turner on one of his Welsh peregrinations.

The way that Turner recast Loxidge Tump as a rearing dark monster, mist-shrouded and alpine. The way he whipped the stream into a raging torrent, restored the priory, flooding it with heavenly light. Thus: the eternal Landor forgot the petty squabbles, frustrations and money madness that had driven him into exile; he grasped the essential, underlying, *absolute* nature of Ewyas. The contract could never be broken or set aside like a mere wife – although, there too, he would live by his folly, recognise the creature for what she was, his chosen other. His duplicate. The shape of the vessel, this grove in the mountains, was a sexual instrument: an alembic. His penetrative gaze must run unimpeded from the crooked church of Cwmyoy to the wooden owl-turret at Capel-y-ffin.

Landor, floating away from Siarpal, held on to the sweet chestnut trees he had planted almost two hundred years before. He noticed how they were dressed with white blossom; but I, labouring up that deceptive slope, away from the priory car park, saw an eldritch semaphore of bare branches, a procession of twisted wood, lifeless silver corroding to black. Landor's great vision undone by cruel winds and remorseless winters, the 'boisterous' weather of the Hatterall Hills.

In the deeps of this clamorous silence, Landor was tormented by voices, projected presences, friends and familiar strangers who infected him with their imaginary conversations.

Meeting, shade to shade, we embraced most pathetically; one of us condemned to quit the earth, the other to live upon it.

LANDOR. I could never undertake a work of fiction. Romances are an abomination. Leave novelty to milliners.
NORTON. Your *Imaginary Conversations*, dialogues between Barrow and Newton, Diogenes and Plato, aren't these a form of fiction?
LANDOR. They're dull enough, certainly. Now they tell me entire volumes are contrived through dialogue. Ivy Compton-Burnett. Elmore Leonard. George V. Higgins. I confess to a weakness for *The Friends of Eddie Coyle*. I unreservedly admire Mr Robert Mitchum. Did you see the movie? Woonderful, woonderful man. When Miramax get around to a Landor bio-pic I want Mitchum above the title.

NORTON. The inconvenience of having to dig him out of Forest Lawns won't affect his performance, that's true. He demanded overtime rates for lifting an eyebrow. You can only think of Mitchum in terms of geology. He made the heads on Mount Rushmore look like speed freaks.

LANDOR. It's the wardrobe, sir. Mr Mitchum isn't dressed, he's wall-papered. I never could describe clothes. The very act would be an impertinence. Draping a woman, article by article, is more of a provocation than a chamber of naked harlots in a bawdyhouse.

NORTON. And yet, don't you find, that's the very thing wives ask? When you've been out somewhere, lunch with a woman journalist. What was she wearing? How should I know what she was wearing? Black probably. Loose in places, tight in others. You can't tell how much underwear is supposed to be on view. Safer not to look.

LANDOR. Don't do women, sir. They're not a fit subject for literature. I attempted the first Queen Elizabeth, but royalty doesn't count. Elective hermaphrodites. Mistresses, on the other hand, under suitable pseudonyms, are a legitimate subject for verse.

NORTON. Would you agree that, disqualifying yourself from writing fiction, displaced autobiography, made it inevitable that you would become the subject of fiction for others? As Laurence Boythorn, for example, in *Bleak House*? The energy you squandered on your life, the famous mood swings between irascibility and generosity, couldn't be wasted. The way you would force gifts on the unwary, send them staggering away with a sackload of favourite books from your library.

LANDOR. Look around you. A noble estate: it produces everything but herbage, corn and money. It is about eight miles in length. I planted a million trees. I lived here little more than eight months altogether and built a house only to pull it down again. Invent a hero, if you can, who has performed such exploits.

NORTON. I don't do heroes, never could. Lowlifes, book scufflers, retro-bohos, that's about it. No writing, just editing; misremembered anecdotes.

LANDOR. Memory is not a muse. You must wrestle with and conquer time. This park is my most eloquent poem; read it from horizon to horizon, then exclaim: 'It is done.' In one session, forty hours at a stretch, my wife hammering upon the study door, I wrote a thousand deathless lines.

After walking abroad, never setting foot on land that was not my own, I would bring before my eyes various characters, men of science, poets, philosophers, and give them voice. If a tenant interrupted my reverie, I would knock him down.

I enter – see, there, *there*, the dog fox rush from the alders – into the consciousness of these animals; into the curled fern, the snowdrop, beads of dew on morning grass. The Welsh don't deserve this valley. They don't have the language to describe it. They were always an irritation, a barrier between myself and nature, as useful to the landscape as masses of weed or stranded boats.

NORTON. Poetry is pith. Fiction is what you leave out.

LANDOR. Who said that?

NORTON. You did. Or you will. I've always believed the writer must dig in for prose, stay in one place, find a single subject and cane it to death. Poets can afford 'capricious migrations'. Doing anything fictional with Llanthony would be tautologous. Leave it to the low-flying Harriers.

Giallo, Landor's faithful cur, bored with our creaking conversation piece, pissed on my shoes.

My feet had come out of the bed. The curtains were pulled back. The hotel room was silver-bright. Waking into a negative, my mouth was dry. I went into the tiled bathroom and filled a tooth glass with water. Stretching, up on my toes, I could see over the panel of frosted glass: two men walking by the river.

As I twisted and turned in the bed, trying to find a comfortable position in which to resist sleep, Landor was still with me. Now he had the face of a dog. A dog in a snuff-coloured suit. His sharp, shrill barks acted like Morse code; a blood-hammering headache. I spoke dog. I slowed the tape, smoothed the pulses into language.

Landor was digging his tower. *All shafts are to be solid.*

'A tower,' he explained, 'is a well that has been upended.' Wells are telescopes by which wise men read, anticipate the clockwork of the stars. Landor's tower went *down* into the earth. *Shafts may sometimes be independent of the construction.* Landor hearkened to Ruskin.

The house, Siarpal, was widowed and tumbled – but the tower was undisclosed. Landor's tower chased gravity towards the fire at the centre of the earth. From seething, magmatic depths, the molten eye of the poet stared out and up, catching its own reflection in the night. A shard of broken glass, many thousands of years old, winking from an ink-blue quilt.

2

Halogen haloes twinkling on water. Within the speeding car I experienced the shocking cold of a gravel pit. I recalled swimming here; better than chlorine, better than sea-soup. I should be up in the air, flying back to my dead father: Henry Armstrong Norton. I was older than him now. I still had work to do.

The ridges were dropping from his skin. Fearing an exchange of souls, I wouldn't look into his grey eyes in the mortuary chapel.

Floating high over the Thames Valley, I watched light-slicks sport on pools and puddles and reservoirs; rivulets wriggling their way back to their recent ancestor, the Rhine.

I drove out of London, my bags not yet unpacked from that futile excursion to Terry Waite's cottage: seeing nothing, noticing nothing, experiencing nothing. I could jump-cut like one of those American crime novelists. Wounded time would heal itself. The elements fitted, no detail was extraneous. Plot mechanisms are so smooth that life appears to be fated. Bad things are there from the first sentence.

That line from the poet Ed Dorn, talking about Sendero Luminoso in Peru: 'You don't disappear, you reappear, dead.'

Remember negotiating the fence on Stanwell Moor? An afternoon of grandiloquent purple-black clouds coughed straight out of the lungs. The short steep slope to the King George VI reservoir: that volume of mysterious water, flood potential, waiting in reserve, just outside the city. Airbuses in procession trafficking out of Heathrow. I couldn't believe this was London.

Here now, beside the perimeter fence, were fields, woods, the River Colne, bands of impact-radiance squeezed beneath the iron bulkhead of the western sky. On the horizon, the M4, headlights were dipped; bug-eye beams in the limbo of transit.

I never like to stare too long at any one car, that intensity of gaze might bring about a fatal accident. If I watched a plane coming in low over the Stanwell Moor Road would I be responsible for that swollen silver belly bursting into flame?

What the hell had happened to Kaporal?

His caravan was lost in darkness, somewhere in the shadows of Harmondsworth Church. There hadn't been any tapes since he reported the bizarre happenings in Barnstaple. I guessed that, with his ramblings about a talking dog, he'd finally lost it; succumbed to Henry Williamson syndrome – animal ventriloquism, the compensations of dog breath. The last resort of the muzzled visionary: a four-legged pal (going steady in a platonic, non-penetrative, mutual admiration bind).

Kaporal was expendable. I liked him. He was crazy in a quiet way. His tapes were the most soothing – voice flat, language functional, zero content – of books at bedtime. A mug of cocoa and Kaporal's latest dispatch from the leafy Devon lanes would have the most determined insomniac crashing the security barriers at the Land of Nod. Kaporal was John le Carré without the literary pretensions: his conspiracies unravelled like a roll of dental floss. Until your cheeks swelled in protest and you choked on it.

The Thames Valley gravel pits were Kaporal's stalking ground. He'd checked them out – access roads, security cameras – for Jamie Lalage. Lalage wanted a key sequence from *Amber Lights* to be played against this bleak backdrop: motorway sounds and incoming aircraft as his event horizons. The audience never worked out the motivation of Lalage's central character, the one who feels obliged to slouch his way westward to Bristol. The director couldn't help. There *was* no motivation. The man's existence began with the film. But, as the story progressed, so Lalage, prompted by Kaporal's researches, decided that his anti-hero should work for GEC/Marconi on computer simulations. He had a past and he was running away from it. A woman he'd been involved with had died in peculiar circumstances: wrists cuffed behind her back, gagged, ankles chained – and yet she somehow managed to totter in high heels, twenty or thirty yards, from her car to a gravel pit on the edge of the motorway. The marks of her heels, one shoe had come off, were found in the sand. She drowned in a couple of inches of water.

Lalage hadn't enjoyed shooting the scene, those complicated moves, half as much as Kaporal had enjoyed inventing it. 'Kaporal,' Lalage always used the surname, 'is very good at going over walls. He'll breeze in to Sizewell or Porton Down and have the security guards pour him a cup of tea. The insulin grin does it, unfeigned innocence. A guileless mug who will listen to any yarn, however preposterous.'

Lalage never knew if Kaporal had stumbled on a real story or if he'd made it up. He didn't care. What he wanted was this gloomy, mist-lifting-from-cold-ground, early-morning murk; a slow pan across black water, a frieze of pylons. He wanted to do the girl in one take from the far side of the pond, so that the absurdity of her walk, her hobbled suicide, wouldn't show. He was embarrassed by drama, by action. He needed to feel he was betraying someone, laying the ghosts of his childhood. Even after a couple of hours in the bar, he wouldn't drop his guard. He had an atavistic terror of revealing secrets of the confessional: they had to be displaced, converted into abstract imagery. Once he had the scene cold, a gesture of the head, an involuntary hand movement, he knew that time was fixed. His film wasn't prophetic, but the chemistry of place and weather (and minimal human intervention) was both a response to signals from the past and a marker that would affect any future reading of his nominated site. Malfate, he called it. The wound. A shadow on the lung. The cinema of malfate was pathological, flick-book X-rays.

It was Kaporal, at one of our early meetings, at a roadside coffee stall just off the M25, near Shoreham, who explained the material he was trying to work into the gravel pit scene. He'd picked up, at a car boot sale in Elstead, a few battered cans of flammable 16mm film and an album of photographs: recreational stuff, Savile Row farmers posing on brand-new tractors, slick bints. Very sixties: leather caps and dark glasses on winter afternoons; men with equipment (cameras, Purdeys, nonce motors) and decorative companions, rather cold, doing their best to raise a bleak smile. Designer leisurewear: zipped sealskin, white silk turtleneck, Hermes headscarf with balanced spectacles as optional extra, frosted Aquascutum trenchcoat. These were people who liked taking photographs of themselves. Nothing happened until they recorded it. It was an age of conspicuous consumption. Gadgets went out of fashion as soon as you bought them. The faces in Kaporal's album vied to outspend each other. They swapped Nikons and Leicas like kids trading differently coloured Smarties. Non-event snapshots, bored Sundays in Windsor Great Park (Kaporal clocked the distant ugliness of the Castle), were presented as the aftermath of a *Vogue* shoot by David Bailey. Men were iconic and women were waiting for something. They'd done it, swallowed it, shot it: what now? Brand-leader lethargy in a queen-sized package.

At first, Kaporal ran the 16mm reels and refilmed a couple of sequences, fashionable ghosts mugging for the camera. By the time he'd finished with them, they were unrecognisable: minor crims, floorshow girls who did it for food and a cleanish bed, unfunny comedians, land-rich snappers, amateur junkies. It was when he had the highlights properly looped, cut against TV speeches by Wilson, Heath and Enoch Powell, found footage from Soho dustbins (dope rallies in Hyde Park, Vietnam War demos in Grosvenor Square, White City tower blocks, Jayne Mansfield entertaining the troops), that he realised what he'd got. Home movies featuring Peter Sellers, Tony Snowdon, Britt Ekland and PM: a celebrity foursome in Windsor Great Park and the Bray Marina. Sellers, Kaporal guessed, shot Snowdon doing fancy passes on water skis. Snowdon tried a tricky focus pull with his two-shot of the girls, pouting Britt and stern-faced Mags, who everybody said had the talent to go pro. A tractor shot, evidently taken by PM, was signed: 'With love from Margaret, 1966'.

Very useful for future showbiz biographies. But Kaporal was more excited by what he swears he found in the last, heavily taped can: a different kind of charade, indoors. Nothing very extraordinary in Surrey wife-swapping circles: amyl nitrite, cannabis, a bit of dressing up. His private agenda, with the *Amber Lights* sequence at the gravel pit, was to get Lalage to restage one of Britt's chamber performances. She'd always been more of an accessory than an actress: game female, good egg. She let them truss her up. You could hear giggling and raucous asides from Margaret on the soundtrack.

Britt was in the coat and the heels; she staggered around the sandy edge of the marina, before falling flat on her face. The camera was swooping incontinently in a sort of mindless Dick Lester/Gilbert Taylor mock-actuality pastiche, kamikaze-panning from a banking Jumbo to the road, to the abandoned Land Rover with its headlights and open door. A big, out-of-focus, CU of Britt's face. Black-ringed eyes, spidery lashes; see-through tape that squeezed and distorted her mouth. A cruel joke. The others walked away and left her wriggling, kicking small circles in the wet sand. The scream was poochy and high. She kept trying to pull herself up, but only succeeded in slithering further down the short slope towards the water.

This was one story I didn't want to know about. I told Kaporal he could dig up whatever he liked about politicians, radiation leaks, weapons deals with corrupt regimes, but leave royalty out of it. Magazine-fodder and the royals had always gone together, shared a bed. It was a perfectly natural conjunction: that lovely German sense of fun mingled with a taste (acquired by the showfolk) for field sports. Let them get on with it. In private. Between consenting millionaires. If we breathed a whisper of this we were dog meat. Peter Wright had no serious trouble getting his whistle-blowing MI5 saga into print, but nobody in Britain would touch a mildly frisky biography of Prince Philip.

Seeing the lights of the Severn Bridge, and seeing them doubled, I realised that exhaustion had finally caught up with me. I had to risk Bad News Mutton and his midnight crew and take a break at Aust. The crossing into Wales would be like walking across the ribs of my dead father, fording the flood on a raft of skin. For most of the journey, my father sat beside me. He didn't speak. He'd had to stop driving, at the same time as he put aside the bulk-bought Craven-A fags, when his heart began to give out. Now after all those years at the wheel he was able to enjoy landscape. He turned away from me, breathing quietly and steadily; breath sweet as grass.

It was a cold, clear night: star-points breaking through the black umbrella. As ever, the car park was deserted; a solitary Merc at the outer limit of an otherwise empty grid. The car's colour, under the yellow lights, was suspect: self-destroying Agent Orange. The classic trifoliate Mercedes symbol glinted like an ice crystal, a quest badge.

It was hard to resist a peek inside the car – if only to check on who I might expect to find waiting for me in the service station. I looked at the books piled in the back, but they weren't books – VHS tapes. Dozens of them, dated, initialled. It wasn't a random decision. The Mercedes had been parked at this perverse angle, across the lines of the grid, because it was a blind spot. With one door open, a sneak thief would be hidden from the CCTV system. The car as I suspected was part of an art project. I was being invited to help myself, to stitch together a narrative to exploit this doctored evidence.

I ignored the tapes and picked out the only book I could find, along with one of those large brown envelopes that are so useful in spy stories. And I made my way, shivering, towards the low, flat-roofed building. The spirit of my father stayed in the car. He had faded as my speed dropped, vanishing altogether as we turned off the motorway.

I watched the hands of the counter woman as she scooped beans, black sausage, bacon, refried potatoes, onto my plate. This was the school/prison/brewery labourer experience: the choice that is no choice, fuel you don't want. It's a social not a culinary event. I had to stop myself reaching out to squeeze her fingers in gratitude. I was starving. Sitting by myself, in the window seat, this would be my funeral feast. A homage to all those other meals and treats, in Kardomahs, red leatherette and Formica booths with salt-caked windows: Celtic Americana. Fast-food in slow motion. Polite chat with an ageing waitress, her veins and her sturdy arms, wedding ring disappearing into a ruff of fat. Eating these overcooked, juice-less, nourishment substitutes – vinyl bacon and a glutinous slop of beans – would be an act of patricide. I was devouring the memory of my father. As he binged after post-war austerity, appreciating chrome, plastic, liquid soap in the toilets.

'Aust,' I said, 'best in the west.' I was echoing him, the old man.

It was happening already, his body lying with its eyes open in a cat-
alogue-selected coffin, and I was parroting his favourite phrases.
The need was there, fixed in me, the GP's reflex: to chat on easy
terms with whoever stood in front of me with their tongues out.

'Aust,' said an American voice, over-educated for the time of
night. 'I'm thinking, Skip – how do you *spell* that one? Aust? You
know what austenite is? I'm not talking about a bunch of lady
professors of both sexes from the Midwest misinterpreting the great
Jane; I mean the solution of carbon in gamma iron. I'm talking *austere*. Rigorous. I'm talking loci. You with me, Skip? Aust. One of
the empowered places of the earth. The bridge, Skip? You read
Hart Crane?'

'Orst,' said Skip. 'You should call it Orst. That's how you pro-
nounce it. I grew up on the mudflats. I still go elvering. It's spelt
A-u-s-t, but you say Orst.'

I knew Skip. Who didn't? Skip Tracer, Skippy the Hippie. He
had a cleanish licence (inherited) and ferried poets around what
was left of the circuit, Dartington Hall, Isle of Wight,
Aberystwyth. Most of the Americans, these days, could be booked
for the price of a curry and a backstreet B&B. They had one stip-
ulation: 'Anywhere except Cambridge.' Skip with his
pudding-basin hair, his genially wiped expression and unrevised
beard, made them feel comfortable. The guy lacked a bone armature, he was as soft as a head cartoon, or a refugee from the Three
Stooges. He was both local and universal, an estuarine survivalist
from the Northwick Lowlands and also a man of education; he'd
been thrown out of universities on three continents. The flash of
consciousness delivered at Buffalo, New York, by the partial ingestion of rhapsodic monologues from the poet Charles Olson and
total ingestion of psychedelic boosters, toasted his synapses.
Everything subsequent to that period was playback. His parturient
belly counterbalanced the screeching T-shirt: the look of the man
both whispered and shouted. His provisional smile commented on
itself in such a way that casual acquaintances couldn't tell if they
were confronting a Zen master with a flatlands drawl, or a trout-
fucking inbreed who kept a collection of trailer-trash skulls in the
basement.

I joined them at their table. Skip nodded. The poet he was

escorting into Wales was a Horus-headed dude of some personal magnetism. The hair was feathered gell, the nose hooked. He stared at me and he didn't. His eyes belonged to a magician; one bored into you, right through the lens into the depths of the vitreous humour – while the other popped and wobbled in the style of Ben Turpin. He folded in on himself, profile sharp as an axe. A labrys. The man would have no problem seeing around corners.

'This food is divine, better than you'd locate any place on the road in the States,' said the poet. 'Do you ever feel, Skip, you could *taste* a still life by Juan Gris? Sound the flatness of a lemon? Lick an oyster till it rang like a silver bell? Goddammit, we're eating jazz tonight, clashes and contrasts that force you to improvise, make the moves. Aust, Skip, is an Eleusinian shrine. Dig into this stuff, boy. Then say it aloud, Aust!'

'Orst,' barked the stubborn driver.

'Oww-st.'

'Or-st.'

'Owwst.'

'Orrrst.'

'Owst.'

'Orst.'

'Owst.'

'Orst.'

'Owst.'

'Orst.'

I turned my back on them. The Owst/Orst combo sounded like Meg Ryan's orgasmic simulation in *When Harry Met Sally*. This was a duet nobody was watching, apart from the security man deputed to check surveillance monitors.

In the solid darkness beyond the window the dead gathered. They pressed white faces against the glass: Dryfeld and Billy Silverfish, Terry Waite and Francis Kilvert, Jos Kaporal and Jeremy Thorpe, the Clifton suicides. Slow, flamelike entities resolved into a single figure: Prudence. Her face bound in strips, her lips fire-truck red.

I put the book from the Mercedes down on the table, hoping to distract the hyperventilating sound artists. And the poet fell for it.

'I knew Kees, strange guy. *St-range*. Gifted, sure, but incapable of walking the line. Too much Browning in there. Weldon Kees: great name for fiction, a character, no use for a poet.

'I mean, Jesus, the big play with the bridge? The abandoned car? A broken-assed metaphor, Skip. Too specific. You see what I mean?

'Kees was saying: "I want poetry and I want pulp to deliver an equivalent resonance." Well, that's simply not sustainable – as an argument. Can't be. In poetry every gesture carries an intolerable ethical burden. Pulp can never forget its origins as a service industry. Something has to *give*. Poetry fucks with you, pulp fucks at you.'

He reached for the book and, opening it at random, began to declaim.

> 'History is a grave and noble pageant,' Landor said.
> His family life at Gherardesca proved impossible.
> In 1844 his daughter gave him Pomero, a dog.
>
> On the neglected lawn, the iron dogs and the deer,
> Rusted among the weeds, alert, indomitable, keep watch.

'Lowell without the pedigree. Letters written with a trembling finger in whisky spill. You want a sharper take on Landor? Go for Apollinaire. What did he call himself, marooned in the smoky horror of London: *The Emigrant of Landor Road*? "Tomorrow my ship sails for America / I shall never come back." We gonna go there, Skip, we got time? "Guider mon ombre aveugle en ces rues que j'aimais." Landor Road, where is that?'

'Stockwell/Clapham border,' I blurted. 'I used to live there once, when I was in film school, between the railway and the hospital.'

Skip, bored with the direction the conversation was taking, began to doodle on the brown envelope I had retrieved from the Merc. His style was to have no style, portraits made by knitting with barbed wire. He collected, so he told us, all the poets. It was as if, in attempting to isolate the poetry gene, he saw them, various as they were, as beings unravelled from a single bobbin: squat, foreshortened, hairy, with heads that grew directly from their shoulders, hands like fins.

Taking the envelope from him, I ripped it open. Inside were a number of landscape-format b&w prints: the bridge at night, a woman with rather elegant legs sliding out of the Mercedes. There were also some far rougher video grabs: a self-portrait, taken at arm's length, that I took for my old friend Nicholas Lane. It wasn't Lane. This man was younger than Lane had ever been; he had the same wasted but genteel air, pushing himself towards romantic debaucheries, tapping the spirit of the times. There were the usual minor mutilations, anti-cosmetic improvements worked with a blunt blade; a moustache that seemed more painted than grown. And a single, flaring nostril offering easy access, a powder-passage to the brain.

This guy, coming after Lane, had taken his place in the loop: doomed rock star, a performer with more language than the medium could use. He was scripting, through this pack of images, journeys the young Lane had not yet attempted. Time at Aust was a backward spiral. Those influenced by us, by the clues we scatter in our random lives, act out what we imagine – and, in doing so, ensure that we experience them first.

'Hey!' Skip said, 'that's Richey. Richey Edwards, the Missing Manic. A strictly off-planet kid. I drove him that afternoon when they said he disappeared. Where d'you get these, man? They're the snaps Richey took. He was right on the edge. Been in Cardiff, hospital. Living by himself, reading too much.'

'Did he know Nicholas Lane? In London? Was he a customer?'

'Didn't say. Only met Richey one time. As a favour to a friend. I said, I said, "No, man, I'm strictly poets." Richey was a special case. Sat shivering in the back or slept beside me, head lolling on my shoulder. He read everything, so he probably came across Lane: as a bookman who, like Rimbaud, walked away. "It's been annulled, Skip," Richey said. "Nothing to live for. No books left." I drove him to Weston, through Portishead, Avonmouth, out on the mud flats. To stare back at the bridge.'

'But what happened? Where did he go?'

'Hold it, right there. Will you take a look at *that*.' The American poet, seizing on a photograph from the bottom of the pile, was enraptured. 'That picture is straight ace: the absolute coexistence, simultaneity, of . . . I tell you, Skip, listen to me now . . . A profound incident of the immediate transcending chronological time. I mean, *wow*, the gestural profundity of the boy's casual stance, the hoodlum slouch. The – what? – Hasidic confidence, *blood* confidence . . . yes . . . dandyism of man in his own being beside a wet road, travelling nowhere, at the end of the world. Waiting for a ferry that ain't never going to come. That, Skip, is one of the defining images of our era.'

It was a print that didn't belong with the Edwards set. It had none of the throwaway volatility of the Missing Manic's snaps. The Manic hit the release button with his eyes shut. The piers and struts of the bridge lurched at wild angles, in and out of focus. The video grabs might have been retaken with an underwater camera, printed through somebody's shirt: colour was intense, non-documentary. Figures distorted into cabbalistic signatures. A woman with a knapsack became a fire-angel walking up a wall.

The print that the West Coast poet had isolated was a considered composition: Bob Dylan, heavy shades, hands in pockets, frowning at the photographer. Skip, or one of his family, lounging alongside an Austin Princess (numberplate *540 CYN*). The road is rain-slicked, a cobbled causeway on the edge of a marsh. There's no definition in the sky. A clapboard shack with a Park Drive sign. Something that might be the beginnings of a suspension bridge. An arrow points to the ticket office: AUST FERRY. End of everything. Nowhere to go. The crossing into Wales.

Dylan stares back at the camera: he knows how to act as if *knows*. Just where he is. The hut, the car with its open door; salt-stiff marshes disappearing into an unseen river. Waiting for complimentary transport under a Medusa-shake of dirty hair. From behind those dark lenses, he sees the thing that is always there, lurking behind the man behind the camera. The thing that sees him.

Dissatisfied, I followed them across the restaurant, down the stairs; towards the automatic doors. Skip hadn't finished his story. Where had he taken Richey Edwards when they crossed the bridge? Where, exactly, in Wales, did Richey want to go?

'Skip,' I shouted. 'Wait.'

The poet with his Moroccan shoulder bag was gliding towards the car park, but Skip paused, midway, on the zebra crossing; he faced me, nodding with a benign absence of recognition. I wasn't there. Another revenant from the album of those who needed a guide to get them over the water.

I had to reach Skip before he drove off. I had to know. Richey Edwards and Nicholas Lane, never seen together. Lives, I convinced myself, could be rehearsals for lives. The younger man showing the older man the way. In places like Aust, the future pinches.

The system had broken down, the doors wouldn't part. I tried to force my hands between thick rubber lips. 'Skip!' I banged on the glass. It might be years before I met him again. I shouted, kicked. Gulls lifted from their perch on the walkway that acted as a barrier between the service station and the car park. They landed, ruffled their feathers, settled.

I thought I saw the whirlpool opening. / Kicked all night at a bolted door.

Weldon Kees. I remembered those lines. Something about 'blue fluorescent light' and staring towards a river. I remembered, or flashed ahead, the road out of Wales, the empty strip of motorway running between Abergavenny and Monmouth: how I'd seen, in the beam of the headlights, a decapitated hare rear up on its hind legs and dance. And, worse, how it tried to fly. Before the over-ambitious magpie let it drop. Inauspicious: an omen to be stored away as the signifier of some horror still to come.

'They don't respond to force.'

The uniformed security operative took me by the elbow. His feet were abnormally small and delicate for his trade. He had to dance to move. The rest of him, crackling with static, was ironed and shaved and polished; he seemed, like a customised wreck, to have been assembled from separate body parts. His shoulders were heavy, his chest pumped, but he had the legs of a malnourished child. His forearms were a Popeye quote but his hands wouldn't have looked out of place on a mongoose. He was a flatlander, taking what work he could find.

He didn't have much to say as he eased me towards the control centre, a cupboard room with a wall of rolling monitors. If he could rustle up a decent cup of tea, I'd be happy to spend a few hours surfing the screens: car park, entrance hall, stairs, restaurant and, best of all, the view from the high gantry; traffic flowing over the bridge.

I felt pretty good. The security man quickstepped out of it, leaving me to the multichoice channels, Aust in real time. How serious could it be, abusing a faulty door? I could probably sue them for skinning my knuckles, preventing me from pursuing gainful employment as an investigative reporter.

I was tired. I let my eyes close for a moment and I was gone. When I opened them, nothing made sense. I woke in a state of arousal. I couldn't stand up without doing myself a mischief. The deprogramming might have lasted a few seconds, there had been a sensual reverie.

'Do you recognise this woman?'

'I don't, no. Not at all.'

Two of them, backlit; fuzzy in outline. A man and a woman.

'You've never seen her before?'

'No.' I spoke without conviction. When anyone puts that degree of challenge into their voice, you feel guilty. You *are* guilty. I was guilty. I could quite easily have done whatever they thought I'd done. Done it in my sleep.

'Look carefully. And please take your time.'

There she was. They had photographs of what I'd dreamt. A woman in water. Eyes closed. Aust was a zone in which nothing advanced or decayed; everything happened at once. Photographs were the only evidence of an exterior world. Images laid out on the table like tarot cards. You could pick them up in any order and invent a narrative. Therefore I must say nothing.

'Mr Norton?'

'Yes?'

'Your name *is* Norton?'

Is it? They passed my driving licence from one to the other, made notes. Born? Married? Number of children? Purpose of present journey?

'Please look at the photographs.'

It was like being interviewed for a job at the National Portrait Gallery. Images: overlit and harsh, unsympathetic to the subject. They were of that school where the artist shoots herself in a variety of *film noir* poses. Casts herself as victim, spends a lot of time on makeup and wardrobe. And it still feels wrong. It's like Weegee but it isn't Weegee. Genuine scene-of-the-crime material has a particular smell: fixer, testosterone, dried blood, spit cooked on the stub of an extinguished cigar. Light fries. A white lizard-flash stays in the emulsion. Shake the print and the body will slide.

A figure lying in shallow water. Marks in the sand. A face, distorted by clingfilm, shocked by the explosion of the bulb. Sections of the body: the angle of the leg. Handcuffed wrists. A decorative anklet. A naked foot and a foot in a flimsy sandal. What was I supposed to say?

'Do you recognise this woman?'

Which woman? The artist or the model? Were they the same?

'Sorry. No idea.'

The man sat down, opposite me, but the woman was still standing behind the light that was shining into my eyes. 'Pelham. Do you know that name?' she said.

'No.'

'Are you absolutely sure?'

'I don't know any Pelham. Never have. There was a film, after my time. Walter Matthau. I've forgotten.'

'Look at these.' The man again.

I needed a drink, a glass of water. The woman fetched it. The man passed some papers across the table. Photocopies. Hotel registers: the Three Cocks, near Talgarth, the Bear at Crickhowell, the Valley of Rocks, Lynton. Names in a familiar scribbled hand: Norton & P. Pelham. I'd never been to Lynton. Lynton was the wrong side of the channel, north Devon. It must be Kaporal. With some stray he'd picked up on the road. Kaporal using my name, dropping me in it. It wouldn't surprise me if he'd got hold of my credit card.

'This make no sense. I've never been to these places. Somebody is using my name.'

'Should we know it, your name? Have we missed you on the television – *Newsnight, Crime File*?'

'Never, no. Things aren't that bad.'

The woman: 'Do you mind telling us what you do, sir? Your occupation?'

'Writer. I'm a writer.'

'Nice,' she said.

'*Very* nice,' the man echoed. 'A writer. What sort of thing do you write? Do they make your books into films?'

'All sorts, you know.'

'Horror? Serial killers with exotic tastes? Stephen King, Thomas Harris? Or is it more like . . . journalism?'

'Investigative journalism?' The woman chipped in. 'Do you smoke at all?' She held out a box of matches. I shook my head. She lit a match, blew it out. Lit another.

'We're having trouble,' the man said, shifting his chair closer to me, 'understanding how you can have visited these establishments, a grand tour of the west, with a P. Pelham, sharing a room, all facilities, and still say that you have no idea who that person is. Like to think again? P-e-l-h-a-m. Pelham. Ring a bell?'

'What happened?' I said. 'Who is Pelham?'

'She was a government employee, Mr Norton. A signatory of the Official Secrets Act who had recently taken a relatively minor position, on a trial basis, with an electronics company in the Thames Valley.'

'Was?'

'Good family. Been travelling, as they do. Roughing it, odd jobs here and there. Grape picking, chalet girl, bar work. Decides – tell the truth, it's decided for her – to settle down. Interview arranged, no obvious flaws. We checked, discreetly. Nothing serious in the way of drugs or men. But we did come across your name, Mr Norton. As having enjoyed a close, but short-lived friendship with the young lady. Was there a problem?'

'With who, whom, who?'

'With Prudence, Mr Norton. The woman who was found dead, drowned, in a gravel pit. Hands tied behind her back, face smothered in six yards of clingfilm. Is that what you were into? In those hotel rooms? Did it go too far?'

What had Kaporal done? It was his territory, the gravel pits. This absurd killing was a scene from Lalage's film, a scene which Kaporal must have taken too literally. The Prudence name was coincidence. This woman looked nothing like the girl I remembered. The hair was wrong, the clothes were wrong. Prudence couldn't drive and she'd never have traipsed about the countryside in thin gold slippers. Kaporal had borrowed my name, picked up a girl from one of the spook establishments, got her drunk, pumped her for information, taken her back to the caravan – then shown her where they'd filmed the snuff scene in *Amber Lights*. She might have been persuaded to play a role, tripped in the dark; he'd panicked, taken off. If the police found the caravan and searched it, this could get serious: the VHS tapes, the Thorpe material. Everything he'd recorded about the Money Tree.

I was a middle-class boy. I never had trouble with the police. When pulled in to a lay-by, I played the genial dolt. 'Sorry, officer, complete oversight. Pressure of work. Won't happen again.' Allow them to patronise you, give them a whiff of the officer class, solicitors on tap; don't get their backs up. And you'll walk away from the smoking gun on the table. 'Hackney's overrun with foxes. Have to keep them down, you know.' They understand a metaphor when they hear one. Not this time.

The woman came out from behind the light. She was attractive in that over-painted style air hostesses have, too early in the morning. A mask over exhaustion, flight miles. The perfume knocks you back. You could plough a furrow with those eyelashes. Crack an egg on the powdered cheek. Her lips were small and brilliant, like the knot-end of a balloon. But, under all the cosmetic enhancement, she looked closer to Prudence than the dead woman in the photographs ever could.

'Mr Norton,' she smiled, 'we have statements from a number of witnesses confirming your friendship with Prudence Pelham. A bookshop manager from Hay-on-Wye, a publican, waitresses, maids. Your relationship is a matter of public record.'

'But unless you're frank with us,' said the man, 'we will be unable to eliminate you from our enquiries and may require you to accompany us back to Maidenhead.'

'Can't do it. No way. I have to be in Wales tomorrow. My father, he's dead.'

They exchanged a look. This was better than they thought. I was obviously a mass murderer, the Fred West of the borderland. First the girlfriend, then the family. Stiffs piling up like the last act of *Hamlet*.

'You don't know Prudence Pelham? Never met her? Can't say anything about the entries in the hotel registers? Is that correct?'

She sounded so disappointed that I was on the point of fabricating a complete and unconditional confession.

'Yes. No. Yes. I knew *a* woman called Prudence. Didn't give me her surname. I stayed with her for one night in a pub. I've never been to any of the other places. The woman in the photographs is not the Prudence I met in Hay. And I haven't seen or heard from her since I left Wales.'

'And that's your final statement?'

'That's it, yes.'

'Then how do you explain this?' said the man, sliding a tape into the monitor.

Explain Aust? That would take a better writer than me; that would take a collaboration between Walter Benjamin and Edgar Allan Poe. Up on the screen, filling one window in that wall of windows, was the date-coded car park. Present time, the true 'now' played against this captured sweep of the past. There were the corridors and cafeterias, the bridge and the view from the bridge. Cleaners buffed the floor of the entrance hall. Deserted telephone booths. Toilets where dealers met and exchanged their packages in what they imagined was unwitnessed security.

All on tape. It ran whether or not anyone stood in the doorway to watch: to watch themselves watching – because this secret room was also on camera. I could see myself looking at myself looking at the screen which showed the nocturnal car park. There, under foggy lights, was my past life: Bad News Mutton and Davy Humpp.

Speed the tape. My car. A woman leaning against it. A woman in a ratty fur jacket. I am walking towards her. Very hip, Dogme-95 film-making; no close-ups, reverse angles. I ought to do something about that walk. 'Foot foundered,' as the poet John Clare wrote, in the account of his escape from the Essex asylum.

'Freeze that frame.'

I am chatting to Prudence.

The technicians had been playing with their Avid: in tight enough to let professional lip-readers make an accurate transcript of our conversation.

'Sorry, I'm heading back to London. With no detours.'

I didn't think much of the dialogue. Might need a rewrite, a script doctor. But the cops had the whole thing nicely word-processed in a red folder.

'Quite right, Mr Norton. "Back to London, no detours." Your car is waiting.'

'Sure you won't have a cigarette?' She had the packet open, pushed towards me. 'Small cigar? We know you indulge, from time to time. We've got the matchbox you gave Prudence. It was still in her pocket, a bit damp. And now we have your prints on that glass of water.'

She put her hand on my head, a kind of benediction, as the uniform held open the door of the car. Why do they do that? The abandoned vehicle at Aust is mine. I'm one of the disappeared.

In the back seat, next to the woman, I turned to get a last look at the bridge. The cops were chatting to each other, office gossip; they'd got a body and they were cruising back through their own country. The woman was humming.

'Bung a tape in, Mart.'

'Right, guv.'

Bob Dylan. Who else? A thin sun polishing drowned fields, shining into our eyes. *Not Dark Yet*.

3

Take the taps.

Four-prong silver stars with white porcelain eyes. Morning light polishing silver spouts into distorting mirrors. Take the look of the taps: armless mermaids. Take that fascinating device the bath plug, which comes in the form of a leadweight periscope. Twist it and it drops. Take the title: *The Arcadian Bath*. Run water if you will. You'll never use this deepwater trench. It's out of your league.

Water rusting the basin. Sunlight nudging the ridge of the wooded hills. A mirror steamed over. No mirrors. No mirrors in my bedroom. In this narrow bath-place there is a slate disk and it is not to be trusted.

A sharp pain in my lower back. A weakness in my left side. Heart? A lesion in the brain? I emptied myself into the view. The landscape captured in the steamed-over glass was a scan of the lump in my head, the clay foetus; a pouch of springs and rivers, nervous tissue, cerebral viaducts. A drowned child in a casket of bone. The pattern of fields, ridges, outcrops and abandoned excavations was analogous with the contents of my skull. Dig your heel into mud-stone, I experience the pain. Spit in the swirling current and I wipe my eye.

A violent knocking at my door predicted the headache that was soon to come. The door of the outer chamber. It might have been a natural sound, such as timber expanding when the central heating is switched on.

I'd forgotten how to shave. Should I risk this slate panel? Or simply look out of the window and rely on the enlarged version of myself that has always existed in the definition of the hills and fields?

I kept the razor moving, scratching at overnight corpse-fleece, wire wool; steady downward strokes peeling layers of skin, an easy rhythm. Shaving blue mould from a cheese. But cheeses don't bleed. Carve through the quilt of white fat and into bone. I wanted to expose the skull, the shape you can feel with your fingers. As we grow older we learn: meat is the parasite, bone is the host. Bone is where we are. We don't need eyes. The deep sockets are wells. Inside that bone, which will, in its own time, crumble away, is earth.

The basin was splashed with blood. The knocking wouldn't stop. We school ourselves, in cities, to shut out marginal interference: dogs that whimper and howl, car alarms, sirens, drills, rucks, blows, the sobbing child.

There he was, every morning, across the lower meadow, down by the river, a ragged figure with a huge knapsack, a stick, walking west; his shadow ahead of him on the dewy grass. I could feel how damp his feet must be. See hot breath leaking from his lungs. The determination in his stride. I tried to imagine the rest of his journey, where he could be making for, and why; but the impulse towards fiction had died. He was outside me and there was nothing I could do about it. He told me it was morning, another day.

The taps were running, to wash away the mess. There was still some skin left on my face; the fleshy protuberance of the nose, ear flaps I'd failed to trim. Keep cutting: cheek pouches, dewlaps, wrinkled lips. Throat. Tongue. That's why they produce razors with two blades, three blades, diamond-tempered wafers of steel. To peel without pain.

At twilight, standing at the same window, I would have no excuse. I'd be holding my cock in my hand, waiting. And there they would be: the same two walkers, one leading the other. Not so direct, so focused, as the morning man; poking about, picking up stones, sitting on the bank. What frightened me was that I recognised one of them: a younger, older version of myself. But I couldn't remember the incident, perhaps it was still ahead of me, this walk, searching for something not to be found.

The maid who dressed like a nurse stood in the doorway, wanting, I suppose, to take my breakfast order or to clean the room. 'It's
all right,' she said. 'We'll tidy this up. You sit in the chair by the
window. You like that, don't you?'

She was a pleasant woman, not Welsh – from Australia or New
Zealand; strong with good legs and a nice smile. The sort you're
happy to obey, like a dental hygienist who climbs mountains and
paraglides. The nature of our relationship, her professionally ami-
able role, my pampered subservience, made conversation awkward;
beyond meteorological gambits and mutual congratulations on
finding oneself in such a privileged place. She said that after I'd had
something to drink and taken my pills, she'd fetch the doc. It was
time we had a chat.

I sat at the window and waited. The light was more than I could
cope with, I didn't have the words for it. That was the problem
with so many of these country house hotels; they were part of a
natural progression, from coal-owner's mansion with Italianate pretensions, Tuscany on Usk, to coarse fisherman's billet, to software
salesperson's breakfast bar, to genteel old folks' euthanasia facility. I
was a fraud. I didn't have the cash, even with a second mortgage,
and conned advances on more books than I could cobble together
in three lifetimes, to hide here longer than a month, six weeks at
the outside. The trick was to stay sane enough to play mad; to shift
between the dream of life and the promptings of the clamorous
dead. To fix the assessment.

I dreamt my father dreaming me into existence. I summoned
memories of his father, who I never knew, holding up seed cake so
that his dog, a Scottie, would jump; an incident witnessed as a
home movie, film so pale and grey and fogged it looked like a
posthumous fantasy.

These Welsh borderlands, as Arthur Machen knew, are passages
where sights and sounds break through the mantle of unconvinced
reality with grail hints, chthonic murmurings, earth spirits and
strange atavistic impulses. I feared, shading my eyes against the
autumnal clarity of the light, the savagery that counterbalanced
Machen's sense of the blessedness of the countryside around
Caerleon. Exiled in London, he married the gothic horror of the
alleys and courtyards he walked so compulsively, the conjurings in

suburban villas, with invocations of prelapsarian bliss. If I didn't have the language to describe the place in which I found myself, the technical terms for the processes of nature and weather, how could I be said to be here at all?

The doctor was a brisk little chap. If he was a doctor. There were two things that made me wary of his introduction, his breezy: 'Doctor Vaughan.' He was too small. And he was English. My father, and his father before him, had been in the medical game. Six foot three inches was the basic qualification. It was like the police force in the valleys, when they had to take on the Irish, bullet-headed Paddies with size twelve boots; hard-drinking Papists who could clear a bar or break a strike. Doctors, being authority figures of a sort, big houses, gardeners, laundry maids, chauffeurs who once looked after the horses, were, without exception, foreigners: displaced Highlanders with a qualification from Aberdeen, ambitious Glasgow boys, Ulstermen with impenetrably grim accents. Genial eccentrics capable of sustaining the mystique of otherness. The gullible industrial proletariat, displaced from Cardigan and Carmarthen, shacks and byres, believed they were listening to Latin, or Hippocrates in the original Greek. Size was taken to be the visible symbol of ascendancy. Anyone who climbed above the native five and a half feet was gifted with an honorary doctorate from Cambridge University. Bone-setters, more veterinarian than Harley Street, treated everyone alike: a horse drench or a dose of castor oil. Some drank, most smoked and many, exhausted, died young. Carcinogenic clouds from the steelworks on the coast hung over the hills. The doctors worked long hours and drove everywhere, even to the end of their own front drive. They kept second cars to motor to where they'd parked overnight. Physiologically they were a different species to the folk they treated: they were sicker, with twisted spines, locked knees, shot livers, the shakes, double vision, and first call on all the latest viruses.

This man, Vaughan, didn't belong. He didn't have a 'Mac' prefix to his name – where the best of the genuine breed had two or three. Vaughan was from London. He admitted as much and asked me to call him 'Francis'. He was a psychiatrist, so perhaps the usual rules didn't apply. The old Scots, the displaced Dr Camerons, didn't recognise this newfangled science as a branch of medicine; they graded it with mesmerism, syndicated astrologers and Jewish Americans who charged you a premium to kip in their offices. And I agreed with them. I'd rather nail my tongue to the table than delve into the traumas of my past, accidents in the pram, schoolyard horrors, guilty dreams. Shift that lot and I'd disperse my entire stock of angst, I'd be too well-adjusted to write another word. A 'clear', as the Scientologists have it, is an elective Californian; a toffee-coloured freak who babbles on demand, with an explanation for everything and no reason to get out of bed.

I knew this Vaughan, despite what he said, as the younger son of one of the other doctors from the valley where I'd grown up. He'd been my age then, now he was younger and smaller. But apart from his colouring, his face and his name, he was the same man. No wonder he was shifty. He couldn't keep still. Nervous and speedy, he picked up objects from my dressing table, closed the curtains an inch or two, then spread them wide. He was on something, if it was only adrenalin. Perhaps he'd shrunk in memory, stayed the size of the owl-spectacled child. Perhaps, surging restlessly backwards and forwards across the carpet, he'd worn his legs to stumps. In a sense, paying what I did for bed and board, the man was my employee; a medical retainer in the old sense, summoned to the big house, let in reluctantly at the front door.

The Cambridge voice worried me; if I gave him half a chance, he'd be spouting poetry and Marxism. All I wanted was the piece of paper, the verification that I was a chained-to-the-wall loony. Intelligence, of a self-devouring sort, lasered from his eyes. I had to get the interest of the man, wean him from metaphysics. If he let me stay here for a while, in his clinic on the edge of the mountains, I could keep the police at bay. Reports, assessments, the stern-to-be-kind care that patched up coke fiend comics and woozy footballers, mended electrically insulted bodies, stealth pilots traumatised by after-images, politicians hiding out, were on tap: a sliding scale of payment for government agents. And potential prisoners of the state.

The doc poured himself a coffee. 'What we have to understand,' he said, excusing himself the sight of my Elastoplasted face, 'is that we are sharing a voyage into the unknown. Do you keep a dream journal?'

I could have thrown him from the balcony, but that would be overplaying my hand. 'No,' I growled. 'Why don't you ask if I piss the bed?'

'You can't recall a single dream from last night?'

'Not one,' I lied. Usually my nights were black as coal measures, leavened by fitful, waking hours recalling cricket statistics, the undercasts of obscure Westerns starring Tim Holt or Audie Murphy; then a kicking of sheets, mortality sweats, the sound of sandfalls behind damp paper, birds trapped in the chimney. But, on the night in question, I'd moved through all the cycles of sleep, deprogramming my ambulance journey to the west, which followed on my release, after hours of impertinent questions. I'd dreamt of beaches, walks. I'd rehearsed this interview. And written chapters of a book that interwove truth and fiction, the insistent dead and lovers I'd never loved.

I was in one of the padded crypts beneath Broadcasting House with a bright little thing I barely knew. We were talking on a couch when she insisted on showing me a map she'd knitted. We were kissing. In life, I'm sure there had never been anything beyond the usual maw-maw, airbrush of the cheek. Now we enjoyed a feeding frenzy, face-gobbling, tonguing for cavities, drowning in drool. She wore a ratty suede jacket and had recently had her gold hair cropped. I had to sink to my knees. Either that or rick my back. Her sparky humour and the impassioned engagement with the case she was pleading, the way her map gave entrance to the past, the family she honoured, moved me. Disposed me to express my approval in physical terms. That and her boyish shape, her big grey eyes. We were banging on the floor.

'Did it occur to you,' Doctor Vaughan said, when I let him in on this steamy cartoon, 'that the girl's height, the fact that she was unusually small and filled with so much energy, was an invocation, in some sort, of your mother who, I believe you said, was rather . . . petite?'

Actually, no. It was an invocation of another episode entirely, a night of snow, driving from the ten-pin bowling rink in Llanelli to Roath Park in Cardiff, with another gold-haired Celt – and what happened then, and how strange it was to return to the street in which I'd been born, but which I scarcely knew. All fascinating, no doubt; better left to simmer in its own gravy. Nothing would do more damage than to bring this muck out.

Vaughan was disappointed. Or mildly miffed. It was clear that his problems were much more interesting than my own. *He* thought so; he juggled with the bright red pills I hadn't taken, shot them into his mouth, washed them down with the dregs of my juice. He left his fleck-moustache, the orange ring around his mouth, unbrushed. 'Is sleep a problem?'

'Sleep's fine,' I said. 'It's the bits between that hurt. Like now.'

He didn't take the hint. He liked the look of the pile of papers on my desk. Scholarship as therapy. Without invitation, he began to skim a page or two, humming something melancholy from one of the Germans.

'Have you come across your namesake, the poet Henry Vaughan?' I asked. 'He finished up as a quack in these parts. When he wasn't mooning about the hills.'

Francis Vaughan perked up at the prospect of a literary chat. He'd been too easy to tag, a poet/doctor, affiliated to William Carlos Williams and Gael Turnbull, rather than the local boy, the serial sentimentalist, Dannie Abse. It might have been the book by Geoffrey Hill poking out of his jacket pocket, or the way he ripped through my papers, checking to see if he'd stumbled on a rival. The relief when he discovered it was only prose.

'I suffer,' said Vaughan, clapping his tiny hands at the prospect of talking about himself, making a confession, 'from a growing horror of the onset of a syndrome I've had before: the dissolution of short-term memory – as, for example, knowing who you are or what you are doing in my room. It makes the act of reading impossible. I *hear* broken units of words as pure sound: screams, wolf howls, laughter. Ricocheting fragments of external actuality bombard my stretched nerves like advertising slogans from an alternate universe. The brain loses all sense of location, even the psychomotor relation with the body. I am assaulted by script from an alien cosmology, a Linear-B code I can never hope to break.'

Sweat beaded his prominent forehead. The guy was coming apart in style. 'What does Vaughan the metaphysician say? "And man is such a marigold." He understood the sun-seizure in the fields, the crows of madness: Van Gogh recovering the starry firmament from a pot of marmalade. Space without end, inside and out.'

'Do you take any medication?' I asked.

'All I can scrounge,' he answered, 'but the most effective cure lies in a scheme I've considered marketing under the slogan "Inward Bound"; in which rugged mountain walks, bathing in ice-cold becks, will be combined with guided meditations on the extinction of the human soul. Wales is the perfect locale. An hour's tramp would lead the most vacant optimist to thoughts of suicide. Exile Lord Archer to Builth Wells or Aberystwyth for six months and you'll have a second Wittgenstein on your hands.'

'How are your bowel movements? Libido? How frequently do you masturbate? And with what success? How many pieces of fruit do you consume in an average day? How long do you sleep?' Sinking back in the chair, making a steeple of my hands, I fired questions at the pacing Vaughan, whose pedestrian circuits were growing tighter and tighter – to the point where I felt that he would soon be corkscrewing through the floorboards in a puff of yellow dust.

'I miss my solitary breaks,' he groaned. 'Pressure of work. We should never have accepted sponsorship from the defence industry. They're going down like flies in the Thames Valley. Those who don't spend their working days downloading the vilest porn, or cruising bookdealers' catalogues for first editions, are ready to sell out to the Chinese or the Yanks. It's a culture of deceit. Climbing into bondage uniform, or topping yourself from Clifton Suspicion Bridge, is the most straightforward response. We can't cope. I need a place, a landscape, where this unrelenting verbal pressure can be run to ground.'

'Henry Vaughan practised sleep deprivation,' I told him. 'He feared the loss of control that comes when you allow yourself to wallow in dreams. He believed that nights were given to us for meditating upon the coming hour of death. We must make ourselves ready for the Bridegroom. Vaughan knotted his sheets. He lay in a draught. He would quit his bed and take to the fields, rage through a cycle of prayers. "High noon thus past, thy time decays," his brother Thomas the alchemist told him. Sleep was a deceiver and not to be endured.'

'Yes, yes,' the doc replied, 'but Vaughan was already in a state of *virtual* sleep. Like one of the hermit saints who first colonised these hills, Vaughan saw immortality in the corruption of the flesh. The house where he lived, the ancient tree, his father: eternal forms.'

He scrambled through his pockets until he found a notebook in which he had transcribed one of Vaughan's visions, as if the late Metaphysical was there on the couch.

I went to bed: and dreamed, That I lay full of sores in my feet, and cloathed in certaine Rags, under the shelter of the great Oake, which growes before the Court yard of my fathers house and it rain'd round about mee. My feet that were sore with Boyles, and corrupt matter, troubled mee extremely, soe that being not able to stand up, I was layd all along. I dreamed that my father, & my Brother W. who were both dead came unto mee, and my father sucked the Corruption out of my feete, soe that I was presently well, and stood up with great joy, and looking on my feete, they appeared very white and cleane, and the sores were quite Gone! Blessed bee my good God! Amen!

Reading these words aloud brought the doctor out of his reverie. I couldn't direct his actions to fit the plot. I knuckled moisture from the corner of my eye. I found myself responding to some triggered reflex; just as, reaching the end of a chapter of Dickens, I'd blubber on demand. Cheap tricks but they worked. Vaughan's fable hit me hard, the oak tree, the dead father and, especially, the feet. Walking these hills, as a youth, in clumping black boots had introduced me to schools of boils and blisters; infections that had to be lanced, stinking, in a tin bowl.

'It might be useful,' the doctor said, as he fiddled promiscuously with the cache of unpaginated dross I'd bought from Becky, 'if you sorted out your papers. I'm delighted to find that you're research-ing Father Ignatius and the founding of the abbey at Capel-y-ffin. An outing might be arranged if the weather breaks. Meanwhile you should go downstairs, join in, explore the grounds. I'll be back tomorrow, we can talk about your work: the difficulties that can arise in editing a problematic manuscript.'

I came down the wide stairs like Gloria Swanson at the climax of *Sunset Boulevard*, clutching the balustrade, blinking in the bright morning light. There was no welcoming party of hacks and flashbulbs, no staff at all. I wandered through empty, high-ceilinged rooms, fearful of the larger-than-life furniture, the loud chintz; brass coal scuttles and warming pans polished to an offensive sheen.

Autumnal foliage draped itself over complicated ironwork at the edge of the terrace. I wanted to show willing, to oblige Doctor Vaughan and 'join in', but there was nothing to join. On the oak sideboard, overlapping newspapers, *Telegraph* and *Times*, were shingled, waiting to be claimed. A folio ledger, when I examined it, contained nothing but lists of fish caught, weights and lengths.

The dining room, which was L-shaped and vast, offered a river view to the south, and an expanse of lawn, with cedar, cypress and hornbeam, to the west. A handful of punters, ancient and dejected, were waited on by sturdy antipodeans who treated them with boisterous indulgence. The food was excessive, they tucked it away with good grace. The room was panelled and hung with heavy drapes; the only sound was the creaking of stiff jaws, straining to crunch and tear and gum: the squirting of eggs, the cracking of dry toast. You couldn't tell which would snap first, teeth or biscuits. And all the while the attendants, in their inappropriately short, tight skirts, bent to whisk away soiled plates, retrieve crumpled napkins, recover sticks. Conversation was entirely food-based, comparing this meal, to its detriment, with the previous day's offering.

I stepped outside onto the terrace. I decided to make a turn of the estate, which was still something of a mystery, even to the locals, screened as it was by dense woodland. I knew, because I'd walked the canal on the far side of the Usk, that the asylum, with its blue-grey brick and its odd, Italianate towers, was lost among clumps of oak, chestnut, beech, complemented by more exotic nineteenth-century plantings. The walks, on their various levels, linked by steep stone steps, became a metaphor for degrees of sanity. As your mania was brought under control, so you were permitted to wander, in ever wider arcs, away from the house.

I trembled that first morning out in the air, the privilege of this light, with the stereophonic babble of the river, hustling against rocks, rattling pebbles, sweeping broken branches downstream towards Crickhowell. Dry red leaves caught in the fuzz of the hedge, giving it a wounded look. The gardens had been designed as shadow traps. Avenues, abandoned tennis courts, in which speckled paths appeared and disappeared, as fast-moving clouds masked the sun.

The most disturbed among us, hugging themselves, shocked by the immensity of space outside their pounding skulls, dragged their feet in a slow circuit of the gravel, leaving curious tracks when they were helped back inside. Bolder spirits set off recklessly across the damp lawn in the direction of the fishpond. Then something unexpected would occur, a fountain would spurt, a motor mower start up, and they'd run back to the shelter of their rooms, regretting their futile bravado from beneath a tent of sheets. Solitary melancholics, nosing out potential suicide nooks, crept down to the river terrace and gazed longingly over the low stone wall and into the meadow. They decided, reluctantly, that it was too modest a drop, their plunge would be defeated by pillows of bracken and bramble. Catatonics, left on benches to be thoroughly aired, were themselves furniture.

One old man, who reminded me of the television personality Lord Bragg (reduced to agonising silence), hooked himself over a sundial, where he would spend the day watching the needle creep around its verdigris-enhanced copper disk.

Another veteran, with close-cropped politic hair, was wheeled out and placed in a position that he indicated by a sequence of bat squeaks. Facing two heraldic animals, he became the third point in an equilateral triangle. After many months, his pale skull, peeking out from a tartan rug, developed, in sympathy with the weathered stone, an alopecia of grey-green mould.

I was reluctant to return to my room, to face the indisciplined and unpaginated heap of Brother Jonah's manuscript. I'd never had a problem cranking out labyrinthine fictions that tottered and tumbled under the weight of their conceits. Those days were over. Even with my leathery ego, I couldn't face the labour of dredging this (Llanthony and Capel-y-ffin) utopian community material for another five years. The landscape, the garrulous river, mocked me. I stared at the campanile with its red brick bands, its ledges and lips, its barred windows. The brickwork was rimed with threads, out-of-season Virginia creeper, encouraging fantasies of escape.

I found, beneath the main terrace, a walkway screened by overhanging foliage, lianas, ivy and thorns. A dank passage led to a

small bricked cave that offered a view of the fields above the treeline on the opposite bank of the Usk, and which promised, at the
same time, the illusion of privacy. Walking around the grounds had
been a pleasant experience; the temperature, according to a giant
thermometer on a outbuilding, was well within the comfort zone.
But, sitting on a stone bench, I began to shiver. I'd obediently let
my mind play over the incidents of the last few days, in the same
way that in better times I'd have rehearsed the elements in the
chapter I was about to write. Now, hands on knees, looking down
at one of the York stone slabs, I let its greyness melt into photographic emulsion. The pattern of watermarks and stains became a
body lying in mud. A face. A woman. Britt Ekland. The actress,
whoever she had been, in Lalage's film. I strained to call up the
name: Pippa Guard, Sandy Ratcliff, Coral Atkins? None of these.
The eyes in the stone winked. There was a particular perfume in
the air, the damp canvas of a folded sun umbrella, leaves rotting in
a water butt: the face was the face of the dead woman, Prudence
Pelham. Who was not, and never had been, the Prudence I'd
known in Hay.

The smell was stronger, closer to hand. Not macerated leaves but
tobacco, foul shag tempered by wet dog, Irish terrier. The air in the
cave tasted red.

'Nice day for it,' said the man who was hiding in the shadows,
behind a cloud of blue smoke. If he was burning leaves, it was in
the cauldron of his pipe. A gardener on the skive, lounging on his
rake. I had a sudden panic that he'd been deputed to keep an eye on
me, track my movements, wrestle me to the ground if I tried to
walk out of the gates. The man had a nasty, pubic-graft moustache
in ginger, spiky clumps of hair bristled from his greying temples,
despite his best efforts to grease them down with quantities of lard.
Even in the open air he smelled of the kennel, rutting hounds. He
dressed like a POW in grey-blue serge, buttonless battledress,
trousers tied with twine, one foot booted, one in a carpet slipper.

If he hadn't been dead for years, I'd have tagged him as Mr
Lydd, a neighbour from my childhood, an ex-policeman in the
RAF who finished up as an enforcer in the local asylum, a place of
brutal reputation. Lydd was a widower who lived rough in his own
garden (a hammock in the Anderson shelter), while turning the

family house over to the Irish terriers that he bred. This extended
and incestuous family roamed through every room, sleeping on
unmade beds, shitting on rugs, fighting like tinkers, and barking day
and night at anything that moved across the garden, birds or clouds.

There was a rumbling in the valley, distant thunder, and the
walls of our damp cave shook; but the day was still scoured and
sharp, with not a wisp of white.

Remember?

The ferns growing out of the loose brickwork brought it back.
Red dust on the roped parasol. The smell of green canvas cushions,
sun flaps, the swing-seat at the bottom of our garden.

Remember? How I would climb into the old oak which over-
hung the garage, then drop into the next garden, a bramble
wilderness; through green tunnels, filching soft fruit, fat earth-
tasting raspberries; sunstreaks firing the veins in pale leaves? The
only guardian, a cat, nested and yawned. This was a tame invasion,
the house belonged to a woman who was so short-sighted she
couldn't tell if it was the postman or her father, a long-dead head-
master, at the door. The bushes this disciplinarian planted had
spread into a wilderness. His daughter, had I asked, would have
been delighted to let me pick all the fruit I wanted.

Lydd was another matter. Approach his hedge, into which he
had woven strands of barbed wire, and the terriers would bark, yelp
for food – or from resentment at his return. He was frequently
absent, his hours at the asylum were unpredictable. By temperament the man was a nightworker, patrolling empty corridors,
listening at doors. He wasn't a drinker or chapelgoer and he never
went near the RAFA club. He wasn't seen at rugby matches. So the
stories of his explosive temper, his violent assaults on patients, hap-
less females, were rumours that crept out from behind high walls,
carried by kitchen staff or handymen.

*It wasn't thunder, but a bell. A bell whose dull clanging made the bricks
shake.*

One afternoon, tearing my sleeve, I squeezed under the wire and
down onto the roof of Lydd's shelter. This bunker had, in the years
since the war, been heaped with earth that had evolved into a
grassy mound; a tumulus in which Lydd could incarcerate himself.
The bunker was sheltered by a dying apple tree, wrapped in sticky

black tape; from its withered branches hung strips of flypaper on which numerous insects hummed.

I walked on tiptoe, in expectation of mantraps, pits filled with snakes. The shelter was an ice house in which meat would be left to survive a hot summer. Flies were drawn to the place by this sweet, rotten smell; by the oven of dog shit. By the gummy-footed fellows writhing on the blue tongues that decorated the tree.

The dogs at the window of the house spotted me. They jumped on one another's shoulders in a frenzy of barking. They butted the glass. I had to pee. I couldn't wait. I was wriggling with it; hopping from foot to foot, between the racket of the dogs and the manic zizzing of the flies. I ran towards the house, with the vague notion of calming the beasts by demonstrating that I meant no harm, but that only provoked them to further ecstasies. I could see that some were half-starved, others lay unmoving on the late Mrs Lydd's best armchair.

My bladder was burning. I lifted my shorts and pissed deliriously into the drain. I couldn't stop. Even when I heard the footsteps and the turning of the key in the gate that guarded the narrow passage that ran down the side of the house.

'Can you hear it?'

The gardener had moved alongside me, puffing on his pipe, happy to initiate a conversation that might postpone the moment of returning to work. He had a strange way of walking, or hopping, punting himself on his rake. I was happy to indulge him, to cut off the spontaneous eruption of a misremembered childhood. I was born yesterday, when I gritted my teeth and typed that fatal sentence: *I watched them.*

'The bell?'

Of course I could hear it. They'd hear it ten miles away in Llanthony. The foundations shook. The bell was a storm prophecy. I could see moisture being drawn from the river by the vibrations as they ran through the earth. 'No,' I said. 'Can't hear a thing.'

'Good,' Lydd replied, slipping the pipe into his pocket, 'because they call that the Lunacy Bell. If you hear it, you're mad. If you admit that you hear it, they'll take you in and burn your brain. And if you say you still hear it when they come a second time, they'll open up your head, put wires inside. Your head, see, is like a bell

without a clapper. *I* hear it but I don't say. There's some inside that
say they hear and hear nothing but the river and the swallows
diving around the tower. I see and I hear and I don't say. Never let
them catch you sitting with nothing in your hands. They'll think
you're listening for the bell. Always have a book about you. Not
much of a reader myself, but I've learnt that dodge. Here, borrow
this.'

He pulled back his battledress tunic and dragged a lurid paperback out from beneath a grimy vest. It was hot in my hand. Picking
up his rake, he moved away. *Arthur Machen: Tales of Horror and the
Supernatural. Volume I.* Published by Panther. Priced, second time
round, at 5p.

Father Ignatius, it seemed, had a pathological fear of dogs. The
rabble he gathered at Capel-y-ffin would have put my present
asylum to shame. That's if you trust Brother Jonah's forgery, the
papers he tried to punt as a commentary on Ignatius's unrecorded
autobiography, *Wheel of Heaven, the Recollections of a September
Soul.*

The old poseur, kipper-breathed (as Kilvert noted in his journal),
rounded up a posse of paedophiles, underwear thieves, morphine
addicts and Irish drunks that no other monastic order would touch.
Ignatius's abbey was an architectural freak peopled by inadequates
who, according to the locals, lived 'a good deal on milk and allowed
no woman to come near them'. Naked beneath their coarse habits,
these sunken-eyed runaways took the brunt of the weather as they
drudged, potato digging or diverting streams, on the cruel slope
beneath the sandstone cliffs of Tarren yr Esgob.

Ignatius, meanwhile, was on the train – back to town, or shipped
out to America on a reverse Billy Graham crusade; performing, like
Oscar Wilde, for savages in the Wild West. The man, dripping with
jewels and dressed like a pope, was accompanied everywhere by his
ape, a precocious child, bought from his parents and made to dress
as his master's miniature: the Oblate Infant Samuel, or 'Baby
Ignatius'. An idiot lama, elected by the abbot, as a future king of the
mountains.

Sitting in my window seat, with a pot of Nicaraguan coffee and
one of the excellent Don Ramos cigars available from the bar, I

passed an indulgent afternoon; the founding of the abbey was a great, page-turning yarn. Ignatius was one of those late-century sports like the Bensons and Frederick Rolfe, Baron Corvo. Corvo spent some time as house guest of the Pirie-Gordons at Crickhowell, being called 'Hadrian' and granted the title of 'Protector of the Peacock and Puppy'. But the hierophant of Capel-y-ffin lacked Rolfe's talent, the compulsion to write and draw, to fill page after page with fastidious calligraphy. Rolfe, by transmutation, made himself into the first English pope. Ignatius settled for a rustic retreat.

He tried, without success, to purchase Landor's estate, the Augustinian priory, the felled mansion and the pit where the foundations of a Florentine tower should have been laid. Landor's executors sent him packing. So Ignatius walked, for the first time, the hard miles uphill to Capel-y-ffin. He walked, setting a curse on Landor, who had died five years earlier. He cursed the ground, the flocks, the forests and the fields; he cursed Landor's descendants and his dogs. He cursed his literary reputation and lived to see it wither. From that day, there was a fault in the land, the weather; one side of the valley would shimmer, each stone marked with Mediterranean clarity, while the other would be lost in clammy mist.

Ignatius took on the same families of local bodgers and brigands who did for Landor, and he paid them cash up front. He wanted a precise replica of the priory church. They disappeared and didn't return till all the public houses from Talgarth to Brecon had been drunk dry. Ignatius was helpless, all he could do, miming a Pilot-like laving of the hands, was to work his magic, causing a chunk of heavy masonry to fly through the air, crushing the foreman's leg – then, with secret signals and a few passes of incense, he cured the man. The ruffians fell into line and the chapel was completed. They offered to work for nothing on Ignatius's tomb. 'Be sure to have the ground prepared, your honour, for who shall know when his day is come nigh?'

The chapel tumbled within a few years, access is now forbidden. There's nothing to see beyond the priest's futile memorial, the symbol of his final exile. 'To live on the edge of eternity' boasts the inscription. A lion, a bull, an eagle and an angel are arranged at the

four points of the compass, summoning the guardian spirits who
nursed Ignatius through his follies.

Darkness, when it came, came fast; I could hear scufflings in the corridor, nurses with trays of pills and exotic cordials. I rolled the cigar
between my fingers and let the legend of Ignatius fade. There had to
be very real differences between this healing place, with its gardens,
its river, and the small community of miscreants digging themselves
in against a culture (and a geology) that couldn't tolerate amateurs.

The story of Ignatius was, for Brother Jonah, a mere settling of
scores. He depicted himself as the voice of reason, driven to quit
the monastery by the excesses of a schismatic regime. The community, at the death, was reduced to three monks and the Infant
Samuel, who would chirp on demand: 'My father, my father, I'm
the monastery baby.' Brother Augustine was an escaped child-
molester and Brother Stanislaus a con man and petty thief.

Jonah wanted to be named as Ignatius's successor. When that
honour was withheld, he ran off; first to Bristol, then Oxford. He
tried to interest various newspapers – for no more than the price of
a drink – in the scandals of a remote and enclosed society of mis-
fits. Ignatius would, apparently, offer his surrogate child, the Infant
Samuel, a choice of punishments: physical or spiritual. 'Take a
good caning before your communion and without complaining.
That will prove to me, and to your brothers before God, that you
are truly sorry.' Later Ignatius would rub holy unguents into the
raised weals on the child's buttocks and thighs.

The site of the monastery had been chosen on the shady side of
the valley, its arrangements laid out with 'a masterly eye for inconvenience'. The monks had not left the world, the world had
expelled them. Capel-y-ffin was a spiritual gulag. Ignatius was a
curious creature, unworldly, high as a rotten pheasant, yet capable
of mesmerising large congregations of Nonconformists and
Dissenters. He raised huge sums of money and saw them disappear
into ill-conceived building projects – into Brother Jonah's wine
cellar. He floated through metropolitan society as the latest miracle-
working Puseyite charlatan, but couldn't remember the name or
the face of some local dignitary to whom he'd been presented a few
moments earlier; Ignatius unfailingly addressed Francis Kilvert as

'Venables'. Jonah, in snivelling and bitching and sniping at the man who had once been his model and his inspiration, was abusing himself; doing dirt on his aspirations.

Despite Jonah's journalistic bile, his desperate, unrequited longing for this charismatic man came through. The expulsion from the abbey was a festering sore. He had rusticated himself from a cold country Eden. He denied himself the sight and smell and touch of a great teacher. Judas-Jonah was driven to ever more frantic researches to turn up the stories that would discredit and bring down the only man he had loved unconditionally. He knew, even as he ridiculed them, that the legends of Ignatius's magical powers were true. Devils had been cast out in Norwich. When the abbot told him the earth was flat, he accepted it. He scrambled through the woods to the mountain path; he climbed to the summit, waited for the mist to lift. Seeing the circumference of the earth, range after range of hills leapfrogging into the west, he denied his own vision. He willed blindness on himself. And he *was* blind. He stumbled about the lower meadow, spilling earth from his wheelbarrow. Ignatius could move stones. He could draw the stone from your heart and make it translucent, alabaster.

Put them in auction. Run them to Hay. I couldn't take any more of Brother Jonah. His papers were a come-on for a hungrier hack, a blocked novelist ready to work the old Catholic scam. Advertise in *The Tablet*. Give Piers Paul Read a bell.

Then Wellclose Square caught my eye. Ignatius in east London? Ignatius cruising the purlieus of Wapping? I had, for old times' sake, to read a couple of pages before I black-bagged Jonah's manuscript.

Word was brought to the Mission at Wellclose Square that the Father's presence was requested by the family of a young woman, Lizzie Meake, who was not expected to live through the night. What business had mere females disturbing Ignatius's meditations? These Cockney grubs had no understanding of the rigours of spiritual life. The Father, whose vanity would answer to the slightest tickle, was called upon to attend to the whim of every low person, harlot or villain from the Ratcliffe Highway. Every Lascar or Jew who presented themselves at his door with a hopeless cause, some opportunity for the Man of God to stroke their sores with scrupulously gloved hands, and perform a miracle.

Ignatius had recently acquired, from auction rooms in Islington, a frag-
ment of what purported to be the True Cross, and he let it be known that
he sought an opportunity to test the efficacy of his not inexpensive purchase.

The night was wild. The Father swept through those mean streets in a
rough serge cassock, with the hood drawn close; his eyes upon the ground,
so the credulous reported, to prevent him catching sight of a female person –
but, in truth, this show of modesty grew from Ignatius's horror of setting his
foot in the excrements of horses, dogs or the barely human denizens of the
lower depths. I accompanied the Father, under instruction to keep a full and
proper record of all that would be spoken and enacted during that long night.

The child Meake was despaired of; weakened by fever, she was rapidly
approaching the climacteric that is the lot of all creatures upon this earth. In
sin she had come into the world and incontinent she would quit it. Her brow
was clammy, her hair like strands of salt-caked rope, but she seemed to rally
when her mother, taking her hand, informed her that the Father was pres-
ent in the room. For an instant, there seemed to be a feeble brightness in her
eye, then it was gone. The child was saved from the inevitable shame and
licentiousness, the certain damnation, of an existence as a woman in this
hideous quarter of the city.

Ignatius put his knuckle to the deathly pallor of her lips. He drew down
her eyelids with an affecting sigh. He ordered the wretched mother, the sis-
ters, and the chorus of attendant harridans, from the garret. He would pray,
so he said, over the corse. I alone remained. I alone witnessed the Father's
most notorious miracle; the blasphemy of reversing the will of Our Lord and
raising a sinner from the Dead.

Much has been made of the fire that Ignatius ordered me to set in the
blackened grate, and how he caused it to ignite without the aid of a spark
or a lucifer, and those legends are beyond dispute. Ignatius, by what means
I cannot surmise, commanded the spirits of Fire and Water. It was within
his compass to cause bushes to blaze. He might, at whim, fill the cupped
bowl of his hand with Holy Water. Water streamed from his breast. He
suckled the child, the Infant Samuel, by lifting him to his bosom and part-
ing his robe. I cannot explain such phenomena, but I witnessed them on
occasions too numerous to catalogue.

It has been said that Ignatius drew his fragment of the True Cross over
the bosom of the expired female, Meake, and dragged down into her cold
corse the spark of Life by commanding her with these words: 'In the name
of Jesus Christ, I say unto thee, Arise!' And that he called for soup. And

so he did. Though the soup, a humble broth of bones, was for his own lips. He had exhausted himself utterly. He might have fainted away if I had not, at that instant, supported him with my arm.

Much has been made of Meake's virginity, which was itself a miracle in that riverine district, at such an age; she was said to be almost fourteen years old. I have speculated in idle moments on the afterlife of a person returned from the embrace of Death, an afterlife before a second casting off of the envelope of Mortality. Meake was a ghost, a near mute, living out the shame of her rescue from the Eternal Ocean. Ignatius had taken possession of her Immortal Soul, and of such souls must Fire be created.

What has never been revealed, and what I now transcribe, freely admitting my own sin, as a Witness, a gulled disciple of that false Messiah, is the means by which Ignatius worked his terrible conjuring. He whispered incantations into the ear of the dead child, waiting, as he said, until honey spilled down her cheek. Honey which he tasted as a sacrament. He drew the Cross, repeatedly, with signs and strange, outlandish words, over Meake's uncovered breast. He pressed the sweet cedarwood against her mouth, then, before my affrighted gaze, he assaulted her; physically, with his person, forcing apart the stiffening lips, the creaking jaw. I will never, however many years I am fated to live, forget that pathetic sight: the healing ravishment, the heretical and obscene acts Ignatius performed with the splintered wood which had soaked up the bright blood of Our Saviour. He made the corse his bride. And I was damned for witnessing this and keeping the truth hidden away for so many years.

After Jonah's lurid fantasies I couldn't sleep. I paced the room. I washed myself, lathering my hands until they looked like gloves of foam. I returned to my chair. The house was hushed now, a few distant moans; water gurgling in the pipes. I picked up the paperback that Lydd the gardener had forced on me; a couple of pages of *The Great God Pan* by Arthur Machen would be light relief. But I couldn't concentrate, I was as bad as Dr Vaughan; my short-term memory couldn't retain any part of a sentence beyond the first clause.

Machen has 'two men slowly pacing the terrace' in front of a doctor's house – while, outside my window, I tricked myself into hearing their distant Victorian voices. Keeping the open book on my lap, but not attempting to read the words on the page, I caught echoes of fictional dialogue as it floated upwards in the still air. I heard footsteps, I smelt the smoke of the doctor's pipe. Machen offers a moonlit landscape. Such is the power of his intricate rhythms that the covert pulses of language mimicked the irregular beat of my heart. What if, in surrendering ourselves to the magic of a text, we enter the dream at such a level that we are unable to break free? Machen describes *this* house, the experiment the doctor attempts on a young woman given into his care, with more conviction than I could bring to measuring out the dimensions of my room. His story is so driven, I would have to abdicate my version of reality and live through his savage fable.

'By what seemed then and still seems a chance, the suggestion of a moment's idle thought followed up upon familiar lines and paths that I had tracked a hundred times already,' wrote Machen, 'the great truth burst upon me, and I saw, mapped out in lines of light, a whole world, a sphere unknown; continents and islands, and great oceans in which no ship has sailed (to my belief) since Man first lifted up his eyes and beheld the sun, and the stars of heaven, and the quiet earth beneath.'

I had to prevent this brutal operation, rescue the girl. The doctor was going to shave her head and cut away a portion of her brain. She was waiting in a room at the end of the corridor. I had become the narrator of Machen's tale, the witness the doctor invites into his house on the Welsh borders.

'Thoughts,' I wrote, taking over from Machen's mouthpiece, 'began to go astray and to mingle with other recollections; the beech alley was transformed to a path beneath ilex trees.'

Who *was* this willing victim? What was her name? Was it Mary? Or H.V.? Or Helen Vaughan? Was it too late?

Reading the words aloud, carrying the book in my hand, I opened my door. I crept down that creaking corridor towards the locked room. If I entered Machen's grisly tale I would have to play by his rules. Nothing could be changed. The order of words on the page is an absolute. Sanity hangs on a single misplaced comma, a printer's error, the slip of a lazy compositor.

Her face grew white, whiter than her dress; she struggled faintly, and then with the feeling of submission strong within her, crossed her arms upon her breast as a little child about to say her prayers.

From outside the room I could smell the sickly sweetness of the syrup the doctor kept in a green phial. I rapped on the door. Someone dropped cutlery onto a steel tray, tiny saws and bright blades. A ring of hair was being scorched over candleflame. The door wasn't locked. Prudence was waiting for me with out-stretched arms. In the moonlight her thin white nightdress was transparent. Her head was shaved, but there was dark hair beneath her arms and between her legs. Her legs felt rough as I drew her to me.

Not Machen's chloroform, but the stub of a joint smouldering in a dish. Thick grassy air. Not moonlight, a beam on the creepered wall; a silver searchlight playing on the tower. Prudence, backlit, her nightdress damp, pulled me towards the bed.

Another superimposition, another layer to the dream: Mastroianni in *La Notte*, in the hospital, being dragged, with a pout of reluctance, a mime of exhausted charm, into the room of a nymphomaniac. Another vampiric cameo: the pleading voice of this prisoner woman whose sexuality is defined and discussed by a panel of excited doctors.

Fantasies of rescue, gratitude, the sobbing victim throwing her-self into the arms of her protector, burn the already overexposed film. Sleep-language disintegrates into its constituent elements: growls, obscenities, yelps, chokes of swift, strangled breath. I tasted the dope, the spearmint, and, behind both of these, something copper. As if, with her mouth open, Prudence kept a wet penny on her tongue.

She hugged me, wrapped her legs around mine until I was sup-porting her weight. Beneath the nightdress, which was plain, institutional, I felt the passage of her blood. Instinctively, I smoothed the thin material, where it was riding up her thigh. I drew a stubbly chin across the soft pad of her shoulder; a thing which previously she had liked. I held her away from me, to post-pone and sharpen the pleasure of having her again.

This was very different from our earlier tryst at Three Cocks. Then we had made love, now love made us. Unexpected as my sudden appearance must have been, if she remembered who I was, she seemed to be waiting for me. She had the window open and you could hear the river. 'You *are* the river,' she said.

Being a stranger, a figment of Machen's imagination, I had learnt how to wait; to let Prudence set the dictation, come in her own time to what she wanted. 'Take your clothes off, all your clothes,' she said. 'I want to see you standing there, by the window. No, don't come towards the bed. Not yet.'

I waited. I watched her, what she did. The bed, when I came to it, was made up from two single beds pushed together. Sometime in the night, they divided, leaving us wrapped together; thinking of new ways to please ourselves and to delay conversation. Explanations of her disappearance and my arrest.

It was already light when Prudence listened to the tale I invented in compensation for the loss of her company; my ridiculous story of suicide, murder and conspiracy. Then she made herself into the character I sketched, a thing of impulse and mystery. She was my woman in white. Willingly, she pleasured herself that I might feel pleasure, pleasured me with the idea of how I would want her to seem and be.

There was nothing to say. The bars of the window projected onto the high ceiling. Lying close, the sheet pulled back onto the bed, we did not dare to break away; lose heat. We feared the loss of each other, the risk of sleep. Alarmed by this novel tenderness, we watched. Waited for some insignificant shift in the light. A sound from the corridor.

4

I'm back. In Bristol. Staying for a few nights with a poet I met on the Downs. What's rather disturbing is that his room is entirely papered – even the light bulb – with newsprint. Yesterday's headlines, when you wake in a sleeping bag on the floor, are horribly prophetic. All Archer. From back then and now come around a second time. Money scandals, tarts, rent boys, three-in-a-bed footballers. A fall guy like Aitken gets sent down for a few months and the real players tut-tut in feigned shock, ringing their hands in dismay. They rap the knuckles of one self-made miscreant – before advertising for the next.

I had a bad turn, on Exmoor, trying to find the lab rat who knew about Thorpe and the talking dog. I thought I was getting on quite well with the yokels in the pub. You have to talk dog to crack it. Know the jokes. Down here they do Jill Dando, not Diana. I let them buy me a few drinks. Ex-army, most of them. Belfast they'd like to have you believe. Fetch out the red berets if they think you can introduce them to a literary agent. When they've had a skinful they go looking for stags: pickup trucks, bull-bar jeeps; searchlights.

So one night, I know this sounds like something out of Peckinpah, they decide to visit 'Jeremy's bum boy', as they call him, for a bit of fun. They've got the rope, the cattle prod and a gallon of castor oil. I can't get out of it, without risking a dose myself.

Light's on, door's open. No barking. That freaks them out. This dog can chat. He's probably on the blower to the old bill. They're half expecting the Great Dane to jump from behind a bush and tell them to piss off. 'Think it'll bellow like Peter Schmeichel?' one guy asks. 'And call you, with your muddy face, a black bastard?'

They're for packing it in before the Beast of Bodmin picks up the scent. Then one of them steps inside and, shamed, most of the others follow. TV's on, Paxman grilling a professional liar. Hair that doesn't move, spray-on dandruff.

Cup of herb tea steaming on the kitchen table. Bowl of dog food the size of a baptismal font.

Where's the dog?

Have you noticed how upwardly mobile rough trade has a weakness for how they think the horse and hound mob live? Baggy armchair with chintz covers and dog scurf, cushions in burnt orange velveteen. Late Victorian chest of drawers with Georgian ambitions. One shelf of leather bindings, one with bottles – whisky, gin. Famed photos of nags and royals. A family portrait of someone else's family. Threadbare carpet. Damp stains coming through the distemper. Snuff boxes. And no snuff.

He was hanging from the shower bracket and he'd brought it right out of the wall. Water dripping on his rubber corset. Ladders in his fishnets. Tangerine in mouth. Auto-erotic asphyxiation. Standard spook job. They don't have much imagination.

I walked back to the pub, picked up the car and drove straight to Bristol. I'm sending you the only tape. I don't want to keep a copy. I'll stick around here for a few days, then come over the bridge. I'm about ready for Wales.

Kaporal's voice, the hesitancy, the drawling inflections that hinted at irony or imminent collapse, suited the asylum. I sat in the conservatory with a bunch of other overfed manic-depressives and watched the weather. With my headphones on. My wife always hated them. She said they made me look like a Nazi war criminal sitting in the dock at Nuremberg. But it was one way to disguise the subversive material that bombarded me from across the Bristol Channel. Every few days another padded bag would arrive with Kaporal's latest monologue from his voyage through the west. My instinct, evaluating the unimaginative nature of his paranoia, was that he'd lost the plot. He was doing a Donald Crowhurst. Remember him? The round-the-world yachtsman who, very reasonably, settled for fiction. Making up dispatches while sailing the Atlantic in ever-decreasing circles – until the moment came to go over the side. That's what happens when you can't contrive an acceptable climax.

Jos Kaporal, to keep my cheques coming, was beavering through book pits and rural libraries in search of discounted Thorpe biographies: Auberon Waugh, the *Insight* hacks, and Dan Farson's frolicsome conceit, a pseudonymous chapbook (as told by the dog). Kaporal insisted: Farson, the least reliable of the journalists, a florid drunk, had been the only one to approach the true story. His canine satire wasn't funny but it guided the discerning reader to the crucial fact all the serious investigators, with their files and tape recordings and signed witness statements, had missed: Thorpe's pal, Norman Scott (a.k.a. the Honourable Norman Lianche-Josiffe), was *never* the target. They were out to get the pooch.

Quotes from revenants. Cut-ups from conspiracy mags (funded by the Secret State). Extracts recorded while channel-hopping (stoned out of your skull). Cobble those together and you get the flavour of a Kaporal report. The guy was drifting at random between Bristol and Barnstaple – as if he were lost at sea.

He slept in the car, or found flophouses where the film crew had suffered an overnight when Jamie Lalage was on the road. At the worst moments, soaked in cold sweat, hands shaking too much to unscrew the cap on the whisky bottle, he watched *Amber Lights* – all the way through.

The Mondeo was still in colour, still dark blue, but the landscape was monochrome. He cruised the Weston esplanade and saw it as a reservation of the dead. He tried to check in to the room that overlooked the flyover in Bristol and found the flyover was gone.

The only solution was to restage Lalage's anticlimax, the scene at the quarry, when the guy in the car drives to the edge, reverses, thinks again; wheels spinning and a song he doesn't recognise on the soundtrack. Kaporal had the right tape but they wouldn't let him through the quarry gates. Cash upfront or fuck off.

In a lay-by near Brent Knoll, trucks and caravans, holiday traffic covering him in spray, he whispered to the mike. 'I'm back. In Bristol.' And he was. I bought the story, withdrawing the rain that was bouncing from the tiles of the terrace, cattle huddled together, steaming under the trees, the tannin Usk, and settled instead for Clifton Downs. Kaporal, his car parked by the water tower, striding over the grass to the circle of trees where the defence worker killed himself.

Misremembered pleasures return as present pain: such is the curse of indolence, quacks ordering us to indulge ourselves by keeping dream journals, dredging all sorts of properly suppressed bilge from the primal swamp. Clifton, before Kaporal inflicted his tape on me, was totally erased. Who wants to return to short pants (down to the knee but tight in the crotch), grey corduroy? Or sandals that never had the right spacing for the holes on the strap? They were either too tight, bringing up small bruises, or so loose they slipped from your feet at every second step. Did they really have white corrugated soles – like folded lard?

My father enjoyed zoos. We came out of Wales the long way around, crawling through Chepstow and Gloucester, no bridge then; Bristol was as remote as London. I took the Downs for a reservation, wild animals restlessly pacing their pits and cages. Burrowed into the cliffs above the Severn Gorge, they protected this boundless prairie.

Later it would be a Black & White charabanc to the school, Clifton College, for rugby matches. The noise of the crowd packing the touchline enhanced by auxiliary effects from the imprisoned beasts on the other side of the wall.

The snapshots of the progress of a life become a frieze of failures, refusals, skulks: my insistence at being, mentally and morally, elsewhere. Brought back to Bristol to promote a book, I spent the time between performances revisiting the Downs. Strolling up Park Row, past the University, I remembered a futile interview with the poet Charles Tomlinson – who asked, quite reasonably, what I was reading just then. And how I took this for an unwarrantable intrusion. I was a strange youth in a bad suit, tweedy but of Teddy Boy cut with a neon-green lining: a metaphor for the awkward mix between imposed respectability and elective subversion. Always overdressed and underprepared; arriving early, after a fierce walk. Eager to be on the move.

Grilled about Dylan Thomas, the subject of a juvenile dissertation, I sat before a committee in one of those university rooms and blurted out the story of the coffin. They were bringing the bloated poet's insulted meat back from New York in a fancy box and hired a Welsh mortician to fetch the corpse from Southampton; to ferry it to Laugharne for burial, brawls and riots at the graveside. The driver, well-bevvied in the fashion of the times, auditioning for future literary anecdotes, or simply confused, arrived at Bristol, that pivotal point in the culture, and took the wrong turn. He headed into Somerset, Devon, the deep southwest. When the police red-lighted the hearse in Cornwall, the driver came up with an immortal line: 'Nobody said to me this bloody country was forked.'

He should have used the spare petrol can to torch the coffin in one of the stone circles above Land's End, calling on the spirits of D.H. Lawrence, W.S. Graham, and Mary Butts; or launched it, as a fire ship, from a spray-soaked rock. Let the dead make their own choice of landfall. The suit they buried Dylan in, loud as Handel, carnation in buttonhole: my interview outfit. The waxed complexion and painted lips: my mask.

On impulse I bought a ticket for the zoo. It was summer. Boys were playing cricket on the college fields. Buses decanted damaged folk. Hothouse geriatrics who could out-lizard the lizards. Gecko heads with gaping, toothless mouths, scaly skin, hands like claws. The keepers must have been working from a manual of sympathetic magic, treating like with like. They'd wheel some codger to the tiled pit in which a giant turtle lay unmoving in its own shit. The whorled shell with its separate panels was a bony shield under which the creature had withdrawn. Its useless legs were tubes of primeval mud. The small head, when it emerged, parodied the old man – but was more oracle-like and hurt. Dragged from the ocean, kept alive too long, the turtle had seen everything. Ronnie Reagan had the same look: an idiot savant pickled in brine, blackened by corruption, sanctioned crimes. Not many of us achieve this state, nodding in a Shaker rocking chair while victims of our benign indifference fry in their own fat.

The zoo was a nightmare. Many of the animals of my childhood had died and never been replaced. The survivors were often mongrels stitched together in hideous combinations imported from *The Island of Dr Moreau*: birds with monkey's tails, fish with hands instead of fins. Huge Asiatic lions dozed in the sawdust as if they'd been tranquillised or fed on foetuses.

Middle-aged innocents with smooth, careless faces gawped open-mouthed at the antics of spider monkeys who played out the masturbating, shit-throwing, swinging-through-trees adolescence they had been denied. There was often a marriage between child and parent, the mother seeming younger, more tired than the son. Autistic and Down's syndrome teenagers, once exoticised as 'mongols', were dressed like the Famous Five – in very clean Aertex shirts and baggy khaki shorts. This area had an intimate connection with the crocodiles of special needs excursionists brought here by their watchful minders. The word 'Downs' took on a double meaning as the procession faltered among empty glass units and deserted lagoons. You no longer saw gorillas on the Gorilla Island, you listened to megaphone lectures about them. You left money in a box to keep the tiger in his own land.

My father would have to make do with the reptile house and its peculiar blood-temperature warmth. The Amethystine Python, with diamond-tread skin, was the symbol of the city; an aerial photograph of the lazy, dangerous Avon wriggling through the gorge. My mother would demand her cup of tea in the Pelican House, having endured the tanks of silent, creeping, sticklike things, pests and predators who bide their time, waiting for aeons to take their revenge. As she would have endured my father's traditional joke: 'Pelican Restaurant? Who wants to eat pelican?'

Even the entrance gates to the zoo had been painted with silhouette animals from Noah's Ark, so that it felt like visiting day in a children's ward.

The tall trees of Clifton brought me back to the park around the Usk asylum: cedar and beech, ash and elm. I reprogrammed myself with these green wands, switched to Kaporal. Now – thanks to his white noise – I could track him, watch him carrying a cup of coffee back to his car. He had the map of Bristol spread across the passenger seat. He took his time finishing the hot drink, then he locked the driver's door and set off across the Downs, video camera in hand.

The thing Kaporal wanted to check was the camera obscura tower, which overlooked Clifton Suspension Bridge and the wooded gorge. It didn't open early, so he mooched about. He read notices the Samaritans left at the entrance to the bridge and thought immediately about going over the side. He tried to calculate why the first

Sikh, the Marconi jumper, had missed the water. And what was wrong with Archway, or Tower Bridge, or bombing out along the M25 to Staines? There was a peppery local pride in this; Kaporal refused to acknowledge that anyone would be crazy enough to think there was a better place to top yourself than London. It made him want to kill the man.

The edge of the Downs, he had to admit, sent ripples through the belly, waves of vertigo; sonar effects fled like recalled echoes from the Romantic chasm. If he'd been Wordsworth, he'd have paced the paths, chanting transcendent rhymes, awed by the immensity, the pathos of lives tossed away like rusty pennies into a measureless well. In hock to a lesser god, he switched on his Hi-8 and played with the touch screen, fuzzing the focus, squeezing colour into discrete bands. Brunel's turrets were command posts on the Great Wall of China. Dense woods on the far shore became ridges of broccoli spears. Kaporal panned listlessly, not bothering to watch what he shot. These days he preferred to let the camera do the work. He might stab a finger at the greasy screen, deepen the contrast, initiate a strobe effect, play with his paintbox like a depressive in therapy.

The tower opened and a witch at the window took his money. He opted for the ascent, rather than the cave with its view of the gorge. The stubby sixty-foot folly with its crinkled crown had been built in the 1760s by James Waters – as a mill for grinding snuff. Now it was used by solitaries who stuffed their nasal cavities with fiercer powder.

William West rented the tower in 1837, completed the conversion, and took up residence. This was the year when Daguerre fixed light impressions in a form in which they could be exhibited. Kaporal thought the fact, picked up in a brochure, was significant. He had some vague notion of using the camera obscura dish as a scrying bowl; a device in which he could trace events, life lines, out of the past.

Internally, the tower was in a distressed state, paint peeling from the walls, graffiti carved into the window frames; Kaporal followed the arrows, scampered up wooden stairs. He dripped, soaked his shirt and undervest; he considered, for one wild moment, dispensing with the military greatcoat. He came close to fainting, out of excitement, fear or dehydration, before he reached the secret chamber.

'Small Room. Close door. Rotate handle anti-clockwise.' Said the handwritten notice.

Door duly shut, the solitude was overwhelming. Kaporal was imprisoned in a sweat box. Glistening beads slid from his forehead to ping into the upturned dish. The Downs floated like a wash of infinitely thin light. Kaporal staggered: there was a jolt, a white flash that kicked in like the automatic exposure on his camera – struggling to come to terms with the way he zapped from skulking shadow to sunburst. The agoraphobic, widescreen expanse of the Downs, gorge to water tower, was tattooed on his eyelids. On the curved lens of his eye.

The world had been stood on its head: landscape was a scum of dancing particles, rocked in a soup bowl. Kaporal cranked the handle and the Downs *moved*. Half the sturdy beggars in the town were taking their ease on the grass, indulging in improvised meals, swilling from giant, party-pack cans.

This wasn't *now*, it couldn't be. The camera obscura was a trick, a precursor of the video camera, offering – at a turn of the wheel – instant playback. Clouds raced. Kaporal believed they came from the nineteenth century, made from olive oil and egg white suspended in alcohol. He whipped out his Polaroid camera, flashed the dish. He wanted hard evidence. The pop of light proved nothing. The print that curled in his hand showed the pitted white surface of the drum: naked as the moon. You had to take the vision of the Downs as an article of faith.

The little world within this concave five-foot table was intolerably sensual. The groaning of the wood became a sequence of autoerotic sighs. Kaporal gripped the hot handle like a male member carved from ebony; he lost himself in the waving and weaving of the trees. He was seeing the past. He was outside time. The lens, within its revolving cowl at the pinnacle of a conical roof, provided Kaporal with an extensive view of the Downs, from the base of the tower to the horizon. The cowl was linked by rods to the handle Kaporal cranked greedily. He gasped out the various names by which this device had once been known: 'conclave obscurum', 'cubiculum tenebricosum', 'camera clausa'. Everything was arranged for the 'gratification' of the observer; the paying customer in the panelled sweat box. A geological peepshow. Kaporal wondered if his actions cast a giant shadow over the grass.

The heat was unbearable. He stripped to his boots, never taking his eyes off the copper dish of the viewing table; allowing an uncensored gaze free play over puffy clouds, paprika-trail paths. Each bush a site of potential transgression. If he worked the handle in a counterclockwise direction would he rewind time? Access visions of an earlier landscape?

The close chamber encouraged such notions. Naked Kaporal ground this reverse projector, running film backwards, seeing *what actually happened on the night when the Sikh threw himself from the bridge*.

He tracked the path that led towards the lip of the gorge. He saw the low river and the muddy pink banks, cut with sharp lines. He saw the hard, serpentine road; woodland shadows snaking through shallows. He saw – and the shock stopped his heart – a man and a woman, in the shelter of the bushes, in a hidden glade, a dip of the field. He was astonished to discover human presences invading his movie. If *that* could occur, then he was no longer the director of his own fantasies.

He let go of the handle and was pumping his cock. What a strange threesome: the unseen Kaporal in the tower and this couple sitting on the ground, playfully intimate, but not, as Kaporal willed, getting down to it. They were very young, Indian, Bangladeshi. That was the thing, the fear: the man was certainly not a Sikh. This was now: Bollywood, a song under a sacred tree. 'Go on,' Kaporal screamed. 'Give her one, you bastard.'

And he did. Spattering the bowl. Raining hot gunge on the blameless meadow. Kaporal's come hung from the branches, above the heads of the couple, like a treacly web.

Smoke drifted from a burning bush. A motor mower was parked alongside. Kaporal, hooked, gasping over the viewing table, could smell the smoke: grassy, nostalgic – medicinal. His arthritic shoulder ached at the memory, the desire for one good, deep, lungful of that herbal remedy. He saw a van, farting black gouts of pollution, twist its way down Bridge Valley Road towards the A4.

The camera obscura didn't offer vulgar close-ups: this was pure cinema, detached and impersonal. Kaporal, with one last, monumental, spine-arching shudder, shot his load; and, in the melancholy of that little death, he captured every detail of the hard-travelled white van – red mud-crusted, threadbare tyres, rear doors roped to prevent tube-like objects falling out, lettering on the side: DIKKON'S DISCOUNT CARPETS PYLE.

Listen, Norton, we were in danger of losing it back there. Thorpe, Farson, the dog. We weren't reading the larger picture. It suddenly struck me – I was retracing the movements of the Sikh across the Downs – that I was blundering, as all the Marconi suicides had blundered, into a landscape whose salient features had been laid out thousands of years ago. I was tiptoeing down a causeway of buried skulls. How could I begin to understand this pattern of sacrifice – voluntary or state-assisted – until I visited, surveyed, meditated upon the sacred sites, the Celtic Fields and the Stokeleigh Camp? How could I send you another word until I understood the geology of the Avon Wetlands, the Triassic rocks of Aust, the interbedded sandstones and silty marls? What right did I have to compose a single sentence until I'd spent months annotating the advancing weather fronts, the cloud streets six miles up above the Avon Gorge? Then there were the holy wells, the springs, the healing waters. I'd have to plot them all.

And trade. Cabot's Bristol. Mercantile records. The growth of a city. Industrial archaeology: railways, bridges, canals, water mills, pumping stations, docks, ferries. Port industries: Bush's Warehouse, Harvey's Wine Museum, W.D. & H.O. Wills's Office and Factory. Cigarettes, sugar. The City as myth. Bladud.

Jesus, man! Chatterton! The muniment room at St Mary Redcliffe. The epitaphs in the graveyard.

And Southey, Coleridge. Pantisocracy. Republicanism. Unitarianism. Cottle the Bristol bookseller.

Douglas Cleverdon, Eric Gill's patron, had a bookshop in a turning off Park Street, on the road to Clifton. Easy to miss it, as I did, the vital link that's been lost between those intimately related functions – bookselling and printing, publishing. These guys did it all. Their shops were centres, meeting places. Cleverdon offered a refuge to Gill, an excuse for getting away from the Welsh mountains. He published handsome books by David Jones. He finished up with the typescript of Under Milk Wood.

Then there's Landor. In retreat from Llanthony, taking the waters, enjoying such society as Clifton offered. This was where he met his beloved Ianthe. He kept an engraving of the view from Clifton Church, after a sketch by S. Jackson, fastened inside the lid of his desk. 'Clifton in vain thy varied scenes invite, / The mossy bank, dim glade, and dizzy height.'

You're going to have to send more money, man. We haven't scratched the surface. I got most of this stuff from a gardener I met; he's a poet really, lives above what used to be Cleverdon's shop. He's going to incorporate this amazing material into an epic which is the story of a city as told through letters and postcards and cuttings and quotes and statistics and observations and 'effusions' as he calls them, immediate perceptions scribbled without mediation or censorship into his notebooks, free jazz – and scholarship and practical information, facts, *gathered as an ordinary working man; how to mow in straight lines, how to peel an apple, roll a joint, mend a puncture. Everything, all of it.*

Name's Tunstall. Gwain Tunstall. Says I can stay with him, a communal house. Mean draw. Scores from some Welsh character who delivers, door to door, in a carpet van.

Oh no. Tunstall and Kaporal. Together. My narrative was folding in on itself. I'd heard about Tunstall's flight from London, his elopement and subsequent adventures in the Channel Islands. Tunstall wrote great letters, in purple ink (with scarlet corrections and additions); but, always, the rapture took off from a bedrock of plain statement. The guy had spent so much time working alone, trimming verges, laying out municipal flower beds, mowing the Downs and going deaf from the noise of it, that he spoke, when the opportunity arose, with great precision: footnoting each statement with the relevant authority. Solitude made him a pedant. Dope loosened the flow.

Tunstall and his girlfriend crossed the sea in a state of visionary excitement. They hitched down to Weymouth. She was reading John Cowper Powys and he was *living* Jack Kerouac, with sidebars of Gary Snyder. England was too small – but, as they filed up the gangplank, the lights of the ship dancing on the oily dock, they understood that this was one of those rare, snatched, must-be-appreciated moments, when you break through the membrane of the dream and *experience* your own story. A long-rehearsed event

was being enacted *as Tunstall knew it would be enacted*; he was scripting fate. He reached out for Jean's hand. And, probably, she felt it
too. This hair-prickling sense of decision, rightness, inevitability;
his hand closing on her hand closing on the smooth wood of the
rail. The warm smell from the kitchens of the boat. Their bodies in
heavy sweaters and duffle coats. Voices of other passengers, ahead of
them. The night, salty and wet, on their faces.

Then, walking to the stern, as they left the harbour, looking
back, Jean setting down her guitar and Tunstall taking from his
pocket the papers he'd liberated from the office – as a safeguard
against retaliatory action; slipping the rubber band, letting the
sheets blow away, a wheeling gull race, into the broad wake that
stretched to the last of England. Goodbye to all that.

A jaundiced moon floated above a quiet sea. They didn't want to
go, immediately, below decks. They didn't want to lose anything of
this voyage out. Their future plans were vague. Tunstall had a job,
arranged by advance correspondence, at Gerald Durrell's wildlife
park. Jean would take whatever seasonal work she could find: hotels
or bars.

It was getting chilly, so they took a turn around the boat. And
almost walked, on the cabin deck, straight into a man with orange
skin; a man who was hammering at a door, begging for forgiveness,
asking to be let in. Lucky to find him preoccupied: this shifty individual had seen Tunstall in the dining room above a Fleet Street
pub, when the timorous clerk had delivered documents, witness
statements in the Thorpe case. What was Thorpe's bagman doing
on the Jersey packet? Had Tunstall been tracked from London?
Surely not. Who would be mad enough to pick a freak in a cream
turtleneck sweater, Roger Moore blazer, bootpolish hair, skin like
a nuclear accident, to shadow a premature hippie? The bagman was
the kind to give cancer a good name.

Tunstall convinced himself, retelling these events, years later,
over a glass or two of home-brewed beer, in his cottage in the
Neath Valley, that Thorpe's goffer brought about his downfall; the
reception that awaited him when he walked with Jean down the
long pier in Jersey. The strip search, the grilling about dope habits
and sexual preferences, the Prevention of Terrorism forms. All he
wanted was a job. The letters from Durrell were produced. They

had to let him go. If old Jaffa-skin hadn't telegraphed ahead, tipped off the port filth, then he was bad luck incarnate, an agent of Mephistopheles. Goethe reckoned the devil took the form of a dog. Tunstall swears that when the cabin door stayed shut, Thorpe's spook began to bark. His eyes green as a guttering candle.

Dressed in a safari suit, hair in a ponytail, Tunstall mucked out the cages in Durrell's zoo. Looking for action, his first weekend on the island, he was offered a spliff by one of the local freaks. Pub life hadn't been all he'd expected: trippers, drunks, head-banging sounds. He accepted, lit up, and was braced in an armlock, arrested, informed as to his absence of rights, chucked in a cell. They told him he was looking at five to seven years. Jersey was like Texas without the enchiladas and refried beans. They didn't relish outsiders unless they were prepared to graft at dirty jobs the islanders didn't want. They didn't bury wetbacks and drug mules in desert graves some-where outside El Paso, they shipped them straight out. Drug cash was fine. Sacks of it came in on every flight. Their serial killers were homebred Satanists, fond of rubber hoods; mustard-keen Freemason types. They didn't drag black men behind pickup trucks. The roads were too narrow and crowded, most of the citizens ran two cars.

Three days after stepping ashore at the beginning of their new life, Tunstall and Jean were heading back to Weymouth. Thorpe's man was collecting campaign funds from an Indian philanthropist. And making phone calls – collect – to the Bahamas.

Landor's honeymoon in Jersey wasn't much of a success. Mrs Landor called him an old man. She hadn't learnt to read the danger signs; the trick Dickens noticed, Landor's 'noticeable tendency to relaxation on the part of his thumbs'.

The thumbs curved back, flaccid and boneless, limp wicks. The new bride, testing the limits of her influence, had dressed with care for a promenade, and was confronted with the reality of this large, shambling, snuff-stained man. Greasy waistcoat, scuffed shoes. Landor stormed from the room, shipped out for France on an oyster boat.

Bristol, Tunstall told Kaporal, was the next move. Obviously. Kaporal as a video poet – with wheels – could join them. The plan was, when they'd chilled out for a couple of months, to make excursions to Glastonbury, the Quantocks, Nether Stowey, Alfoxden; to revive the suspended dream of the Pantisocracy. Move on to deepest Cornwall with John Michell's *The Old Stones of Land's End* as their guide. Also: *Long Shout to Kernewek* by Allen Fisher. 'The Avalon causeway reaching out for old unions.' Right!

Meanwhile, Tunstall cut the grass on the Downs. Saw the carpet man from time to time and let the dirt of London drain from his pores. In the high, fast light, the gentle curvature of this exposed (but domesticated) heath, there was a sense of ecstatic release: diurnal impressionism building, through swiftly transcribed journal extracts, into a torrential overview. Coleridge in his letters, or the *Biographia Literaria*, paddled the same pool; the poet climbs through the poem, exposing himself to sympathetic metaphors: 'All Truth is a species of Revelation.' Plus: nitrous oxide, cannabis resin, cheap red wine, cider and a weekend tab.

Language worried him, arriving at the most inconvenient times; while, say, he was scouring filth from the windows of the toilets by the water tower. Or when furious rotor blades spun a shower of fresh dog shit into his eyes. 'I am spying,' he would write, seeing himself keeping watch on a passing world, schoolgirls and biddies, lovers, workmen on bikes. 'The isobars are tightening.'

Things were cool, in a diary sense; scarlet geraniums in a pot on the window ledge, Jean in a rocking chair; music, letters to friends. A network developing, books exchanged, readings given. Bristol corresponding with Cambridge, gigs at Mordern Tower in Newcastle; Keele, Durham, Colchester, Brighton. Despite all that, it might be time to move on. Into Wales. Follow Wordsworth up the Wye. Track Coleridge and Tom Wedgwood down the Usk. Establish a community of equals, away from the hassle of the city, the drag of clocking on.

One other factor concerned Tunstall: the request, made by Howard the Carpets, that one of the municipal glasshouses be given over to cultivating dope. Howard was laughing, it's true. He'd been good as gold, up to now, nothing heavy. But, after Jersey, Tunstall was in the files; they had his mugshot and his dabs.

The whole gang, in the light, airy room, with its crumbling balcony and view over the wild garden and the Somerset hills, watched Kaporal's road footage, and smoked. Like Norton, Tunstall was a Beefheart fan; 'Moonlight in Vermont', 'Frownland', 'The Dust Blows Forward 'n' the Dust Blows Back' – laced with the String Band, Dr Strangely Strange and other of Jean's folky-trippy friends.

Kaporal looped time. Who knows if they spent an entire afternoon watching an hypnotic procession of lighting poles on a section of the M5? Then there were stuttering pans across midnight reservoirs with planes taking off on the far shore. *Right!* Roads and hills and water and clouds: the sprawled observers, from that state of boredom called enlightenment, forged their separate narratives.

If Norton had been able to tap these contradictory versions, edit them into a coherent strand, his book would have written itself. Unfortunately, just as the boys were on the point of achieving total paralysis, the person with the van, who'd been roadying for Nicky Lane and his mob, Minehead to Porlock, broke in with the news that he had to collect a cowboy poet from Temple Meads, and did anyone want a ride?

They were, the ones who could get to their feet, up for it. Of course. Skip had the poet's name written on a piece of cardboard: Ed Dorn. The wheelman, when Kaporal, still the investigative reporter (get names and ages), asked, was revealed as: Skip Tracer, 33. The age of the dead Jesus, with hair to match.

Tunstall was excited about this event, down on the docks, a new gallery/bookshop/coffee bar with a flash moniker, the Arnolfini. Dorn was one of his gods: *Hands Up!*, *Geography*, *Idaho Out*, *The North Atlantic Turbine*. The dude knew Olson! And was reputed to be the epitome of cool, literary gunslinger in ice shades: words as weapons, facts punched into the ground like fence posts. Delivery. He understood when to let a line walk and when to break into anecdotal mode. Dorn was a frontier moralist living by the Apache code: abstinence and endurance. And he looked like Clint Eastwood with a torch inside.

There was more. Skip announced, as they tumbled around the back of the van – Kaporal cradling his camera – a guest star was promised. 'One well-known yet unknown' the flyers puffed. An

English support act – equal billing – some character who refused, on grounds too complex to explain, to give public readings. Wild! This gig, on a sweltering dockside night, would change Bristol forever. Diminish the pull of the gravity of ignorance that warped the city. Hit the burghers (living on the fat of slave-trading ancestors) with bottled lightning. West and East on a collision course. Good cop, bad cop. Punches coming from every direction at once. After this, Tunstall reckoned, they'd *have* to move out. His old consciousness, like a tramp's overcoat, could stroll off on its own. Dorn was the messenger of outward, bringing hard wisdom from the desert.

Faces. That's what Kaporal shot. The febrile excitement and the barely disguised apathy of the gang gathered on the dock, waiting to be let in. Yawns. Strategic cigarettes. Chancers sucking at discarded plastic cups. Through a plateglass window you could see poets checking the shelves of the bookshop for their own work; and, if they found it, rearranging the display to achieve a cover-to-the-front vantage point. It was important to be here, naturally, in terms of boasting about it later; but embarrassing also. There was so much hanging about, paying cashmoney to listen to a poet who couldn't – could he? – be better than yourself. What if, on the night, he *was* – visibly, audibly, triumphantly – good enough to blow the socks off a corpse? The rest of them would have to skulk home like rats with tails up their assets.

The flutter and fury, the amnesty of this special evening, Kaporal understood, showed in his freeze-frame close-ups. Rivals rushed to the Gents and couldn't pee. There was no point in shooting the reading, robbing it of spontaneity – which, as a selling point, was all it had. Instead, Kaporal reckoned he'd pick one dockside lounger, and shove the camera up his nostrils; provoke an angry monologue. Bad will to underwrite the reckless self-congratulation of the lecture hall.

Elbowing a path through the stragglers – he could see Skip's van jolting over the cobbles, ferrying Dorn to his fate – Kaporal located the face he needed: a silver-haired presence who burnt a hole in the frame. He was about to switch the camera on when somebody nudged his arm. 'Wouldn't do that, mate. Mr Undark, he don't like to be filmed. He clocks you, you'll finish in the dock.'

The thing was, Kaporal knew that this buff-coloured Brummie lung fluke was right. Undark didn't register. Shoot the guy and his aura would act like a black hole and swallow the rest of the data. Melted tape would run like treacle from the Hi-8. Undark, the guest star, had manifested in Bristol; nobody could recall seeing him, on any previous occasion, west of Milton Keynes. Even now, most punters, recognising the legend, nodding acquaintances with some of the work, refused to accept that he had any existence outside the printed word. They convinced themselves that the Undark *oeuvre* led a life independent of its author. You could, if you insisted, work back to *assume* an authorial presence – but that conjecture had still to be proved. For one night only, Undark was in two places at the same time. It was beyond belief that he would leave Cambridge, so he must have cloned himself.

He was unnervingly present to Kaporal, bringing back, with that laugh, the firm handshake, grey flannels and goldfish tie, memories of schoolmasters; uncompleted assignments, essays that fell apart when exposed to the air.

Shuddering, he let himself be steered to the bar by the fragrant Brummie (fragrance of charity shop, overnight bus, station waiting room). The Brummie's mate, by using his lack of height to dip under authoritative arms, and spreading a hand of stolen books, had managed to reserve a couple of seats at one of the communal benches. He helped himself to the yellow pack of Petit cigars that stuck from Kaporal's jacket pocket.

The first bum, the one who had taken Norton's latest tenner from the traumatised film-maker on the way in, returned to the table with three pints of the black stuff.

'Your round next. He's Humpp. I'm Bad News. We're mates of Norton. He puts us in all his books.'

They bookended the unfortunate Kaporal, blowing his own smoke back in his face, while he scanned the room for some means of escape.

'I caught that film you showed at the ICA on the *Crash* weekend. Very dull, actually. Imitation Peter Whitehead. Which, let's face it, doesn't give you anywhere to go. Ballard bought us a drink afterwards.

'It's really strange, man, Humpp thinks it's bollocks, but I reckon the bit where you pick up two hitchers in a service station and then come on to Bristol – and one of them explains his theory about Third World debt – has to be based on Humpp and me. Look. I wrote the whole thing out – *before* it happened. Coincidence or what? You mobile? Any chance of a run into Wales?'

5

Standing on the doorstep in Bath, Kaporal was getting flashbacks from the Arnolfini reading. He'd shot Dorn and forgotten he was doing it (where *this* fitted into the story he didn't know or care: 'continuity of emotion' was his new catch phrase). Burnt light danced around a wasted profile. War and chemistry and a life truly lived: Kaporal was sharp enough to read the signs. He had no idea how he could exploit them, use the afterprint of this lustrous man to bargain for his own survival. Was Dorn a *witness*? Kaporal understood, eavesdropping on literary chat around the fringes of the Arnolfini event, that the gaunt Westerner had lived for a time in England, Colchester (if that counted); he'd hung out in London and noticed things. Poets enjoyed the privilege of slack time, notebook mornings, afternoons on the drift, TV at illicit hours; the midnight monologue that doesn't have to be put to bed.

The shift in consciousness was so severe that Kaporal obeyed Undark's killjoy prohibition, he hadn't recorded a word the Cambridge man uttered, nor treated him to a single pulse of the camera. Undark was inviolate, the dark velvet against which Dorn's bright eloquence could be displayed. Undark, Kaporal considered, behaved like black leader at the top of the reel: he edited the necessary darkness into his film, suave nightstuff that would allow Dorn to flash like a diamond.

Tunstall skinned his knuckles on solid English oak; there was no bell and nobody within responded to their shouts. Dorn was staying in a safe house in Bath and had agreed to a short interview. Tunstall, awed by the prospect of meeting one of the legends of his library, assuring himself that such a being moved and talked and held out a hand to grasp his own, accompanied Kaporal on the run from Bristol. He'd already decided that the moment was propitious. After the Undark reading, Bristol had no more to offer; it was time to move across the water, into Wales. Dorn, he hoped, would offer a blessing.

The house spooked them, there were too many steps up from the street. The windows were too wide and the stone too old. Instinctively, they searched for the tradesman's entrance. They expected dogs. The square was too sure of itself and its period – in which they had no place. A gaff like this might be squatted or broken down into units, student pits, disbarred solicitors, dentists dodging sexual harassment indictments, but the idea of one family having the right to all that space was more than they could handle.

'Oh, hi.' The lad who'd set up the meet (he must be pushing forty now, but Kaporal remembered him peddling paperbacks in Spitalfields, getting his kit off for sculptors who predated Gilbert and George) tried to wave, but one hand was caught up with plastic shopping bags and the other with hounds. Undark and Dorn had taken off to sample the waters, kill or cure, but might return for lunch. Kaporal and Tunstall could find their spot in the garden.

The stone-flagged hall, as their bustling genial host shepherded them through, was further evidence of their unsuitability for this task: elephant-foot umbrella stands filled with odd clubs and muddied sporting sticks, maps so faded only the rivers remained, white ferns in bell jars, discarded garments on which dozed animals that doubled as trophies. Cats hissed from the stairs. The smell of burnt breakfast rose above layers of inherited damp, poor drainage, casual personal hygiene and exotic plants dying in black earth.

The lad carried it off in style, he was comfortable in other people's houses; he made a career out of it, issuing invitations, mixing poets with decayed gentry, New Georgians and old slappers; keeping on the move, a couple of hours ahead of the bailiffs. He was the best kind of pest, nagging and wheedling and misinterpreting with style, stepping aside just before some disgruntled author gave him a slap.

Tunstall squatted, cross-legged, making multicolour entries in his journal, much taken with the state of this wild garden. Kaporal decided that he would film from behind a bush; comfrey, wild garlic, tangles of thorn. Dwarfish apple trees with bullet fruit. Blackberry grenades. Fat rubbery leaves that squelched like bath mats. Coarse grass wound itself around their boots, slashed at pale ankles.

Kaporal was lost. He sneezed. He was allergic to excess, nature running away with itself, a chaos of seeding and oozing; indiscriminate stickiness. He didn't have the palette to handle seasonal shifts, the discriminations of this parallel universe of buds and pistils and spiral shells. His touch-screen responded best to diesel fug. Take it away from the M5 and it choked.

Tunstall, on the other hand, was a pedagogue; he worked through his guide books, from fungi and lichens, horsetails and club mosses, to gymnosperms, monocotyledons and dicotyledons. And, more to the point, he lifted from mere recognition to analogue. He became what he saw, spilling language like a silvery secretion.

And here, while they've been absorbed in their private worlds, vulnerable to the breeze from a fly's wings, the breath of mortality teasingly present in that late-summer garden, is Dorn. He's the only one dressed for where he is, the kindness of the day: linen jacket, open-necked white shirt, grey-white trainers. The hair is light wool, the skin tanned and composed, written over by weather and experience. The face is long; his hands move expressively, pointing or clutching, supporting a chiselled promontory of chin.

There's a lot of chat, skirmishing, homage paying. Kaporal decides to ship Norton an edited tape. Dorn comes across like someone from the Administration who has been put out to pasture, a wise man whose advice is no longer required. The Bath garden, in Kaporal's conceit, is the embassy in Saigon. If you listen hard enough, you can hear the growl of the choppers, coming in along the Kennet and Avon Canal.

Kaporal found himself confessing. He rambled about his visit to the Aztec West Business Park. What did the English West mean to Dorn?

'Well,' he said, 'it's all relative. You get on a train at Paddington and there's the thrill of heading west. And the country does have a broad base and it does open out and it does go all the way to Land's End and people who only buy shirts that are chainstore in America are amazed to learn that there's actually a *place* called

Land's End. Yes. It's the West and things get a bit louder out here.
You can feel it in the people. There's a certain kind of pride of
being farther west than whatever is east. And they've got the
eclipse – which is a big, big event. A big solar event.'

The eclipse, right. Anoraks scouring the skies with cardboard
periscopes. Handholding disbelievers among the grumpy stones
on the boot of Cornwall. A psychedelic bus rusting in the rain. The
eclipse was an event that couldn't be filmed, the cosmic equivalent
of Mr Undark. The clockwork of the world in remission. Kaporal,
toying with his own dismal attempt to link the temporary blinding
of the sun with Jeremy Thorpe's political eclipse, asked Dorn for his
impressions of that extinguished meteor.

'I like Jeremy Thorpe actually,' Dorn replied. 'When I lived in
England, Jeremy Thorpe was quite active. He could talk. He was
intelligent. He had a brain. He wasn't bad looking. He was *there*.
And all the other politicians suffered in comparison. He was obviously minority, so he didn't have to be responsible. He suffered
because he stood out.'

This gave Kaporal pause: Thorpe shifted as he listened to the
hours of recordings, speeches, interviews, witticisms; he changed,
floated in and out of focus. He was courageous, timid, shifty, true
to his cause. But he was *never* there. That was the one thing he'd got
right in his exile. In winding down that green lane, he stretched the
thin thread of his substance to gossamer. Nothingness. A bag of
bones propped in a tall chair in a sunlit room. Thorpe had gone,
leaving behind a croak, a raven cough.

Conversation meandered, moved away from areas Kaporal could
pitch to Norton. He retreated to the far end of the garden and left
his camera running on Dorn's face; patterns of dappled sunlight,
wavering foliage, high cheekbones and creased skin. The poet was
absorbed by accident, the place in which he found himself. His
voice was steady and remote, swift and sure in response to Tunstall's
questions; the rush of words as another target appeared on the
screen, another connection was made.

Dorn, bending to the task, signed one of Tunstall's books.
Tunstall tried to explain how much the Arnolfini reading had
meant to him, this coming together of – what? Two modes of
consciousness.

Graciously, Dorn helped him out. 'I think last night's reading was historically interesting and significant – but things of that nature have to be borne away by the witnesses. Sometimes I think it's a shame that it's not captured. But, in a way, it's such a moment that capturing it is – defeating it.'

'Yeah, right. *Right.*' Tunstall nodded, as Dorn fished under his black sock to scratch a troublesome ankle. 'Umm, yes.'

Kaporal, spotting the youth who had organised the event struggling with a bottle of something pale, was on the move. *Capturing*, he knew, was everything. If it wasn't recorded, it didn't happen. If you couldn't play time back, chop it against another riff, you would never achieve fiction. And, much more important, you would have nothing to sell.

As the van cornered, Bad News lurched against Davy Humpp. There was no view, not much light; they were buried in shifting sacks of books, clothes, records, household goods, and they had a captive audience. What could be better? Mutton bellowed above the struggling engine and the amplified cough of a sawn-off exhaust pipe.

'Blame it on Landor. They were taking me down and the copper said: "Go straight through that large door." *L'Age d'Or*, I thought. "Hold on a minute, squire. I'm getting weird vibes here." They were doing me for performing a gross act, behaviour liable to outrage public decency, when all I'd done was take a dump in a graveyard. Then I discovered . . .'

Tunstall wasn't really listening. He was still high on Dorn, on quitting Bristol, the realisation of his long-cherished vision: the Pantisocracy. Jean had handed in her notice and Filo Sparkwell, a gentleman carpenter from Montpelier who had a few bob put by, a licensed Transit, was up for it. Get into Wales, check out the sacred sites (Tintern, Abbey Dore, Kilpeck, Llanthony Priory), rent a property from a hill farmer, or offer work in lieu of rent. The New Life.

He dozed, lulled by the fumes, the narcoleptic drone of Bad News Mutton. He dreamt: the saturnine figure with the fox-pelt helmet kneeling behind that fat, white mountain of blubber. Inserting his tongue, rimming the crusted rectal eye. The Templar's

Kiss. It was another reason, the best, for fleeing the city. Acid flashbacks to the scene in the Temple Church: Thorpe and Witold
Grossman. Grossman turning, seeing him, making the identifica-
tion, pointing the finger.

'. . . that Landor was a character in a tale by Edgar Allan Poe.
And visiting a ruined Welsh priory was like infiltrating the House
of Usher. The magistrate turned to me and said . . .'

'Put a fucking lid on it, B.N.,' Humpp muttered. 'You're doing
my head in.'

'Listen, man, when they had me in the cell, after the kicking, I
was reading this book on Derrida. I flipped the pages and, lo, there
was the heading OR in French. "Or" is never stable. This playing
with words recalls "an occult grammar" where "accidents occur".
I see these coincidences with names as undermining the natural
order of meaning required by logocentric texts. Jack Derrida (no
less!) underwrote my thesis.'

'So what happened?' Good-hearted Filo, one hand on the
wheel, the other resting lightly on Jean's bare, brown thigh, found
that he actually wanted to know. Did Mutton get off?

'Conditional discharge, fine of £30. Anyone care to contribute?
I pleaded guilty but asked for the court's indulgence to make a
statement in mitigation. "I'm not well," I explained. I told them I
was under treatment. "There are periods," I said, "when I'm not
myself. I am, in fact, on a part-time basis, a fictional character in the
novels of a man called Norton. I enact whatever he imposes upon
me. The man has little imagination but, like a vampire, he makes
steady withdrawals from my vital essence. His romances are vul-
garised versions of my autobiography. I inspire, he betrays. This
picaresque episode in the churchyard was an invention of Norton's.
He is the man who should be standing before you. Sadly, his books
are little read, and, for the most part, out of print. Give me leave to
walk from this court a free man and I'll fade into oblivion. Or burn
these damned books and return me to the condition of a blank
page, radiant with potentialities." The beak was gobsmacked.'

Filo applauded. He was the kind of Englishman who might very
well work in a Welsh landscape. He was unobtrusive, economical in
his movements; quizzical without giving offence. Prepared to graft.
With his own wheels. He shared Tunstall's vision of a self-supporting,

grow-your-own-dope, poetry-writing community – but he realised it wouldn't happen on magic mushrooms and peddling purple candles around craft markets in Abergavenny and Brecon. Filo was a forerunner of the opt-out homeworker, the ex-futures trader who operates on Tokyo time from the Outer Hebrides, by way of a satellite dish. On-line hermits. Money men, in denial, juggling Third World debt by playing at trout farms, or breeding exotic pigs.

Tunstall, Jean and Filo checked out the pub car park. The vibes were hard to interpret. Skirrid. 'Wales's Oldest Inn,' it said. They liked the conjunction with the conical hillock, the real one on the far side of the road, but they weren't sure about the version on the pub sign: a sharp-pointed Madonna breast split by lightning. While they were musing on the polarity between holy and demonic mountlets, the Brummies let themselves out and scuttled towards the bar.

Tunstall and Filo, on the whole, favoured a drink; but Jean, using her casting vote as den mother, decided they should move on, try for Llanthony, the priory pub, before closing time.

Llanvihangel Crucorney felt right, it stood on the edge of things. They would twist away from the main road, through a fold in the hills and into the secret valley. A proper beginning for their experiment in communal living. There needed to be a small ceremony, a baptism, a tasting of the waters; the River Honddu, a homage to David Jones.

Filo and Jean scrambled down beside a grey stone bridge, towards the fast-flowing, white-crested stream. Tunstall stayed in the van, writing up his journal; purple ink giving way to an excited green. He noted how the passage of the van was linked with a 'warm, turbulent wind' that rushed wildly across 'the flat limestone plain'. Theirs was a benevolent invasion. The window of the van was wound down (there was no way of winding it up again) and Tunstall relished his first, heady hit of Welsh air. A butterfly – he didn't have the book to hand – alighted for an instant on his thumb, and seemed to taste its own reflection in the nail. These particulars, swiftly annotated, without egoic interference, shaped the page. The poet was persuaded by joyous recognition; morning haze lifting from the warming ground as from his exhausted sense of self. Leaving behind the hesitations and false starts he associated with the city, he was ready to stride forth into the fresh, silage-smelling day.

Light, that is heat, coming from within, fused with the light of the world; in movement, definition. And memory. A transitional landscape fractured within the frame of Filo's rusted wing-mirror. Tunstall pressed his hand down hard on the book he'd been dipping into, David Jones's *The Anathemata*. Here was the solution. To carry his projected cycle of poems, *The Ladder of Light*, beyond the form of the diary (which had prepared the way); beyond quotation, recycled love letters, colour, sound and scent; beyond everything that comes together to initiate a sense of being *in* the present. Beyond the rush and stutter of the personal – race memory, stone memory. A riot, a ravishment; a chaos out of which he, Gwain Tunstall, poet, would retrieve, or recognise – order. And form. A unitive commingling with the pollen of the cosmos.

Tears were running down his face. At the work that was still to be done. The magnitude of the task he had set himself. The hard research: geology, prehistory, climate, palaeontology, industrial relations, ufology, ley lines, mycology, shamanism. Jung, Eliade, Castaneda, the Vaughan twins, *The White Goddess*, the *Mabinogion*. George Borrow, Gary Snyder, Jack Spicer, Robert Duncan, De Quincey. Mrs Leyel on *Elixirs of Life*. And, above all others, David Jones.

He had his fingertips on the first rung.

Filo gripped Jean's hand to steady her, as they waded out into the river. Weed wrapped their naked legs like angel hair, drowned wheat. The high sun floated across the surface in a silver bowl, but the water was icy, small stones sharp underfoot. Jean's long, thin skirt slapped against her thighs, clung to her. Filo bent forward to let his fingers dangle against the current, then he outlined an Egyptian eye on Jean's hot forehead.

Later there was bread, cheese, olives, a bottle of wine left to chill in the stream. The meadow had run wild. They walked through the long grass towards the embankment, looking for the site where the station had once been.

The diminishing ladder of the railway shone like frost, leading the eye towards the promise of the distant hills. David wanted to drop to his knees, but Gill was involved in detraining the troop and their animals.

The porter, Dilwyn Rees, said later that he took them for Russian folk, a travelling circus. Gill was an extraordinary figure; bearded, bespectacled, bundled against the cold in a style it would take thirty years of solitary life, scraping a living in the Upper Neath Valley, between 'bleak moorland' and 'coal spoil', for Tunstall to achieve. (Picking his way tentatively through the Camden mob in later days, Tunstall looked like a survivor from the Eastern Front; a political prisoner returned from long exile in Siberia. He shook when anyone spoke to him and couldn't find the language to shape a reply.)

There was a cigarette holder, such as you might see in the film magazines, the man Rees reported. Behind the holder, stained teeth and a greying beard. The eyebrows were fierce, but they were offset by laughter lines. A Frenchman's beret. A greatcoat. Stockings. Polished brogues. Whether the gentleman wore trousers on no, Rees could not confirm. There might have been something in the style of a golfer or country walker under that coat.

Gill challenged him, wanting to know if the conveyance he ordered had arrived.

Proper hands, he had. So Rees said. Workman's hands. Always fetching up on his hips. Like a bloody commissar. With a sense of humour.

Two families, it seemed. And numerous children. Cats, chickens, dogs, goats, geese, one pony and two tame magpies. The smoke from the engine rose, a pale plume in the darkening sky. The lines hummed. The engine hissed. The pony coughed. David was the only one standing still, trying to understand, the where and the why, the how of this potentially fatal decision: the flight into Ewyas. He adjusted the brim of his soft hat. He shivered inside his herringbone coat: fine tailoring was no protection against the elements. Unframed space was not to be borne. He was dizzy. He wanted to lean on Petra, but she hadn't noticed his plight. She was helping her mother with the trunks.

Gill, nominally in charge of the disembarkation, left practical matters, the shifting of cargo, the stacking of the lorry, the rounding up of infants and animals, to his wife and daughters. The paterfamilias, ostensibly discussing the lettering on the nameplate of the train, was, very sensibly, checking the times of the Newport link, the connection to the mainline and Paddington. You couldn't commit yourself to the wilderness without first securing a return ticket and a means of maintaining an income on which your dependants could rely.

The first light, damp flecks of snow settled in his beard. He climbed up beside the driver, a taciturn Calvinistic Welshman, and let the rest of the tribe settle where they would, under canvas, in the back of the lorry. Picturing Father Ignatius's abbey – its remoteness, the inward-looking quadrangle, the 'female' essence of the place, warm milk and cold water, a plain table, the baking of bread – Gill saw how well the community would work: without him.

Capella ad finem: the chapel at the end of the world. It was his duty to go into the city, among the wealthy and the devout, to seek patronage, to labour as a simple craftsman; to celebrate God as the male principle. Christ the carpenter. Carving his own cross.

Staring out at the darkening landscape as the lorry lurched around the bends of the narrow, muddy road, and the luggage shifted, the dogs worried the geese, the goats pissed, and his daughters led the children through a medley of hymns and folk songs, Gill allowed himself to drift into reverie. A fire. Candle-flicker. The plates not yet cleared from the table. Another weekend in a Thames Valley farmhouse.

Such lovely spirited conversation. Such plans. Such projects. Poring over papers and inks and fonts. Then the food, the wine, the cigarettes, the brandy; the sanctity of firelight. Chunks of pear wood glowing white in the blackened grate. The heat and the splash of perfume that Moira wore.

Then, as now, Gill wore a camisole next to his skin, and under the smock, silk; a spiritual vestment, sensuality and discipline. His friend and patron, the hot, bearded man, had a beautiful voice. They sang together, the three of them. And they danced. Naked. In the firelight. Round and round. Moira laughing, embracing her husband, brushing against Gill. 'Your bones are so sharp. You're all edge. We'll have to smooth you out.'

The husband, clearing a space at the table with a sweep of his arm, pressing his wife down, entering her. Gill panting, after the dance, hands on knees. Now. The warm-hearted, childless woman reaching out, grasping him, holding him, stroking him – while her husband pumped and swivelled, clutching the sides of the table, his long white feet slithering on the tiles. Now. The discomfort, her belly rubbing against unyielding wood; the bones in her broad, childbearing, childless hips, the pelvic cradle bumping with the rise and fall of her husband's thrusts, willingly borne. Now! As she closed the magic circle, squeezing Gill, breathing his excitement, until her husband shouted aloud; then coming down from the table and, wet, taking the other man, their guest, on the rush mat by the fireside.

Headlights caught the glittering eyes of a sheep trapped between hedges, they slowed to a walking pace as the panicked animal skittered uselessly from verge to verge. Petra Gill, leading the pony, had no trouble keeping up with the lorry. It was much colder now. The countryside was strange and dark and deep, not a farmhouse light to be seen; late in the year, their move seemed more than ever a banishment, a mad flight from the duties and complexities of civilisation, a wilful descent into paganism and perversity.

Gill couldn't give up his weekends. His true Arcady was Berkshire. It was too late to recant, but this Welsh adventure was a mistake. He was committing his wife, family and dependants to a prison colony, a pastoral hell. And they hadn't arrived yet. They might never arrive. The whole thing was madness. He wanted to be back beside the Thames. The collection of old hats, yellow and smelly and battered, for use by men and women, protecting fair skins from an English sun, light reflected from water. Rolling up a mean cigarette, sitting on the cold stone surround of his friend's swimming pool; all of them naked, misshapen, figures from Cézanne. He wondered, after so many years of making art, tracing and carving the shape, what it felt like to take the head of a man's erect penis, the shining helmet, into the mouth. And now he knew.

The Eye of the Father, the chart that hung on the wall of his childhood breakfast-room, painted on card, faded. 'Thou God seest me.' Watcher and watched. Gill delighted in couples who thought themselves hidden in the bushes of Hyde Park.

There was another eye scorched into the palm of his hand when his father held out a magnifying glass to demonstrate the concentrated power of the sun. An eye that was the engorged tip of his friend's sex, in the scald of the act which cleansed sight.

Blindness, the Welsh night; the stalled lorry, wheels skidding uselessly on mud, the engine causing the seat to throb beneath him, the cab to shake.

David tasted the first flakes of snow. The bones of the land shivered. He trembled. He longed for a second coat, a thicker scarf, gloves to wear over his gloves. It crushed him. The immensity of the task for which he was so ill-equipped and underprepared: to feel and see and believe. The heavy, quilted silence and the sharp purity of the mountain air, the lull that preceded the next bombardment. He wanted to recover that primary vision by dropping the tailgate, climbing down from the lorry, paddling across the stream to the ruins of the Augustinian priory that had once been the hermitage and shelter of the mendicant Dewi Sant.

After the battle, wandering through a blasted wood, a forest of crosses, he came on the shell of a farmhouse, an improvised communion service. 'You can't beat whitewash and candlelight. That's about as good a thing as you can see in this world.'

The corpse candles of the Welsh peasantry, foretelling death, haunted Jones. He tried to work the shiver into his watercolours, the exhalation of other worlds.

They all climbed down. The road was flooded. There was no road, a misdirected rivulet. The lorry could carry them no further. Mrs Gill organised the division of the load, the porterage. Children with cat baskets. Men with trunks. Daughters with bedding. There were no torches. The driver stayed with his vehicle. It was three or more miles, uphill, from the priory to Father Ignatius's abbey at Capel-y-ffin. Wet snow was falling, sticking to their dark coats.

David felt for Petra's arm, her strength. He wanted to resurrect feelings that were dead, the proposal he had made, the anticipation of a fuller life: hope, hurt, the hunger to possess, to have her entirely to himself. He wanted the risk of that unique afternoon at Ditchling. Gill had been up on the Downs, walking to the Beacon, with his other daughters. He had picked up a stone, a flint, shaped, so he thought, somewhere between a blade and a prick. Petra had been gifted to Jones, as a sister – for his use, certainly, but more as a way of engineering a bond of blood between the two men. The feel of that stone in Gill's hand was electrifying. He willed Petra to freeze, he gifted her with a kind of involuntary autism.

David relived the scene as an event framed off from the rest of his
life. Petra, obedient, benign, impenetrable in her passivity, accepted
his proposal. The drama survives in his coded painting: stiff-necked
geese rushing through lopped trees, the red brick V of the path and
the dropped doll. He holds her, lightly, and she fends him off;
twinned profiles make up a single face. She was busy, at something
else, interrupted. Geese in flight. The gash. Her shoes. His goose-
neck arm.

'Repressive silence' and an inflamed wound that wouldn't heal:
these were the conditions of Petra's pact with her father. In this
painted embrace, Petra reclaimed a stolen virginity and Jones was
excluded from the garden he was struggling to design. The
engagement was broken off; Jones, in remission, with the monks of
Caldey, trying to iron out the sea. Passing boats were matchboxes.
He found himself stroking the red-gold hair of the girl who carried
milk to the monastery. He was banging his head, over and over,
against a plastered wall. The crushed letter dropped from his hand.

The procession straggled out over the last mile, snow was no
longer falling, a clear night; they climbed, breathless, under a
canopy of stars. Mrs Gill took her husband's arm; resigned to
spending the night wandering the countryside, she saw a light
moving ahead of them, a lantern to guide them to their future
home. She gathered up the exhausted children. They could hear
the sound of a rushing stream and they saw the outline of the owl-
tower church that was their marker.

The light she had taken for a lantern must have been some
strange natural phenomenon, marsh gas, fire-flies: it swerved and
swayed and flittered over the fields. Gill had seen nothing and told
her she was talking nonsense. Petra saw it. Jones felt it, believed it
should be so. A terrible place. But the right place. A place that
recognised his spirit and welcomed him home. The spring-pool of
his dreams.

Horses, brought down from the hills, stamped in the stables.
Each person took another by the hand; and, singing, they made
their way up the steep and twisting lane towards the sharp-sided
abbey.

6

I no longer believed that I could write my way out of this. Dr Vaughan – 'call me Francis' – found an excuse, most evenings, to drop in at my room. I didn't share any of my friend Moorcock's prejudices about persons of restricted growth ('fucking dwarfs', as he called them, 'evil little sods'), but Vaughan's height, or lack of it, did seem to gift him with a curious inability to stay still; as if movement could somehow disguise this deficiency in inches.

'Why is it,' said Francis, 'you feel obliged to quote Moorcock? Think about that. Is it something to do with the name? By way of example, you rarely mention – Jack Trevor Story. Too painful? A story? A task uncompleted? Then again you collaborated, didn't you, with Christopher Petit? We don't hear much about him. Significant? Your choice, Moorcock rather than Petit?'

Vaughan riffled the loose sheets, looking, I suppose, for dirt: confessions, insights he could pinch or neutralise. He found it increasingly difficult to feign interest in the Ignatius journals, the past had a value for him only in so far as it echoed or prefigured current difficulties. He became excited if he found a passage in Shelley that read like a paraphrase of his own notebook. Coleridge attracted his attention only when the troubled metaphysician plodded through a landscape that was familiar to the doctor. Vaughan walked compulsively, roamed the local hills, scribbling precise meteorological observations, reams of stuff about light shifts, psychogeographical displacements. His large head, hair aflame, bobbed above dry-stone walls. He talked to himself, yelping with excitement; the rush that signalled the next dip into catastrophic, knees-to-chin melancholia.

I miscalculated badly when I thought I could perk him up with one of Moorcock's yarns. Mike had been standing on the platform at Earl's Court underground station when he felt a sharp pain in his lower calf. He turned around, but noticed nothing out of the way in the usual mob of dispirited London travellers. He resumed his vigil, felt the pain again, sharper than before. A dwarf was hacking at his shin, squeaking: 'Watch where you put your great feet, you fat bastard.' Moorcock attempted an apology, but his assailant was having none of it. He spluttered and booted until Moorcock found himself saying: 'Why don't you pick on someone your own size?' For ever after, Mike swears, he has been followed through the streets of the West End by groups of drunken, Celtic miniatures, film extras, occasional hitmen, hissing and banging cans of export lager in a hideous cacophony.

This was not the most tactful anecdote to deliver. I realised that as soon as I launched it. Vaughan reacted badly. He was a Caius man and had a rather stiff sense of what constituted ethical behaviour in relation to less privileged (all) sections of society. Setting himself as judge and jury, watchful for episodes of class treachery, sexism, racism, partiality to bogus shamanism, inauspicious similes, he was an elitist in the best sense. Before he could attack me for my failure of taste, he checked the verbal aggression that, coming from a superior intellect, might leave him open to the charge of insufficient sympathy for the underdog (i.e. myself, his patient). He therefore crumpled into a vast armchair; and, as a penance, begged me to read him a few pages from my edited transcript of the fraudulent journals of Father Ignatius's amanuensis, Brother Jonah (the Noseless).

By now, having worked my way backwards and forwards through the unpaginated sheets and misbound chapters, I was reasonably confident that I could identify the passages that were pure Jonah (salacious, stumbling, sticky with self-love) and those which were quotes or paraphrases or pastiches of Ignatius's original. I no longer doubted that there *was* an original and that Jonah, or one of Kwilt's little gang from the abbey, would be sniffing around for a buyer.

'Try the chapter that deals with the Marian Vision,' Vaughan said. 'I'm interested in the elective delusion element in group hallucinations. Adolescent fantasies. Pre-menstrual dreams that turn water into blood. Fetish animals, don't you love them? A mongoose with human hands? Phantom lights conjured out of psychic crisis? Better than the movies.'

The Father was absent on one of his ever more frequent and extended missions, preaching to Western savages, converting the Jews, or luxuriating among the silken snares of metropolitan society, when a child of the village, a youth who had been making a retreat, learning at first hand of the rigours of monastic life, saw the Infernal Lights moving across the Lower Meadow. Instructed to follow the path, down from the chapel to the stream, where he would commence his True Ascent, until he was crawling, barelegged, over the stones, meditating on the Passion of Our Lord, he was — as I surmise, and I was observing his progress, or lack of it, from the security of a grimy upper window — diverted by the company of several ne'er-do-wells, clerks and office grubs, who had been lodging at the Abbey, in the pretence of acquiring Grace, but in truth as catamites to Ignatius's ill-favoured deputy. One of these godless fellows had procured an optical device, a Magic Lantern, with which to cast vile images, filth from Brussels or Paris, onto our plain, whitewashed walls. I believe that this villain, encouraged by his success with the lowest of the Brothers, a rabble of Hibernian drunkards, disciples of Onan, attempted what he saw as a fine jape, a blasphemous prank: he caused the simulacrum of a harlot to be projected by his hideous, smoking engine out into the trees.

The credulous farm boy, dizzy with his exertions, intoxicated by the misunderstood Latin of his prayers, gaped as the bedecked slattern drifted across the meadow. 'A Vision!'

How the peasantry fell upon these rumours. And how swiftly did Ignatius transport himself back to Wales, so that he, and he alone, should be the auditor, examiner and author of this fantastic episode. The child's misinterpretation of a ghostly woman's body, a thing with which he had no acquaintance, became the Holy Virgin.

And thus it began, the sightings, the emasculation of our community. Every peasant girl with cramps was visited by Our Lady. Stones leaked milk. Legions of the insane plagued us, seeing the Dead claw their way out of the ground, seeing verses from the Revelation of St John the Divine scorch

themselves into mountain rocks. It was impossible not to be affected by an
atmosphere of mounting hysteria. I have to confess that one autumn evening,
after several days of fasting and flagellation, as I was passing along the ter-
race towards the chapel, I became aware of an Immanence, an intense and
overwhelming Essence of Celestial Blue, dispersing, disposing, hither and
thither, as if honouring the passage of an unseen tributary, darting in the
direction of the Honddu river. This was undoubtedly a natural phenomenon;
unseasonably warm temperatures teasing moisture from the damp ground,
curious metamorphoses, pulses of previously unrevealed igneous strata.

I felt it was my duty to inform the Father that I too must be numbered
amongst the recipients of the Blessed Vision. He was astonished, with-
drawing from the Brothers to pass the evening in private contemplation.

After Prime, on the following morning, Ignatius summoned the entire
community to let it be known that henceforth there would be an annual pil-
grimage, from the Chapel of St David at Llanthony Priory to our Abbey,
in remembrance of this day – when Our Lord, by showing us a Sign, con-
firmed the Blessed Father's Wisdom in the choice of this wild fastness as a
Place of Worship and a retreat from the sinful world.

'Sanctimonious piffle!' Vaughan piped. 'Why can't the wanker
write a simple English sentence? It's so frustrating. How many of
these manifestations were there? Who was present? And what *pre-*
cisely did they think they were seeing?'

Mass hallucinations spreading like the pox through a closed community were all very well, but I was having problems of my own. I
saw a woman, glossy as a seal, making her way down the gravel
path; disappearing behind the yew hedge to emerge in the lower
field. She was heading for the river. I was sure – I wanted it to be
so – that it was Prudence. My Prudence.

Dr Vaughan, thinking I was struggling for breath (instead of
simply putting my respiratory system into suspension), released the
catch and eased open the window. Clean air. The sound of the
rushing, tea-coloured Usk. Spidery shadows across the asphalt of
the tennis court. Fresh-cut stripes in the lawn. The glistening negative of Prudence clambering over flat rocks beneath the
fisherman's hut. A woman who finds it difficult to remember how
to walk upright. A woman who has become an animal, a fish. A
woman returned to life by being dipped in water.

Mr Lydd broke cover, from the woods on the far shore; sunlight glinting on his binoculars.

Cars. They always had problems with their transport, poets and medics. Doc Vaughan banked on it; a clapped-out station wagon that never left the asylum without overheating, excreting an oil trail, was his way of justifying the eco-damage he was inflicting on the environment. On his self-esteem. Vaughan was a hiker, a Romantic; he belonged in the high hills, navigating by starlight – but to travel *between* these hills, between hill and hospital, required wheels. Travel as an aid to composition. In the car, a heap of books on the passenger seat, he talked to himself: ricocheting fragments of reality, mottoes on hoardings; the brain abdicating all sense of location.

In town, commuting between Bart's and his Wormholt Park fuck pad, he thought of himself as 'spinning west'. How many times had he circled the Shepherd's Bush roundabout looking at that horrible phallic plunger, the Perspex hypodermic filled with Jeyes fluid? He seemed, always, to be driving through rain curtains, mudwash from high-wheeled juggernauts, into a drowning sun.

Vaughan despised the car that made his life possible. It wasn't, in the end, cars in general – it was this one, the one with no colour. The one that wouldn't go where he wanted it to go, unless he did a whole lot of stupid things with gears and wheels and pedals. He tried ordering the car – he nicknamed it Leviathan – to turn left at Crickhowell, up to Llanbedr and Lower Cwm Bridge, along the skirts of the Sugar Loaf to Llanthony. And it worked. The car behaved immaculately, did what it was told. There would be trouble later, payback time. Fine. One more bolshy episode and Leviathan was scrap metal.

Brother Jonah's slippery account of the miraculous light at Ignatius's abbey niggled Vaughan. If something verifiable had happened once, it must happen again; it was still happening. 'I've always been good at working the field, laying out everything that surrounds the action, but nothing touches me,' he thought. 'I'm a disposable factor on my own event horizon.'

It was, by one of those coincidences about which Bad News Mutton makes so much fuss, the day of the Llanthony pilgrimage, the Procession of Grace, the bearing of the effigy of the Virgin from the Augustinian priory to Ignatius's tumbledown chapel, his grave. Vaughan decided to join the mob, treating them as if they were Peruvian peasants, shutting himself off from the high-throated gargling of aboriginal voices, becoming one with the spirit of place.

The car died as it splashed through a stream. Vaughan was delighted. He had no idea where he was. The rain wasn't too bad: it was that soft, insinuating, dripping-from-overweighted-leaves kind. His spectacles were steamed over, so he flung them through the window that wouldn't close. He slammed the door. Like a cop in a TV drama, he walked away without locking the vehicle, leaving his keys in the ignition.

What he saw fitted nicely against what he felt: a thatch of old woodland, undifferentiated trees, a narrow winding road carrying him uphill. Sound led him to a spring that bubbled from a wayside shrine. Sound was the hinge of memory. Vaughan was blank: as he dipped his hand into the reviving chill of the water, clear and swift, he remembered nothing – his breakfast, the purpose of his journey, who he was. Tasting wet fingers, he *was* remembered. Clammy stones with their slimy necrotic mouths remembered him. They had anticipated this arrival, Vaughan's dissolution into the green wood.

His boundaries burst. He was in London, an attic room, someone's house, on a long Sunday afternoon. And his head was being crushed, squeezed of language, emptied of all it knew. 'Concentration around wood lice.' Final words. If there were to be final words. Left on a scrap of paper. He would never know if they were his own or a whisper from the thin volume left in the open car. A book he travelled with but didn't read.

Vaughan rested at the gate of Patricio Church, a climb of a few hundred yards from his stalled motor. Sheep were grazing among the gravestones, beside the stone lectern where Geraldus Cambrensis preached the Third Crusade.

'I have deserved a thick, Egyptian damp,' Vaughan quoted. Quoted Vaughan. The other one, the poet. Satisfied now. A piece of his life clicked against a long-forgotten sentence.

'That's Turner in the bag, time to nail Gill.' Marc Pyratt, the Corby culture-broker, sprang from the Jag, shut his eyes, topped up his lungs with mountain air, waited for the ancient stones to settle in their slots. As he came slowly down from his levitation, he knew that he had found the right place, *Llanthony prima*. 'Western towers, aisled nave, central tower and transepts, aisleless choir.' He bullet-pointed M.R. James, then pressed his hands together in a gesture – 'om-mmm' – that echoed Tom Maschler's 1967 snap of Allen Ginsberg.

'Silly sod,' the painter Ruthven Cobb muttered to the driver in the tugboat skipper's cap. Cap'n Bob was chewing on a black stogie; gripping the cork, while he revolved a bottle of inferior champagne in the proper manner. A decorous pop lifted a few lazy crows from the tower where Walter Savage Landor had bivouacked through several miserable Welsh winters.

Cobb liked sketching in the rain. He liked the way proud structures, such as the gothic nonsense of the abbey, dissolved, faster than he could get them down. He thrived on discomfort, the corkscrew smile. The side-of-the-mouth witticism nobody hears. He could deface good paper for hours at a stretch; hurt gave his narrow eyes a truculent shine.

'There's only one position from which to work,' he told Bob. 'Close as you can get to the bloody car park. If you bang the odd tractor or TV aerial into the composition, so much the better. If not, try an owl or a heron. And make them big. Big enough to hide a mess of fiddly detail.'

Cobb had been here before, been everywhere, ticking off the gazetteer of the sacred, getting the measure of mysticism; taking the piss out of his latest patron – of whom he was quite fond. Art was a tough racket in an age when yobs, who would have been lucky in Cobb's day to get a job cleaning the karsy, picked up all the prizes and the best metropolitan gigs. Cobb was a craftsman. He had the splinters to prove it. Nights on his knees working an oversize woodcut with a bent spoon.

For his most recent tour, featuring notable Welsh landmarks rendered in gobstopper colours, Cobb used Pyratt's windscreen as his framing device: menhirs, brochs, holy islands, follies and fountains, all within the landscape format of smeared, flyblown glass. But Pyratt valued Cobb's eye, his experience; his contacts with lost artists and discontinued reputations were cash in the bank. The boys from Corby hoped to use the Procession of the Virgin as a way of infiltrating the abbey, digging out a cache of pornographic etchings by Gill, ethereal watercolours by David Jones.

'And after the mist, lo, every place filled with light.' The parson was stronging it and the rabble were spilling from the car park towards the little church of St David; happy to busk as temporary pedestrians. Tunstall brandished one of Jean's candles, while Filo darted about, shaking hands with strangers and taking photographs.

Becky had motored from Hay with a golden youth (less young, more blusher-enhanced on close examination) who took everyone's eye by his gift of conspicuous modesty, being always on the drift – tensed, watchful. His steady gaze was blue-chip, money in the bank. Cretan lapis lazuli. The unacknowledged director of any scene in which he appeared: the mythologist Bruce Chatwin.

Chatwin was adept at placing himself in positions, at the back of the crowd, where he could be effortlessly acknowledged by the notables, folk with country piles and A-list connections. Sunstreams, stained by their transit through the mulberry windows of the church, followed him like a hot spot. You couldn't take a bad shot of the man. He did the concept of 'used' with preternatural delicacy; shirts that looked as if they'd been borrowed from Stewart Granger, sandals that smelt, in the nicest way, of camel. Pernickety notebooks from a shop in the arcades nobody else knew.

What Pyratt realised, but couldn't figure out any way to exploit, was that each of these characters was writing a different story. The procession dispersed before it began. Some moved, some posed; some registered the particulars of the church. Some flashed ahead to the service of thanksgiving that awaited them at the end of the dusty trudge up three and a half miles of narrow country road.

Cap'n Bob, so drunk that he let his massive belly steer Pyratt's vintage Jag, brought up the rear, cruising in second gear, just below walking pace; chucking empties into the hedge, honking at stragglers. Offering lifts to fillies with freckled Ascot legs and sunhats.

The Believers tried to get a hymn going, but it didn't take. The problem was that after the first half-mile there were no pubs on the road, nothing to lubricate the throat. Essentially, this was a decent country walk spoiled; instead of hacking up onto Offa's Dyke or

following the river path that led to the low-roofed white farmhouse
named after the original Ignatian 'vision', they were stuck on the
road. The hedges were high. There was nothing to see. Ugly vehicles with bull-bars, going full tilt out of the high country, had
them hopping for the verges, pressing themselves into nettles. Dogs
barked at every farm gate. Carefully considered hiking outfits always
got the weather wrong. Jackets felt heavy, awkward. Underwear
rode up, scuffing lurid ridges around the crutch. Shoes pinched.
Toes swelled and blistered. Dodging horse droppings, they would
find the human variant, a bag of baby cack chucked from a car.

The lads carrying the plaster Virgin wanted to roll her into a
field. Book-reading incomers never really got into the spirit of
fiesta. You needed a more rigorously plotted agenda: a cathedral,
labyrinthine streets overlooked by balconies, drums, firecrackers,
masks; increments of inebriation, a rising sense of panic. There had
to be the understanding that it wouldn't take much to tip the gig
into riot; blood-spattered penitents running amok, crucifixions in
the town square, massacres of the ungodly; sexual licence, and full
confession in the morning.

The pilgrimage to Ignatius's abbey plodded in resentful silence
like a school crocodile, soggy-souled pedestrians locked into their
own thoughts. The morning rain let up. It was a perversely brilliant
afternoon. Gwain Tunstall, as Llanthony disappeared around the
first bend, regretted the knitted skullcap and the floorlength coat.
He tried to explain to Filo what it had been like for David Jones.

'I am a man in search of memory,' David thought. Memories provoked by cloud shadows racing across the anvil-shaped hill, Y
Twmpa; memories he had not earned. The woods, with their
abbreviated branches, were loud with ghosts. Robert Graves had
walked Offa's Dyke, weeping and grinding his teeth and talking to
his comrades, the ones with wounds instead of faces. He shuddered
from the impact of the guns. Tanks churned the slanting fields into
mud. This was Annwn, the hidden kingdom of the dead. The
tank was Twrch Trwyth, a boar whose ferocity had no limits, one
of the hunted who becomes a hunter; leading his pursuers through
forests and swamps, over mountains, down rushing streams, through
precipitous declivities, towards the broad Severn river.

The tracks of the boar were still hot. Unappeased, he would swim the flood, pass into the Lands of the West; the hounds that followed him would be destroyed, washed up on sharp-toothed limestone pavements, their eyes pecked out by crows.

David sat at a high window, watching himself move off with the other men. He shivered. His earlier self shivered. Two coats were never enough. He had come to help them dam a stream. He didn't care much for outdoors. He liked Petra carrying a mug of steaming tea to the cold cell where he kept to his bed, huddled under a downy cover. Spiritual art has a domestic base: the tobacco tin, the gentle parenthesis of the roll-up, hands warmed on a thick china rim. A pattern of harebells around the rim. Nothing better than candlelight, flickering shadows on a whitewashed wall: the carved Christ figure, black and naked and maimed. Nobody understood the tremble in the landscape better than Jones, gauzy bride-veils like the gossamer bird-spit that decorated the high hedges in the lanes around the abbey. A theatre of the sacral, the Sangraal; the quest for the restoration of memory. For restitution.

The other men, jackets off, sleeves rolled, were wrestling with rocks; working boulders out from the red earth, with staves and boots, curses and laughter. David was paralysed by the dimensions of the sky, the wet weight of cloud-sea; the depth of ground falling away through coal measures to ancient forests. A furnace hot enough to melt Christ's nails.

The women were in the fields, calling to the cattle; thin dresses, hands raw. They were kneeling; bare, bruised flesh on stone flags, scraping out the embers of the fire; chopping wood, chopping vegetables, pulling the necks of chickens, skinning rabbits. Driving the cows, chapped fingers squeezing hard teats. Weaving, sweeping, preparing soup, singing, mending; accepting the ordinary urgency of the demands of the paterfamilias as a natural hazard, a sometimes tolerable, sometimes importunate force of nature.

Gill came on them as the whim took him, obedient to his instincts. The justified craftsman. He unbuckled his belt, lifted his smock and presented the chosen partner with the proof of his affection. On the kitchen table, in the byre, on the mountain path. In quiet bedrooms, damp with night. Remote stars visible through a narrow uncurtained window. He ruled, he penetrated. They indulged his heat, the unwashed maleness, the long pale body with its scratchy tufts of hair. He might corner them, excited by an experimental encounter with goat or dog or duck, and speak of Saint Francis. Outsiders would never understand the undramatic, diurnal nature of these affectionate couplings: an old ram with a barely inconvenienced flock, uninterrupted in their quest for sweeter cud.

The sculptor with his rasping cough, his stained fingers, enjoyed the consolations of solitude. This was not a community, it was a purpose-built, self-generating harem; wife, daughters, domestic animals – kept clear of wagging tongues (except those labouring at todger rejuvenation). In purdah, safe from outside influences. Capel-y-ffin, in its remoteness, was a colony in thrall to the solar eye of Gill's prick.

It was not enough: where David Jones froze on the hillside, losing himself in what he saw, becoming the image, Gill seethed and boiled. He puffed, laboured at prose sermons, clunky, rabble-rousing essays. Art as duty. Art as function. A coal cellar filled with tight lines, hieratic pornographies of god lust: to be the Prime Force, the creator, rather than merely giving that force entrance – as an instrument. To ravish with a nib. Carve with a hard pencil. To force the V of a woman out of stone. In dust-flecked, cobwebby darkness, he caressed a sharp-pointed lingam, the flint from the Ditchling Beacon.

Gill thought of water, oily prisms of flow; small waves lapping against the side of a swimming pool. He was ready for another excursion to London, a weekend in the Thames Valley farmhouse; naturists drinking real ale from pewter mugs. Mugs always. The medievalist spurns glass.

They lunched well, a roast (bread, cheese, beer, apple pie with cinnamon implants); then retired to bed. He'd sunk so deep, it was a kind of death from which, an hour or so later, he returned: chastened. Nothingness was absolute. No image, no sound; no content he could exploit. Gill wasn't present in his own dream. There *was* a dream, but he was no longer a part of it. Gentle light burnt through muslin curtains. He hearkened to disembodied voices by the pool. He wondered who he was and what he was doing in this strange, lavender-smelling bed.

He'd slept in his camisole. Now he stood at the window and watched. One of Moira's friends. The young Bloomsbury woman who had dominated the luncheon conversation with her loud, harsh voice, the tedious orthodoxy of her fashionable cant – Strachey cynicism and godless socialist propaganda. He'd seen the art they bastardised, years before, in Paris. These creatures learnt to talk too early and felt the want of restraint, a kindly slap.

He watched her mouth, sensual, greedy; the ugly overbite. Lipstick smeared nicotine teeth. A circlet of fat yellow beads hung about the folds of a porcine neck.

What depressed him was the conservatism of her lefty opinions; opinions backed by a discreet trust fund, a network of smart bohemian friends, Cambridge socialists with merchant banking cousins.

A thread of meat lodged between her teeth. She sucked at the beer with a horrid urgency. As she talked, she revolved an ivory napkin-ring between finger and thumb, occasionally giving emphasis to her argument, something to do with 'significant form', by squeezing a thick thumb into the ring.

This woman, parasol protecting her from the low afternoon sun, was floating in a rubber dinghy at the centre of the homemade swimming pool. Moira, wearing an extravagant pair of sunglasses and an old straw hat, was dozing in a deck chair. Gill noted with approval the firm, womanly rolls of her belly, the thick black bush. Her husband sat at her feet, reading, glancing from his book to their house guest – as the dinghy revolved, slowly, propelled by a lazy hand. A lily spun by a subterranean current.

Gill gripped his hurtfully engorged cock. The sagging, half-inflated craft became a kind of rubber overcoat, folding around the white nakedness of the young woman with the bony knees. Her lazy breasts curved, as she tried to sit, into horns.

He wasn't a swimmer. She was out of reach. He wasn't properly awake. He was dizzy. He bandaged himself in the muslin of the curtain. He could hear calls from the tennis party in a neighbour's garden. The sound of the ball struck by catgut.

He pumped. He groaned. He could feel the coolness of the limpid, slightly muddy water, on the woman's long feet. She splashed herself. The rubber under her would be damp, uncomfortable. She worked the flaccid boat in slow circles; mindless, slack-bodied, beyond his reach.

He gushed into a strip of old sacking. He was back in the coal cellar at Capel; hungry, dirty, sweating. He emerged into the grey Welsh twilight and went searching, urgently, for his wife.

Pyratt's naked feet stood up pretty well to the sharp stones, tar twists and horse shit. He must have cracked the gimmick fakirs use when they skip across burning coals. And, now he'd dropped the fags, he had the wind for the final twisting climb, up the lane from the hamlet of Capel-y-ffin to the abbey. Watching him glide, dogs forgot to bark.

The procession straggled back over most of the stretch between St David's chapel and the finishing line, the tomb of Father Ignatius. Bruce Chatwin pranced between his minders, those seasoned aristos, the Ladies, Diana M. and Penelope B. Ma Betjeman had trekked the Himalayas for years, and felt the want of a good pony between her knees. But she was game. Chatwin was taking cleverly out-of-kilter snaps. The Tyrolean Christ. A lozenge of bright yellow moss on the stump of a tree that aligned with the summit of Y Twmpa. A spotted pony in a field that seemed to have been standing there since it posed for David Jones.

Tunstall and Filo were in the abbey kitchen chatting to Conor Kwilt, an acquaintance from the grass-cutting days on Clifton Downs. Nicky Lane was showing them a folder of Jones's sketches that he'd rescued from one of Kwilt's bonfires. Tunstall's hand flinched as it touched the paper with its jumble of broken lettering, runic scratchings, ordered compressions of Latin and Welsh. Most of the pages looked like rubbings from standing stones, memorials to forgotten mercenaries. There was a wartime ration book, worked over. A heavily annotated out-take from *The Anathemata*. Doll women, boneless men. A study for Prudence Pelham. A threadlike figure with antlers that belonged on the wall of a cave.

When you lay your hands on such things, life changes. Tunstall had been brought up in the old faith. True art stops the world.

Through the open window they could hear the skypilot going the full Branagh, hammering the footsore celebs and turncoat Papists. Even as wormbait, Ignatius pinched the glory from the peasant lad who first saw the vision of the Lady in Blue. Like all British attempts at ceremony, this one locked off into low-grade embarrassment: light rain from the west, Masonic handshakes, and a panicked youth from the *Abergavenny Chronicle* trying to get the correct spelling for unpronounceable Welsh names, the ages of a bunch of batty dowagers.

'Give a bit of rope to left-footers and they'll unspool the bloody lot, caecum to rectum,' growled Ruthven Cobb – who had a touch of the Western Isles, the Wee Frees, about him. Cobb was punting himself along on a shooting stick, keeping pace with Cap'n Bob, who slipped him the odd snifter from the Jag. Pyratt's motor couldn't negotiate the lane to the abbey. Bob parked on the bridge and fell asleep, dreaming of lazy Mediterranean afternoons, a fishing line dangling over the stern of his white and gold cabin cruiser. A dusky lad with a tray of iced drinks.

Cutting at hedgerows with his stick, Cobb hobbled after his barefoot patron.

The Corby entrepreneur was lounging against the base of the statue of the Virgin. Her eyes were blind as dead haddock. She was chubby and a little sullen: birdshit on her cowl. Her hands were half-raised, wide apart, in a gesture of surrender, recognisable even to the LAPD.

'She must be remembering Gill,' Pyratt said. 'It was *that* big.'

Cobb didn't bother to laugh, he hissed. He decompressed.

'Let's get the fuck out of the rain and see if these druggies have got anything worth buying. Show them cash and they'll chew through concrete to dig up Gill's bones.'

As the speculators from the east Midlands stood in the porch, pulling at the bell, Nicholas Lane, dainty-footed, the folder of David Jones ephemera under his arm, vaulted the back gate and scampered into the woods. A London dealer with an optimistic Volvo was waiting in the village. This material, within the week, would be well-sorted in Berkeley, California. Lane would be treated to new choppers and a set of strings for his guitar. And the Charing Cross Road middleman would purchase another barn in Suffolk, to store his accumulation of futures: sacks of concrete poetry, Punk staples; books about radio, books about computers, books about suicide, books about books.

Chatwin knocked off the last shot on his roll: a CU of the Virgin's right hand, floating unsupported over the dense greenery on the far side of the valley. Over the partly eclipsed, slate roof of the farmhouse they called 'The Vision'. Tucked, well away from the sight of the uninitiated, in the lee of the Black Hill.

1

I was going mad. Which was no more than I deserved for taking up residence in a four-star asylum. It gets to you. The complacent weather, always spring or autumn. Often at the same time. Then there's the way everyone I met, medics and retainers, pretended they wanted to listen to what I had to say. With such concern in their eyes, nodding encouragement, murmuring sympathy. Even if I was totally out of my tree, they'd been there before; they could coax me down. The other loonies, of course, yapped in your face, or had their jaws wired.

I was undone by my natural tendency to keep a low profile, to fit in. It goes back, I suppose, to being sent away to school in England with an accent somewhere to the west of Max Boyce; an exile's romanticism about the weary, corrupt and despoiled colonial out-post from which I'd come. South Wales thrived under occupation; first the Romans, then the English, now the Japanese. A welcome in the valleys. We were quislings bred in the bone. Now those valleys looked like the far side of the moon, industrial debris rusting in apocalyptic mounds.

My throat was as dry as sandpaper. I tossed from side to side in order to clear the blockage in one or other of my nostrils. I wasn't ill, not really. I was getting older, lying awake for hours listening for the crow's beak, as it pecked against the glass.

Not trusting my perceptions, nor being sure how much dope they'd managed to smuggle into my food, I didn't panic when I couldn't lay my hands on the Ignatius papers. I assumed that I'd given them to Dr Vaughan and forgotten about it: short-term memory loss leading, obviously, to fullblown Alzheimer's, the geriatric ward, a cardboard overcoat and a high-intensity barbecue. The disappearance of all the Landor research was another matter. I'd kept *that* secret. The novel, when I pulled it off, would be my ticket of release. As a certified manic depressive with a murder rap hanging over me, I'd be on the circuit with Howard Marks, Eddie Bunker and 'Mad' Frankie Fraser. Work up the anecdotes, smoke enough French tobacco to roughen the voice, drop the pitch a couple of tones (to around the Thatcher growl), and I'd be fronting a King Mob gig in some fashionable slaughterhouse.

My books and papers had been removed in the night. There was nothing left except a heritage booklet featuring homiletic quotes from local heroes (Machen, the Vaughan twins, Alexander Cordell, Raymond Williams and H.J. Massingham). There were photographs of beauty spots within an hour's drive of the madhouse. (I was intrigued by the car park named after Colonel Harry Llewellyn's famous medal-winning horse, Foxhunter. Who, it transpired, was buried there.)

A snippet from the alchemist Thomas Vaughan also caught my eye. It was illustrated by a computer-enhanced snap of what appeared to be pretty much the view from my balcony; same meadow, same trees, same river.

'The soul of man,' Vaughan wrote, 'while she is in the body, is like a candle shut up in a dark-lanthorn, or a fire that is almost stifled for want of air. Spirits (say the Platonics) when they are *in sua patria* are like the inhabitants of green fields, who live perpetually amongst flowers, in a spicy odorous air; but here below . . . they mourn because of darkness and solitude, like people locked up in a pest-house.'

As I was, I thought; responding as all the madmen do – by turning everything back towards themselves. The seething world as nothing more than a poorly transcribed autobiography. But, standing on my balcony, breathing that 'spicy odorous air', the piney resin, fresh-mown grass, jasmine, river, cattle – plus: coffee, bacon, frying eggs – I knew that Thomas Vaughan was right. My soul was separate, a woman.

I let my weary body slump while I took flight, out above the green parachutes of the trees. I searched for Prudence, my Beatrice, as she made her way down the steps and along the terrace. There was no sign of her. Blue smoke curled from the alcove where Mr Lydd would be leaning on his broom, puffing his pipe, watching and waiting. Pulling his lower lip up over the grey moustache, retasting the sweat of food.

Taking my morning constitutional – they insisted on it – along the riverbank, between discreet security fences and cameras blinking among high branches, I decided that the time was right to give old Frank's Polariscope a try. The instrument, hidden among folded shirts, had escaped the attention of the midnight searchers who had removed everything else that might be capable of triggering memories of an increasingly Xeroxed and faded past. The Polariscope might have been mistaken for a primitive self-administering enema device. Not taking any chances, I kept it hidden under my long, flapping coat until I reached the blind spot by the fisherman's hut. Lydd, I had already checked, was skulking behind a curtain of Virginia creeper, peeping in at the leotard women as they free-danced and swayed; stately, slow-moving, or rigid as aftershock victims, still smoking in the electric chair. The anodyne tapes, late Beach Boys, early Boyzone, were unnecessary; this chorus line was wired to its own unheard melodies, jitterbug frantic, then torpid as setting concrete.

Lydd grinned and barked.

I heard the sound, fearsome, safely distant, as I gave the lens of the Polariscope a wipe. The only dead I expected to find were the cattle who had roamed the riverbank for generations. If, as Frank promised, I saw people who weren't there, *where* were they? Would this be a *Mabinogion* moment, the revelation of a fairy kingdom, a meadow of clover and bones? In those Celtic twilight stories the innocent hero, granted access to a parallel world, never returns; the music was too sweet, the ice queen wouldn't give up her human cavalier. The unsuitable suitor.

The Usk was in flood and the steps, cut into the riverbank beneath the fisherman's hut, had been washed away. The guide rope trailed in the water. I had to hop from stone to stone, until I reached a suitable boulder on which to lie, flat out, belly down, and look through the Polariscope at the race of the river.

Light splintered and danced. It multiplied, poured in prismatic bands, divided to race around rocks, glacial debris; shattered into foam. Each bubble a flashing diamond, so brilliant that it hurt my eyes. Spray splashed the lens. If I hadn't been lying down, I would have swayed and fallen, been swept away.

The roar of the river was converted into light.

As a party trick or hippie buzz the Polariscope was a winner: a psychedelic kaleidoscope, a kaleidoscope with attitude. A customised tool for the inarticulate. There was no way to describe what you saw. Once upon a time, I could have made a fortune punting the Polariscope in the *Whole Earth Catalogue* with an encomium from Timothy Leary: 'Buy the Eye. Spy the Why. Scope the Hope.'

I wondered if this gimmick worked like a Stone Age camcorder; a DVC contrived from a war surplus (slightly damaged) torch, gaffa tape and a set of slides with views of the Isle of Man. You didn't see into the past, you optioned a distorted version of the present.

What would happen if I dipped the nozzle into the water? Would I capture visions of a drowned world or would I stun trout with a jolt of bad electricity?

The rush of different layers, the currents and velocities of the river – reflections of leaves, light bands bending as they glanced from pebbles and stones – was overwhelming. The river-beast was a living entity, complex, violent, indifferent to its manifold parasites.

I saw the most shocking of all sights: myself – twinned, divided. A grinning ghoul with a tube instead of an eye. My bloated death mask leered back at me; an oracle of the drowned. A white skull framed and duplicated in sea-green glass that shone like a lantern.

I panned upwards, tracking the *memento mori* as it surfaced, revealing itself as a pair of diver's goggles.

Eel-slick and sudden, she broke from the medium that contained her. She emerged; waxed, dripping – like a part of the river flowing uphill. She was black. As if she had coated herself, painted herself, neck to crotch, in mud. If this was the Ursula Andress moment, my Polariscope had earned its keep. Prudence, a woman whose fleeting appearances in the poem of my life in Wales were more emblematic than essential, held out a hand for me to help her onto the wet rock. When required, at each significant hiatus in my story, I teased Prudence out of the eternal into the actual.

Dr Vaughan, the Cambridge moralist, was right. My fantasies had taken me over. They were polluting the landscape. I couldn't walk beside the Usk without frightening the cattle, spoiling the fishing. My bad karma was leaking like Sellafield. There was no borderline between film and dream, fiction and the enactment of unrepressed mental playlets. Pastoral melancholy, the lack of streets and aggression and bagels, had undone me. I was thinking in Martini images.

The madhouse. The wicked gardener. The swan-necked aristo climbing from the river in a wetsuit. Now we would escape. And later, I suppose, get rich, married, envied. Not necessarily in that order. Then fall, brought low by duplicitous enemies. Rise again. It had an Old Testament feel.

Prudence shook out her hair. The late-season river was nippy. Swimming was therapeutic. She had established a pattern. She swam for an hour every day, coming down with the flow, from Gliffaes fach, around the long curve, navigating the boulders and the small rapids, bruised, exhilarated, to the fisherman's hut; where she could use the rope to pull herself up onto the bank. Lydd, she knew, watched her. Made his report. She had played the game for months, waiting for this chance. Today Lydd had an assignation with one of the catatonics. Or so he reported to a cook Prudence had cultivated. She had always been good with the servants. She understood when to muck in with the potatoes, advise on which claret to liberate from the cellar.

We would swim downriver, beyond the woods and the standing stone that I'd never located, to Crickhowell. If we waited for twilight, plunged underwater at the right places, we would avoid the surveillance cameras. Prudence had bribed the cook to leave spare clothing in a room that would be booked for us at the Bear. Then we could make our way, by the back roads, over the hills to Hay, where Prudence had a chum with a bookshop.

I was following her into the water before it occurred to me to wonder: how did she know I would be coming with her? Didn't she realise that I was suspected of killing her, leaving her strangled body in a Berkshire gravel pit? I had no other reason for hiding out in the asylum. The plot hinged on one simple fact: Prudence was dead, murdered.

The familiar tea-coloured water woke me, expelling breath, making me weightless and powerless. I was swept along in Prudence's wake, away from the big rock, out into the stream. I tried to check myself, test the bottom with my foot, but the river's momentum was irresistible. I turned onto my back and watched the overhanging trees, the sky, a perspective that reduced me to drift-wood; half-drowning, kicking, plunging through sharply differentiated bands of temperature. I was terrified that a false stroke would throw me against one of the submerged rocks. I gave myself up to that terror; swimming hard to come alongside Prudence, losing her; obeying her signal, diving under.

Without goggles, eyes wide open, I saw better than I saw on land. Focus isn't important. What matters is the drift: being a part of the element through which you move and are moved. The per-fect location for the astigmatic. Now rays of light, bent by the refractive power of the water, converged on a single point. For the first time I experienced clarity of vision: the effervescent wake of Prudence's thrashing legs, drowned forests through which shoals of small fish darted. Bright rocks with faults and clefts. Fossils brought back to life. Glacial sand through which I tried to scoop my fingers. The river, with its rusts and suspended sediments, was thawed blood.

I forgot to breathe. Breathing was redundant. The pain of my exploding lungs could be absorbed in this world of drowned light. I could have been washed away through Usk and Caerleon to the Severn and thought myself lucky. But Prudence, that unwritten woman, had other ideas. Her arm around my chest, she hauled me, spluttering, to the surface. We were out of the woods, floating on a gentle current towards the lights of the distant town.

Coming over Gospel Pass, under Hay Bluff, Prudence told me about Mr Black. She was a good walker, long easy strides; I had to slog to keep up. Returned to civvies, she dressed, as I had seen her for the first time in the Hay bookshop, for comfort not effect. She talked in bursts, then kept quiet for miles. I stayed close. I had the feeling that if conversation flagged, if she became self-conscious about her obsession with David Jones and their imaginary relationship, she would disappear.

'The awful thing about Lydd, worse than the pong, which was only dog after all, was his resemblance to Mr Black. Frightful! Black, do you see, was a butler at some house we used to visit.'

'What was so bad about that?'

I thought of Freddie Jones doing one of his turns. Wilfred Lawson, with a skinful, rolling his eyes so that you couldn't tell if this would be the time he'd snap and pantomime would shift into psychosis, and he'd take the set apart with an axe. Lawson once appeared in a film called *Dead Men's Eyes*, from a script written by Kafka. The other one. Hans. Hans Kafka. Sorry, but it's still painful. I have to download the trivia I carry around in my head.

'No, darling, it was Mr Black's feet that gave me the willies. He only wore one shoe. The other foot was bare, d'you see? And white. With bones like a hand. And every time I'd go to another county, find a job, stay with friends, he'd be there. He'd find me. So polite, obliging. So eager to serve, it made my flesh creep.'

'What did he want?'

'Don't know. Don't talk about him, please. I imagine that I've got away, a new place, settling to sleep, blankets pulled up to my nose, and I find myself listening, straining to catch every sound. It'll always be there, the horrible click and drag of a single heel, the slither of a bare foot creeping towards my door.'

'Hold it right there, folks. Complete quiet now. Just give us a couple of minutes. One more take. No, *don't*. Don't move.'

The light was blinding, silver-blue: A metallic UFO blast in the drizzle of the dim hillside. They'd blocked the road. A youth with sculpted hair, razored at the sides, frogspawn on the crown, held out an arm to block our progress. He and his mates, a draggle of odds and sods in yellow parkas, had illuminated a flight path, down from the Bluff and across the road to a patch of flat ground that might, in better weather, serve as a viewing platform from which to showcase the glories of Hay. The shot they had in mind was a spivvy move involving umbrella work, a backward track, a slick pan, a tilt, a gentle zoom to bring the dripping, disgruntled, scarlet-haired presenter into unforgiving CU.

The dye, henna plus industrial additives, was impervious to ordinary rain, but was beginning to wilt, break down into its
constituent parts, under the acid, Steel Company of Wales variant.
Iron oxide streaks gave emphasis to the TV woman's Vorticist
cheekbones. Her eyes, behind pink-rimmed spex, were a chilling
blue. Like Henry Fonda in *Once upon a Time in the West*. She was
fit, well-preserved, with nice legs. A thirtyish body with a worm in
the brain, a noise curse. She reduced all living things within a two-
hundred-yard exclusion zone to a state of abject terror,
chicken-on-a-hotplate frenzy.

It was the voice: the scream of a washing machine hitting the
peak of its cycle. It wasn't a sound television had learnt to mute
under layers of baroque syrup, catgut sawings that signal sanctity.
She screeched at the underlings, then tried to speak to the camera
like a dimwit runner some arsehole had foisted on her. This woman
was everything that TV requires: front, feral intelligence, compulsory rudeness, impatience with the past.

'I want celebs or top-drawer politicians. And I'm going to have
them or you can piss off back to whatever burrow you crawled out
of. Do you know *who* the fuck I am? Stiffing me with a bearded
freak cracking on about a wanky poet nobody ever heard of,'
wailed the Mockney princess. 'Get me Shirley Bassey or I'm out
of here.'

The woman, so one of the pretty young men explained, was
doing a solitary walk across Wales, end to end, accompanied by a
small army of technicians, caterers, wardrobe, make-up, and facilitators responsible for lining up faces for her to casually encounter
on mountain paths or by romantic coal mines; slate workers on
their last lung or Elton John, that was the pitch.

'I'm not taking another step.'

'We could try the Kinnocks in Brussels?' the PA with the girly-
shave phone wheedled. 'Two for the price of one?'

'I'm not fronting *Celebrity Graverobbers*. Not yet,' screamed the
airfix redhead. 'Can't you understand simple fucking English? I
want politicians who *are* celebs. Not Micky Rent-a-gob from
Millbank. I want decent suits, on message guys the kids can look at
without throwing up.'

'Ron "Clapham Common" Davies?'

The sound of the slap echoed around the hillside. They could have heard it in Hay.

It took a while, but we managed to work our way around this light-blasted zone, and back onto the winding track. The Voice, with its flattened consonants and estuarine overdrive, mixed with the howl of a pair of low-flying jets to create a whirlwind of bad noise that had us jogging into the wall of rain.

A shaggy figure, moving slowly as if in shock, was ahead of us on the road. At Prudence's pace we were alongside him in minutes. It was hard to tell, with all the hair and sodden wool, if he was rain-drenched or weeping. Tunstall. Gwain Tunstall on the tramp.

It seems that one of the keener young researchers, seeing him perform in a Cardiff club, had lined up the beatnik poet to deliver a rap on David Jones, Eric Gill and the goings on at Capel-y-ffin. The girl had reasoned that if her boss hadn't heard of these crumblies – who had? – it made a good romp, weirdos buggering each other senseless in a gothic folly at the back end of nowhere. You could rostrum a few of Gill's spicier efforts and bin most of the Jones stuff, no angle there. Another shell-shocked nutter pissing his life away on elitist verse nobody wanted to publish or to read.

Tunstall couldn't crack the code. He was pre-television, a steam radio buff; *Test Match Special*, Beckett plays with Jack MacGowran, the Shipping Forecast. He couldn't hack the embargo on courtesy, the reflex arrogance; yawning soundmen, camera guys who talked about you as if you weren't there. Teenage directors (with the T-shirt) who said things like: 'Does he have to have gig-lamps? Rachel, for pity's sake, do something about the nose thatch?'

It had taken Tunstall – without expectation of recompense, there was no fee for this, he should be grateful to get his ugly mug on the screen – days to rehearse his little speech. He caught a bus to Cardiff, looked at the Jones paintings in the National Gallery of Wales. He found a few reference books in the college library. He read Gill's *Autobiography* and he re-read *In Parenthesis*. He did a few mushrooms and meditated on the knottier passages of *The Anathemata*. He made preliminary notes: 'a sacred, illuminative warmth'. He copied out passages from the critic David Blamires: 'The experience of power through incantation and the stirring of folk memory.'

Then he went outside, walked through the ancient, sodden woods to the stream, rehearsing his litany. He committed it to memory, as he made his way, squelching, back to the farmhouse. He assigned certain loops of his argument to specific locations along the way. A quadrant of four oaks. The sandstone erratic that marked the retreat of the ice. The lone telegraph pole.

A twenty-minute, single-sentence rush of vision and fact, epiphany, improvisation: David Jones revealed and celebrated. Tunstall, a couple of spliffs to the good, was up for it; nervous, dry in the throat, barely able to force the air into his lungs, cold-handed, twitching; *ready*.

When the researcher broke the news.

He'd been up before first light, tramping fifteen minutes to tarmac, then waiting another hour for a lift in the back of a jeep, from Ystradfelte to Brecon. A cup of tea and a current bun. A bus to Three Cocks and another couple of hours half-running, half-climbing to the meeting place under the Bluff.

And all she said was: 'Sorry. Can we get you a cup of something, tea, coffee? Jacqui's changed her mind. The abbey is so, so . . . male. Right? Boy things, pervy pix. We can't go near material that might, you know, get sticky. Child abuse and so on. Lawyer fuss from Caroline Coon. And anyway the building itself is so dull. We're going with the guy from the castle in the book town and a bit of line dancing. But, honestly, thanks so much for coming. Another time, ok?'

Tunstall was mumbling phrases he'd worked on for weeks; he had it all in his head and now, with Prudence on one side of him, and me on the other, he let it out in a voice that was too sincere, too concentrated – too slow for television.

'David wouldn't have given a bugger,' Prudence reassured him. 'He hated interviews and busybodies and women in trousers. What he liked best was the view from the writing room of a dull seaside hotel, a small harbour seen through a salt-caked window. Winter afternoons. Velvet shadows. A cat snoring on a baggy sofa. The feeling that he wasn't really there. Nobody knew *where* he was. The room could go on perfectly well without him.'

'Were you related to David Jones in some way?' Tunstall, putting his disappointment aside, was excited by the immediacy with which Prudence delivered her anecdotes. It was almost as if she had taken tea with the man himself in one of his favourite retreats.

'We were friends, good friends. At one time we were close. Our lives divided but we always kept in touch. All that dope he was taking – uppers, downers and everything in-between – he lost speech. Very sad. Do you know the last thing he said to me?'

'No.'

'He said: "Tell me, Prudence, what's the cruellest word in the English language?"'

'What?'

'Remission.'

Tunstall had to carry that one home. He changed the subject. 'Do you know about the auction?' he said. 'They've got unpublished Jones drawings and two or three notebooks. For the castle restoration fund. Christ knows where they came from. Tonight. Roasting an ox, fireworks, readings. In Hay. We'd better step it out if we're going to make it.'

In the twilight gloom, through curtains of soft rain, window-slits blazing with light, the castle looked good. The town was provincial Wales at its best; boarded up, slick-wet, deserted. Coats over our heads, pressed against shuttered shops, we bundled towards the action, the smell of roasting meat. Would we be let in?

A whoop from the other side of the street. Becky. 'Marvellous! Instinct sure as ever, dear boy, for a *monumental* disaster. The King's gone too far this time, absolutely barking. Dressed up as Walter Landor! An ox has been slaughtered to feed the grockles. You've met Averil? Everybody has. The most glamorous thing outside a Busby Berkeley chorus line.'

Becky was accompanied, and dwarfed, by a gloriously over-stated blonde; a very recent blonde who managed to tidy away most of the excess flocculence under a sparkly turban. She didn't teeter or waver on her four-inch heels. She pirouetted, stamped. Her heels punched neat holes in the odd camber of the road. A weighted cloak, epauletted, leathery on the outside with a scarlet lining, loosely referenced between the Vatican and a Nuremberg rally, spread wide as she gyred towards us. Averil was short-sighted

and wanted to inspect our particulars, before deciding that she
needn't bother. She wasn't a snob, but there were limits.

These *grandes dames* had risen from boilerhouse clubs to become
the new aristocracy of the Marches. They coupled with land. If
they could find it. And the military (assumed or genuine): cashiered
majors with broken veins and palsied hands, spilling Bushmills and
talking fish – grateful for the company, the perfume. Under no
obligation to perform.

Averil was a gent. Old school. One of the sexual utopians who
had bravely opted – before you could get it on the rates – for
gender reassignment in Casablanca. Back in the old can-opener and
bulldog clip days. She'd been famous for a fortnight, Averil Astaire;
morning chat shows, weekend supplements, an autobiography,
rumoured to have been ghosted by Jonathan Meades. *Blue Boy: A
Sexual Odyssey* was rather good. Meades had done far more than
switch on the DAT; he'd finessed Averil's yarns, her bitchy obser-
vational humour, into the borderland novel Nabokov never got
around to writing, *Glans Mauve*. He did the topography of the
wretched town, its permanently transitional status, beautifully. Hay
happened: it was unplanned, skewed, illogical. A do-it-yourself
facelift, learnt over the telephone.

There must have been a few good nights in the pubs, Averil
shifting from sticky green stuff in a thimble to pints of porter, as she
regressed to her earlier life as a Kilburn hod carrier. Meades conjured up music-hall midgets, Korean War deserters, glamour
photographers who had worked St Anne's Court and were now
reduced to cattle shows, loopy aristos with theories about evolution, and sex felons of every stamp. Hay was loud with
disappearance, reinvention, aliases and unresolved identities. Meades
fingered Averil Astaire as the paradigm. He defined her, accurately,
as a person 'uncontaminated by spontaneity'. Every movement was
a quote. She held her pose, leaning on the pool table, swishing back
from the powder room, until the audience of gumbooted topers
chorused: '*Party Girl.*' Or: '*Gilda.*' Or: '*Pal Joey.*' Astaire's life was a
movie quiz. Rita Hayworth, Cyd Charisse. Like the rest of the
living dead, she was trapped; a celebrity in a place that had no use
for it. Hay, not Portmeirion, was the true setting for *The Prisoner*.

Averil took Becky's arm like a duchess conferring a favour.

Weirdly, her pantomimed exoticism, the slap, the costume, the chunks of gold, didn't look out of place. They looked good. Tunstall was impressed. Averil was 'on', calculated, where the rest of the town chose to sleepwalk. You couldn't help glancing at her, checking her out, in the way jaded punters clock a stripper between engagements. The hands that usually give away a gender jumper were slender, resting lightly on Becky's forearm; shellacked finger-nails managing to imply, in the way they toyed with the coarse weave of his smock, an ironic, but affectionate detachment.

The King of Hay – King and Clown – stooped, back to the mob, chucking petrol over the spitted ox. An octane buzz never harmed the flavour. The beast exploded. The King was happy. His retain-ers, reeling with heavy, advanced on the fireball with long knives and axes – one of them pulling on the ripcord of a chainsaw. The pitch was to throw hunks of meat onto paper plates. Blackened stuff, singed on the outside, raw as a fistful of worms, was very pop-ular. The peons thought they were sampling the high life. The lick of diesel duplicated the burger whiff that represented bright lights / big city, the pedestrianised franchise malls of Cardiff; St Mary Street, Queen Street, The Hayes, and all the linking arcades.

You might have fingered Marc Pyratt as a veggie, but he was doing justice to a heaped plate of assorted home farm cullings, served up by Cap'n Bob (who had taken charge of the high table) – invitation only: aristos of the Marches, private-income eccentrics, t.v.s, crossborder journos, oldtime Mosleyites punting the eco ticket. Averil – mewed at, air-kissed, deepthroated by Bob, whose gaping flannels were held together by safety pins – was escorted to the seat of honour at the King's right hand. (As the evening wore on, she would land herself with nursery duties; spooning custard into his raked and drooling mouth, dabbing at the stroke-stiffened cheek.)

Bob kept the booze coming. The idea was: waste the bugger, get him pissed enough to carry off the auction and too pissed to give his speech about the liberties of small businessmen, the dignity of craft; risktaking capitalism blended with Guild socialism, evolution kicking in from the moment some cave dweller decided to mount a horse instead of eating it.

At the far end of the top table, Averil's cropspray perfume is balanced by the subtler – moist from her mountain tramp, dab and dip at the pub, untested on animals (until now) – douche of the TV presenter in her customised geometric crop. The ladies eye each other warily. Without her trademark spex, the high-profile pedestrian sees Averil as a helmet of conceptual blondness, an unsanctified Veronica (part Hollywood diva, part Turin shroud); a Magdalene of the Dock Gates.

You could hear the hiss.

The King, who didn't take television, was having the Jacqui woman explained by one of his former wives. It was going pretty well – Jacqui did other stuff on her afternoons off, edited newspapers and visited cathedrals – until the King touched on the thorny subject of trespass and public access to his estates. Jacqui, from her architect-bespoiled Clerkenwell eyrie, deplored the invasion of the craftsmen's quarter by speculators and media flotsam chasing a trend. She was, electively, and by elocution, of the people. She championed their right to roam. The King was a traditionalist; he favoured tried and proven remedies for unsolicited invasions by the great unwashed. Rope, rack, mantraps, a swift appearance before the beak and deportation to the far west, the Aberystwyth gulag.

Pyratt and Averil hit it off. Ruthven Cobb eased himself gently into the King's vacated throne. The flames from the napalmed ox danced in the windows, revealing generations of woodlice, waxy husks pressed in heraldic patterns against the grimy glass.

'The only way,' Pyratt said, turning to stare straight into Averil's reddish, smoke-freaked eyes, 'to show you care for something is to buy it. Cash down. Book collecting is sanctioned rape.'

'I prefer shoes. They're my little weakness. I can't walk past Russell and Bromley. You should see my wardrobe.'

'I probably should, yes.'

'Jesus wept,' snarled Cobb. 'Why don't the pair of you climb under the table and have done with it?' He ate fastidiously, cutting scorched flesh into smaller and smaller segments, until he could barely fit them on the tines of his fork. After chewing or sucking for a few moments, in comparative silence, he would hawk meat pith into his handkerchief, fold it away. He didn't want to burden a sensitive digestion with coarse fibre, better far, so he insisted, to squeeze out the essence, the alchemised virtue of the beast; leave it at that. 'What's happened to the fucking auction?'

The great hall was laid out with trestle tables on which the plunder that was soon to be auctioned had been arranged. These affairs are usually discreet: quiet mornings in subdued market towns, scruffy chancers picking through the boxes, seeing where they can hide a choice item, shuffle the contents, slip a pamphlet into their catalogue. The opposition is sized up. Arrangements are made. A venue chosen for the divvying session.

I followed Prudence towards the only stack that was being blocked by a man in a dirty corduroy coat. That old trick. It could be a double bluff: you fix yourself, elbows out like John Fashanu, in front of some heap of dross, draw the runners in, make them think you've located buried gold. Stop them getting at the real prize, which you've buried under book club fodder and ballast first editions, the sort of packing material that features in collectors' magazines: late Amis (K.), Alistair Maclean, Deighton multiples, out-of-genre punts by P.D. James, change-of-life novels by exhausted TV comics.

When the man turned and I saw the sweat beading his face, the stub of cigarette bitten to the quick, I knew that the find was authentic. Billy Silverfish didn't make mistakes. If he'd been able to dissemble, hide his emotions, keep his cool, Silverfish would have been a millionaire. Come to think of it, he *was* a millionaire. Several times over. But that didn't heal the wound. The rabbi would never achieve total enlightenment, he would never break the final seal. Silverfish dripped pain, anguish at the stupidity of the world. Dealing was a priestly vocation. By identifying and purchasing obscure treasures, the Torah of value, by preserving them, keeping them out of the hands of the unrighteous, he was fulfilling his purpose on earth. Time was against him, wearing him down; waxy skin, grave breath, fingernails grained like parchment.

It took me a while to work out what was wrong, why the sight of Silverfish was so disturbing. He was missing something, the better half of him, the counterbalance: his deranged sidekick, Dryfeld. What could have brought about this amputation? Silverfish existed, so far as I was concerned, in Dryfeld's manic account of him, the journals of their excursions he published in blotting-paper booklets. And Dryfeld survived, kept suicide at bay, only through his ability to frustrate, annoy and motivate Silverfish. Nothing achieves essence on its own. Provoke a response – love, hate, jealousy, laughter, rage – or quit the stage.

Prudence, by stepping towards Silverfish, then dancing back, feinting left, swerving right, reached the table: the heap of David Jones watercolours. When he tried to block her off, by asking for a match, going into his cancer rap ('oncology is truth, big T; the tumour is the oldest part of me, genetic conscience; smoke is cancer's handmaiden'), I took my chance; breaking up the blindside, getting a firm grip on the trestle's rim.

The women in these drawings – versions of the same model – were strange, stranger than I remembered, doll-like with sturdy calves, no bodily hair, rubber truncheon necks, gold straw wigs. They looked, these crayoned myth creatures, with their fetish (one bare foot, one shod foot), like Prudence on steroids. Prudence swollen by water. Prudence as a plant. A cat. The soft thing that lay on Jones's lap, that he stroked compulsively, when he received the news of his broken engagement, among the monks on Caldey Island.

Here was Prudence, sheet in her hand, studying herself: in a distorting mirror. Here were the drawings that had attracted me for so many years, but which I had never understood. I thought of Jones's images as being fractured, hysterical; built around a notion of the tremble, the shiver in the fabric of things. Veils between worlds. Now, peering closely at the marks on the paper, I realised that the active principle was a form of layering: accretions of symbols, broken pillars, helmets, soldiers with bared, pubescent genitals; spears, chalices, warrior women. Everything was happening at once in a recessive, backward rushing vortex.

It was too much. I dropped the drawing and stumbled to the next table. Sounds of riot from the dining hall, fireworks outside, green and red flashes and flares, competing bands (heavy metal, folk, pub, male voice choir), made conversation impossible. I had been nervously sorting through a box of papers, shuffling the order, when it struck me that this lot, catalogue number 15, had a certain familiarity. The name 'Landor' recurred with irritating frequency. There was an entire apocrypha of Father Ignatius's gospel-mongering. I recognised the studied copperplate of Brother Jonah. These were the books and papers that constituted my unfinished research project. The materials that had been stolen from my room in the hospital.

Cap'n Bob, employed by the King as a basso profundo MC, was calling for order, gavelling the lectern. Some of the mob staggered through, arms around each other's necks, wasted, but eager for the next level of entertainment: watching fools throw their money away.

'These monks were lost boys who couldn't hack it in the real world,' the TV redhead was telling the King. 'Dropouts. Runners-up in the willy competition. They didn't see a decent newspaper from one year's end to the next. If you don't consume, you don't participate. It's just not democratic, grabbing all that good land.'

The King, his Landor costume slightly awry, cravat loose, shirt buttons popped, false eyebrows clocking towards the vertical, liked the sound of this. Land grabbing.

His rival, the sallow Mediterranean with the dubious connections, had got himself up as Father Ignatius. Any excuse, the King reckoned, to try on the scarlet. He'd have them kissing his fucking ring before the night was out.

Later, when the conspiracy theories had been properly aired, run through the *Fortean Times*, turned over to Carlton TV, the interested parties came back to the same question – who *was* Cap'n Bob? Most authorities agreed that the blaze, the destruction of the castle, Gormenghast revisited, was down to the drunken odd job man. Bob always had a stock, god knows where he got them, of Cuban cigars. One of them ended up in a box of papers at the auction; smoulder turned to flicker to flame-dance. A nudged glass of fine.

But that was later. For now, nothing moved. I was trying to remember where I was with the story; with Landor. The research documents made no sense. Clumsy parodies of the *Imaginary Conversations*, topographic scraps, uncredited quotations. 'It wasn't the ghost of his father or mother / When they are laid there's always another.' 'I'm not a snob, I'll drink anywhere.' 'A soft spot in

my heart for Hitler . . . but it's a complicated kind of softness.'
'Certaine Divine Raies breacke out of the Soul in adversity, like
sparks of fire out of the afflicted flint.'

Why would I want to buy this stuff back? Whoever lifted it had
done me a favour.

'Come back. Come home. We'll sort it out.' A tap on my shoulder. Francis Vaughan on tiptoe. The doctor was standing beside me.
'This,' he gestured towards my papers, 'was always the problem. Let
it go. Best way.'

He was right, but that didn't make it any easier to accept.
Paranoia kicked in. Vaughan, the frustrated writer, was trying to
shaft my creativity, bring me back to silence and inertia. A ghost in
a grey towelling dressing gown sitting on a balcony, in thin winter
sunlight, listening to the race of the river. Joseph Cotton in *Citizen
Kane*. A wheelchair and dark glasses. With a cap!

Doctors were always dealers. Remember that old crook who
used to buy proof copies from the back of the car, by the pond,
alongside Jack Straw's Castle? How the cheapskate used to call the
count short? 'I make that 95,' he would say, clicking his retractable
Biro. I had already double-checked them at 112. (Buy a proof of
this, you bastard. Now the market's dropped out of paper pulp.)

Vaughan was a dealer and a thief. Good man. Hope for him yet.

'Wait here,' the doctor said. 'I'll fetch the car.'

The three of them had the dining room to themselves. A certain
amount of smoke and bluster, loud cheers at ever more absurd
prices, seeped through from the auction room. It wasn't like Pyratt
to miss the chance of picking up the odd David Jones (some of
them very odd), but then again he'd never been big on auctions;
the crowded hall, the freemasonry of nudges and winks, the bent
Establishment at its lethal, smiling best. Pyratt liked to do his business at home, on the blower, a chat in the gallery, a run out to visit
one of the reforgotten in a leaky tin shack.

Cobb would have gone through, if only to sneer at the misattri-
butions. But Pyratt and Averil Astaire offered more intriguing
possibilities. The narrow-eyed craftsman was sketching rapidly as
Astaire declined, inch by inch, onto Pyratt's sturdy shoulder. She
was a foot or so taller than her partner, her 'date' as she liked to

think of him, but it took a measure of concentration to slide down in the chair, until she was draped, clinging, all bright-eyed attention, around her potential one-night stand.

Pyratt enjoyed an audience. Cobb enjoyed watching – and recording – human folly (set against the pretensions of the past, tumbled abbeys, standing stones that couldn't, a heap or two of industrial junk, a cooling tower, a fat black crow on a cradle of telephone wires). This conjunction, visionary entrepreneur and parodic diva, was promising: Jove entering Danae in a golden shower, a heavenly deluge of fool's gold.

The pain.

For the first time in months, Pyratt was free of it, that tight circle of silver around his shaven head; the light-flecked, hammering ache that synchronised with the beat of his heart. Averil, whose hands were as strong as a docker's, was standing behind him, massaging his skull. 'Why not?' he thought. 'I've done worse. Why not add another yarn? That's all we are in the end, any of us, a couple of dozen unreliable stories.'

Averil, walking away, looked back at him (Anita Ekberg, *La Dolce Vita*). The smile was enigmatic, but spoiled. Porcelain in Steradent. Her cloak, swirling on the turn, was red under black. She knew how the movement showcased her height, the fishnet legs; the swish of hair, slithery sounds of leather and satin.

Pyratt hadn't touched a drop all evening, but he felt his legs go as he tried to stand. He didn't do ambiguity, pleasure postponed, but this episode might be better unresolved. A cliffhanger. Cobb was poised, pen in hand, waiting. Pyratt winked at him. And they both laughed.

To auction the prize item, the Capel-y-ffin cache, the King had invited a special guest, a major celebrity with established local connections. He'd sold the event to the media on the strength of this scam.

Now the small flames were getting bolder, they were licking the edge of the box; soggy paper curled and shrivelled, submitted to the power of fire. Bob warmed his coal-shovel hands.

Prudence wanted to leave before Dr Vaughan returned – with the inevitable strong-arm assistance, with Lydd and his dogs. I wasn't fussed. I was a dangerous killer, the Gravel Pit Psycho. Jack the Dipper. I'd read the cheap paperbacks with red and black covers: Kray connections, the proximity of Windsor Castle, Marconi suicides, the existence of a 'Green Way' that led into the Underworld. There was a beautiful and mysterious essay by Marina Warner, 'Persephone and the Legend of the Acoustic Double', that brought tears to my eyes. And here I was standing next to the woman I was supposed to have killed. A return to the hospital was the safest option. Wait for the tape. Let Jos Kaporal explain it to me. It took a card-carrying schizo to make sense of these multiplying mysteries. One thing I had learnt, the last person you should ask for a solution is the author. If he knew where he was going, he would stop dead in his tracks.

A loud hum could be heard at the back of the hall, a kind of Buddhist chant: Billy Silverfish. The flies had got him at last. His impatience with the stumbling nature of the proceedings, his need for sugar, had him making noises. His worn brown coat was a swarm of bees. His beard a knot of plague flies. Busy maggots were cleaning the corruption from his wounds.

'For the star item of the evening, an unequalled collection of masterpieces from one of the many communities who recognised the Vale of Ewyas as an earthly paradise, please welcome as guest auctioneer one of the great men of our time.'

The applause started before the bearded giant could make his way to the lectern. Even in his new, diminished form, they recognised him. A Daniel stepping unscathed from the lion's den. A dead man returned to the light. Nothing needed to be said, but the King had to say it.

'Would you please stand to show respect for a man Dr Runcie has called "the Church's answer to Henry Kissinger"?'

The request was redundant. There were no chairs. They clapped and whistled and yelled as Terry Waite, frowning severely, a deep crease between beetling brows, lifted his head to face them. His hands were locked in front of him. They bowed, and waited for the blessing.

Flames leapt at the tapestries. Nobody believed it. A metaphor made real: the fiery furnace as a backdrop to this latter-day prophet. He brought them news of strange revelations. There would, after the auction, be a book signing, a chance to touch flesh with the famous mediator.

Silverfish didn't like it, the pissing around with the auction. Business was business. The rest was foolishness. He started to slow-handclap. He howled like a coyote. Behind him, trying to push through the mob, who were alerted at last to the fierceness of the fire, were a couple of coppers. And somebody hopping up and down between them, pointing in my direction. Dr Vaughan and the heavies.

I felt Prudence's grip on my wrist. 'I can't be here. I can't be here. Please please please, I can't be here,' she said.

I thought it was sympathy over my recapture. Worse. The terror in her voice was absolute. She was staring at the man released from his captivity in the Beirut cellar, at Terry Waite.

'That's him,' she said. 'Mr Black.'

8

A dark and stormy night. On the road again. On the run. Two of them in a car. Rain beating on the bonnet. One faulty wiper scraping against the windshield. Exhilaration. Panic. Pursuit.

'Where is she?'

'Who, she?

'The girl. Girl I had with me in Hay.'

'Blonde hair? Black coat? The drag queen, now she *was* blonde. Crazy or what? The boys used to tell me, flew in from Bangkok, best fuck you can buy. Way out on the rim, unforgiving. Go that route, it changes your life.'

'Prudence was right next to me. Pushing through the crowd. Holding my arm. We got separated. The car park. Mud, headlights, horns.'

'She shouted something,' Silverfish admitted. 'What? Let me get it straight. "See you on the other side." Something like that. OK?'

'Did you talk to her?'

'Sure,' the dealer said. 'In the hall. You know, hello, goodbye. With that medic, the geek. We got into a neat discussion, when she went looking for you. Dangerous lady. So the doc says.'

'Prudence?'

'Know any other with that name? The shrink, Vaughan, he reckons – ho hum – father's a cold fuck out wasting animals, ma's on the bottle, siblings trying to get into her pants. "Come on, guy, she's English," I said. Then there's religion, Magdalene complex; she developed a fixation on some chick who once scored with

David Jones. "That market's peaked," I told him. "Another wacko, an acid casualty, what's special about this one?" Get a life.'

Silverfish coughed, had to slow down; he asked me to hold the wheel while he fumbled through the pockets of his car coat, searching for the silver hip flask of morphine.

'The face. That period look, sure, straight thirties,' he continued. ' "What's special," Vaughan said, "is that she looks very – *very* – like the Jones muse, Prudence Pelham. Same sickness vocation, same bovine indolence. You can't get to her. But you have to try." '

'You're talking about a case study,' I said. 'Prudence does her own thing, takes off from time to time. But she's real. See her down the pub, putting back the Guinness, cracking jokes, holding her own with the farm boys.'

'Vaughan pitches it pretty strong,' Silverfish replied. 'Pelham has this triple identity: wild woman of the woods, moon goddess, figure of death leading virgin males down into darkness.'

The rain was letting up. We could see the black road, the high hedges. Eyes burnt in the silvered rectangle of the driving mirror, a car was on our tail. I turned, looked back; I was sure Prudence was still with us, hunched in the corner, watching those approaching lights.

Silverfish, as I knew, was an unconvinced motorist. He touched the wheel only when it was absolutely necessary – with outstretched fingers, which he ran along the rim, folding them into a hook to negotiate another blind Welsh corner. He tapped a cigarette. The fug was thicker inside the car than out.

Our pursuers were closing on us. Even Silverfish, who never checked his rearview mirror ('tedious as re-reading Henry James'), couldn't help noticing the headlights that lit up the interior. Like being trapped under the beam of a surveillance helicopter. Earlier, as we climbed towards Newton, he refused to glance back at the blazing castle, that vision of demonic consummation; books and tapestries converted into flame. The conceit with which Silverfish operated was simple but effective: no retrospectives, no credit and debit, no reruns. Nothing existed the second time. The vehicle, as he drove through the night, foot hard to the floor, acted, in cinematic terms, as a wipe; eliminating landscape soiled by attention.

Silverfish felt much the same way about women. His girlfriends, ever younger, were less and less infected by experience. Relationships had reached a critical point; the ignorance of his partners, their indifference to the arcane culture of the bookworld, infuriated him by the same measure, expressed as a mathematical formula, that their perky-soft, unshaped bodies, their chicle-sweetened saliva excited him. Soon, Silverfish would find himself, a bag of bones on a cot made from string, talking incunabula to the newborn girlchild cradled in his arms.

He hit the brake, throwing me forward. My paranoia took over. *Silverfish was in it with them.* He'd driven us out to this deserted country lane, back road to nowhere, only to hand me over, return me to the asylum. Or worse.

The car which had been on our tail swept past with a sounding of Confederate horns, bugle blasts. The Welsh don't do obscenity, mild blasphemy is as far as they go. The drunken farmers diminished down the long straight track.

'They've got two ways of driving, these hicks,' Silverfish said. 'Full-beam or no lights at all. Too stupid to work the changes.'

The door was thrown open. Silverfish stood pissing into the hedge, toasting the moon with the last glug of liquid opiate. I stood beside him. The road hadn't changed. But something was missing: apart from Silverfish's rage. The old fires had been banked down. He was melancholy, brooding on the cusp of mortality. There was no past to give him comfort, no future against which to pit his talents; no god into whose eye he could spit.

'Tell me,' I said. The question was troubling me. 'If Prudence is a runaway from Vaughan's asylum, *who* died in the gravel pit?' It went against the grain to concern myself with a coherent structure, but if one part of the story had been 'explained', where did that leave the rest? Where did it leave me, the supposed 'Gravel Pit Psycho'?

'Don't you get it?' Silverfish snorted. 'Prudence, you, me, we're stiffs. *The Third Policeman.* We're trapped within the spiral of a posthumous fable. The circularity imposed upon us is temporal not spatial. "Here" doesn't matter. "When" does. We've returned to the point where we started, but we're not who we were.'

'Right,' I said. 'The third element, the one who walks beside us, is missing. What happened to Dryf? Without him there's no beginning.'

'He's not dead yet, unconfirmed,' Silverfish answered, licking traces of syrup from dry lips. 'Gone west. Too many creditors. Sikhs on his tail. Marriage contracts in Southall. And the cops. They were underage some of them. Typical Dryfeld. The guy was never a pro. He let his personal life fuck up his business. But he was the last of them, the great runners. When he goes, we all go.'

Moonlight on wet asphalt. The long road shining like snail-spit, a mercury highway. I couldn't take any more of the new, subdued Silverfish. The graveyard gab. His method for conjuring up the vanished Dryfeld was to plagiarise the shaven-headed necrophile's monologues. Dryfeld spoke endlessly of suicide, but was in ruddy health, living in obscurity, some backwater without a bookshop. Silverfish, validating no past, addressed nothing but the mechanics of the day in front of him: the next dealer, the next pack of cigarettes, a shot or two in the evening. He was ventriloquised by disease, viral invaders; that stealthy interloper, death.

I decided to stick to the road, moving away from the town of books, towards the border, outwalking the long beams of Silverfish's headlights.

'She's gone,' he shouted. 'You're not Petrarch and she's not Laura. You wouldn't know what to do with her if you did find her. Fucking writer! You've blown it. No plot. You can't do a road movie on foot.'

I was tired. I crawled in under the big stone, but there was no relief from the wind. The Neolithics who contrived these balanced arrangements of rock had more sense than to use them as shelters. They squatted in the dark, under a good thick bedding of earth. With their weapons and their pots. They didn't breathe.

I didn't breathe. It was difficult to accept, after so much hard travelling, so many words, I was back where I started, at Arthur's Quoit. The uncooked notion of a book about Walter Savage Landor.

Wales and the Welsh. 'I never shall cease to wish,' Landor wrote, 'that Julius Caesar had utterly exterminated the whole race . . . I am convinced they are as irreclaimable as Gypsies or Malays; they show themselves, on every occasion, hospitibus feros.'

I shared Landor's distemper, the frustration and life-hatred borrowed from Billy Silverfish. Silverfish knew genocide, dispossession,
bitter intelligence. It was his inheritance on all sides. Nothing to be
done. The pleasure ground of the book, a communality in which
hordes would meet and mingle and speak, discourse on an equal
footing, was overturned. Voices in the head. Quotations scribbled
on scraps of paper. Ghosts and texts and photographs. The vision of
a girl seen in a bookshop, at closing time, by gaslight. In a dying
town.

The melancholy howl of a dog that knows its end.

They were coming for me, hunting me down with mythical
beasts, with Cafall. Stag hounds and lurchers and Appalachian
mountain curs and swamp dogs with slimy snouts. Dogs of the dog
days at the rising of the Dog Star, Sirius. Dogs that could track a
scent to the depths of Annwn, revenge a blood crime.

One dog. On his own. Tethered to the fence that surrounded
the burial site. I stayed where I was, hidden, hugging the darkness,
holding my breath.

Men appeared. A white van had been parked in the passing
place, but I marked the occupants down as poachers, or sexual
gymnasts: the van was padded with dirty carpets.

'Wants you down Aberavon, by the Lido, to have a word with
him, Friday.' A mid-Glamorgan voice, a nice baritone.

'Yeah, well. There's plenty on here, just now. It'll cost.'

'Money's not a problem, see. Proper people involved in this,
English. From London. You'll be very happy with the terms.'

'Weed's one thing. This is something else, killing.'

'Ka ka ka killing the ka ka cunt will ka cost you. Ka ka cash. You
don't get this one on ak account.'

Joblard. And Kwilt. And someone who sounded very much like
the over-qualified carpet rep, Howard Marks. The boys were trying
it on, stiffing Marks's mysterious employer for all they could get.
Road kill and the odd rabbit, that was the extent of their experience as hit men. But, as performance artists, professional
scroungers, they could busk the slit-eyed stare. They'd grown up
with Hammer Films double bills at the Elephant. Drug-crazed Bela
Lugosi on latenight TV.

Joblard had perfected the one moment of true terror in the

Ripper drama *Murder by Decree*; a tracking camera rebuffed by the mania in the confronted killer's eyes. A turn of the head by the William Gull figure, trapped in a Whitechapel alley. Joblard became Gull. It was more than an impersonation. He downloaded a fictional spirit, granted it a second life. His flesh grew heavier, his suits darker. He carried a Gladstone bag. Then he got bored with the game, shifted to a tramp, a double role out of Conan Doyle, the respectable Neville St Clair and the 'hideous' Hugh Boone, *The Man With The Twisted Lip*. He took to haunting benches outside Southwark Cathedral, begging through the City. Surveillance cameras did for him, but the record might still be there: state art lost in the files.

Kwilt walked over to the dog. He stroked its head, then put his gun behind its ear and fired a single shot.

'Christ, boy, no need for that,' Marks yelped. 'What'll we do with a headless dog?'

'Carry it to the van. Park it on your lap, get it back to the abbey. I've got plans for that cur. I want to cast the skull in bronze. What's left of it,' Kwilt said.

The three of them stood over the body, sharing a spliff, waiting for something to happen; waiting for the film to go into reverse, the dog to rise up, his spirit to take off over the fields like a blue flame.

When they were satisfied that nothing had been changed by this act, the extinguishing of a life, they picked the body up, the weight shared between Joblard and Kwilt, and staggered towards the road. Marks got down on his knees, swept the ground with a small torch, looking for something. When he found the flattened shell, he slipped it into his waistcoat pocket; he set off, whistling, after the others.

I didn't move until I heard the van reversing, struggling to turn in the narrow lane, making off in the direction of Hay. Then I followed them, abandoning my plan of crossing into England, searching for Prudence 'on the other side', picking up with Kaporal; closing down the project, burying the tapes. Where was the last place anyone who knew me, my perverse and obsessive passion for London, would begin a search? The town in which I had been born, the territory I had lived in for twenty years, the memory pit.

There was no chance of a lift and no way I could accept one if it was offered. I had to avoid Hay, work my way over the hills, dodging groups of would-be paras, character-building corporate folk squabbling over homemade rafts, mushroom-gathering New Agers, and squadrons of the unanchored dead. I might hide out for a few days with Tunstall in the Neath Valley, head down to the sharp end of the Gower, look for an unoccupied caravan.

Silverfish's car was still blocking the road, headlights blazing, but of the man himself there was no sign. The key was in the ignition. One of Silverfish's cigarettes was smouldering, just where he liked to leave it, on the dash. The back seat was heaped with books and catalogues, socks, dirty shirts, half-eaten choc bars, cans, bottles, an unspooled roll of toilet paper. The radio was on low, playing something I didn't recognise. Customised gloom: like the end of a Lalage film, when he runs out of puff.

But here was the strange thing, the car had been turned around: it was facing the way we had come. The way it all began, when Dryfeld took off down the road, loaded with bags, muttering to himself, set on reaching Hay by nightfall.

I couldn't resist the crude plot device, the planted car, the spurious mystery. I climbed in, turned the key and drove off, letting the borrowed vehicle take me where it would.

I slept in the car and, early the next morning, travelled over Gospel Pass, cancelling out the route I had taken so many times on foot. Driving trashed memory; the mnemonics of landscape, laboured for in hard walking, were reduced to a gentle blur, a granular irritation. I mean that there was no separation. I inhabited a moving sphere, dividing waves of moist air; centripetally drawing the world through a curved screen, while centrifugally expelling myself from this failed Arcadia.

Any advance in Silverfish's car was willed forgetting; the riff, the dream. It was sensual, lazy, non-specific, lacking penetration and climax. No remembering, re-remembering things you'd rather forget.

From the road, there is no proof of the angular presence of Father Ignatius's abbey; you might be held up in Capel-y-ffin, at the bridge, as I was, by a troop of horses, pony trekkers turning out of the lane. You see the sign for Llanthony Priory, but you catch no hint of Walter Savage Landor. Road reality is other: it flows, it triggers neurotransmitters, sleep substitutes. Coming down through the Ewyas Valley, that fine March morning, the trees and bushes still bare, no farm traffic, daffodil splashes on black earth banks, my journey was pure cinema. No interruptions, no repeats, no faked excitement. Steadycam. Straight weather.

That's why road movies get it wrong when they try for the time gimmick, the flashback – child-self, youth-self, adulterer, victim, killer; that's not how it works. I might make an exception for *Wild Strawberries*, but I can't remember. Can't remember who I was when I saw that early Bergman, only where: the Everyman in Hampstead. Now, stuck for the first time, backing up to let a tractor through, I find myself rerunning, re-editing, a chunk of TV, Kim Basinger in *No Mercy*.

You don't want it as it is, that's no use to you; the narrative vanishes, you hold on to details. A shot of Kim's foot in a burning house – sometimes the foot is bare, sometimes in an incongruous slipper – bringing you back to David Jones and his fetish. To Prudence. Basinger's appeal in this film, swamp girl in the city, sweating dancer swabbing tap water on neck and shoulders, breasts revealed through a diaphanous blouse (Jones again), was both feral and masochistic. The sweet cheat, the captive bride.

The confusion of David Jones's archetypal woman, a pneumatic doll tattooed with quotations, with movie waif Basinger carried me dangerously close to the Crickhowell madhouse. Panicking, I swung left out of Abergavenny, taking a new road, over the hills. Home. I'd been stuck too long in this privileged greenery; the pull was always towards England, the Severn Bridge.

Silverfish's car didn't care for the climb. It laboured, groaned. The grass was coarser here, occasional sheep, filthy and scavenging, trundled into the road. They cropped where they would, untroubled by horns or nudges. As the camera/car broached the summit, craning to an overview of new territory, I realised that this was a harsher border, the transition from Old Red Sandstone to Millstone Grit and the Pennant sandstone of the Coal Measures, than the gentle drift towards Newport, Chepstow, Bristol; the triangle of disappearances marked out by the mouths of the Usk, the Wye and the Avon. A triangulation reprised and confirmed, in diagrammatic form, by the two bridges over the Severn, the new and the old, and their connection with the M4. Aust Service Station, the castle on the cliffs, closed off and protected by security men, was the source, the forcing house of all the mysteries.

I rolled across a barren and blasted tundra that had no connection with the meandering rush of the Usk, with country house hotels and heritaged survivors; towers, gardens, Egon Ronay pubs. The light was different. I'd left behind the subtleties of shade and shadow, splintered beams diverted into dark woodland clearings: the vocabulary of Henry Vaughan. On this scarred and tufted plain, light was a solid. It ground a passage across the resistant topography. It damaged the fabric of place, revealing flaws and schisms and proud wounds.

Here were abandoned mining villages, jerrybuilt units of housing that served a decamped slave population. They reminded me of fake settlements thrown up on the Isle of Grain, on the Thames Estuary, as targets for the military. They roughed it against the prevailing winds, clotheslines whipping free, black rags caught on barbed-wire fences. Stagnant pools. Slag heaps. Rusting machinery.

The sensory hit was marvellous: out of poetry, into science fiction. I came to Blaenavon and Brynmawr as to the promised land; as if I had a copyright on dereliction. This was the kingdom of iron, not coal. I felt like one of those damaged aliens, the artists Josef Herman and George Chapman, seduced by the romance of blight, heroically despoiled river valleys, streams running red, uniform, slate-roofed terraces cut into the hillside. The earlier villages and long, thin towns absorbed scattered hamlets, small farms, pubs set alongside a drovers' track. They had the self-confidence to give this temporary housing, obedient to the colliery siren, these perched terraces, a bloody-minded and resolute permanence. See the gleaming front steps. The shining windows. Net curtains washed to gauzy thinness, laundered against the impossible task of bleaching dirt from the air.

See them today, old women on their knees, old men brushing a section of pavement. Imagine them. Devastated hamlets. Grandiose chapels, ponderous with their brief histories, epic by intention, clotted with voices, repetition, relaunched as cut-price warehouses; cheap clothes, factory seconds, electrical goods, paint, tyres. I saw what was, what had been, what I misremembered.

I took the once-loved road, up from Hirwaun, through Treherbert and Treorchy, as much a spectacle as it had ever been, and I felt, without having any true purchase on it, the sullen anger of these disenfranchised communities. The closer to the cosmetic enhancement of the coastal strip, the marinas and Euro scams, the Millennial Stadium, the tokenist Welsh Assembly, the closer to outrage and perversion. Solitary women, swallowed in cheap raincoats or bandaged in lurid sports tops, hooded against the steady rain, hung on to pushchairs, or let themselves be dragged by small dogs. Their faces were blank, registers of tranquillisers punted by GPs who had been flattered by the Biros and calendars and flimsy calculators gifted by the drug companies. Men in groups stood on corners, staring at the passing traffic with steroidal hatred. Veins bulged in thick necks. Dragon T-shirts took the brunt of the weather. It was a prison rehearsal, prison replay lifestyle: weight training, pill-popping, fantasy women, real crime. Blue lights in breeze-block clubs. Weekend strippers. Vigilante petrol bombings. Punishment beatings that were sexual rather than political. Discharged squaddies. Pensioned casualties. Fat men in chairs waiting for the operation. Smacked-out kids with nobody to blame. The karma of Belfast blown apart and scattered like aircraft debris across bald hillsides.

Then, as the car twisted and climbed, negotiated snakebends that eased the fierceness of the gradient, weak sunlight polished slate; the recessive, river-bottom blue of the roofs.

Smoke plumes climbing straight. Flashes from the windows of a bus. A gap between showers

Slogans whitewashed on the rock, Jesus stuff, Andy Capp cartoons. Water trickling down from the mountain. Men took the trouble to walk up here, following the road, sitting on ruined benches, looking back. They were getting away, above the town; exercising dogs, returning to a sense of nature; seeing where they had come from, mapped out like a postcard. They could read the stark divisions between streets, cemeteries, civic detritus.

I came down through Abergwynfi and Cymmer and Duffryn, past the vandalised bus stops and the mining museums, following the Afon Afan to the sea.

Wet mist capping the coastal ridges, Mynydd Margam; mist mixing with the pestilent discharges from the Steel Company of Wales and BP; nicotine-yellow cloud cover infiltrating the soft grey.

It was twenty years or more since I'd spent any time on this ravished strip, between the dunes and the hills. Even then, in Port Talbot, you could carve the air like cake; a cake made with iron filings not raisins. Sitting in the car, in the empty park, on the edge of the sea, watching breakers smash against the harbour wall, I remembered my first boarding school, something out of Evelyn Waugh, barbaric but good-hearted, a couple of miles down the coast in Nottage.

They marched us through the edge of a caravan park (which seemed bigger than the village, bigger than Porthcawl), to the slippery, slimy, condom and bogroll shore. Shivering, cut by sand grains in the west wind, rubbed raw in saggy costumes that needed to be held up to preserve decency, we were herded and driven into the unforgiving channel. Tumbled by surf, dragged by the tide, swallowing salt drench, bruised by pebbles, cut by shards of glass left by drunks, we fulfilled some deranged notion of what was good for us, the war babies. A dose of cod liver oil. One of the bloodier anecdotes from the Old Testament. Dog Latin delivered by an Irishman on the run. A nature walk with a moustached lady which, mysteriously, concluded at the back door of the pub. Horse rides over the dunes for the nouveau gentry, prize-fighting for the rest of us. A well-rounded education.

Having come to consciousness, at breast or earlier, to the cataloguing of the plagues of Egypt, lepers bathing in the Jordan, fiery chariots, wives transformed into pillars of salt, and having dipped on my own account into pictorial histories of Britain that broke the whole business down into a sequence of morbid Pre-Raphaelite tableaux, white ships, winter queens, burnings at the stake, I passed in this barn for an intellectual. My only rival, known as Mac, was one of those spiky-haired, no-neck, knuckles-grazing-the-gravel gargoyles cloned from the *Beano*. Like me, he claimed Scottish ancestry; he had the accent to prove it. His family were show people, travellers who had come to ground in Coney Beach, the bleak pleasure park which offered a pale imitation of its American original; an outing for the miners. Mac's troop had the toffee apple concession and a few sideshows; they also rented out caravans. Which was why, after all this time, I was searching for my old bugbear and friend. Unlike me, Mac had gone up in the world: fruit machines, clubs, slum property, low-level protection rackets, business. He kept a few caravans, a haphazard encampment out of *Mad Max*, beyond the Hillend Burrows, the Neolithic burial mounds at the end of Rhossili beach. A good place in which to lie low, plenty of the London faces had used it – until they went into convulsions of boredom; the wind, the never-ending sands, the remorseless sea. The sound of it was too much. Some of them went to Swansea and stayed drunk until they were picked up. Others drove straight, first ferry, to Parkhurst and hammered on the door, begging to be let in. One or two topped themselves and finished up feeding the crabs in Carmarthen Bay.

After the fight, Mac and I became firm friends. The system by which the staff – in an entertainment akin to bear-baiting – set the boys on each other was very simple. The school was divided into two houses. Each housemaster wrote on the blackboard the names of all the boys in his house, as he could remember them, in order of pugilistic potential. No reference was made to weight or height or age. Then, starting at the bottom, the lowest ranker took on his opposite number; blood and teeth were swept from the ring, and so on, up the list.

It was a useful diversion. The savages were subdued, brooding on the coming horror for several days; after the event, losers recovered in the san, while the victors were sufficiently bruised and exhausted to be easily controlled. Training was rudimentary, a couple of rounds getting thumped by a military man, whose legs had gone but who still harboured a healthy dislike for the coddled offspring of the rapacious Celtic bourgeoisie. 'Here's one for Keir Hardie and Merthyr Tydfil,' he'd grunt as he split another plum-shiny nose.

The match I didn't want, I would have accepted any other pairing, was to come up against Mac. But I knew, without watching the blackboard, exactly what was going to happen. It was too good an opportunity to miss, two mouthy upstarts, know-it-alls, could be set against each other, with the express purpose of neutralising revolt, clubbing cockiness into vegetoid acquiescence.

That's not how it worked out. I couldn't think of anything beyond the fight. I lost my appetite – which had never been stimulated by cabbage boiled to within an inch of its life, raw carrots and grey beef with a two-inch ruff of fat. I slept fitfully, visualising, as is now fashionable, the coming combat; seeing the inevitable damage, the ruin that awaited me. I'd been in plenty of scuffles in the valleys, territorial disputes, street against street, but that was free-form, engagements were broken off as soon as honour was satisfied. Mac's brothers went around with baseball bats. One of them worked as a second for Dick Richardson, a not notably genteel European heavyweight champion who enjoyed a few good scraps in the Coney Beach arena.

The fight lasted, so I was told, about half a minute. Pure funk, involuntary trembling of the limbs, hyperventilation, gave way at the touching of gloves to primal aggression. Mac never bothered with a guard. He was a suet-white, spongy Tyson. He psyched his opponents out until they froze like rabbits in the headlights, dropping to the canvas in a faint as he took his first lumbering step. Hitting him, sneaking a shot on his blindside, had no effect. He grinned and continued to advance. Those long arms pistoned and chopped until the obstructing object sunk to its knees. Pain was a stimulant. Nothing changed in his eyes, no anger, no fear; no flicker to signal his next move. He didn't need moves. He rolled slowly forward, puffing slightly, until it was over.

I came out with the bell and went at Mac from everywhere at once, a berserker. I can still remember with absolute clarity what it felt like: feather blows that tipped his slippery smooth head this way and that. I was somewhere I never again had to visit. He didn't know what to do. He stood where he was, allowing himself to be hustled into the corner, trapped on the ropes – as I kept on, on and on, hitting him. Until the surprise showed and he tried to hold up a frayed glove in a gesture of reconciliation. The force of my charge threw him out of the ring. By the time they got him back, he'd been counted out. From that day on we were inseparable, co-conspirators in every subversive action.

It was a nice afternoon for Aberavon. So the Arab in the petrol station reckoned; he'd been here seventeen years, one desert for another. Big smile, gold teeth. 'Some of the times is sand, some of the times is rain, always wind.'

He was right. The Parc Hollywood sign was bending towards Harry Ramsden's Yorkshire/Californian Drive-In chip shop. Estates of identical bungalows, thrown up in the boom days, looked like something out of *The Lost Patrol*, a ghost encampment dug in against encroaching drifts. Sand grains wedged behind your fingernails. Sand stuck to the skin. It decorated salt-sticky windows with annoying patterns that were supposed to reveal, if you stared at them long enough, golden cities or winking serpents.

As I tried to push against the gale, across the deserted car park of the multiplex cinema and down to the sea, I alternated between admiration for the Soviet bleakness and long-suppressed childhood snapshots. Fever dreams. The realisation of the horror of being trapped within my tight skin. Sunburn and headache and sickness: the aftermath of a day's outing, a train trip to the beach. With the Lydds.

'Get some sun on your back, boy,' Lydd said, the smell of tobacco in his moustache, prodding me towards the wrinkling waves. A long walk, it seemed those days, from the station to the promenade. Lydd with his own deckchair, to save the pence, and a brace of terriers. I remember wriggling, after the journey, the cups of sweet tea from his metal-tasting thermos, bursting for a pee; being too shy to ask, waiting like all the others until I could get into the sea. It was hard to tell if the sewage was coming in on the tide, pumping out of a broken pipe, or being hosed by the trippers in the general direction of Lynmouth.

Great grey boulders, a giant's causeway of carboniferous limestone, had been heaped against the incursions of a savage sea. Foaming white crests pounded the breakwater. Through the filtered darkness, the death-in-life afternoon, the fret that was neither air nor rain nor spindrift, I could make out skeletal giraffe shapes of the cranes on the Steel Company of Wales dock.

Where was Mac's dive? The layout was half-familiar, the significant elements in place (sea, promenade, oil refinery, smoke stacks, the curdled-cream hotel with its bowed windows, pebbledash porch and red lettering), but the debris that marked development scams subsequent to my childhood threw me off the scent.

The 'God bless the Prince of Wales and grant us the Commonwealth Games' era was represented by the Afon Lido, a chlorine-enhanced alternative to the Bristol Channel. You didn't need a prophylactic wetsuit. The old place was looking bleak, hungry for millennial funds. Various low-level, off-highway, leisure punts – parking facilities, acres of reinforced glass, squiggly lettering, sloping Japanese roofs, fast food in a slow culture – colonised an unredeemable wilderness, making it a kind of Neo-Dagenham. The dollar rinse of McDonald's, with its spiky M logo, looked like a triumphalist arch raised by Saddam Hussein. Moulting concrete penguins and an electric-blue Moby Dick with piano key teeth kept frightened juveniles away from the municipal kinder-reserve.

ERSE BEA H H T read the strange legend on the side of the excessively windowed building at the Port Talbot end of the seafront. Was this the HQ of a druid airline? Windows were boxed off with metal panels, chunks of defunct Concordes. Neon tubes fizzed above the door, a spastic cocktail shaker dispensing bad light.

In its pomp the Jersey Beach Hotel had been Mac's unofficial club. It was comfortable, off the map; a Naugahyde banquette in the corner of the lounge bar gave him an uninterrupted view. With the long mirror, if he could penetrate the cigar smoke, he enjoyed the full panorama, no unwelcome visitors would slide through the door.

Mac entertained on a generous scale, councillors and union functionaries, soft-left yes men and Stalinists in shiny suits; they enjoyed a drink, a capful of free chips at the roulette wheel, a ringside seat for the strippers in the pub across the road. What was its name? And why did it remind me of Kaporal? I had to make contact with my rogue researcher. The Landor project was dead, there might be some life on the other side of the Severn. Resurrect Thorpe? Why not?

Le Fag, that was it. An ex-tapas bar (balcony, Spanish arches) had been reclaimed, rinsed with blue-grey emulsion. A poster of

Belmondo in cap and shades from *Breathless*, a garlic jungle, otherwise nothing had changed: the long bar, the stage, blood trodden into sawdust. A yawn of heavies, off-duty armbreakers, nursed slack pints; none of that fizz-sucking nonsense here. The staff were under strict instructions to keep all bottles safely on their own side of the counter.

The locals were the kind (spiders' web tattoos beneath stubble on ridged skulls) who walked in from a sub-Arctic blizzard in jeans and vest. I couldn't risk asking after Mac, nor could I show myself up by ordering anything exotic like a pint of Guinness. I took a dirty glass of ironically named Brain's (short for brain-damaged), and found a seat as far away from the stage as I could get without putting myself on the breakwater. The precaution was sensible. I'd noticed the poster for the swamp music combo who were booked in for the evening, Mametz Wood, and I suspected, rightly as it turned out, that they might be sophisticates who felt the need for rehearsal. The point of indulging these streaks of piss with their ratty hair and running noses was that they could make enough noise to cover up whatever was happening in the back room. Nobody had to make conversation. Fillings jumped in your mouth. Blood ran from your ears.

A woman, who'd had a near miss at getting herself into a grape-and-verdigris boob tube, ambled over, looking for a light. I didn't discourage her. She was on brandy and ginger. Twenty minutes' chat and the ashtray was full, smouldering, our round table planted with little bottles. She wasn't fussed about the ginger. She smoked Park Drive. Four or five hungry pulls before she let the butt go. A very civilised person. For the neighbourhood. The spikes on her dog collar had been given a good polishing.

I was happy to float with it, the on/off monologue that required no audience. I stared out of the window at the empty car park with its LOCALS ONLY (subtitle: Wankers) graffito, the colourless sea.

'Can you think of a colour for the Bristol Channel?' I said. I had my notebook open. She was a seamstress, with the punctured fingers to prove it, an outworker; she designed her own clothes. It hadn't occurred to me that they *were* designed. But I was delighted when she offered a Western-style shirt with pearl buttons, slashed pockets and a picture of William Burroughs on the back. For fifteen quid. Which was very reasonable.

'Endurance,' she said. 'A quality, not a colour. It's what I think of when I look at the sea. Which I don't, not much.'

'True,' I answered, keeping it going. 'Chewing gum parked under a table for years.'

'What about these?' she said, putting one of her hands over mine. 'The nails?'

'The colour?'

'Yes.'

'Pretty much what you're wearing. Nice match.'

'I'm colour blind. Great sense of line. Colours? I've got to hear them. My feller's with the band.'

They were out on the stage, nurdling instruments and amplifiers, arguing amongst themselves about who got them into this gig. Trying, unsuccessfully, for free drinks.

Fortunately, I couldn't see them too well in the half-dark. It was that time of day when strip lighting argues with twilight's last gleam, the odd headlight out on the road. And leaves you feeling sick. 'What's his name?' I asked.

'Nicky,' she said. 'Nicky Lane. He's been through more groups than Jenny Fabian and he's better looking. Fast hands. But every time they're about to land a deal, he makes his excuses. Congenitally modest, Nick. I have to lift the money from his pocket before he shoves it up his nose.'

Nicky Lane, the Sutton Sufi! One of the Capel-y-ffin mob. I hadn't recognised him; beard, moustache and barnet crammed into a Rasta hairbag. But now, watching him smoke, fiddle with the tuning, laugh, drink – Adam's apple bobbing in tensed neck-sock – sure, ok, it *was* Lane. The man.

And what a bunch he had backing him.

The girlfriend had run out of straights and wandered over to the stage to cadge a needle spliff from Lane's bass player. He might have been Nicky's younger brother, wasted with equal dedication, but with a crazier light in his eyes (in their kohl-emphasised brackets). When he bent down to torch the girl's smoke, I saw the fretwork in his arm, the self-carved signature: 4 REAL.

'Who put this lot together?' I asked, when the groupie wiggled back to my table.

'Some local head. Travels in carpets, but gives good future.

Booked a shitload of gigs on the other side – St Paul's, Minehead, Bridgwater. Finishing up, at the bottom of the page, in Glastonbury. They all like Howard. You can trust him, one hundred per cent. Gift of the gab. Does bullshit in that lovely deep voice and you know it's bullshit and he knows it's bullshit, and he knows you know, and that's part of the craic. You're in it with him, he'll never let you down. He's got the connections.'

Howard had assembled – for one night only, at the end of the world in wet Aberavon – a super group of phantoms and revenants and never-weres (alchemised from fanzines, junk sickness, road smegma). He had the hippie bluesman, putative genius Nicky Lane; shuddering through cascading riffs, yowling half-toothed of mysticism, the Old Man of the Mountains; heresies, bayous and bagels.

He had a tall Londoner called Bruce (who for some reason never bothered to change his name) gutting his guitar, but otherwise keeping his back to the room. Bruce was post-punk before punk came along, a stooped stoic in sinister Nazi spex. A noise technician. Bruce looked as if he'd wandered onto the stage to check the amps, adjust the sound levels, and then picked up an instrument, to see what it sounded like.

Bruce – slouched, vulture casual; with cropped head, leather slimjim tie, bondage trousers, polished shoes – was as fast as Lane. Faster. At the climax of some amazing, skull-splintering duel, which gave the audience time to nip home for tea and then come back, he might ghost a grin. But he wouldn't sing. Or speak.

He left all that to the beret, the chocolate-muncher with the complex tattoos and razor runes. The Milky Bar Kid was no musician; he went through the manic motions, but words were his thing. He was East Welsh and it hurt. He was playing to an audience of two (plus armbreakers and barman) and he found it worthwhile to spit like a preacher ridden by an alien spirit. I've seen Methodist blackcoats in their pomp, standing in front of a congregation, running on for hours, to a chorus of responses and affirmations. This boy interrogated himself. Damned himself for his chemical intelligence.

The drummer, a genial alky, wouldn't abandon his new, best mates at the bar, so Howard sat in. He was famous, around Kenfig, Bridgend and the Ogmore Valley, for his Elvis routines. He was launched on 'Jailhouse Rock', the rest of them were somewhere else entirely, when Mac walked in.

I was waiting for the man, so I recognised him at once. He hadn't changed anything except the outer wrappings: a spherical schoolboy in a Paul Smith suit. He looked like one of those old rugby stars on television; chewed up, scar tissue blistering under studio lights, slightly uncomfortable in business drag. He wouldn't spot me, back in the shadows. Keeping company with a woman.

He nodded to the barman and gestured to Howard – who put the sticks down, vacating his place, to follow Mac into the back room. Mac was shadowed by another man who had either outgrown his suit or ordered it, sight unseen, from a Hong Kong catalogue. Colour contradicted texture. The stretched waistcoat had too many buttons, not enough buttonholes.

This lurching associate was all shoulder and belly; he walked like someone who had learnt the skill from a correspondence course. He was trying to remember where to fit his Cuban heels into the white footprints on the diagram.

The hair was wrong. It was wrong on the donkey from whose tail the raw material had been docked. Looking on the bright side, this cowboy would never be run down in the dark.

I walked over to the bar, my young friend was ready for another brandy. I thought that if I placed myself at the optimum angle, I might be able to scope what was going on in the back room. The barman, before I said anything, slid two doubles, the best, the palest stuff, in my direction. 'Mac says if you're not too busy, you should go through and have a drink with him.'

A chair was pulled back, ready. I could look at Mac and his associate and see nothing of what was going on around the stage.

'Long time in the smoke, Norton. You've withered, boy. London's put a print on you. Come home to die, is it? Sorry to hear about your old man. Well respected he was. Fair do's, they gave him a lovely write up in the *Advertiser*.'

'Hello, Mac.'

'You'll want a bit of a favour then?'

'Something like that.'

'You know Howard. Got his own room, so he says, in the Strand

Palace. And this is his boss, down Kenfig. Norrie. Norrie Dikkon the Carpets.'

Would you buy a used carpet from a man who couldn't fit his own rug? The wig, as Dikkon sweated in the whisky heat, slid down his Cro-Magnon forehead. (Think: *Planet of the Apes*.) Norrie was a bad name, a near anagram of noir: Mr Black shapeshifted to another malign disguise.

'We're political in Wales now,' Mac told me. 'Realigned. You're a writer. You should move back, do your bit. I can fix you up with a nice place to live. Quiet. No trouble. I know all the boyos from Yr Academi Cymreig. Grants from here to Christmas. But give me a little bit of help first.'

I didn't like the sound of this, but I smiled and accepted another drink. 'Sure, Mac. Anything you want.'

'Easy as putting down a sick dog. That's all it is, two minutes for a vet. Not worth the call-out.' He nodded to Dikkon who opened his briefcase and whacked a heavy revolver and a box of shells onto the table. 'Politics by other means. You have to be flexible in business these days. You know that better than I do, nobody can get by with one job. Diversification, boy.'

It would have taken someone as skewed as Kaporal to understand Mac's proposal. The old Labour alliances were finished, so the fixer thought, gone with the mines. There was no point in having a union base when there were no workers to pay their dues; no leverage in fixing local party bosses and housing contracts. The game these days was too big for the Cardiff bankers with their first-class tickets to Paddington, their flats in Dolphin Square. Hospital redevelopments, dormitory estates on poisoned land, cronyism; none of the old standards played. This was the age of the facilitator, the man with the numbers. You don't have to get your hands dirty but you know somebody who will. For the right price. Carpets, ex-rental televisions, strip clubs: finished. We've moved into the favour market, dirty tricks, creative villainy, black propaganda – PR. There's no history, it's been forgotten. We improve the present before it happens.

Money men, English gents, non-political (i.e. Liberal), wanted a dog put down, a nuisance frightened off. Was that unreasonable? Obviously, Mac and Dikkon couldn't take care of it personally.

There were Rotary Club lunches, entertainment packages at the Millennium Stadium, rugby shirt concessions, karaoke evenings for sushi-suckers from the trading estate.

The whole thing would take – what? – two or three days. Howard's tour through the West Country was the perfect cover. A pair of lowlifes, artists, had been set up in case bodies were needed to take the fall. They'd act as roadies, drive us over the bridge.

And here they were, right on cue. Mac was shaking my hand, wishing me well, slipping me a few quid. Joblard was getting along famously with Bruce. They had the same interests: drinking, sitting in pubs while the world settled on its axis, sampling sound, over-laying it, cutting it up, distorting it – until Paddington Station became a swarm of chanting Tibetan monks. They understood the parts of a city in which you could lie low, reinvent yourself, incubate covert mischief.

Kwilt was keen to be away, on the road. He leant on the horn of the white Transit, until the whole sorry bunch, musicians, roadies, girl in striped top, Joblard, Marks – and the reluctant narrator – stumbled out into the bitter night.

The bridge again. Faces in the car. Black water.

9

The crown of that silvery head, end-of-season stubble growing out, butted through green water. The swimmer was purple-faced, his red-veined eyes bulged behind tight goggles. Thick skin had been grated into cheesy white flakes. Daily immersion in chlorine-soup was peeling the man. But, week by week, Kaporal had to admit, the attendant was looking better, fitter, less haunted.

Both of them, athlete and spectator, looked better; a little weight gained from regular pub lunches – fish most days; stamina from long afternoon walks. Gayness was not obligatory for hanging out at the pool, but it didn't hurt to cultivate an air of sexual indecision, a wounded past. Which was something Kaporal could play without breaking sweat. Choices of life style were provisional in Appledore; talk, bitching, anecdotes nobody was required to authenticate. There were no predatory shirtlifters, none of the old queens had the energy; shirts, or faded Breton smocks, were worn outside elasticated slacks for the short hike between the 'perfect little white cottage' at the edge of the sea and the bar of the Royal George.

Kaporal decided that Appledore, on the mouth of the Taw, convenient for Barnstaple and the Pannier Market, close enough to Thorpe country to pick up on whispers, was where he would spend the summer. Why not? The Liberals welcomed him. They were very helpful with paperwork, social security payments. He had media contacts, didn't he? Phone numbers in Bristol? He had lunched once with Mike Kustow, in the days when Channel 4 were doing high art.

But Appledore was like rheumatism, it crept up on Kaporal by invisible increments; it slowed him down. He ached. It took him slightly longer, each day, to get moving. Each day he did less work. He'd given up on the tapes. TV reception was lousy, he ran the *Amber Lights* VHS – with the sound off. Or, better, *just* the sound, picture phased as interference, white light. Bits of Lalage's dialogue were mesmeric. How did the director come up with this stuff?

Kaporal made a loop of the German woman saying: 'And where should we go?' Played it back as: 'Anwar shaygo.' 'Wee shah goo.'

What Kaporal did was to walk every morning from his terraced cottage, along the seafront, good weather and bad, to the municipal swimming pool. He didn't, he couldn't, swim; but he could watch and, as he put it, 'exercise by default'. Leathery senior citizens, a fat lady with a bald head, ground out their laps, while Kaporal teased a squirt of lukewarm, coffee-flavoured water from the machine. Then he settled, feet up on a white plastic recliner, with the one Petit small cigar he allowed himself each day.

Barnstaple had run out of yellow. He was making do with limegreen packets, twenties, to save petrol. Sumatra, 100 pc tobacco. E. Nobel (in gilt relief). *By Appointment To The Royal Danish Court.* Overpasted: 'Tobacco Seriously Damages Health.' And on the flip side: 'Smoking causes heart disease.'

Smoking was of course forbidden. In Appledore. Under the grubby corrugated roof. The flooded greenhouse.

The wobblies were too absorbed in the agony of their exercise to take any notice of Kaporal's apostasy. And the attendant, a fanatical non-smoker (recovering dope freak, Kaporal reckoned), didn't see anything he didn't want to see. Which was mostly himself, full-length, bulging suggestively from a striped Edwardian one-piece: down a line of poolside mirrors. Huge hands, huge feet. Wedding tackle awkwardly nested. Like a pecking bird.

This man, who never spoke when he could bark, nodded approvingly as he spotted Kaporal with a copy of *Haunts of the Black Masseur*. The burnt-out researcher waved his tiny cigar in acknowledgment, and a relationship, however tentative and open to revision, was struck. What Kaporal did not reveal was that the jacket of Charles Sprawson's laborious account of man's relationship with water concealed another, slimmer volume beneath: *The Dog*

Who Knew Too Much by Miss Matilda Excellent (a.k.a. Dan Farson). Water, Farson reckoned, was a way of spoiling a good glass of whisky.

Both books had been found in the rented cottage. Farson's campy fable, a coded recasting of the Thorpe scandal, was impenetrable – unlike most of the cast, a swish of ingles and catamites, pub bores and party fixers. What did any of it matter? Thorpe was in retirement, blacked by the charity quangos (strange that he dropped out of the game at the point where Lord Archer got his start, tapping disasters for guilt cheques). The withered public man had been incapacitated by a wasting disease named after a working-class quack who was born in Hoxton Square, east London: James Parkinson. And the victim of the notorious assault on Porlock Hill, Norman Scott, had a new life, somewhere in the West Country, with horses and dogs, silver-framed photographs and stories told too often, stories that would never be told.

This, Kaporal decided, was England. There was nothing he could do about it. The Yanks had Kennedy and we had Rinka the dog, the Great Dane who failed to respond to Norman Scott's heroic kiss of life.

'Norman Scott,' he mused. 'Of course. A *Norman* Scot, one of the Templar bloodlines; Priory of Zion, St Clair, Rosslyn Chapel. The usual suspects. Start anywhere and it keys in a cycle of victims and sacrifices, redemptive crimes, bloodlettings, white chapels.

'Thorpe? Didn't that name suggest the birthplace of the Victorian surgeon Sir William Gull? Thorpe-le-Soken, Essex.'

Farson, who was a relative of Bram Stoker, had been paid to hack out a Ripper book, proving that Gull was not involved: no links to Freemasonry and the Royals. Farson had fingered the fall guy, Montague Druitt. And then found himself, like all the other conspiracy theorists, like Colin Wilson (who is puffed in the foreword to Farson's book as knowing 'more about the subject than anybody' – any body), exiled to the West Country; a remote view of the Bristol Channel. Wagner and a black bag of empties on the porch.

'His brain trembled for a moment,' wrote Farson, 'and he realised what he had done. He revealed this knowledge in papers left for his brother William, and then took his own appalled and appalling life.'

What if Farson, in his turn, had left papers among the boxes in his white cottage? The pattern never changes: once again the Establishment, in the person of Thorpe (removed from the scene as Gull was removed to a private hospital), confronts a whistle-blower, a tale teller, and is supposedly caught up in a plot to silence an insignificant, socially defenceless pest. Once again a smokescreen of atrocious, theatrically staged crimes, murders and suicides, disguises the main event. Trashy books, wild accusations pour from the presses. Forged journals are discovered, the Roger Casement scenario: sex scandals to divert attention from the brutal realpolitik of the state.

Kaporal drew the acrid, slightly sugary smoke deep into his lungs. His nominated exercise-substitute, the swimmer known as Dryf, ploughed the pool, rising and falling in a desperate breast-stroke; teeth gritted, taking in water, battering his lengths like a man trying to run, face down, through a liquid nightmare. Kaporal (think: *The Sorcerers*) relished every nuance of the anguish Dryfeld endured on his behalf.

That was when, after Dryf retired to towel himself down, and Kaporal had the building to himself, the memory door opened.

The researcher hauled himself up from his lounger. He stood at the edge of the pool, about to send his cigar stub – with a practised flick of the first finger – arcing across the rippling water, all for that small, satisfying fizz as the hot tip was extinguished.

It happened.

He drew away from himself, the consciousness of his being in this place. He was trapped, heart in mouth, between Appledore and somewhere that was not Appledore, had never been Appledore. For the first time in months, he lost it entirely. The connection with Lalage's film. He was no longer an unseen participant, the ghost in the frame. Life wasn't fated, wasn't scripted by a troubled man smoking small cigars in a north London bunker.

An ugly bucket chair cast its outline onto the wave patterns of the pool, the unsteady aftermath of Dryfeld's thrashing breaststroke. The attendant, emerging from his cabin, in yellow silk shirt and cranberry kecks, moving across the radiant lozenge of light, had Kaporal transfixed. Dryfeld's head, with its shocked mercury stubble, became a floating signifier, a moon. The elements of the scene – moon, shadow of chair, reflected shape of the handle with which swimmers hauled themselves out of the water – disturbed Kaporal. He spoke of this vision, when he exploited it, years later, in a film of his own, as 'a memory door'. It was nothing of the sort.

What was there to remember, to reinvent? Childhood, when he forced himself to think of it, was an album of badly chosen locations, faces he didn't recognise. It was the journey between two places where he didn't want to be; long hours staring at dull fields, avoiding his reflection in a dirty window. Childhood was waiting anxiously for the sound of a car, sitting on a cabin trunk in an empty gym.

The epiphany in the Appledore swimming pool – haunting, emblematic, arbitrary – was of a different order. It carried Kaporal towards the reading of time as a recurring carousel of images. The brash yellow of a young girl's rucksack on Margate Sands. The sick orange of the kerb in a small town in west Texas, driven through, after a sleepless night in a motel that smelt of drains. A poet's white suit in a hot garden. A wire basket filled with broken statuary, chipped hands, under the Heathrow flightpath, on a walk from West Drayton to his caravan.

These were not true memories. He could reassemble them in any order, fabricate any story that took his fancy. They belonged as much to the archives as to his own experience.

What the scene needed was a woman. Without one, a slender figure passing across the diamond of sunlight, Kaporal's meditation wouldn't play. The tarot dealt him the wrong card.

He wanted a woman, he saw a woman. Towel roll under her arm, toddler hanging on to her long skirts. The pool was open to the public. You could hear the noise, the amplified squeals and slaps and lost shoes, the West Country voices. It was time for Kaporal and Dryfeld to pick up their books and move on.

Down at the Royal, doorway still draped with black crepe, the Farson wake was running into its third month. Dryfeld fisted his usual orange juice, Kaporal nursed a bottle of sweet German wine. They were easy, at a window table, staring out at the milky estuary, enjoying the melancholy notes of the sea bell, the sardony of distant horns. It was good to be out of the story, off the case. If only – it was a source of deep regret – they were capable of staying shtum, keeping their heads down, sticking with the slow rhythm of the days: pool, harbour walk, pub, doze, pub again. Both of them, without admitting it, to the other or even to themselves, were bollocksed, done up by futile ambition: the compulsion to write a novel.

Dryfeld lived a life that was better, faster, heavier with contradiction, slapstick, perversion and petty tragedy, than any ten works of contemporary fiction. He was costive with content. But he couldn't open his mouth without pitching a synopsis. Men in dirty raincoats followed him around with open notebooks. Street-market scufflers secretly taped his monologues and turned them into concrete poetry. Journalists risked feeding him mung beans and seaweed shavings, until the trumpetings of his belly-compost blew them across the restaurant, on the off-chance of buffing up a profile for the *Guardian*; another English nutter. Blocked hacks, who hadn't come up with an original idea in years, willingly drove him from Totnes to Lincoln, in the hope that he'd pitch a legend of insider dealing, sexual high jinks, conspiracy and suicide. Dryfeld's mistake was to start believing his own bullshit. He decided to copyright eccentricity, peddle his image to the media. In return, they offered a gnat's blink of fame, then banished him as a pest who didn't know when it was time to pick up his coat and slip out by the tradesman's entrance.

Kaporal was excited by Dryf's rantings, the way he spat out chunks of bread roll and pounded the table. Dryf rekindled latent desires that Kaporal never admitted to harbouring: get it down, all of it, these contradictory fragments. Invent a conclusion. That was the thing with Dryfeld: manic excitement redlining midwinter depression.

'Three jugs of inky coffee and I was busting for a pee. Bookshops assume you don't, or that you've developed a superglued bladder. Chucked the flowers in the bin and filled the vase as soon as he locked me into the private room. Sneaked upstairs where the offices are and that's where I found the torture chamber, the rack, the whipping horse. No discounts without a trade card.'

Kaporal had no idea who Dryf was talking about. He had zero interest in antiquarian bookshops or superannuated dealers. Becky,

Silverfish, the Portsmouth transvestite, the Corby Clamp and the one who follows you around asking what you want (answer: to be left alone): none of these figures had the remotest attraction for the M4 researcher. He swallowed Dryfeld's vitriol, hoping that sooner or later the motormouth would run out of steam and bring the story back to Farson.

'Basically, I came to Appledore for the golf. Wouldn't know one end of a stick from the other. But the books fetch a premium. Memorabilia, Bernard Darwin, menus, commemorative teaspoons, can't get enough of them. I bunk in with a couple who collect, pay cash. *In advance.*'

The nice thing about Dryfeld was that you didn't need to prompt him, you sat back and waited. Kaporal watched, out of the corner of his eye, while a Farson disciple, brick-red, baggy shirt in deckchair material, shunted an unsuspecting tourist towards the corner table. 'Sit there. I'll order. You'd never manage the patois. What? Couple of bottles of fizz to start?'

'Flis decided to cook a herb omelette.' Dryf was on a roll. 'Don't know what time it was, early, around three or four in the morning. I turned up on the bike. We were in the kitchen, books out on the table, knife and fork at the ready – Athol hears a noise in the wine cellar. Fetches a torch and we go down together. He gave me a club to carry, a driver. And there it was, a brick sliding out on its own! Then another. We see this arm, toothpaste-stripe shirt, identity bracelet. "It's fucking Farson," Athol shouted. Grabbed my wrist, before I could give the bugger a smack.'

'Did they know Farson?' Kaporal couldn't help himself. He had to find a way to sneak a look at the old drunk's papers. He knew there'd be nothing worth finding. The Limehouse exile had sold every scrap he had and most of it twice over. Music hall, Soho, murder, celebrity tittle-tattle, holiday snaps, he'd peddled the lot. He was a credit to his profession. He could cobble a book out of a three-hour lunch and write it in less time than he spent at the table.

'What did Athol do?' Kaporal asked.

'Laughed and shook Farson's hand,' Dryf said. 'They thought he had a bit of a thirst, but, all things considered, was a decent cove. Dan was barred from all the local pubs. They invited the old sot round. He polished off my omelette and kept us amused until

breakfast, when Flis did a huge fry-up. Fell asleep at the table. Left
his carrier bag behind, the book he was working on. Three days
later they found him dead.'

Farson, Kaporal decided, was one of those who never sat down in
a pub without having a photographer on call. He wasn't bad with
the Leica himself, not if his subjects enjoyed a drink: Kingsley
Amis in Swansea, Brendan Behan anywhere. Photography wasn't an
art, it was inspired accident and a good printer. But unlike so many
of the journeymen who defaced their work by scribbling their
autographs all over the margins, Farson was a modest man. He
didn't bleat about having his name above the title. He took useful
snaps that reminded him of where he had been and who he was
supposed to be writing about. An aide-mémoire for an expense
account.

Dryfeld's carrier bag, when Kaporal opened it, having purchased
it sight unseen, was disappointing. A few late photographs; Farson,
ruddier than the leatherette sofa on which he's sprawled, boozing
with Gilbert and George. Why are those pub tables so small? Three
or four hours into a session and there's no room to fit the glasses.

The notes for the Gilbert and George book were rudimentary.
Hotel bills, cab receipts. Nothing of interest in the pink folders.

'Walking is hell,' Farson had written. 'If it wasn't for the dog, I'd
never get out of bed. I hate being old. Apart from my prostate, up
several times in the night, I'm quite fit. But the dreams are so
hideous I fear sleep. Last night I was wandering through a landscape
redolent of Munch; moorland, a hill I laboured to climb. There was
a meeting for which I was late. In Barnstaple. With Thorpe. He
begged me, yet again, tears in his eyes, to appear as a witness at the
trial, to reveal what I knew about Scott. The whole truth. That
man is extraordinary. He believes what he wants to believe.

'Money was available for a book, Thorpe boasted, a vanity press
in London, media friendly. I could make up a story about the dog.
I liked animals, didn't I?

'Nothing had happened, nobody had been threatened. I'd get
the jump on the other hacks. I'd write my book *before* the conspiracy unfolded, before the hitmen were hired.'

Kaporal put down the folder, walked into the garden. He liked

Appledore and he would be sorry to give it up, but Farson's dream struck him as prophetic. Whatever it was that he had been circling for all these months was about to occur. And he knew *where*, it was in the book, the notes that preceded the book. Porlock and the steep hill that led up to Porlock Common. Scott's Great Dane was Jeremy Thorpe's albatross.

'The dog was excited,' Farson wrote. 'I could hardly hold him. He'd picked up a trail. Stink like crusty arseholes, shit in the bed.

'Moors on one side, sea on the other, thick, wet darkness – and the dog stops. Stops dead. Won't take another step. The thing he's chasing halts too, turns. Its eyes! Hurt. Unable to blink. Thorpe's eyes.

'I wake up drenched in sweat. No sound in the room. I brave the cold to make a cup of hot lemon tea. Open the curtains to noth-ingness, the fret of a never-ending night. I run my hands through the dog's warm hair as she lies panting beside me.'

The noise was excruciating. Jos Kaporal, after months of estuarine hibernation, was sensitive to it. The side windows of his royal-blue Mondeo shuddered in their slots. He'd hung on to the BBC car and the mobile (which was now dead). He'd been squeezed, by a badly parked Transit, into the only available niche, alongside the Castle pub in Porlock.

In self-defence (know your enemy), Kaporal completed a break-down of the elements that constituted his acoustic torment. A pub band made up of disparate, irreconcilable parts (rate them at around the threshold of physical pain, 120/130 decibels). A mob of drunks larging it, howling to make themselves heard above the drum and bass; men shouting in each other's faces, women screeching with jack-hammer laughter (110 decibels). Projectile vomiting, pres-sure-hose micturation, gurgling water pipes, rushing conduits, beer pumps, grumbling cisterns, clinking glasses. Spike heels piercing rotten floorboards, hobnail boots striking sparks from fancy tiles (80/90 decibels). A large dog barking, its face pressed against the windscreen of the Transit (70 decibels). TV sets in which sound levels rise and fall against the baffle of Porlock Hill. Vats of hot fat sizzling in the chip shop. Yelps and sighs and mews and long-delayed roars of lovemaking – in beds, cars, caravans, kitchens,

churchyards, and, in one case, a kennel (60 decibels). A camper van
straining on the brow of the hill (50 decibels). Dialogue between a
man who has decided not to leave his wife and the wife who
wishes he would (40 decibels). The cicada tick of Kaporal's Swatch,
the synchronised beat of his heart (20 decibels). Caterpillars
munching. Slugs balancing on droopy hostas. A rook shifting from
claw to claw in a dead elm (10 decibels).

And something gross, formless, at the limits of audibility: the
sepia drone of a Brummie with a doctorate in boredom, GBH of
the tympanic membrane. He has nothing to say and can't stop
saying it. And Kaporal, the compulsive auditor, can't stop himself
tuning in, sifting meaning from headache preliminaries.

I saw the face at the window, put it down to the drink, then had
the hallucination confirmed: as Kaporal, older, greyer, tighter-
skinned, backlit by a passing car, froze in the pub doorway. He
looked like George Best, back from the dead, feeling his way down
overlit stairs at some awards ceremony. Shock waves were palpable
as he recognised me, the man whose story he was supposed to be
telling: his paymaster. He didn't miss a beat as he worked his way
through the crowd, finessing the presentation he would offer in lieu
of the missing tapes. No excuses were asked for or offered. I welcomed the man. He might drown out Bad News Mutton and the
sullen Humpp.

I wriggled in my seat, shifting to a position in which the gun
stuffed into the waistband of my trousers would lie more comfortably against my hip joint. Kwilt reckoned that this was the night.
He and Joblard had some guy who lived up on Exmoor pinioned
between them at the bar; his dog had been left in the van. Kwilt
was waiting for the word. Joblard was waiting for another round.
Nicky Lane and the boys stormed on, unshamed by the lumpen
yobbery of their audience.

'Your books, man,' Bad News shouted, 'no fucker can tell them
apart.' The Ketamine Kreeps had tracked Lane's band, Mametz
Wood, down the coast from Bristol. They'd picked up the scent at
the Aust Services coffee shop. Bad News wanted to sit in, he had
his guitar under the bench. Lane was too canny. He encouraged
the errant bluesman to talk me through the conclusions of his

definitively aborted thesis: 'W.G. Sebald, Andrew Norton: A
Heritage of Malfate.'

'Don't you have any imagination?' the Brummie droned, tempt-
ing me to imagine him, face down in wet concrete with a heavy
roller smoothing out his creases. 'Every novel starts with a stalled
car, a squabble of bookdealers. What are you, a fucking Catholic?
What's with this three-part structure? One: lowlifes running
around, getting nowhere. Two: a baggy central section investigating
'place', faking at poetry, genre tricks, and a spurious narrative
which proves incapable of resolution. Three: *quelle surprise*. A walk
in the wilderness. What a cop-out, man!

'Your women are a joke and you can't do working-class. Or
blacks or Jews or immigrants of any kind. As for kids – where are
they? Frightened of being taken for a nonce?

'You rely on portentous hints, bits and pieces stolen from better
writers. The ethics are shit. You think you were satirising Thatcher?
You were celebrating the bitch, delighting in the ruined riverscape.
The worse it got, the better you liked it. That's an elitist programme, man. You've become part of the accepted apparatus of
disapproval, the so-called – lily-livered, sponsored by Beck's –
counterculture. The rest of us, man, resolute non-metropolitans,
have learnt, in the Age of the Floating Signifier, not to believe that
things are what people say they are.'

It wasn't, despite Humpp's sarcastic snorts, a bad riff. I'd read
much worse in the broadsheets (at least Mutton didn't bang on
about verbless sentences), but the white-lipped alky was only just
coming up to speed. I felt as if I were trapped in some off-piste
New University in the Midlands, taking a kicking from a sixties
harridan, a born-again slapper who had run through the catalogue
of bad behaviour and was now taking revenge on white-world
daddies who soaked up attention that should rightly be hers.

'Get 'em in, B.N., you're starting to dribble,' Humpp said,
scratching at a parasite that had come to life beneath his Ketamine
Kreeps T-shirt.

'Let me,' I said, as I doubled over in an effort to stop the revolver
dropping onto the floor. I was quite ready to walk up behind
Thorpe's chum, the Exmoor man; then, while Kwilt and Joblard
pinned his arms, to take out Mac's gun and blow off the top of his

head. I'd be doing us both a favour. He'd be released from his role in an increasingly clapped-out narrative and I would abjure my claim to be the author of my own story. Give it to the judiciary. It worked for Thorpe. There's always an interesting afterlife for the publicly shamed. Their biographies are ghosted. The past is improved as it is trampled over by researchers – sponsored by clients who insist upon cliffhangers, punchlines, conclusions. Thesis writers are forced to drag in chunks of Walter Benjamin and the French boys, brand-name intellectual franchises unknown to the victim. Impoverished grubs tease out sex scandals. Why there haven't been any. What's he trying to hide?

Piss on the confidence men and before the stain dries, doughty souls will be rushing to their defence. Nobility in defeat. Courage of their convictions. A gong for Profumo. Dig it *all* up, the dirt. That was gist of Mutton's thesis. You're doing them a favour, son. The writer needs to look very closely at the source of his obsession. He envies the glamour of the guilty man, the charisma. The novelist (in this case) is a nasty piece of work, living vicariously, incapable of separating truth and fiction.

Kwilt wasn't there. Neither was Joblard. Neither was the slightly foxed young man from the moors. The Porlock mob sealed the gap like proud flesh around a wound. It was on. The signal must have been given. I was released from my contract with Mac.

'Another brandy, sir?'

'I'll take the bottle.'

It was B.N.'s lucky night. With the noise coming from Lane and his boys, you'd never hear the shots. They could butcher the sad fuck in the karsy, with Kwilt's machete, and it would sound like a first solo by the preternaturally morose (one name) Bruce.

'Too many Ks, wasn't it?' said the man at the end of the bar. Howard Marks, toking on a jumbo spliff, was foot-tapping along with the band. He was the only person in the room who was totally relaxed, present through absence; a bent Illuminati in a beach shirt with compulsory gold-chain trim. 'Too late now, see. They thought your mate, that bloke Kaporal, was the signal for the off.'

'What off?' I asked.

'Who cares?' Howard laughed. 'These boys, they take everything for a sign. They were expecting a man, a message. All the Ks, see. Kwilt, Ketamine Kreeps, now this Kaporal. KKK. Ku Klux Kunts. What a fucking freakshow!'

He was right. It was coming apart. I thought I was tracing a palimpsest of David Jones, the *Mabinogion* and classic Welsh mythology, and found myself, up to the oxters, in Mickey Spillane.

I thought of the dog's face in the dream, in the Transit, staring out at me. And I remembered what happened at Arthur's Quoit. Thorpe's friend, the young man from the moors, could look after himself. He'd be taking calls from Max Clifford and Murdoch's jackals before he'd wiped Rinka's brains off his Barbour.

I moved rapidly across the contours of the sound-map, from Nicholas Lane and Mametz Wood, the bar, the Dionysiac thumps and screams that tracked me into the night, the throbbing silence of the town. The Transit was still there, unlit. I couldn't see the dog, but I could hear it panting and scratching against the rear doors. I tried them; maybe I could force them open. Release the animal. Take off, find Kaporal.

The doors weren't locked. The dog didn't bark. I hauled myself up into the van. There were no windows. The doors slammed shut. Someone hammered on the roof. The engine started and the van pulled away, crashing through the gears as it struggled with Porlock Hill.

Joblard, who had a weakness for theatrical effects, illuminated his face with a torch held in his lap. He winked. Cheap *film noir* lighting turned the smooth mask into a craggy landscape. The nose was huge and twisted. The eyes, in their shadowy pits, were ice. And the hair, a thatch of silver needles, looked as if it had been gelled with Viagra.

This was my Frank 'Mad Axeman' Mitchell moment. The switch. The hole in your stomach when you feel as if you've fallen down the lift shaft of Canary Wharf Tower. Joblard, the boy from the Elephant, as Albert Donaghue ('Henchman and Final Betrayer'). Kwilt, seated beside him, hatchet-headed, gun in hand, was Freddie Foreman, the fearsome enforcer; the mechanic who tidied up after the Krays, took care of business while the Twins were fannying around the clubland circuit.

Remember the rumours? When Foreman's associates, down in the country, performed their own crude autopsy, retrieving the bullets from Mitchell's head, they found a brain-jelly you could cup in a child's hand.

'The size of a d-d-donkey,' Joblard said, patting the dog. 'He'll take some burying. I hope you've brought your bucket and spade.'

The stutter was going, gone. That sound was the chattering of my teeth. Bad News had got it wrong. My obsession with the number three had nothing to do with Catholic doctrine, the Trinity. It was superstition; two men walking down a road will conjure the presence of a phantom third, the secret auditor. Three men sitting in a van are an argument about which one is redundant. Who will be eliminated, so that the world can retain its necessary balance, the play of contraries.

My doctrine of the three interconnected spheres derived from Dr Dee and Agrippa, Hermes Trismegistus: an elemental world of chancers and clowns, a celestial world of astrology and alchemy, a supercelestial world in which, through communication with the spirits, a true understanding of the relation of things is achieved. The mysteries become transparent and the faces of the dead are lit with numinous radiance.

The conceptual brownness of the Brummie boys, the Ketamine Kreeps, led me back to Bruno. Giordano Bruno, his missionary enterprise; a Hermetic faith, love and magic and the grand curvature of everything. Ending in repression, torture, death. Bruno or Bruin. The ancient bear, lumbering and shaggy, baited by dogs. The bear that was a star, an archetype: Arthur. The collared bear scratched into the surface of a window in Southwark. The bear that David Jones, a sick child, saw from his bedroom. His first crayon drawing.

Fear provoked glossolalia.

Joblard on a beach, an attaché case in his left hand, a coypu, suspended by the tail, in the other. Joblard edging his way across a limestone cliff, searching for the Paviland Cave, the bones of the Red Woman of Gower. Gower the poet memorialised in St Saviour's, Southwark. South Walk. The tramp Joblard on a bench. Joblard, hands in pockets, at the grave of Sir William Gull. Joblard, Job. Torments still to come.

The Transit was never going to make it up the hill. Kwilt was humming. Joblard tapped out a rhythm on his knees. The sack I was sitting on started to move, to groan. Joblard kicked it. We pulled off the road, the engine was still running.

'Dump the bugger, over the crown of the hill. Traffic out of Lynton will take care of him,' Kwilt said.

'Hang him from the signpost like the man wanted. By the heels, under the Countisbury/Lynmouth arm.' Joblard fancied a touch of ceremony.

While they argued, the Great Dane whined and sniffed at the damp patches on the sack. Joblard passed me the torch. I swept the beam around the parking place. Somewhere behind me I could hear the sea.

Bad News had been right about one thing, the Landor novel was a disaster. Landor with his senatorial fantasies, his withdrawal from the world, with a few books and a stout stick, was a kind of Prospero. Llanthony was an island with plenty of aboriginal Calibans to provoke him. Prudence, if I'd had more wit, should have been presented as an elective daughter, a Miranda. Instead, through her repeated disappearances, she was revealed as a literary device; a figure that symbolised virtue in an anaemic masque. Virtue with the smell of onions on her hands.

Thorn trees with a frosting of white blossom. Deep red earth. Springy turf cropped by sheep whose eyes flashed demonically in the beam of my torch. Joblard and Kwilt were going head to head over the fate of their unfortunate cargo. What would happen to the witnesses – when it was over? The writer and the dog? Our destinies, I understood, were linked. They'd never let us walk away.

I'd shot a rabbit, a couple of crows, a bucketful of frogs, and I had them all on my conscience. Could two men be any worse? Struggling to pull the revolver from my waistband, where it had snagged, I was more likely to blast off my own foot.

Lights came on. We behaved like nightclub villains caught in a strobe. The lights went out. I cocked the gun and fired, heard the shot ricochet off the signpost with a loud ping. Compensating, I aimed too low and heard Joblard swear. The second bullet ploughed into the ground.

The lights came on again. A car. Joblard was hopping up and

down. He'd been hit in the foot by a shot that must have passed straight through the sack, which was soaked with blood.

'Get in, get in,' Kaporal was shouting. He moved across the throw of his headlights, camcorder low on the hip, aping the style that his mentor Jamie Lalage had made famous. The whole crazy scene, nobody saying anything, random gunfire, wrong man shot, was a homage to Lalage's 'lost' masterpiece, *Russian Dolls*. He'd shot it in Leningrad with a cast of KGB stringers, local hookers, Czech surrealists – with guest appearances by Jean-Pierre Melville and Francis Stuart. You'd have to go to a long way east of Minsk, if it still existed, to find a copy of the deleted video.

This comedy, the unseen driver trying to get some purchase for the spinning wheels of the Transit, was a reprise of the final scene of Lalage's *Amber Lights*. Kaporal had lost the plot. He hadn't kept up with current theory. A person called Darke, in an essay in *Film Comment* (retitled 'Named & Jamed' by Soho wits), suggested that Lalage's aesthetic freedom was purchased at the price of political naïvety. It was time for *Amber Lights* to be studied from a post-feminist perspective – which would demonstrate, conclusively, that most of the credit should go to the editor, a fast-handed woman who had been left to improvise, during the period when Lalage was 'off colour'.

In the face of the critical neglect that followed Darke's polemic, Lalage retreated to his bunker, leaving his editor to shoot and record the last days of *Amber Lights*. The man had *never* been on the road. He'd been on the telephone. Kaporal's transit of the M4/M5 axis was a big mistake, first to last.

The Transit bucked, rocking in an ever-deepening groove, going nowhere. And Kaporal kept on shooting, doing a Borges, making a new work by precisely re-creating Lalage's script. Everything happens twice but it's never the same.

I grabbed the dog's collar, dragged the beast with me towards Kaporal's car. The shoot-out was unreal. It didn't count. It was like a bar-room brawl with balsawood chairs and bottles made from sugar. You can't die unseen. It might be another dog, another coypu, in the sack.

The keys were in the ignition. The dog sat, panting, beside me in the front seat. 'Put your foot down, boss,' he said. 'Don't hang about, forgive the pun.' Even the Great Dane had an accent that was closer to Smethwick than Elsinore. Maybe it was the length of the beast, the rings in its ears, but its voice reminded me of a photographer I'd worked with in the past, a man called Axel Turner. What was it that was supposed to happen, first time as tragedy, second time as farce?

We hit the road. In the rearview mirror I could see Kwilt and the limping Joblard shoving at the Transit. I cut the lights. Let them figure out which way we would take; across the moors in the direction of Exford, down to Porlock, or on along the coast road.

When in doubt, go west.

I put the headlights on full beam. 'Swing over, four-eyes,' barked the dog.

'Belt up,' I snarled as White Fang slammed his snout against the windscreen. (Think: *Lassie: The Road Back*. In which our hero is 'dogged' by amnesia, after being struck by a car – while trying to rescue a small girl.)

A woman, arms aloft, was straddling the thin yellow line; waving us down. The power of the beams threw her shadow back down the road. A negative of *Kiss Me Deadly*, the movie, not the book. My reflexes were shot, I was haemorrhaging film clips. An asylum runaway, Secret State conspiracies, nuclear secrets, a quarrel of character actors meeting grisly ends: if I remembered Robert Aldrich's plot. A rhythmic sequence cut between squealing tyres on the Californian coast road, headlights sweeping out of blind curves.

I wrenched the wheel over, felt the rear end start to slide, brought it out with a splash of power and almost ran up the side of the cliff as the car fishtailed. The brakes bit in, gouging a furrow in the shoulder, then jumped to the pavement and held.

So wrote Mickey Spillane. I couldn't match his dash, the way he ran those slurpy 'sh' sounds (splash/fishtailed/shoulder). *A damn-fool crazy Viking dame with holes in her head.* What a pro. You can't do prose like that without an old-fashioned typewriter, a Remington. Every sentence carried an invisible exclamation mark. Spillane had mastered the Zen art of converting capital letter prose into lower case.

But this woman was the reverse of Spillane's short-lived escapee, a Nordic goddess dressed in white. Cloris Leachman. This woman had black coat that shone, glistened against the saturated fields.

She wasn't going to budge.

As I wrenched the wheel over, felt the rear end slide, braced myself against impact, I saw her face. Pictured her as Prudence.

Then the sickening bump.

Loose chippings. Thorn bushes. Nothing on which the wheels can grip. Losing it, bucking over short fast grass.

Read it that way: that I should, through the exigencies of the plot, commit an act for which I had already been charged and found guilty. I must kill the woman who provided the motivation, the only drive in my narrative. Kill her again.

Damage her legs with a glancing blow from the skidding car; so that she hobbles, staggers towards the edge of the abyss.

I lost control. I couldn't remember if I was supposed to turn into the skid or fight it. 'You're taking pathetic fallacy too literally, squire,' said the dog. '*Sturm und Drang* went out with Goethe.'

Headlights raked a black sea; signalling, like wreckers of old, to nightcruising oil tankers. There was nothing under our wheels; salt air, a perfectly still night. A lightboard of stars.

A chance to develop a theory of flight.

I wondered if Mac, waiting in the bar of the Jersey Beach Hotel, on the other side of the Channel, would get my message. The bright wink of acknowledgment. Task concluded. I counted them out; leaving the return count to a better man.

Book Three

RESURRECTION AND IMMORTALITY

'None of us has anything to hide.'
— Jeremy Thorpe

BOOK THREE

RESURRECTION

IMMORTALITY

'None of us has anything to hide.'
Jeremy Thorpe

1

I remember the day they brought my father a foot in a box, a club foot. And how well he took it. This, you might think, would be just the kind of incident he could work up into a serviceable after-dinner anecdote. But, no. The story of the foot and the man who left it to him was kept in the family.

After he died (my mother too), their house with all its curious contrivances — rooms within rooms, garage makeovers, blow-heaters scorching dust and sweating paper-covered breeze blocks — passed into other hands. After the two funerals, and our luck in finally disposing of the freakish place in the middle of a slump, we got a call from the local police.

It wasn't the foot. That, I understood, had been cremated with all the proper documentation: a bequest that couldn't, legally or morally, be refused. The foot had received a better send-off than the rest of the man; the Tupperware box in which it had arrived, freshly amputated by a forensic surgeon, replaced by a pine casket with a small inscription on a brass plate. Name, date and a tag from Henry Vaughan: *As strange an object brought.*

The bereavement technicians in their short black jackets must have wondered what they were dealing with, what thing had been set on display, before disappearing on rollers through the curtains into darkness, the furnace, the bone-crushing machines. Too old to be a child, a stillborn infant: the dates didn't fit. This dwarfish lump was more than sixty years old. They thought of *The X Files* and wished their white gloves were made from asbestos. They

imagined, instead of this bruised and bulbous drumstick of bone
and tissue, a perfect miniature, an homunculus with eyes like lapis
lazuli disks.

The police had been summoned because of the partial skeleton
found in the garden shed. A junk dealer with a wallet of trade cards
had taken the contract to clear the place. He'd managed the house,
but given up on the sheds with their mounds of rusting tools,
brown bottles, sacks of old magazines, card photographs of forgotten ancestors. The upwardly mobile retirees, who were trying to
clear a space for their edging irons, powered handsaws and telescopic tree pruners, were appalled to discover a sack filled with
bones, an articulated skull. They feared Satanism, serial killers,
Health Service vampires. The truth was soon established.
Mementos of an Aberdeen medical student. An anonymous
Chinese or Indian man (or collection of men), pickled, wired and
assembled for export. No exorcism was required.

I don't know why I thought of that foot. The original owner
had still been alive, limping around town, obsessively collecting and
washing milk bottles, when I set out for Llanthony Priory in a car
owned and driven by a medical student, Francis Vaughan. It was my
first visit. Frank lived in the same town, his father was the other GP;
we had been to the same school.

Why, I wondered, wondered now, not then, did this melancholy man with the inward-twisting boot, pack the padlocked,
razor-wired passage down the side of his house with shining milk
bottles? Why did his front room disappear under bundles of
newsprint? He sat on chairs made from slithery blocks, back numbers of the *Guardian*. He slept on a pink couch, supplements of the
Western Mail. He wouldn't have radio or television indoors. They
leaked, so he believed, while he slept. They indoctrinated him
with alien whispers. Bottles must be scoured so that the watchers
couldn't lift his fingerprints. Newspapers, properly evaluated, when
you learnt to break the code, were replete with messages from the
secret masters, the Illuminati.

Mr Ford smelt sour. Milk had got into his skin. His thick lenses
were filmy. His breath fierce. Like chlorine. He knew they were out
to get him. He was living on borrowed time.

Frank, on an Easter break from Cambridge, suggested a walk. He knew a place. I'd never been much of a walker, but I was up for the drive, a breath of air. This excursion to some ruin on the border-land afforded the time, staring out of the car window, to brood on the contradictory impulses that landscape provoked in me. Vaughan was the first provocation: by training a scientist, by inheritance a Lloyd George Liberal, a true Celt. By recent inclination, a poet.

'The truth has lately been / Welsh & smoke-laden & endlessly local,' he intoned, quoting some Cantab genius they were doing that season. I could hear the ampersands, rattling like pills in a small plastic bottle. This was a new kind of verse, conversational, horribly sure of itself and its doubts, negative capability in spades. No more Dylan Thomas, no more water beads; no incantations, no belly-banging rhetoric. Bad news for bards. It wasn't compulsory, so Frank said, to drink yourself to death or to behave badly in pubs. Which, careerwise, was quite a relief.

'The poet,' Frank told me, as we dawdled through the infinitely dull suburbs of my birth city, Cardiff, 'no longer insists on domi-nating the foreground of the poem. He hears, if you like, a voice in the next room. And he interrogates it.' I had no idea what he meant, but it didn't sound too painful. The reading list was more problematic: a lot of French names, books on trade routes, anti-psychiatry, ethno-politics, whaling records, glaciation, Mayan glyphs, toxicology and baseball. 'The path to the truth,' Frank blus-tered, 'detours through the small print, the innocuous detail. Read everything, trust nothing.'

I'd been to Abergavenny before, with minibus sportsmen, oxy-moronic combinations, such as a Bridgend hockey team. We were always slaughtered, but in pleasant surroundings. A bluebell-scented backdrop you noticed as you picked the white ball out of the net for the eighth time. The country beyond the Seven Hills – sugar loafs, ice-carved altars, mammary outcrops – was a new thing: deep green lanes, high-hedged, dawdling up a wooded river valley.

Frank namechecked long-eared owls and lesser spotted wood-peckers, wild flowers in the spring verges. I might be pushing a fancy here, but I believe it was Good Friday. We were between showers; the late-morning sun, breaking through fast clouds, pol-ished dewdrops caught on spears of grass.

I'd have been happy to sit for a few minutes in the car park, beside the small chapel at Llanthony, with the window open; in silence. But Frank was already out and bustling, pulling on well-dubbin'd climbing boots.

'Certaine Divine Raies breacke out of the Soul in adversity, like sparks of fire out of the afflicted flint,' he recited. 'That's my great predecessor, Vaughan the Silurist. Half of a pair of twins. You can't set foot on these sacred hills without making obeisance to his quest-ing spirit.'

We didn't hang about admiring columns of stone, the neuras-thenic beauty of a place with no practical purpose. Frank had little sympathy for Neo-Romanticism and its pale washes. 'Reactionary tosh, moons and herons and impotent kings,' he snapped, vaulting the monastery wall and setting off at a clip towards a stream we'd have to wade through or take at a run.

The lower slopes were deceptively easy, the going soft; when we paused, by the stile that led into the wood, I looked back. The priory, with its arches and jagged, ivy-clad stacks, was unfinished; a sentence the monks lacked the wit to complete. Patches of yellow and greeny-white mould flattered dull slabs with the patina of antiquity. Mean slits in the tower demonstrated the fact that this structure had been built for defence. But the thing from the forest had undone them all the same.

Frank was getting away from me, jumping from outcrop to out-crop. I remembered why I didn't like walking, it was unnatural. You sweated, panted, gasped for breath. My antipathy went back a long way. I was a small scrubbed child in shoes that were too tight. We had to make an epic journey, every Sunday morning, down the hill, along Talbot Street with its windows of uninhabited clothes, past the eccentric town hall and its U-boat clock tower. Past the black, bayonet-wielding soldier on the war memorial. Dragging and flinching every inch of the way, shadowing the rusty Llynfi rivulet to the lower town, to Garth.

Frank had a bigger house; part of it, with access to the street, set aside for his father's surgery – which Frank was due, one day, to inherit. The garden was as big as the town park; walks, lawns, coppices, vegetable patches, fish ponds. Bringing a cullender of freshly picked raspberries into the kitchen, hands honourably scratched, we tipped the red fruit out on copies of an exotically radical publication known as the *New Statesman*. In the living room was a collection of green plaster frogs.

What I couldn't cope with, even then, was public walking. I progressed at the whim of the women, the old folk who stopped to hold long conversations with everybody they met; elaborate exchanges, repositionings, shifting of feet. I remember: high kerbs, layers of unnecessary clothing, hats. Patient dogs. Babies maggot-swaddled in fluffy blankets full of holes. Gossip, when it got interesting, shifted into Welsh. I was expected to know everyone who knew me. There were few cars on the streets and they were all polished and gleaming. Our car had running boards and those hanging leather tongues with which you could haul yourself out of the seat. But on Sundays, as on other days, my father worked.

It took me years to discover that cars could move. I thought they were exhibits, kept in the drive; buffed and waxed like an additional front room. Occasionally, neighbours would come around to visit, to inspect the new vehicle which replaced a previous model that had, so far as I knew, never been out on the road.

At least in chapel, in Libanus, up the steps, you could sit down, duck out of sight. Hard wooden benches. Excited, choral voices in a language I refused to learn, but which I interpreted in my own way. Much calling on Jesse Grease. A god name. Chanted approval from the elders. 'Ie, ie.' Ee-ah. Ee-ah. Donkeys in a stable.

Once I was prodded to the front of the congregation to recite a few verses, learnt phonetically. The shock of that reverse angle: pebbled, pink heads nodding before the diminutive Elmer Gantry.

I preferred Zoah, the place of worship of a schismatic, my grandmother's unmarried sister. The walk was shorter. The chapel aligned directly with the hill on which we lived. I could lift up my eyes and there it was, the road out. The way to the sea.

When rogue hormones kicked in and chapel-going was abandoned for token attendance at the Church of England, I spent Sunday mornings climbing the mountain (as we called it) behind the railway station. Rough pasture, rundown farms, pit scars, bog and wind. Strange things were to be found in the chest-high fern jungle: sheep skulls, grey pictures of large-breasted ladies, a wedding ring inside a half-full sardine can.

The hit was the view back over the narrow, flinty town; Sunday smoke, meat in the oven, angled gradients of slate. This modest panorama imprinted me, followed me to London. When I started to write, the shape that I saw – the cottage hospital on the edge of the park, the conifer plantations, the despoiled river – was my nightly dream.

I'm standing with a group of lead figures, Sioux warriors, clutched tightly in my fist, trying to make them stand on the hot bonnet of the new silver car, the Triumph. I can't take in what they're telling me: that I am to be left in this place, this is where I am to live. Forever.

I was seven years old, it was the end of home. That wasn't too bad. I was a fatalist. It could be worse. The food was wretched, cabbage boiled to death, grey meat so flavourless it didn't belong to any particular animal. It was generic: dead stuff. Onion-mush in white sauce. The anticipation, the way the smell infiltrated corridors and classrooms, was as bad as the miserable process of pushing it around the plate. But it was well meant, they were doing their best for me. As they saw it. In future times I would eat anything that didn't move.

There were, in those first days, quiet moments. I lost my solitude. A life lived in public. A few tears in the vegetable garden, an apple to munch, that was it. The invention of a mask capable of surviving this, or any other, environment.

I accessed a parallel world and delivered reports. The other boys in the dormitory were enthralled. These were not lies exactly, they were improved documentaries; documentaries that couldn't support their own weight. Nothing too fantastic, versions of what *should* have been; real people pushed – helped – into the acceptance of an identity that made them more than they were, closer to their uncensored potentialities. Dangerous territory, if you start to believe it. If you forget your way back.

'Those who are not worthy will have cause to remember.'

I remember. Everything. I can't get shot of these images. The crocodile of boys in brown and red caps, shepherded by a duty master, straggling over the sand dunes, the burrows. Sharing sticky Spangles when they were too dirt-encrusted for personal consumption. I had no idea how long the walks would last. We enjoyed no right to roam. We picked up spent cartridges and Neolithic axe heads.

Frank's school was on the far side of the dunes, upstream. It looked different, broader, reedier, but it was the same river; the one that ran through our town. Frank never lost touch with where he came from, where he stayed. He fished. He understood about water-plantains, goat's-beard, beetles, butterflies, foxes, ravens, hawks. All we saw were rabbits. In the evenings when we turned for home, for school, bunnies with powder-puff tails skittered mockingly through the marram grass. It was hard walking, polished shoes sinking, filling with sand, picking up sharp stones.

Henry Vaughan, in his house, gazing out on the broad-skirted oak, dreamt of lost people; people he had never known but who had vanished. All he knew was a single fact: they were gone. Not here. The play of the sessile leaves invoked their presence. The tree absorbed them into its furrowed bark.

Vaughan lay in his bed, holding sleep at a distance, on the far side of the room. In the shadows. Sleep came off him like flaking skin. Powdered snow on the boards of his bedchamber.

He kept paper, a pen, ink, close at hand. He would question the spirits. He lay with his eyes open, under the dark beams of the low ceiling, hearing cattle move restlessly in the fields, hearing the river, the small, common noises of that thick night – and he saw himself reach out for the pen. He transcribed this non-dream, the story one of the vanished dictated. About a man in a bed. Reaching for his quill.

He fell into a deep sleep; in wch he dreamt, that he saw a beautifull young man with a garland of green leafs upon his head, & an hawk upon his fist: with a quiver full of Arrows att his back, coming towards him (whistling several measures or tunes all the way) and att last lett the hawk fly att him, wch (he dreamt) gott into his mouth & inward parts, & suddenly awaked in a great fear & consternation: butt possessed with such a vein, or gift of poetrie, that he left the sheep & went about the Countrey, making songs upon all occasions, and came to be the most famous Bard in all the Countrey in his time.

Frank was orienteering strenuously through the wood, while I slipped and slithered at every turn. He'd chosen the wrong path, I was sure of it. But he was too far ahead for debate about the vicious slope he was about to provoke. You know the kind, seductive at first glance, pastoral idyll, butter wouldn't melt, Lurpak pasturage. Until you fall for it. Until you are hanging by your fingernails, plunging through hidden streams, slashing your wrists on barbed-wire blossom masquerading as heather. The first gentle summit reveals another. And another. Disappearing into gloating, wet mist.

Mountain becomes metaphor.

Never trust anywhere picked out by monks, that's what my Nonconformist upbringing tells me. This deal with the paths is a *Pilgrim's Progress* test and we've been suckered. We haven't noticed how the rim of the bowl is split by a plunging rivulet, frantic to join forces with the Honddu in the valley below. The lines on Frank's map are grain in wood, flowing around a knot or obstruction. There's no easy way to ford the vertical stream, or bypass the cleft it has dug out of the red earth. Clearing the woods, it's quite obvious – now it's too late to get at it – that there's another route, a sheep track digressing, hands in pockets, up the gentler, southern slope; the one we didn't option.

This, Frank tells me, when he pauses at last, sitting on a rock, was the route the monks employed when they went to Longtown for beer. Across the valley is another crease in the hills, another rivulet; another visible track. Visible from here, when you are halfway into the clouds.

The fish path, Frank said. The monks went over to Llangorse Lake with empty baskets. In winter it was quite an adventure. Glittering freshwater fish laid out on the frozen grass, edible ice-skates. You could hang them on a tree and play them like a xylophone.

Restless Frank, before I'd caught my breath, was away; on all fours, arms becoming legs, as he pounced from fingerhold to fingerhold. Invigorated by oxygen debt, he let rip with a fresh improvisation: 'You must allow the shallow parts of your mind to fill with landscape. Notice how the blurred tilage is pocked with rain, pleached hedgerows shadowing a road we will never take. The folk in those cars, down there, are listening to their radios. They want news of the weather confirmed. They don't trust the evidence of their own eyes. But if we weren't here, we wouldn't need to be here. Or anywhere.'

He disappeared over the rim. And I followed. Contradictory tracks offered themselves like glossy postcards in a King's Cross kiosk. Seductive, but over-egged. Not quite believable. Frank was nowhere to be seen. I branched to the left, on the curve, able at last to walk upright; to breathe without turning blue. Bumps in the ground, flat stones laid on a peaty track, encouraged me to go forward in better heart. I could move without stooping, without resting my hands on my calves, working them like a reluctant machine.

The sky reared above me, oceanic, untroubled; blue waves tipped in a glass bowl. A steady gale blew back the skirts of my coat. I made for a heap of loose stones, knowing this was not the summit, but hoping that the cairn would suggest a direction in which to walk; some notion of the route Frank Vaughan had taken.

After all that sweaty effort, the weight and mass of shale and marl over which we had climbed, this path was too narrow: a ridge suspended between contrary worlds. The secret valley, behind us, we trusted would still be there on our return. And the open patchwork of countryside terminating in the distant Malvern Hills. This, I supposed, must be Offa's Dyke.

The cairn, on which I was advancing, shifted to a slippery black coat, another walker. My interest was pricked. The person, male or female, turned away and stood so perfectly still that I thought I'd been mistaken. The wished-for presence reverted to its identity as a rain-splashed rock.

Then she lifted her arms, advanced on England. She didn't care if there were other hikers about. It was a possibility she hadn't considered. I began to wonder, with no sight of Vaughan, if I *was* on the mountain. The girl, light caught her hair, was so much a projection of what I wanted and lacked in my life. I trusted what I was seeing, but I didn't believe it: that it was happening now. I'd come on the scene too easily. She belonged to a part of the story which had not yet been told.

Working, a holiday job, in the post office, dragging mailsacks on and off trains at night, I'd been trying to read the *Vita nuova*. It was an American translation and I hadn't got very far. I kept breaking off to enjoy the rush of whichever pulps were lying around in the shed, Chester Himes, Mickey Spillane, Simenon. But one comment I did pick up on in the Dante introduction: the poet David Jones saying that the whole Beatrice business (he calls her 'Beatrix', which made me think of the rabbit woman) had been overestimated. This threw me, because I'd been told that a girl, spotted in a Florentine church, became an obsession, the incarnation of poetic inspiration, the key to the journey through the labyrinth. Every poet, as I understood it, should be on the lookout for the two elements vital to the plotting of the true life: the elder guide (Virgil) and the fire-source (Beatrice). And here was Jones quoted as saying that Beatrice 'is not a compelling girl of total pulchritude in all her members, impossible to resist because of the radiance in flesh and blood, not a "smasher" as the pre-Raphaelites would say'.

She took off her coat, her jersey and whatever she wore under that. She was standing, thirty or forty yards off the path, facing Longtown, its church and single street, naked to the waist; her back to me, arms lifted in a gesture of affirmation. Not a girl, a woman. Strength in the shoulders. Pleased with herself, I guess, for being part of the mountain.

It happened, it is happening. Now, not then. Then it was antici-pated, prefigured. Now it's awkwardly transcribed, invaded by a recapitulation of what it felt like to be younger and stronger; the breath knocked out of me. I've lost all sense of a proper order. There's no Norton, that's for sure. Or, rather, there is a Norton, but I'm not him, not the narrator. Llanthony Priory is a location you can find on the Ordnance Survey (Landranger 161) in gothic script. You could very well repeat this walk. They issue leaflets telling you how to go about it. All anyone needs to know about Walter Savage Landor.

I knew nothing about Landor's connection with the Vale of Ewyas when I made that first ascent – which I'm making again. In Hackney. Vaughan wasn't called Vaughan. He was a collision between two other doctors; one dead, a probable suicide. A man I never met. But a more intelligent and troubled person than my caricature allows.

The fiction of the tower dissolved as Norton plunged over the headland above Porlock. With the talking dog and the aftershock of the collision on the cliff road. Joblard and Kwilt reasserted their original identities, but my unresolved avatar was suspended, in the rake of the car's headlights, out over the Channel; waiting for a coda that could never be written. The trajectory of Norton's non-life was over, spiked. A blink of white light, unoptioned, barely noticed on the far shore.

The grand scheme remained uncompleted. Landor planned to restore parts of the priory, towers squatted by hunters, walls slimy with animal blood. The remnants of his villa can still be found. But the tower with a room at its summit belonged in a southern landscape, with a philosopher/aristocrat like Montaigne. With another writer. Landor never got much further than laying out the foundations, planting trees in his wild park.

The quickened memory-taste, the clarity of light on the mountain, is only there for an instant. A milky, Alzheimer's illumination. Far-off things can be held snugly in the hand – but the climb, earlier that afternoon, is already forgotten. The Norton novel meant nothing; a folly of the worst kind, forged narratives, faked climaxes, bent history. A disservice to all concerned. This is not what I felt about Wales, not what I set out to say.

You can make as many charts as you like, plot graphs with different-coloured inks, predict movements, the arguments of ungrateful characters. You can spend years ploughing through biographies, reminiscences by tourists in search of the pastoral; libraries of geology, church histories, mythology. You can visit every site a dozen times, live on the road. It makes no difference. The first sentence on the page and the game's up, the story goes its own way. A fly that refuses to buzz.

My mother on a gold, mock-Regency chair; benign, plumper than she had been, eating the same meal so many times, wandering over to the deep drawer for another sherry. She confused me with my father. He'd ceased. She couldn't place him. The anger and the extraordinary will, to make the world conform to her picture of it, had faded. She rehearsed often-told episodes: how she had run away as a girl, taken a train up the valley to stay with relatives, and how her father came to fetch her home.

Before she settled to this calm, the reliving of events that were seventy years gone, it hadn't been so easy. Family meals, on our infrequent visits, were eccentric. My mother was still under the illusion that she was, as she had always been, preparing an elaborate roast, dishes of vegetables, carrots, sprouts, mashed potatoes. Over the years the preparation took longer and longer. We might get to the table by 6.30 and not taste a scrap until 9 p.m. We'd be light-headed with sweet, pink champagne before the carrots arrived, stone cold, and the joint was carved with a humming electric blade.

Discreetly, my father took over, allowing my mother the usual tributes for such a feast. Much of the food would, in fact, be cooked by my wife and brought down with us in the car from London, ready to be heated up. Each visit was an occasion, a party, a premature Christmas. Crackers and paper hats were out.

It had rained all the way, the children were tired. They had eaten the peas, pulled their crackers, and were waiting patiently for the sausagemeat to be scooped from the spoon. My mother made one of her final gestures in the general direction of Delia Smith and tipped orange cordial into the gravy boat.

'That'll be mam and dad,' she said. 'Dead on time. Very Welsh.' They'd been buried for years, gilt lettering faded on their shared headstone.

But it was unexpected, the door bell. My parents were too old for it. Before retirement, in the other house, up the valley, every meal had been interrupted. Not a night passed without the phone ringing. My father was always on call. That's why they moved. Neighbours in this quiet street didn't socialise at night. Their friends, the ones who were hanging on, in remission, recovering from their operations, their surgical interventions, wouldn't drive in the dark.

The ring was insistent. My father, carving-fork in hand, cardigan and slippers, pottered out to answer it.

I dished up and we carried on eating. We could hear muffled voices in the hall. The intruder wasn't invited to the table, so it couldn't be anyone they knew; it must be an official or a tradesman they'd forgotten to pay. We put it out of our minds, my father's absence. My parents never sat together at the table; if one was eating, the other would be clattering in the kitchen. We moved on to the trifle, and were sorting through odd half-inches of duty-free liquor left over from their travels – peppermint cordials, Lindisfarne mead, Cointreau, cherry brandy – when my father returned.

He told us about Mr Ford. It sounded to me like the man needed a dentist not a doctor. He'd limped out of the rain, on one of the worst nights of the year, having endured a ten-mile bus ride, and a long walk from the terminus, to present my father with a carrier bag of papers. He was convinced that government agencies had planted a miniature radio in one of his molars.

'Radio tooth,' he insisted. 'They've given me a radio tooth.' Ford was a scholarship boy, a physicist. He'd worked for an electronics company. Then later, after refusing a transfer to the outskirts of London (Enfield, Borehamwood), as a teacher in a school for disturbed children. He wouldn't involve himself with weapons systems, the tools of mass murder. If he prostituted his god-given talents, he said, he would be branded with the mark of the Antichrist.

When war came, Mr Ford was a conscientious objector. On his way to a detention camp, he'd fallen – or been pushed – from the platform at Reading. His foot had been damaged. It would never recover. They – the Brotherhood – would see to that.

The foot was true. It was the one fixed point in Mr Ford's autobiography. Prove the incompetence, the malignancy of state-suborned surgeons, and the rest would follow.

This was the foot my father received in a box. Ford's papers, transferred to a Jiffy bag, had passed into my keeping on my father's death. I'd never read them. They belonged in a book I wasn't ready to write. For years I carried those papers around. This might be the moment to open the packet.

We were into the second layer of the chocolates, squinting at the chart, when my father finished his story. Ford was troubled. The tooth had warned him: he would be dead within a fortnight, without a drop of blood being spilled.

2

The habit was still there, the impulse, to get out into the country on Good Friday, to make a pilgrimage. Joblard, his rucksack freighted with home-baked pies, pasties, samosas, black Italian cigars, Jamaican rum, was up for it: the run west. I didn't read fiction (didn't write it either), but I was moderately addicted to earth mysteries, Alfred Watkins, E.O. Gordon (*Prehistoric London, Its Mounds and Circles*), John Michell; sacred routes, animism. Poetry was my other indulgence: George Herbert, Henry Vaughan, David Jones, Vernon Watkins – and now this newcomer, the London/Bristol runaway who had settled in the Neath Valley, Gwain Tunstall.

I wanted to bring them together, Joblard and Tunstall; very different writers, to whose work I was equally committed. I'd started to put out their books through a small press, editions of a few hundred copies that could be sold at readings or traded at one of the independent bookshops (which always came down in the end to Compendium in Camden Town).

'Abandoned precision', that was what someone wrote in a Cambridge magazine. Reading this tribute sent me back to poems that cropped up from time to time in *Second Aeon*, a counterculture publication that came out of Cardiff: pink covers, pulp paper, explosive typography – star-bursts, chopped-up women.

Tunstall floated, Joblard burnt and branded. Tunstall named names; no deflecting shields, influences lightly worn. The random gaudy of a working life: open-field discourse, bright colours – the time to notice red geraniums in a blue pot. The way language ran with him: 'The analeptic, giddy shock, deliquescent flood of wood-grain.'

Joblard would never do this, let the blank page take the drift, the improvisations, the shift of consciousness; he hoarded his terms, under enormous pressure, until they were torn from him with a physical wrench, converted into savage marks. Specifics of place and person were, at all costs, to be buried. His was a purposefully high form of composition, mediumistic and life-threatening. The task: to create a parallel world in which words were objects; an enigmatic zone from which he, the author, would be banished.

Tunstall and Joblard had never met, but Tunstall's mates, when they saw Joblard give one of his performances, when they witnessed the conjuring of phantoms, the hypnotic scoring of jagged fragments of sound, sidled over to ask the inevitable question: 'What are you *on*, man?' The recipe, that's what they wanted. They refused to believe he was clean. Give or take a modest half-dozen of Russian stout and cider, rum chasers, shag cut with gunpowder, atrophied cigar stubs, the dude was pretty much an abstainer. All those hippie dope clouds – puff, pills, cough linctus – were too tedious to be worth the blather, the sale-speak, that went with them. Joblard was a control freak. An out-of-control freak: psychotic acts disguised by genuine and unforced charm. Like Böhme, he put the wind up his punters by letting them hear a creak from the wheel of anguish.

So that was part of it, to bring the poets together. And to get in one of our Easter walks. I'd told Joblard about Llanthony, how I'd been there years before and it had stayed with me. The idea, this time, was to take the fish route, up Bal Bach and Bal Mawr, through the forest to Crickhowell, along the Usk and across the Beacons, over Fan Fawr to Ystradfelte, to stay with Tunstall in his farmhouse. I was pretty vague about what this involved, and how long it might take. We would spend the first night drinking in Crickhowell, check out a standing stone I'd spotted on the map, somewhere along the river, then sleep in the woods. Easy.

I kept quiet about the covert plan: to locate and experience the Holy Grail. Or, at least, pay our respects to the place where it had once been, Strata Florida Abbey in Cardiganshire; the area from which my mother's family had migrated to the industrial valleys of south Wales.

There were other things about this undisclosed quest: Strata Florida was the burial place of the poet Dafydd ap Gwilym, whose bones rested under an ancient yew. It was also the site of a curious relic, the left leg of a man called Henry Hughes who had emigrated to America, after organising a funeral for his amputated limb. I'd seen photographs of the stone with the graceful, Cocteau-on-opium doodle of the leg lifted in a chorusgirl kick, and the inscription: 'The left leg and part of the thigh of Henry Hughes Cooper was cut off and interr'd here . . .'

Hughes was a cooper. So was Joblard. Cooper with a capital C. His birth-name, before he was adopted.

In my pack I carried the testament of Mr Ford, the only surviving history of Ford's foot. Missing limbs, shifting names, there had to be a connection. At worst, if I could pull off this quest, Ford's papers would metamorphose to that posthumously amputated lump. The foot shaped like a rubber hammer. Somewhere during the journey, trekking over mountains, passing through the *Mabinogion*'s dark forest, the foot would be restored; made ready for burial in the churchyard, beyond the perimeter wall of Strata Florida.

The thing about Joblard is that you can't rush him. He is where he is. Sitting in the priory car park, seeing it through his eyes, as for the first time, Llanthony was a different place. We left the doors open and waited, without talking, allowing the car to empty itself of the accretions of the early-morning drive out of London, across the Cotswolds; the talk, the tapes played, the discontinued business of the city. We took a leisurely stroll through what was left of the Augustinian retreat: which was nothing more than a device to slow the pulse of visitors, preparing them for the move into the surrounding countryside. The priory, this geological freak, had no centre; it was all view, the further you walked away from it, the more it made sense.

But it felt odd or wrong to turn our backs on the sharp ascent that led to Offa's Dyke (memories of the bare-breasted woman). There was something heretical about crossing the road, taking the little metal bridge over the Honddu.

Our path was easy to find and we climbed steadily, without effort, through fields of sheep, onto the hillside. After about half an hour, when we were sure we'd located the right track, we saw that there was only one way through the bracken, the winberry; one viable groove in the long ridge, the chain of hills that ran from the Bal Mawr summit, north, towards Capel-y-ffin. Follow the swift rivulet, stick to the edge of Cwm Bwchel, that was our instinct. Attempt this walk in Black Mountain mist and you'd better have a compass.

Joblard sat on a log, rolling a cigarette. 'Great,' he said. 'That's the first time we've walked more than ten minutes in Wales without you leading me to the edge of a limestone cliff or a crumbling ravine. Things are looking up.'

I fixed the priory in the lens of my camera. I didn't bother to click the shutter. Post-monastic conversion work – hotel and pub – distorted the impression; space was compressed between arches, a narrowly selective view swivelled as you panned across towers and vaultings and cloisters. There was no single, privileged spot on which to stand. The priory was simply the conflux of a number of paths. From where we sat, flicking at midges, it was child's play to work out the best route, the route I should have taken when I made that first climb with Francis Vaughan. The track was so accessible – once discovered – that you could do it drunk, as the brothers did, reeling back from Longtown.

Sacred ruins, at a distance, have such resonance. I thought of a grimmer day, a long walk in steady rain, over Margam mountain; hours blundering through a conifer plantation, sweating, soaked, heels rubbing in ill-fitting boots – then coming, unexpectedly, on the sight of Margam Abbey and its maze. Maybe that's what Llanthony needed, a few petrochemical plants, a permanent curtain of red smoke; a slimy, grey sea.

It was getting dark. The kids, who had been excited at first, skidding around the paths like the tricycle boy in *The Shining*, jumping up and down to try and see over dense box-hedges – always to see in, to the heart of the labyrinth – were beginning to ask questions. Like: 'What happens if we have to stay all night?' 'Does anybody *live* in the middle of the maze?'

'Mazes don't have middles,' I said. 'They're a straight line, tangled up like a garden hose. If we get bored, we can cheat and push our way through the hedge.'

The two girls were shocked by the idea, but my son was off, plotting his own course, treating the choice of paths like a computer game, with himself a bolt of white lightning.

I was waiting for the closing bell. And I was worried about my father who had come with us on this outing to Margam. We'd given him the tour of the orangery, a turn around the gardens, then parked his wheelchair. He said he'd been fine, watching the sun drop behind the crematorium. He'd use his binoculars to follow white sails on Eglwys Nunydd reservoir and to penetrate the fiery blanket of the steel furnaces, which had provided him with a steady stream of afflicted clients.

He pulled three chocolate bars from his coat pocket. 'If you meet the minotaur,' he said, 'feed him Fruit & Nut. That'll stick his teeth and give you time to escape. Take as long as you like. I'm happy sitting here, seeing where my patients came from. And where they're going.'

When these things happen, they happen fast. The phone call when you least expect it, as you're sitting down to eat. 'Very sorry. Your dad's passed away. In his chair, a heart attack. Been to Tesco's. He had carrier bags all round him on the floor. Fair play, not an egg was broken.'

It wasn't unexpected but it was a shock. One part of your mind moves at the speed of light: what's to be done? The content of a life, where is it now? The other part, the part that takes charge of speech, shuts down, switches to autopilot. You walk towards the table: 'Grandpa's dead.'

There's a lot of projection here. Seeing yourself – myself – in that red chair. Hearing the race of a heart, too big for the cavity that contains it. It was obvious to all of us, even though we did nothing about it, that my father was in an impossible situation: taking over my mother's work, cooking, keeping the place tidy, while that big muscle, already damaged, raced and surged. There's a natural entropy to things. The system runs down, I had no problem with that. But my mother, in her confusion, was getting up at all hours of the night, wandering the street; her short-term memory had failed.

Would it happen to me? And when? How would I know?

Boundaries between events were breaking down. Son as husband. Her father, my grandfather, restored to his pomp, leading her into the farmer's field to find the pony with the bright new saddle; her tenth birthday. The fall that would break her back.

Researching a novel in which these incidents, transmuted and transposed, might have some place, I returned to Margam. I didn't know where my parents' ashes (or what passed for their ashes) had been spread. I couldn't say with any certainty that their names had been entered in the Book of Remembrance. Had that line from Henry Vaughan been written out in copperplate? Or had I scribbled it in my notebook, as a linking device in the Landor novel, a way of folding back to Llanthony? *Then I that hear saw darkly in a glass.*

Rain and the aftermath of rain, a glistening black road with bent arrows pointing to an empty car park. A bleak concrete cross. A burning stack made from Carl Andre slabs.

Fast-travelling showers puckered the deep-green waters of the reservoir; low dunes, burrows. Sometimes, according to legend, you could hear a bell from the drowned church that lay, with the rest of the town, under Kenfig Pool. Kenfig Hill, Pyle, Sker Point: names on a map. Discontinued romances; novels by R.D. Blackmore, who spent his childhood at Nottage Court. Motorway and mainline railway divided a landscape that was heavy with evidence of early settlement, the manufacture of primitive tools. In more recent times, off-road speculations (discount carpet warehouses, chip shops, gloomy pubs) had been the testing ground for a bright schoolboy with overlong hair, the Elvis impersonator and future narcotic entrepreneur Howard Marks. A person who would, like an American evangelist, turn an absence of shame into a marketing device.

Chopped cypress hedges on the private drive of the crematorium. One of the staff, a young man in a short black Eton jacket, striped trousers, knife-bright shoes, points to a square of turf, represented by a coded number in his book.

'Near as I can say, that's it. Where the ashes would have been scattered.'

Behind the hedge is a plantation of bare trees, inky tendrils in a solution of milk.

I decide, then and there, to give up my trip to Port Talbot beach. I would never hold it together until I reached that point in the novel: the absurdist hitmen, Nicky Lane's band, Mac the fixer. I couldn't nail them in one place at one time. Everything I described had happened, was happening – but not now. Not here.

I wanted to do a short walk, as recompense for the things I'd left undone, an unfocused act of remembrance; a way of stretching the maze into the hill that overlooked it. A way of linking the crematorium, the abbey, and the small church at Llangynwyd, where my mother's parents were buried.

Sometimes it feels right to go backwards. Following the path into the forest, allowing one walk to fade into another, I was straining against earlier versions, other tellings of this tale.

My mother's spirit was unappeased.

When we were clearing her flat, getting it ready for the relatives and friends who might come back after the funeral, a vacuum cleaner lifted into the air and landed on my wife's foot, breaking a toe. She limped, in some pain, through the afternoon's ceremonies.

Strong winds threatened to close the Severn Bridge. We were the last car out of Wales that night, buffeted and tugged all the way over; relieved to make it into a pub on the English side. Touching hands as we waited for our second drink.

I'd been over Mynydd Margam many times, but always the other way, south, in the direction of the sea. The scramble into the Sychbant valley, with its little stream and its railway tunnel, is an abiding memory; picnics, paddling boys daring each other to crawl through one of the pipes that carried the stream under the farm track.

Once, I took Joblard to Llan. They were suspicious of his voice, his size: that ill-omened stutter. A couple of pints was enough. Coming over the mountain, the way I used to go with my grandfather, I explained how, when he was a young man, he thought nothing of walking to Neath Fair, and back at the end of the day.

It was a spot, a dip in the ground known as Cwm Goblin, that the farmers avoided. They would cover the extra mile to keep clear of it. Joblard clutched his chest and toppled over in a seizure. He couldn't have been pissed or exhausted. We'd only done two or three miles along an easy route I used to take with my grandfather, when he was over eighty years old and visiting the churchyard where his wife and brothers were buried. These were very Welsh excursions: a stroll in the hills, stories of what had been, a rest on a bench under the yew tree; chatting to the sexton who would, at the right time, help to dig your grave.

Joblard, taking a steady pull on the rum, recovered quickly. Natives and landscape, as far as he was concerned, belonged to H.P. Lovecraft; malicious inbreeds, spine-sucking parasites with ancestral grievances. I'd never get him back here. A butterfly of an astonishingly pure blue fluttered out of the ferns. As we came onto the crest of the hill, away from the treeline, a glider – which we took at first for a child's toy – drifted slowly towards us, getting bigger and bigger, until it passed a few feet over our heads, forcing us onto the ground. The masked pilot waved his arms like a character in a comic strip.

On the top, once the arid darkness of the conifer plantation had been cleared, the sense of the track as a migration route was strong: making the present desolation louder and harder to bear.

When I walked with my grandfather I questioned him about the tattoo on his right arm, the boats he had worked on as a purser, the times when he had to collect colliery wages from Bridgend and come home in the trap, knowing that highwaymen were waiting on the road. A good time for dogs. They roamed, disappeared into the verges, but they weren't sheep-worriers. I'd get him to tell me again about Colonel Cody's Wild West Show.

We would meet other old men and there would be conversations, drifting between Welsh and English, as the landscape shifted between the scars of industry (feeders, stagnant ponds, overgrown railways, Soviet estates) – all the ugly, dangerous, provisional things that interested me – and the walks, trees, animals that were his memory.

If I was taken to Llan, the church on the hill, the village that had been there before the mining town spread along the broad base of the river valley, taken by women (mother, grandmother, great-aunt), we would travel by bus. We'd put flowers on graves and tidy things up, pull out weeds, rearrange sea-green chippings. It was a favourite outing. And it would usually conclude – a nice cup of tea – at the cottage of one of our relatives, the last keeper of the Mari Llwyd.

The Mari Llwyd was a strange shamanic thing, a horse's skull that was taken out once a year, on New Year's Eve, decked in ribbons and paraded around the houses. The revellers, who represented the dead trying to gain entrance to the hearth and fire of the living, made their rhyming challenge. Householders responded. When invention failed, they had to let the shrouded strangers with their white horse inside; they had to feed them on cakes, offer them spirits to keep out the cold.

I remember the voices, the bells. I remember standing on my bed to see what was happening in the street, pools of rusty light in the snow. The shadows of the singers distorted by the frosted glass of the porch. A great white horse who would kick our door to splinters.

Coming from the crematorium, over Margam Mountain, on my return walk to Llan, these earlier walks, memories real and imposed, rushed at me. If memory went, I went: I knew all too well how my mother and my grandmother, after years of work and involvement in everything that happened within the force field of domestic existence, let it go. Suddenly, shockingly, the blood-pudding of the brain was reduced to a rind, a desiccated cap. The mechanics of daily routine were suspended. There was only a shimmering past, events made fabulous by repetition: over and over, with no means of progression or resolution. No escape.

I thought about that summer day when I'd walked over the hills from Maesteg to Glyn Neath, to visit Gwain Tunstall and his newly established community for the first time. I was consciously repeating a walk that my grandfather and grandmother had taken to Neath Fair.

I set off early, bareheaded, on a morning of treacherous, milky sunshine. My cheap boots, picked up in a London street market, began to rub before I found a way to ford the Afon Afan. This wasn't hiking through the Cotswolds or the Lake District; there were no designated paths, no fell guides. The only folk who blundered from valley to valley, microphones in hand, were radio essayists navigating 'the roof of Wales'. The trouble with this roof was that you kept falling through the skylight: a bog, a plantation of future pit props, an abandoned colliery. Then climb again, claw your way up the next coal-grit slope, through farm dogs, midge clouds; a view from Resolven Mountain towards the ranged Fans of the Brecon Beacons.

I remembered something the Helpston poet, John Clare, wrote about rambling until he got 'out of his knowledge', until he went beyond what he knew. Clare defined this point by his conviction that the 'very wild flowers and birds' seemed to forget him. The natural world no longer registered his presence. He was a new man, or he was nothing: he cast no shadow. There was no echo when he spoke.

The skin on my neck was tight. I massaged it with butter that I picked up in a village shop. My arms were burnt. For the last leg, I followed Tunstall's directions, over fresh tarmac; nursing a bottle of fizzy stuff, paddling along the sticky road on spoiled feet. Nails had come through my boots. But I wasn't tired. Tunstall's hand-drawn map was detailed: 'Follow the white stones, swing left before you get to the shop that services visitors to the falls.'

Out here, in the middle of nowhere, was a red telephone box. I had an irresistible urge to use it, not to waste this opportunity. There was no one to ring. The box was loud with flies.

As I came to the stream, in front of the farmhouse, I took off my boots and paddled in the clear water; tied the boots together, slung them around my neck, and stood there, giving my swollen feet a chance to recover while I watched the figures on the grass.

A girl with long hair was strumming a guitar. Couples were lying around, talking, smoking, drinking from a jug that a man I guessed was Tunstall brought out from the house. Thinking back on that afternoon, I can recover Filo Sparkwell and Tunstall's wife, Jean; the others remain shadowy, generic. Pleasant pastoral drones. Weekenders whose toes would curl up at the first frost. (Already the scene is transposing, taking colour from a lost weekend in Jack Kerouac's novel *Big Sur*. There may well have been readings from that book, but it was less frantic in the Neath Valley; fewer comings and goings. No sense of San Francisco on the horizon. No anxiety over big ideas, big careers.)

My physical discomfort, T-shirt sweaty after the long hike, kept me at a distance from this idyll, the conspiratorial ease, the purposeful indolence. I was expected. They knew that I wanted to publish Tunstall's poems, but they expected a metropolitan figure with contacts and hot news, not this tramp, blundering in like an undercover agent, with a shirt tied on his head and a rucksack of books and cameras.

As the weekend progressed – picnics, soft-ball cricket, home-brews, dope and mushrooms, day into night, talk around the fire, music, the declaiming of poems by Tunstall and others – I felt sympathy for what they were attempting and also my own separation from it. There was enough reality in Tunstall's cultivation of the sodden ground, the work he had done in mapping out precisely where he was. He just might carry it off. And, win or lose, there would be the book, the continuing story of his quest for language.

On that first evening, when things were mellow, couples had taken themselves off to the woods with their sleeping bags, and Tunstall and I were inter-monologuing about David Jones, the farmer came knocking at the door. He could smell something strange. He couldn't work out what Tunstall was after: how he would make the money to survive.

Evans was a gloomy man, a solitary, waiting for the best moment to sell up. Tunstall was a good labourer, useful at lambing time; ready to be called out at harvest. Why did he tolerate these free-loaders? What did he want with poetry? Evans's idea of entertainment was reading aloud choice extracts from the local paper, recent crimes, a killer who preyed on young women. 'Her clothing was in a state of disarray,' he pronounced, moistening dry lips. ' "Signs of sexual molestation." They want to be careful, your friends. No bugger's safe these days. It's like Sodom down there in Cwmgwrach. They're all on drugs, mun. I blame the Common Market.'

He didn't take off his coat or cap, and he wouldn't sit down. 'Where's the wife then?' he asked, sniffing, wiping his nose on the sleeve of his gaberdine. 'Upstairs, with the candles, is it? Lovely girl, but she don't make the best of herself. You want to tell her, Tunstall, about swimming by that brook. There's funny people about.'

Evans was a bring-down, so Tunstall said, but he owned the land. 'Evans-on-Earth' the topers in the New Inn called him. Nothing to be done but suffer his morbid silences, sepulchral readings from folded newspapers, sex crimes wished on sun-worshippers.

When he had finally given up waiting for an invitation to step behind the curtain (furtive glimpses of nubile young women, deranged by laudanum, gobbling in sapphic congress), he wandered off, muttering, into the night. A dog had been troubling his sheep, maybe he'd get lucky and shoot it; maybe those Australian lasses, all legs and hiking boots, would slip off their shirts, down by the Dan-yr-Ogof caves.

There was a long, grateful hiss as Tunstall let out the grassy smoke he'd been holding, so it seemed, for the duration of his landlord's visit.

'Where we are,' he quoted, reading slowly from an early draft of his new epic, 'is registered mainly in terms of the earth's climatic systems, present and past; emigrating air and the detritus of glaciation. Memories and dreams of deep suburbia impose themselves, allowing me to work through the unanchored scree of personal history.'

'When do you think the book will be ready to publish?' I asked.

'Not in my lifetime,' he replied. 'Over – what? – the next half century, *The Ladder of Light* will evolve as our community evolves. It's the only way. Emotional highs and nigredo glooms syncopated with the rhythm of the seasons.'

He didn't need to convince me. I was sold. Small groupings, dispersed from the city but retaining a healthy relationship with it, in terms of barter of services, readings, some casual teaching, retreats for pressured workers, would maintain a network of contacts. The communards would grow their own food, cultivate the land: leaving time for study, practical scholarship, play, loving exchanges. No gurus, no rules. Come and go as you like.

I was dizzy with dope and sunburn. I'd been sneezing all day, feverish, drunk on pollen, and now I lay down, in the field above the house, by the embers of the fire, letting the darkness swallow me, as I waited for the appearance of stars I couldn't name.

'O Night, you black wet-nurse of the golden stars!' wrote Thomas Vaughan the alchemist.

The weekenders had been talking about UFOs and sightings and Jungian interpretations of celestial traffic. Comets and meteors that city dwellers don't have the time to notice. The lid of the world was closer that night. Foxes barked. Owls swooped. I could hear the river, water all around me, rushing, making Tunstall's clump of settlement into an island. A woman, in a tepee behind the house, was laughing, swearing, calling out – before her partner growled. Like someone stabbed in the throat. One of Tunstall's cats visited me, sniffed around my sleeping back, decided not to stay.

Talking too loudly, and taking great care where we set our feet, Joblard and I picked our way along the riverbank. Soft rain, indistinguishable from spray, helped clear our heads. I'd set myself to find the standing stone marked on the map as somewhere outside Crickhowell, alongside the Usk, beyond Glanusk Park.

'Hippie bollocks,' Joblard growled, when I tried to describe my first visit to Tunstall. 'Layabouts pissing it away in the grass.'

He wouldn't buy the notion of community, but he liked the sound of the homebrew, the nettle beers, vegetables from the patch behind the cottage; the smell of woodsmoke that drifted across the stream as you wove your way down from tarmac. He insisted on picking up a couple of bottles in the Bear: 'just in case'. He hoped we'd blackbag some decent road kill before we got to the Beacons: skittish pheasants highstepped from verge to verge as we tramped through private woodland.

'If you're stupid enough to leave town,' I said, 'Tunstall seems to have the best pitch: no god-almighty patron, no wacko priest, no sex slaves. He gets a place to live, him and his wife, by giving labour to the local farmer. There's leisure time when he needs it. A reasonable relationship with the provincial capital. He does a bit of teaching, see friends, scores dope, visits bookshops. Travellers pass through.'

'But it's still fucking Wales, isn't it?' said Joblard, who stopped, after a fit of coughing, to gob into the river. 'Thirty miles to a decent curry. Any woman who hasn't got webbed feet and scales down the legs is giving it to ten brothers. Whose idea of a great night out is dowsing a sheep with petrol and trying to invent the first self-delivering barbecue.'

The standing stone was not to be found. Land barons had closed off the riverpath with barbed-wire barriers. Through the trees, we could see the lights of a big house, country hotel or hospital.

'We'll break into a holiday home. They'll blame it on the nationalists,' Jobland announced. 'I'm not sleeping another night in one of your ditches.'

It seemed pointless to stay with the river. Woods with pheasants had gamekeepers with guns. This wasn't good country to creep around in the dark. There were too many trigger-happy SAS psychos on patrol, humping Bergens of bricks and contracts from literary agents for use in emergency. On capture, testicles wired to electrodes, they didn't bite a suicide pill; they whispered their memoirs into a dictaphone.

We left the river, crossed the Brecon road, wandered aimlessly between hedgerows, looking for somewhere to make camp. It was country dark: unfamiliar noises, squelchy matter underfoot, the occasional sweep of headlights. There used to be a surge of traffic at chucking-out time, not anymore. Now they came at you, continually, fullbeam; Range Rovers, pick-up trucks, tractors on rocket fuel.

'Drunker than we are,' Joblard said, 'that's what gives me the pip. I've done a lot of things in my time, but I'd never take a car on the road in that state.'

'You haven't got a licence. And, anyway, you've caused enough chaos, two-bottle sober, in boats.'

We sat on a low wall to warm ourselves with a drink and consider our options. Dim fields, sodden, bordered with nettles, thistle clumps, cow splash: we were in no state to put up a tent. There was nothing like a barn or an Islingtonian second home in sight. We decided to carry on.

'What's that?' I said. I could see the outline of a mound or chimney in the field behind us. Inadequate defence against warring tribes or an OTT cowshed? Whatever it was, the stack might offer shelter for the night.

'Birds,' Joblard said. 'There'll be no roof, it'll stink of birds.'

He was right. On closer inspection – not much use in the dark – the stack proved to be a stone tower. The entrance was padlocked. They were well prepared for this latest invasion. We picked our way across the field and into an orchard or garden; the rain had brought out a delicate smell I couldn't identify, lavender or honeysuckle or old English roses. There was an arbour with a bench, on which I spread out my sleeping bag. Joblard wandered off to try the windows of the house.

I could hear water plashing from a fountain. A romantic notion, but I felt, under my floral canopy, that this was a poet's place: retired, at one with tamed nature, on the edge of a wilderness. Dreams and memories driven by rivulets and secret springs made their way from the Black Mountains to lose themselves in the Usk.

'Mornings are mysteries' was the phrase that haunted me. I woke up mumbling. We had to get moving, we had a long walk in front of us. But, before we set off for Tunstall's farmhouse, we investigated Tretower – which was what this estate was called. There was a manor house built around a courtyard, a restored garden (in which I had slept), and beyond that the stumpy Norman tower, a veteran of border skirmishes. Take in the crabapple orchards, the river, damp fields and broad valley between ranges of thickly wooded hills, and you had all the ingredients for the evolution of a poetry of place.

The family who had lived here, so we discovered, were the Vaughans. Joblard, who was interested in alchemy, wondered if there was a connection with Thomas Vaughan. He'd been down to Oxford, poking about in the Bodleian, using one of his correspondents, a character called Hinton, to get a squint at *Anima Magica Abscondia: or a Discourse on the Universall Spirit of Nature*.

Alchemy. They were all at it. Tunstall through the structure of his poem and Joblard with the fantastic notion of finding, in an alcohol dependency unit on the Old Kent Road, a derelict ('a creature of clay') who might, after repeated treatments with electricity, water and fire, be transformed into an angel of light. He was planning an 8mm film on the subject, which he had provisionally titled *Maggid Street*.

'So we must seek light; but it is so thin and spiritual that we cannot touch it with our hand: so we must seek its dwelling-place, the celestial, ethereal, oily substance.'

Joblard found the relevant passage in his notebook, a quote from Thomas Vaughan, writing under the pseudonym of Philalethes. The quotation was surrounded by doodles of eye-spiders, telescopes, cysts, magnetic storms.

Light was the medium through which the Vaughan twins articulated their vision. Increments of light. Shifts of register. Threads of water made to shine like silver, liquid lead, by propitious shafts of sunlight. The weather from the west came at you so fast, with such subtlety, cloud wisps lowering into a black quilt, splitting with thunder, clearing to the double-arch of a rainbow; a bridge across the valley of the Rhiangoll.

Henry and Thomas Vaughan, twins, poet and alchemist, made the attempt: to turn light into sound. One brother locked to the landscape of his childhood; one in Oxford, with access to libraries and scholars. One, in anguish, recalling another, younger sibling, now dead, walked the hills, a voluntary insomniac; preparing himself for his bridegroom, the bright godhead. 'I saw Eternity the other night / Like a great *Ring* of pure and endless light.'

Thomas Vaughan wrote *Aula Lucis, or the House of Light*. Light as a sympathetic oil. Light synthesised in a dish, pre-Newton. Hermetic light. Light as currency. That is what Joblard was after, with his tappings and scryings, his curious mechanical devices. I, on the other hand, wanted to blunder onto the curvature of Henry Vaughan's light-track, one of the paths he spilled across the cloth of the hills.

In the courtyard of the manor house we found the heraldic shield of the Vaughan family. The stone was worn and weathered. The eight divisions became windows in which strange archetypal figures were trapped. Twins, footless, joined at the skirts; smooth as pawns on a chessboard. I relied on the flash of my camera to catch details which I would have to study at home.

Returned to the lane, striding out, with no likelihood of locating anything to eat this side of Tunstall's place, we came on another early riser, a girl with a complicated camera – which she handled with an ease that bordered on arrogance. She was obviously on some sort of commission, dodging around, trying to get the Norman tower into the background of her composition. Red-nosed, she sniffled, pissed off with having to battle a cold, as well as this unforgivingly immobile stack of rocks. I liked her. She was clearly a person of attitude. She grumped and grizzled, kicked at the turf. Telegraph poles wouldn't behave themselves and stay out of the frame. This was the countryside and she didn't care for it. She pouted, dug her hands deeper into the pockets of her flying jacket.

What struck Joblard, apart from her youth and stamina, the way she moved, was the habit she had of talking to herself. And not just talking, sustaining a dialogue, in a soft Welsh drone.

'Is this the lantern tower?'

The voice came from behind me. The photographer stepped from the hedge. Which was disconcerting, because she was also in the middle of the field, twisting this way and that to get a tolerable fix on the tower.

There were two of them, twins. Soft-spoken. One, local, from a tepee town; while the other had got away, to London.

'Landor's tower – is this it? We've been arguing for hours, there's no one to ask. I'm doing a book jacket.'

'One tower's as good as any other round here,' Joblard said. 'Got anything to eat?'

Finding them as skint as he was, the sculptor lost heart. This doubling had its possibilities, but art schools were full of such things. Youths who couldn't leave the world alone. Conceptualists.

'They look all right,' he admitted, fascinated by the small differ-ences in the two faces; the way a sudden smile could start with one and run across the other. The way they took it in turns to seem con-fused. The dot-for-dot alignment of angry spots. Chatting to them was like folding out a pair of faulty mirrors. 'But they're dumb. Why else would they take this idiotic job? You can find better mounds in Beckton. And make a few bob on the petrol money.'

We left them, arguing. Then hugging. We crossed a bridge.

'Landor,' I said to Joblard, 'what's he got to do with Wales? Didn't he live in Italy with a bunch of dogs? These hacks will bend a story any way that takes their fancy to land themselves a juicy historical narrative. Faked poems, diaries. The pastiched past. I blame A.S. Byatt.'

3

It was snowing as we came out into the car park. American lights and oversized lettering discoloured the slush with reds and greens, tenpin signs flickered in faulty neon. Off-highway in west Wales; you could smell Carmarthen Bay, but you couldn't see it. I was going to drive Luned back to Cardiff. She worked as a legal secretary and she had her own flat.

In those days, the eyes had it. Kohl pencil, eyeliner. Nothing over the top for Luned. An Egyptian wink. But that's where the tease was, in question marks crafted around pale blue eyes. They might have been contact lenses. They had that kind of sheen. It wasn't coke. Not then. She was a good girl. Not too good, I hoped.

Colours stay with you, smell brings them back.

She wore a red coat and a furry Zhivago hat. She was Welsh-sized, her light blonde head came midway up my chest. I helped brush wet snowflakes from her shoulders, then opened the car door with an ironic gesture – I understood that such things were no longer done, but in her case an exception would have to be made.

She settled herself very easily. The small car, an ashtray on wheels, filled with this other smell, her perfume: the bug-burning blast of the heater, her warmth under layers of wool. She kicked off her shoes, paper-thin confections with high heels that made the negotiation of the slithery car park an arm-clutching adventure. Her stockings rasped as she rubbed her feet together.

There wasn't much traffic, going east. Familiar sights lost their familiarity under wet snow. By contrast, the blackness of the night was blacker. The air harsher. My window didn't shut properly, so that while my legs were lightly toasted by the heater, my neck was stiff and the side of my face was cold.

'Weird bit of road,' I said. 'Gorseinon, Llanelli, Bury Port. Not town, not country.'

I liked talking to Luned. I told her about my grandparents coming to Ferryside for their honeymoon. It was astonishing that there was still a railway station, a pub, a windy dip of beach alongside the estuary. One aunt, a famous swimmer (according to family legend), had crossed to Llanstephan. The stories that bore us in childhood are the ones that, despite ourselves, we retain. It had been quite disturbing, that afternoon, when I visited Ferryside and discovered that this much-mythologised place had a verifiable existence. The church, with its weather-worn graves, overlooking the estuary, was *exactly* as I had pictured it. As I described it to Luned.

She chatted about her job.

I have to tell you about this girl: she had a reputation. For being a good sport, a laugh; nice-looking, easy to get along with, no side, warm-natured; shapely, round, firm; with small, very white teeth and a bow-shaped mouth. The lads fancied her. The girls liked her too. But no one, so the word went, was ever permitted to go all the way. That was the rumour. Very lively, but a bit of a tease.

'One woman,' Luned said, 'put in for a divorce. I had to take the deposition. Her old man made her do the housework in nothing but a pinny, court shoes and a pinny. Cleaning and dusting and ironing. She put up with that. It was the cooking she couldn't stand, full Irish breakfast sputtering in the pan. I shouldn't be telling you this, should I? You won't let on? Promise?'

Not a word. Never. Until tonight.

Cardiff was asleep. Silent avenues, private hospitals, old folks' homes: smeared, rubbed out by a single windscreen wiper. A keyhole in the frosted glass. The town was peopled by dreamers enacting Luned's psychosexual games. She didn't mention violence, coercion, child abuse. Marriage truces with nowhere to go. Perhaps, responding to her good heart (those red-tipped, slender fingers poised over the keys of the typewriter), aggrieved victims invented an episode with which to charm her. A domestic peccadillo, an eccentric request that might yet be resolved. In transcribing the history of such partnerships, she made them fabulous. Tale-tellers laboured to reward her bright attentiveness.

It was always the women whose confessions she was asked to draw out and formalise. Men – white-faced with angry, pumping veins – stamped through to the inner sanctum. They talked, words wrenched from them, to one of the partners; a freemasonry of the fairway.

'You won't believe this,' she laughed. 'One bloke, in the Merchant Marine, wouldn't see his missus six months at a time. Gave her plenty of warning, though, pale blue airmail envelope with a fancy stamp the kids fought over. Told her to meet him in a bar in Butetown. Lovely home, a semi in Rhiwbina, nice neighbours, C of E and everything. How she's going to get to Butetown on the bus, with the Christmas shoppers? Doesn't drive, failed three times, anyone from the choir might meet her, wearing nothing but a shiny black mac he's brought back and a pair of tart's heels. Did it for years, never a word. Ashamed, she was. His first night ashore in a place that was next thing to a brothel. See the burns in the orange carpet where customers stubbed out their ciggies.'

'Is it always husbands?' I asked. 'Don't the wives have any imagination?'

'They shouldn't need to talk about it,' Luned said, kneeling to fire the gas. It came on with a hiss, one of those potential euthanasia devices you used to see in doctors' waiting rooms and rented flats in Rathmines (Dublin's finest): chalky columns, hives of gorgeous orange light.

Luned's room had a view of Roath Park. The mud-brown curtains were so heavy they belonged in the Old Vic. There were no cars on the road. The park was as white as St Petersburg. The respectability of the setting, its excessive furniture, gave the flat a heavy erotic charge. I felt the weight of the private dramas Luned had described, the devices men and women stumble on to lubricate ill-fitting lives.

She made a jug of coffee and found some brandy to go with it. Snow muffled sound. I concentrated on the local fierceness of the gas fire. I undressed Luned and she sat in my lap, in one of those unpredictably deep armchairs. There was no urgency. We drank brandy from one tumbler. I liked the way that her eyelashes, pale and unshowy, stiffened into their darker doubles.

I was kissing her neck and her shoulders. She unbuttoned my shirt, teasing and pinching. Gradually, we slipped down towards the floor; a doggy rug that refused to stay in one place. That slithered away from under, leaving you, next morning, with splinters in the knee.

I could taste the powder in her armpits, soft stubble. I ran my lips over her breasts. She mewed a little, bit my shoulder. I bit her back, softly. She climbed up on me, rubbing herself against the lump in my trousers. Laughing. Looking straight at me.

Take care. Prudence, Luned.

We went through into the bedroom. I wasn't married then, not entirely. But in the shift of setting, away from coffee mugs, gas, saggy chair, to the big bed, something changed. Leaving me with a sense of guilt: towards Luned. A reason to stay out of Wales. I didn't belong in this episode. I hadn't earned it. The kisses, the bites, regressed from tight-throated urgency to bruised affection; an act better left incomplete.

The figure in the Cardiff bedroom dissolves into an irritation of the cornea: loosely fictionalised as 'Prudence'. Though Luned is not Prudence and has no part of her. Unmanifest, they co-exist.

Right here.

In Gwain Tunstall's long, cold loft under the roof beams of his remote farmhouse.

After that walk with Joblard, the yomp across boggy ground, I could have crashed straight out. Tunstall had got out of the way of visitors. Around midnight, we picked at brown rice and carrots; smoked weak dope, finished Joblard's rum. Joblard was snoring in front of the fire. Tunstall retired to his hutch. I lay in my sleeping bag, half-dreaming, revisiting episodes from the past, casting fictions.

It was bitter. I was fully clothed, zipped tight in my bag, but my teeth wouldn't stop chattering. I could see stars through the hole in Tunstall's roof, where the slates had gone. A soft snowfall. Flakes, floating quietly down, were settling on the bare boards, turning my bag into a sepulchral monument. Memories of Luned, however mistaken, were an act of compensatory displacement. With the passage of time, my perversion of morality converted prudence into a self-deceiving vice.

There was a terrible groan and it wasn't mine. I reached out a hand and felt another sleeping bag, another presence. The cheek was bearded, the flesh icy. I was sharing Tunstall's loft with a dead man.

After Tretower, Joblard and I stuck with the Brecon road, hoping against expectation to find something to eat: a farmhouse, a roadside tea stall. Nothing. A steady stream of traffic forcing us into the soft verges; the worst walking.

At Llansantffraed we paused to pay our respects to the grave of Henry Vaughan; a brick cabin trunk with a stone slab for a lid. The shallow V of the family's heraldic shield acting as a water trough, a breeding pond for beetles.

'Did I tell you about the blood?' Joblard asked. The past months had been strange for him, stranger than the usual revisions of name on the rent book. Jamie Lalage, when he witnessed a Joblard performance in a lighthouse on the rim of the Isle of Dogs, said: 'Quite extraordinary. The silver hair and dark glasses. He looks like Fritz Lang ingested by Orson Welles.'

Joblard, it seems, was splitting like a rogue cell. Secondary selves were peeling off, moving out on their own trajectories. He could no longer predict the order in which things would happen: the phrase scribbled in a notebook, the sketch on a beer mat, the horror in the real world. The quack told him to lose three or four stone, cut down on the smokes.

'How much do you drink these days?'

'How much have you got?'

A couple of bottles of wine, one of whisky, six pack of cold beer for the bus: fuel for an ordinary life. Heart strong as a dray horse.

'Five spots of blood on the floor,' Joblard continued. 'Nobody, apart from me, used that bathroom. The women had their own. It wasn't the young girl, we checked the sheets. *I couldn't find my face in the mirror.* My hands were shaking too much to try shaving. Blood thick as treacle. Each drop a scarlet jewel.'

He had my attention, so he clammed up. Some fool was leaning on a car horn. One of the twins from Tretower, bored with hanging about outside Welsh ruins, was calling her sister. But the commissioned photographer, in her Ballardian flying jacket, was busy, stropping around the graveyard, firing off shots at all the wrong things. Like Judas goats, we had led them to Vaughan's tomb. Which she now straddled, clunking away with her autodrive camera. Pretending to be Robert Capa.

We decided to abandon the road, cross the Usk, get into the hills. Joblard countered his gurgling belly by slagging off photographers, amateur and professional. 'They all come to it in the end, wanting to be treated like artists. Name in lights. For what? Pressing the trigger without shooting themselves in the foot?' He sounded envious. Something had evidently gone wrong. Students he once relied on to imitate his methods – discomfort, duration, discipline – were running amok; giving allegiance to the new technology, cameras that talked back (took messages, offered recipes, fixed hair appointments).

He returned to the Italian story. 'I was in a church, trying to draw the pattern of blood drops that I'd seen on the bathroom floor, when a section of scaffolding broke free and hit me across the head. The others wanted to take me to hospital, I refused. The pain was nothing. I had discovered the *same* five drops of blood, at my feet, on the tiles. In the chapel. I had successfully materialised a schematic diagram of what was going to happen next. I've got a limited future, Norton, and I've used it all up. Thank god.'

Tunstall's farmhouse was in worse shape than Landor's tower. Half the roof was gone and the windows were covered with sacking. A cat, the last of the line, came limping out of the wood pile; a gaunt starveling with one eye and the smell of gangrene, maggoty wounds. The door which had always previously been open was bolted. Nobody responded to our knock. It was getting dark, we were hungry. Where were they, the rustic communards? Where was the fragrance of patchouli oil, joss sticks and the herb? Where was the wood smoke that should have twisted a welcome across the valley?

Joblard put his boot to the door. It shuddered but held. Tunstall had it deadlocked like an apartment on the Lower East Side. We kicked together.

'I've got a gun and I'm not frightened to use it,' said a frightened voice. Behind us, on the edge of the wood.

'For fuck's sake keep still,' Joblard whispered. 'This clown's wired. He could fart and blow our heads off.'

I turned slowly around, holding my hands up like Arthur Kennedy in an Anthony Mann Western. It was Tunstall with an upraised crutch. He'd done something to his leg, it was swathed in dirty wrappings. With an ear-flapped cap well down on his head, a wild grey stubble of beard, a khaki coat that trailed in the mud, and about as much flesh as an AIDS death mask, he looked like a Balkan refugee. A victim of ethnic cleansing.

'Jesus, Gwain, what's happened? Who did this?'

Rubbing frosted glasses on his shirt-tails, Tunstall stared at me. 'Is that you, Norton? You haven't brought a car have you? Wheels, radio? Too late now. Leave a vehicle overnight on tarmac and they'll winch out the engine, torch the shell. The last mate who came to see me never made it back to Swansea. They found his boots nailed to a telegraph pole in Tonna.'

Later, when he had got a fire going, skinned up, taken the medicine, settled in his elbow-chair, he stopped trembling. Speech didn't come easily to the man. He let it out in fits and starts, while Joblard rummaged around the cold, stone-flagged kitchen for something to eat.

The valleys had died; Swansea Valley, Vale of Neath, Rhondda, Cynon, Taff. The ones without Euro grants were worse. Llynfi, Garw, Ogwr? Send for Tarkovsky. No work, no industry. A generation of Year Zero nihilists, smackheads, vigilantes tanked up on disability pension beer. It was like the postbellum South, the Confederate states: a defeated people living off the bones of the land; angry, frustrated, prey to the worst compensatory fantasies, projections of a mythical past. Easy meat for carpetbaggers, the cynical frontmen of a central government interested only in bribing them with baubles, token gestures that ridiculed ancient freedoms. Knowing nothing but inward-gnawing hatred, they hunted for scapegoats. They petrol-bombed tidy houses occupied by sexual deviants (those who were getting away with stuff the Celts had only seen on video). They lynched petty thieves. They stoned vans that risked psychedelic paint jobs. Nothing had changed, but now it was more visible. Racism, homophobia and greed replaced hypocrisy, envy and benign corruption as the defining elements of Welsh culture.

Tunstall existed in a state of siege. The police had turned the place over, tipping out all his papers, reading his journals a line at a time, advancing the pages with licked fingers. Weekend visitors were harassed until they decided they'd be better off in town. None of the local dealers could afford the kickbacks. Raiding parties from Merthyr, using the Heads of the Valleys road, the heritage switchback, rustled sheep until the farmer, old Evans, decided to sell up. They had most of the slates from Tunstall's roof.

The utopian communities shrivelled, closed the ring, shifted west. The tepee folk of Llandeilo were literally diggers; they spent their days gathering firewood and digging holes in the woods to bury their shit. Nice to visit on a summer evening, hard to endure through a long Welsh winter.

Tunstall spoke of other visionaries who had tried to make it, the move west. He remembered – with proud affection – the poets Harry Fainlight and Bill Butler, both gone; re-remembered, refor-gotten. Death by neglect. Suicide provoked by unsustainable expectations. Out of sight, out of mind. Settling, healing their wounds in these remote places, was a form of self-annihilation. Epiphanies paid for by silence, the crushing indifference of the land.

Fainlight's sister, Ruth, visiting him in his isolated cottage, spoke of 'an existence of peasant starkness', an 'abraded spirit'. The poet slouched around in wellington boots and an old coat of his father's, surviving on sardine sandwiches and Battenburg slices.

Dum de dum de dumb ash: the final words in his *Selected Poems*.

The last I saw of Harry Fainlight was sitting beside Allen Ginsberg on Primrose Hill. Ginsberg, in his hand-painted silk shirt, was musing on the city, the spread of London, a church steeple he located from an earlier poem; the Post Office Tower. He told Harry about his recent trip to Wales, how London should allow the grass to cover it, until it achieved the transcendent pastoral of Walter Savage Landor's Llanthony.

Only one traveller, Tunstall told us, had come through in the last six months, 'a stubborn seeker', an eco-warrior called Rhab Adnam. The name was a whisper of mortality. I'd reached the age when information lost its novelty. I could barely remember the time when newspapers *were* news. I didn't just know the names of the mug shots with their syndicated columns, I'd met most of them; smelt the fear, the sandpaper scratch of media rats trying to keep pace with a speeding treadmill.

I'd been on the road with Adnam, down the Ridgeway to Silbury Hill, to the source of the River Lea, and even, in a burst of psychogeographic delirium, around an anticlockwise circuit of the M25. Adnam, it hit me now, was the man I had seen plodding with his great rucksack along the banks of the Usk. Adnam was the figure who haunted me, every morning, when I sat on my balcony in the madhouse, trying to recover enough energy to start work on the Landor papers.

'The skin was falling off him when he staggered in,' Tunstall said.

Invoking some weird ritual of defensive magic, Adnam had been swimming in the cooling towers of power stations, bathing in the mud of the Severn, upstream of Aust, and off Hinkley Point. He'd crossed the country on foot, from Sizewell in Suffolk to the petro-chemical complex at Baglan, treating these unlisted, secret landscapes as generators of vision. He embraced the sounds, the warning sirens, the hissing, serpentine engines that filled the rest of us with dismay.

'When he walked up to the farm, I could see him through the closed door,' Tunstall continued. 'Adnam's the ultimate green, brighter than the dial of a luminous wristwatch. Wire him and you could floodlight St Paul's.'

After that, we stuck our faces into the rice and carrots. Joblard announced that he'd be turning back in the morning. Much more of Wales and the most extreme of his performance pieces would look tame. He hated to have anything explained or completed. Cutting in and out, between ellipses, that was his bag. Keep the buggers guessing.

Adnam had successfully concluded the grail expedition that I'd only fantasised, the linking of those Cistercian houses; Abbey Dore to Margam to Neath to Llanllyr Priory, to Strata Florida. What he found he didn't say. The message was in the tiles. That's all Tunstall had to go on.

He fumbled in a box for the photograph. It could have been anything, a brick or a Ryvita biscuit. I couldn't tell if it was a rep-resentation of mould, or if it was itself mouldy, ruined by the damp of the cottage. I needed a magnifying glass to make sense of it.

Tunstall reckoned, after holding the card a couple of inches from his nose, that he could make out a horse and a rider in the upper panel and a single figure, handless, facing left, in the lower panel. The saffron dye might have come from the weathering of the tile, or the chemical dissolution of Adnam's image.

Those medieval colours, we loved them: an underlay of pinkish red, grey-mushroom borders, a golden rose.

What Tunstall didn't tell me was that Adnam was still here, in the attic, his downy wrap turned into a bodybag. He wasn't dead yet but his skin had the patina of a spoiled photograph; jaundice over-compensated for by a blush of broken veins. The roseate glow of a terminal alcoholic achieved by this longterm abstainer, the Quaker Buddhist. You could hear grit rattle in his lungs. His breath was liquid stone.

I couldn't sleep with the rasp of Adnam's breathing, unseen snow drifting through darkness. This part of Wales always had its own microclimate. I'd come from the Aust Services once, on a location-hunting expedition with Jamie Lalage; we crossed the bridge in two cars. I witnessed sunlight dancing on a broad river. Lalage swears that the rain never let up and he had the shots to prove it. You accessed the light you deserved. I'd pushed west towards the Gower with not a cloud in the sky. Lalage was snowed in before Newport; he skidded off an icy road, spent three days in a country house hotel, waiting to be dug out.

Sleep was out of the question. I didn't want to rerun memories of Luned: I had the sound of her voice, the light Welsh intonation; every statement a question, a tease. A phone call that could no longer be returned. I had the scent she used, her soap, the hot excitement of one night. But her face was gone. I wouldn't know her in the street. I could walk into a shop and ask if she had a par-ticular title on the shelf and it would mean nothing. There would be no moment of recognition. Which is why Prudence took over, usurped Luned's part; stepped across the threshold from wherever she had been before that dank evening in Hay-on-Wye.

I dragged my rucksack downstairs. Tunstall and Joblard were both snoring, tenor and basso profundo in perfect counterpoint. Joblard took it down and Tunstall, in his musky cabin, gave it back.

Embers glowed in the wood fire. I found my torch and settled myself to read Mr Ford's papers. Now was the time.

Joblard groaned, talked to himself, wrestled with some minor demon. But he wouldn't wake. I'd seen him sleep through riots, hurricanes, nights pitching on a running tide at the mouth of the Medway – while the pilot fought the DTs and nosed his way around a sandbanked munitions ship.

I pulled the tightly packed wad of papers out of the Jiffy bag. It was strange to find the fable of the foot confirmed in the language of lawyers. There were ten partners and five assistant solicitors on the letterhead. These boys had the town sewn up: property, rent collection, conveyancing, council, the election of the next Archdruid. They had more consultants than Harley Street, those Evanses with their superfluous initials and featured middle names: J. Howell Evans, W. Trehearne Evans, Owen Evans (Cantab).

Dear Dr Norton,

Re: *Thomas Oswald Ford, deceased,*
                   Late of 39 St Cadog's Road, Maesteg

We act on behalf of the executors of Thomas Oswald Ford, deceased, who was a patient of yours.

In his Will, Mr Ford expressed a desire that his right foot be offered to yourself.

We confirm the same has been removed and is preserved and shall be grateful to know whether you wish to avail yourself of this bequest.
                   Yours faithfully,

               p.p. J. Howell Evans & Partners

The papers, as I worked my way through them, disclosed a pathetic tale. Ford was an obsessive. The damaged foot became the focus of his life. The story as my father had told it was pretty much true. Ford, a Cambridge physicist, a valley boy made good – intelligent, arrogant, socially uneasy – researched electromagnetic fields. He'd been drawn into the same spooky defence industry nexus that later made use of the Sikh suicides, the Clifton Suspension Bridge jumpers. He moved to London, the outer suburbs, and worked on pre-computer simulations, parallel-world scenarios; equations so elegant they confirmed future discoveries. For a time, Ford was hot. He served.

Out of hours, he listened to music, attended concerts, cultivated a beard. Otherwise, mathematics was his world – until he read Eliot, then Wyndham Lewis, Spengler. World conspiracy. He started to keep a journal, in which he referred to company officials, insurance agents, members of the orchestra, as 'Jewish'. He believed that he had uncovered a pattern, alien influences brought to bear on the purity of his research.

The bank manager in Welwyn Garden City is 'balding, with a single greasy strand of dark hair pasted across his shallow brow'. He is 'thick-tongued', drooling as he talks. He has a 'fleshy' nose.

When war broke out, Ford's work took on a new urgency: weapons systems that exist on paper, theoretical conundrums, have to be given a material form. He hides his calculations away, takes them home. He develops complex codes, practises mirror writing. Experiments with acid-splashes on his fingertips. But they're watching him, watching him eat, sleep; pleasure himself. In the bathroom. At stool. He won't allow his landlady to wash his sheets or his underclothes. He will do it himself. If he remembers. He's scribbling through the night.

He decides that he's had enough. Why should his research be exploited by warmongers, the conspiracy of industrialists and Satanists, the little Jewish cinema-owner with his foul cigar and his fur-clad whore? Doctors try to poison him, bend his will with drugs and potions, food additives.

He resigns. They send a false message, that his father has died, back home in Wales. But the old man is still alive, fit as a monkey, smoking Sweet Afton cigarettes and quoting Karl Marx. A German Jew. They've got to him.

Ford is conscripted. He burns his papers. They arrest him. Subject him to mental and physical torture, make him march and drill on a diet of crusts and foul water. Then, as they are transferring him to an assessment centre, they push him under a train on Reading station.

After the crisis, the foot assumes the narrative burden.

My father took me to a music hall once to see an armless man who could paint, smoke a cigarette, juggle, tie his tie; all with his feet. A novelty act. Ford invested everything in the catalogue of medical indignities perpetrated on him, on that harmless clump of tissues and tendons.

He managed, in the postwar years when educational standards were fairly relaxed, to get a job as tutor at a school for delinquents, 'special needs' pupils as they are now called. In Wanstead. He lasted ten years before they had to get rid of him. Nobody was too fussy about methods – so long as children were not actually killed without a good excuse. He dosed them on Nietzsche, G.K. Chesterton, Bernard Shaw. And multiplication tables learnt by rote. He ran a quiet classroom.

His evenings were spent composing long letters, urgent with dates and details, to Patrick Jenkin at the Department of Health and Social Security, and to Richard Crossman. He sent file after file of medical reports, clinical notes from various hospitals: *Swabs from wound: Aerobic culture – a few colonies of a coagulase negative gram positive micrococcus growth. Patient rather hot and restless. Cannot sleep very well. Remarks: Dark specimen amber colour. Mucus deposit. Bile – salts nil, pigments nil. Acetone nil. Patient complains of frequent colds. Rash consisting of pale conflating erythematous spots on limbs and neck, face. Washed up specimen: Acid urine. Trace of albumen. Pus cells +. Red blood cells ++. Culture sterile.*

His salary is spent on trips abroad, visits to specialists. He is convinced that servants of the Secret State crushed his foot, smashed the bones, made a cripple of him.

He is convinced they have implanted a radio transmitter in his teeth. They send false messages. They say again that his father is dying. They want him out of London. If he resists, the pain is intolerable. Steel rings expanding inside his skull. He would happily throw himself off a bridge, or fix a rope around his neck and hang himself.

Following a dying sun, he quits the city. Creeps west. To the memory lands, the bosom of his mother.

He seeks appointments with specialists in Munich and in Sweden, forensic scientists in Berlin; Germans who appreciate what feats creative scalpelwork can accomplish.

A 'Jewish surgeon' in Gothenburg is appalled at the length of time his foot was left in plaster. An 'eminent' German professor of orthopaedic surgery asserts that the maltreatment must have been deliberate: 'This foot has been arthrodesed. The fact is beyond question.' The joint had been *intentionally* destroyed.

Scotland Yard refuse to X-ray the limb, as does the radiologist at St Bartholomew's Hospital in Smithfield. The voices in the head are getting louder. If he does not withdraw to Wales, they will kill him. Unmarked, he will be found dead – no matter where he hides. They can control his movements at any distance. They hear blood pump through the valves of his heart.

The typescript ends. The last entry is handwritten.

Eventually success came. At St Alban's Infirmary I finally saw a lateral X-ray of my right foot. The X-ray showed clearly that there were no injuries to the bones of the outer side of the foot, but that two bright wedges had been inserted which held the foot respectively in a position of maximum equinus deformity and in one of partial varus deformity.

A telegram arrived ORDERING ME BACK TO WALES. *I wouldn't obey. I decided to start again, make a new life in London. That night a messenger informed me that my father was dead; a few weeks later my pension was suspended. I had no option but to return. The Establishment wields a mailed fist against any who challenge its* SATANIC *power.*

Paranoid delusions, firmly held for so many years, become the truth; they are activated by repetition. Mr Ford's world picture – industry conspiring with government; hospitals, doctors and school governors obedient to their paymasters – was confirmed by his death: the body, with no mark on it, in a cave of newsprint.

But he had outwitted his oppressors. His journals ensured that the foot would survive the rest of him.

I poked the fire, pitched the yellow packet into it; sat in Tunstall's elbow-chair, watching it burn. Like the Landor novel, this was a story that should never be published. We have to learn when to turn away. When to keep our own counsel.

Walking out of Crickhowell, a crisp clean afternoon, knowing that our car was on the other side of the hills, I chatted to Joblard about another excursion. The stretch of rugged cliff between Port Eynon and Rhossili, on the Gower peninsula, beyond Swansea. We'd been looking for the cave in which the Red Lady of Paviland had been discovered. We didn't find it, this midden shelf occupied by snails. And, as it turned out, the Lady was no lady, but a Cromagnon youth; a pattern of bones coloured by red ochre, lying on a bed of periwinkles. That walk, with its vertiginous swoops and scrambles, its needle rocks, was special.

Back in Camberwell, Joblard made a series of black ink drawings: quivering vertebrae, burial mounds, fissured limestone pavements. I tried, without an adequate vocabulary, to write a piece linking a sense of inheritance, the women of my family, with this locale. With the caves. Redness was a quality that intrigued me.

The poet Vernon Watkins, when I visited him in his bungalow further along the Gower at Pennard, told me that he had been born in Maesteg. He was unwell, sitting up in a narrow bed, wearing a cricket blazer over his pyjamas. On the wall that faced him was a photograph of Dylan Thomas, impossibly young and tousled, brandishing a croquet mallet. His new wife, Caitlin, stood beside him in ankle socks and a spotted dress (that looked like something given to her by nuns). A womanly woman holding firmly to her mallet, not yet ready to bring it down on Dylan's curly head. 'July 1938,' Watkins said. 'The golden wife.'

Watkins was a benign (but stubborn) presence. His long ears and his quick eyes gave him the appearance of a startled nocturnal creature, a bat who navigated accurately by his own radar. Dropping out of Cambridge and working as a junior clerk at Lloyd's Bank in Butetown, Cardiff, he suffered some sort of breakdown. He returned to the family home in Swansea and the lifelong practice of a poetry focused on 'the conquest of time'. He synthesised a version of Neo-Platonism, like that of Henry Vaughan, through which he could re-experience the ecstasies of childhood. He developed a notion of the 'replica', the moment which is all moments; a condition of consciousness activated through response to the particulars of place.

In his first collection, *The Ballad of the Mari Llwyd*, the dead return, challenging householders, those who grant entrance to their thoughts. Watkins worked within a secret tradition (the Black Apple of Gower); memories prompted by loss, sporadically witnessed immanence.

'Light screams,' he wrote – of Rhossili beach. 'Turning-place of the winds, end of the Earth.' The thing seen reminds us of the thing seen. The place that is always the place we meant to visit; somewhere we can't quite recall. An event we *will* to happen for the second time. When there is no time left.

'Do you know,' Watkins said to me, as I was leaving, 'the first piece Dylan ever wrote for the *Herald of Wales*? An account of Walter Savage Landor's connection with Swansea. Mostly cribbed, I'm afraid. But a good place to start.'

Continuing in the general direction of the priory, we stuck with the narrow road, but gave up on the map; we climbed, descended, splashed through streams. Tight-chested, we spilled hot air, sucked a clammy chill. We stopped talking. I forged ahead by a hundred yards or so; I could hear Joblard behind me, muttering and wheezing.

It was a stiff ascent from the valley of the Grwyne Fawr, tight contours squeezing the puff from Joblard's lungs. The morning mist, which lurked in hollows, grew more opaque as we marched through a clump of ancient woodland. I couldn't tell if we were advancing in the direction of Llanthony or dropping back towards Abergavenny. We were somewhere between the Sugar Loaf and the Black Mountains, beyond that I didn't have a clue. Joblard didn't care; the closer to the car (and the priory pub), the greater his stamina. He came alongside.

Low clouds, damp and clinging, reduced visibility to half the length of a cricket pitch. The woods made it worse. Interknotted greenery, leaf mulch; muffled sound. We could hear the odd shriek of a bird, the trickle of running water. The road dwindled to a path, then a concept, a fanciful reading of broken twigs and sheep droppings.

'Look for lichen,' Joblard said. 'Which side of the tree it's on.'

'What does that mean?'

'Haven't a clue.'

'I thought lichen only grew on stones.'

'Check these trees. Most of them *are* stone.'

Time slackened; swirled and eddied around oak, elm, alder. Mosses squelched underfoot like surgical dressings. Everything oozed and ran. The mist was silent rain. It didn't spatter on leaves, it infiltrated our clothing.

Purples and browns, fecal yellows: colour stopped down. Filtered to a uniform grey.

Then Joblard found a section of rough wall – bricks, mortar, not the usual freestanding heap of stones. Some of the bricks were missing, forming a kind of ledge or votive shrine in which had been placed a number of copper coins, one or two silver ones. The Welsh were tight, even in their superstitions. Alder cones and a stub of candle completed the modest offering to the spirit of place.

Joblard reached in. I don't think he helped himself. He might have touched something, performed a ritual of his own. I left a pebble that I'd picked up on the Gower and which had been wearing its way through my pockets ever since.

After the shrine, the way became clearer: a stream, then another abrupt climb. We were gasping so hard we swallowed the mist like a ball of chalk. The road had a polish Joblard compared to melted lead. He spoke of the damage he had done himself, over the years, with no mask, grinding and burning and hammering in his studio. His lungs, he boasted, were scratched and laddered like a tart's stockings.

It was clearer at the top of the hill, we could see across the woods to the ranges on the far side of the Usk. A grey fret threaded the trees, soothing distance.

' "Died at the Chain",' Joblard read aloud. 'I like that. A touch of the Charles Laughtons.'

He had pushed open a wooden gate and was surveying a broken-backed church. St Issui at Patricio. The characteristic redness of this stubborn building, perched against the side of the hill, was silvered by the moisture: another of my white chapels. As far as I was concerned, it could take the place of St Mary Matfelon (a pilgrims' church, on the road out of Whitechapel); rebuilt and destroyed so many times that the authorities had settled for a rim of bricks in the grass, a skeletal outline.

Our church, I imagined, must have served Llanthony; it must, with Cwmyoy and Capel-y-ffin, mark the borders of the Ewyas Valley. We had stumbled on another pilgrims' route. There was an external pulpit, like the pulpit that once stood in Whitechapel Road. Surrounded by hungry, Sunday evening crowds.

Here, bleating sheep clustered among the tumbledown graves: so many dead souls searching for their names on tongues of slate. Baw-baw. Baw-baw.

Joblard, on his knees, barked back.

They flooded, moved like a single entity (a tipped churn); cropping, scrunching, dropping pellets. The outbuildings were no more than a sheep shed, a sloping roof, tufted with grass. The church itself, hunched and haphazard, was everything a church should be: fixed in a true relation with the pagan shrine and the rivulet. Connected to the priory and the hermitage of St David, but hidden away. Achieved by necessary accident.

The church was open. Whitewashed, plain-benched, dim; high, narrow windows. On the west wall was a painting, in earth colours, of the figure of Death. The design had the scrupulous meanness of a transfer, drawn out from the masonry. No inessential line, no falter in the artist's hand. The head was a smooth bulb on the shaft of the spine, so that the core of the figure became a second spade: with which Death could bury himself.

This personification of Death was older that the church. It hadn't been painted. It had arrived; lifting, vertically, from the ground.

We stood close to the wall, reading the detail, granting the figure with its spread arms and traditional implements, hourglass, spade, dagger, the awesome mystery of a shape found in a cave. The red cartoon followed the flaws in the stone. Uneven plaster gave the *memento mori* a three-dimensional presence.

We walked to the east end, to see Death at a distance; to appreciate the oddness of the way it sustained its pose. The ribs became the map of a fly's flight, a frenzied circling around the heat of some missing thing.

The church door creaked: a niggly family doing the borderland tour on a dull winter's day. The man took one look at the innocent interior and stepped back out, to have a smoke. The woman ushered in a small serious child, a girl.

The mood was broken. Time for us to go. The child, in a shiny red, hooded coat, was placed on one of the benches, where she sat, silent and freakishly still, while the mother scanned the pamphlet that listed all the things she was sure to miss. She knocked off the rood screen; then, shoulders tensed in Anglo-Saxon suspicion, claimed the other highlights.

This was an episode I couldn't photograph. It was too close to Nicolas Roeg's *Don't Look Now*. The girl in the red PVC hood might prove to be a dwarf, a mad old man. Behind her, light-spill from the high window laid too much emphasis on the wall painting.

Snap it if you must, I thought, but don't expect anyone to believe it's not a fraud. A weak quotation. If this was fiction, I could do much better. Documentaries limp so far behind, it's no wonder the TV boys have started to shoot their shock/horror exposés ahead of the crimes.

The mother wanted to go. She called the child, who was gripping the edge of the pew, staring directly at me, at the camera. Now, I thought. *Now*. I saw the face of the woman in the child. I saw what she would become. I saw the whitewashed wall as a mirror; my camera raised like Death's hourglass. Reality always barges in: when you learn to leave it well alone.

Norton: Death. The Red Man of Patricio. After the flash, I knew the little girl's bright blue eyes would be bloodshot, vulpine.

'Prudence,' the woman called from the doorway; impatiently, in a brittle, Islington voice, '*Do* come along. Daddy's waiting in the car. And he's getting very cross.'

The mother didn't hear what the child whispered. I did. I heard it.

My foot was aching. I was almost sure I had a spectacular blister coming up. I'd taken off my right boot, my thick sock. I was massaging the instep.

She was transfixed, looking at me in the way kids do, daring you to blink. 'Ba ba,' she said. 'Black sheep. Mr Black. You're Mr Black.'

FILES
RECOVERED FROM KAPORAL'S
CARAVAN & RESEARCH NOTES
[PRESUMED TO HAVE BEEN
WRITTEN BY NORTON]
PURCHASED AS A JOB LOT AT
A GENERAL AUCTION IN
STAMFORD, LINCS.

DORN Edward Merton (1929-1999). Poet, essayist, teacher. Educated: University of Illinois & - after working at Boeing plant, Seattle - Black Mountain College, North Carolina (under rectorship of Charles Olson). A life of movement, sparsely funded. Dorn's poetry is notable for its intelligence, wit, ease of discourse. 'Suffered fools not at all, and sloppy thinking not for a moment; a lonely position at the best of times' (Tom Raworth). Kept his eyes (& ears) open, always.

Books include: *The Rites of Passage* (1965), *Geography* (1965), *The North Atlantic Turbine* (1967), *Gunslinger* (1975), *Abhorrences* (1990).

Quote: 'It isn't just flatulence. Vegetarians are indolent, very often stupid, their deviousness is legendary. There are exceptions of course.'

DRYFELD (pseudonym). DOB: not known. Father: naval officer. Education: occasional. Occupation: book runner. Appearance: frequently mistaken for the late Raymond Carver, pre-cure. Quirks: a serious newspaper habit, vegetarianism, opera.

Publications: *The Grub's Guide to the Secondhand Book Trade* ; *Grub's Weekly* (single issue).

Fictional cameos (unreliable): *White Chappell Scarlet Tracings* (Iain Sinclair), *Downriver* (Sinclair), *The Cardinal & the Corpse* (Chris Petit/Sinclair), *Play Power* (Richard Neville).

24. 9. 37

Thank you very much for your pictures card
too many irons in the fire — sculpturing, designs
I am most awfully jolly glad that you and
ranted for new stamps for postcards, lecturess & god
the blesed infants are all enjoying yourselves
knows what all. and bills, bills, bills to pay
so much and specially glad that you're Rich
and the scentent is away on holiday. a few more
likes the sea so much. All well here but
years shall roll afew mor seasons pass.....
am completely flummoxed with work — too
much love to you and all.   E.G.

GILL Eric (1882-1940). Stone-carver, craftsman, typographer. Erotomane. Lived and worked at Llanthony Abbey, Capel-y-ffin, from 1924 to 1928 Dominican Tertiary: 'Confraternity of the Angelic Warfare.' Serene depressive psychosis. 'Increasing quietness, a brooding, outward signs (in language and behaviour) of an exasperated bafflement.'

'It is interesting to note areas of affinity between Fr. Ignatius Lyne and Eric Gill. Both had a singular religious calling. Also they shared a love for children and the need to get away from them from time to time.' (C.G.)

Notes: 'Petra found her father wandering across the central quadrangle...and he could not remember who he was at all.' 'Much photographing of nude adults and nude children.'

Philip Hagreen (on Capel): 'It was hell.'

Further reading: *Eric Gill* by Fiona MacCarthy (1989); *Eric Gill & David Jones at Capel-y-ffin* by Jonathan Miles (1992); *Autobiography* by Eric Gill (1940); *Beauty Looks After Herself* by Eric Gill (1933).

FR IGNATIUS AND HIS MONASTERY

FATHER IGNATIUS (Joseph Leycester Lyne) (1837-1908). Founder & presiding spirit of Llanthony Abbey at Capel-y-ffin. A career that could only have been imagined by Fr. Rolfe, Baron Corvo. Ignatius was the embodied 'Hadrian' of the Black Mountains. A charismatic non-presence, hands like gloves of soap. A miracle working fraud. A generator of fictions.

Attracted to the Ewyas Valley by the red stone arches of the Augustinian Priory, Llanthony Prima ('perhaps the most lovely of all Welsh monastic remains'), Lyne conceived the notion of becoming an 'architect of ruins'. He would rebuild the Priory and found a new monastic order. There were two drawbacks to this scheme: no bishop could be persuaded to ordain him and the Anglican authorities refused to support his monastic ambitions. Also: Walter Savage Landor (and his heirs) had no intention of selling him the land. Therefore, he scuttled to the valley's bottleneck and designed his own eccentric facsimile, Llanthony Tertia (a.k.a Llanthony Abbey).

'In November 1869 Ignatius and two others retired to this secluded spot "to serve the Lord in silence." They survived the rigours of winter, and on St Patrick's Day 1870 the foundation stone of the new monastery was laid...Practically all the money for building was raised by Fr. Ignatius on preaching tours.'

Ignatius: 'Now the noisy Honddu shines like silver in the sun & joins its music to the sheep's bleat, the oxen's low, the birds' song, the bees' hum, the breeze's breath. All nature seems triumphant in its wild glad freedom...How majestically the cloud-shades were floating upon the mountains; how calmly the moonlight lay in the valleys.'

Ignatius: 'We don't want any more namby-pamby nineteenth-century-hearted men; we want only downright, brave, faithful, mediaeval-souled Welshmen.'

Ignatius visited America in 1890 and remained there a year. He eventually

436

accepted ordination from a wandering charlatan, the self-styled Mar Timotheos, Archbishop to the Old Catholics of America. After a series of strokes, Ignatius died at his sister's house in Camberley, Surrey. His body was returned to the monastery for burial.

Further reading: *The Enthusiast (An Enquiry into the Life, Beliefs & Character of The Rev. Joseph Leycester Lyne alias Fr. Ignatius, O.S.B. , Abbot of Elm Hill, Norwich & Llanthony, Wales)* by Arthur Calder-Marshall (1962).

Notes: Flat-earther. Incidents of the paranormal in Norwich: women lying in ashes, stinking tallow candles, the caning of youths. Meals eaten off the floor. Preaches to Sioux on battlefields of N. Dakota.

Llanthony: 'a sort of religious casual ward.' 'Arranged with a masterly eye for inconvenience.' 'Faith has its Alchemy.'

As a frail old man in Sheringham, Norfolk: 'Dear boy, dear boy.'

JONES David (1895-1974). Poet, painter. Born Brockley, Kent. Father (Welsh origin) was printer's overseer, mother (English) daughter of Rotherhithe block-maker (& maker of masts). Camberwell Art School, Westminster School of Art (taught by Walter Sickert). Served as private during First War (the defining crisis of his life). Received into Roman Catholic faith in 1921. In the same year he met Eric Gill and joined the community at Ditchling, Sussex. Later moving with Gill's family to Capel-y-ffin. An engagement to Gill's daughter, Petra, was broken off.

'A master of several arts, notably water-colour painting, wood-engraving and, later, calligraphy.' *The Oxford Companion to the Literature of Wales*.

Notes: A man in search of memory. 'A notorious breaker of things.' 'I hate being out of doors.' Liked Blitz, slept with boots on.

Appearance: 'Blue tweed suit...thick ties, huge fat knots...checks hair in mirror...small grey (puttee-coloured face).' Cultivated 'masterly inactivity'.

Books include: *In Parenthesis* (1937), *The Anathemata* (1952), *Epoch and Artist* (1959), *The Sleeping Lord* (1974).

Further reading: *Dai Great-Coat (A Self-Portrait of David Jones in his Letters)*. Edt by René Hague (1980); *David Jones, the Maker Unmade* by Jonathan Miles, Derek Shiel (1995).

KILVERT Francis (1840-79). Curate and diarist. Educated: Wadham College, Oxford. A man of posthumous fame; a life lived, just beyond our reach. Attentive to particulars of place. The status of the 'discovered' journals remain ambiguous, achieving their second birth as a kind of pastoral fiction. The dictation of the dead has rarely been so steady, so much at ease with its own voice; the disclosure of secret springs & motors.

Seven years as curate at Clyro, Radnorshire. Later the incumbent at Bredwardine, Herefordshire. Kilvert's *Diary* runs, in starts and spurts (with mysterious lacunae), from January 1870 to 1879 (the year of his death). A great arc of material in a pre-literary state, not yet cooked & synthesised as poetry: delight, despair, social drama, landscape, weather. A mediative walker & hill wanderer who invented the autobiography that his words (moving out on a generous curve) would require.

The diary cache consisted of 'between twenty-two & thirty' notebooks: some of which vanished (presumably burnt by Kilvert's widow). The notebooks were brought by a nephew, Perceval Smith, to William Plomer - who published three selections (in 1938,'39, '40). Once Kilvert's private observations were exposed to public scrutiny, the original documents began to disappear: Plomer's carbon typescript and the publisher's top copy were destroyed during the war, and it is assumed that Kilvert's niece, Essex Hope, disposed of nineteen of the surviving twenty-two notebooks. 'This literary tragedy,' according to *The Oxford Companion to the Literature of Wales* , 'may be explained, perhaps, by the presence in the *Diary* of a strong vein of erotic sensibility.' But this passionate (and troubling) engagement with a frieze of young women, well-connected daughters, schoolgirls, farm girls, is balanced by the curate's uxorious love of place (in all its flawed beauty).

Further reading: *Kilvert's Diary* (3 vols. Edt. Wm. Plomer), 1938-40.

Notes (from *Diary*): 'We saw the foundation stone which Father Ignatius came down to lay three weeks ago. Then he returned to London.' 'If there is one thing more hateful than another it is being told what to admire and having objects pointed out to one with a stick.' 'Extraordinary visions which had appeared to his brother Ignatius, particularly about the ghosts which come crowding round him & which will never answer though he often speaks to them...that strange unearthly fire which Fr. Ignatius put out by throwing himself into it & making the sign of the cross.'

LALAGE Jamie. Born Kuala Lumpur, 1949. Educated: Ampleforth & Peterhouse, Cambridge. Testing vocation, before joining Carmelites, travelled extensively: Afghanistan, South Korea, Eastern Europe, the Greek Islands. Occasional journalism, trade magazines and special-interest 'life style' publications. Ghosted account of 'Nazi gold' investigation. Gained attention for double-portrait commissioned by *Esquire* : Werner Herzog (positive), Bruce Chatwin (lethal). Agreed, after losing (now legendary) fishing challenge with Herzog (Northumbria), to write film script. Herzog refused to work in Britain, but co-produced what turned out to be Lalage's first feature: *Amber Lights* (1979). Minor prizes: Rotterdam, Montreal. Thereafter, Lalage worked in Germany, Poland and the Baltic (notably: *Russian Dolls*). TV documentaries on J.G Ballard, Rudolph Wurlitzer, Budd Boetticher (in Mexico City); a disastrous TV adaptation of Jean Rhys' *Voyage in the Dark* (shot in Lisbon) was responsible, according to critic Chris Darke (*Too Much, Too Soon*), for finishing career in film. Retirement, North London & Kent coast. Fiction, reviews, American summer schools.

  Novels: (as Pete Wolfe) *Lake of Gold* (1975), *Mouse Passage* (1990), *Kustom Kar Kannibal* (1991), *The Perimeter Fence* (1997), *Malfate* (2000).

  Note: 'You've put up the wrong man.'

Possible sidebar? Moorland setting + mad dog + conspiracy = *Hound of the Baskervilles*. Two photos in file: (1) Man believed to be Lalage & woman in leopard coat standing outside 'Robinsons Depositories' (pencil inscription, 'Bristol'), reflective glass windows distorting street. (2) Lalage by stone cross (pencil inscription 'At Robinson's grave, Ipplepen, Devon.'). Torn photocopy, dedication from 1st edn. of *Hound.* 'My dear Robinson. It was your account of a West Country legend which first suggested the idea of this little tale to my mind...'

LANDOR Walter Savage (1775-1864). Poet, classicist. Educated at Rugby School and Trinity College, Oxford. Father: physician. Intractable temper (see 'Boythorn' in Dickens' *Bleak House*): shot into another student's rooms in Oxford with a fowling piece, justifying his action by labelling his opponent a 'Tory'. Rusticated. Lived in Swansea, fathered a child. Walked the beach, 'violently resenting any intrusion.' Married Julia Thuillier (d. of Banbury banker), 1811. Purchased Llanthony Priory (1807) from Colonel Wood of Brecon who treated the site 'as it were a quarry.' Merino sheep imported from Spain. Lived in shooting box while mansion was planned. Visited by Robert Southey: 'We saw the fox / rush from the alders.' Composed 150 'imaginary conversations'. A future exile, always looking for 'elsewhere'. His tower, he asserted, marked the spot 'where the Ark touched the Mountain.'

Notes: 'Memory is not a muse.' 'Capricious migrations.' 'Quick grey eyes.' 'Wrestles with and conquers time.' 'To others when ourselves are dust / We

(leave behind this sacred trust.'

Malcolm Elwin: 'In his pursuit of the simple life he excluded the conventional pose of enjoying hobnobbing with the working-class folk; the Welsh peasants "were somewhere between me and the animals, and were as useful to the landscape as masses of weed or stranded boats."'

Publications include: *Gebir* (1798), *Simonidea* (1806), *Imaginary Conversations of Literary Men and Statesmen* (1824-9), *Pericles and Aspasia* (1836-7).

Further reading: *Savage Landor* by Malcolm Elwin (1941).

MACHEN Arthur (1863-1947). Born Caerleon, Monmouthshire (a.k.a Arthur Jones, Arthur Jones-Machen). Welsh father (clergyman), Scots mother. Visionary author, fabulist, and longtime Fleet Street grubber. Also actor and hierophant (Golden Dawn). Friend of A.E. Waite and authority on matters occult; profound student of Rosicrucianism, the poetry and philosophy of the Vaughan twins, Henry and Thomas.

Haunted by Grail mysteries and the radiant landscape of his childhood, he was an obsessive weaver of darkness and light. His work is notable for an unresolved dialogue between the labyrinthine metropolis (London) and the memory fields of the Welsh borders. In the story, *N*, which focuses on the search for a mysterious site in Stoke Newington, Machen's characters meet in a room above a inn, near the Strand. 'There were other engravings of a later date about the walls...landscapes of the Valley of the Usk, and the Holy Mountain, and Llanthony: all with a certain enchantment and vision about them, as if their domed hills and solemn woods were more of grace than of nature.'

A compulsive urban walker (see *The London Adventure* or *The Art of Wandering*, 1924).

Other publications include: *The Great God Pan* (1894), *The House of Souls* (1906), *The Hill of Dreams* (1907), *The Great Return* (1915), *The Secret Glory* (1922), *The Shining Pyramid* (1925), *Ornaments in Jade* (Tartarus Books, 1997).

Note: 'Songs of the frantic lunapar; delirium of the madhouse.'

THORPE Jeremy. Born 1929. Father: King's Council & Tory MP. Mother: elder daughter of Sir John Norton-Griffiths, 1st Bt., KCB, DSO & Tory MP. Educated: Eton & Trinity College, Oxford. Barrister. Lifelong politician, the last of the professional amateurs. Former Liberal leader. 'He led the party to its best ever election result in 1967.' (J.Thorpe) Said to be a person of unrestrained charm, resource, energy. A skilled mimic. He was accused ('conspiracy to murder') of involvement in a plot to 'put down' a former protegee, Norman Scott. After his trial (& acquittal), he disappeared from public life into West Country retirement - & an ambiguous status as an inspirer of fictions & conspiracy theories.

Books: *In My Own Time (Reminiscences of a Liberal Leader)* (1999).

Further reading: *Rinkagate (The Rise & Fall of Jeremy Thorpe)* by Simon Freeman (1996); *Jeremy Thorpe, A Secret Life* by Lewis Chester, Magnus Linklater, David May (1979); *The Last Word (An Eye-witness Account of the Thorpe Trial)* by Auberon Waugh (1980).

Notes: 'Wales is a cash cow, so depressed & corrupt you can milk it any way you want.' 'Harold Wilson is like Charlie Drake with a pipe.' Regular trips to S.Vietnam. 'He couldn't have been a journalist, he didn't ask for money.' Parties at Kensington Palace. 'Penetration problem.' 'Darkly apprehensive.' Sees Vater shaving his back in the bath. Marriage connection with Terry-Thomas. Norman Scott: 'He had a bullet but no gun.' 'Roasted sparrows.'

VAUGHAN Henry (1621-1695). Poet, physician, twin. Born Newton, Scethrog, in vale of Usk (grandson of Wm. Vaughan of Tretower, Brecs.). Classical education & introduction to Hermetic Philosophy (Matthew Herbert, rector of Llangattock). Jesus College, Oxford (left after 2 years). Studied law in London. There has been speculation that he 'may have come within the orbit of the literary set of which Ben Jonson had been the leader.' Fought in the English Civil War on the Royalist side (battle of Rowton Heath).

Early poems hark back to London days; later he underwent - perhaps as a reaction to his younger brother William's death, the defeat of the Royalist cause, & a close reading of the poetry of Geo. Herbert - an intense religious experience; a seizure by light which informs & illuminates the work in his collection *Silex Scintillans* (1650).

He wrote prose, made translations (*Of the Diseases of the Mind & Body*). His growing interest in medicine (practical, sympathetic) led to the publication (in 1655) of *Hermetical Physick, or The Right Way to preserve, & to restore Health* (a translation from the Latin of Henry Nollius). Practised as a physician in & around Brecon, without formal qualifications.

'Asked to be buried *outside* the church of Llansantffraid, prescribing for his tombstone the words, *"Servus Inutilis: Peccator Maximus Hic Iaceo: Gloria Miserere."'*

A great spirit: a distillation & distiller of place (water/light). Metaphysician & visionary. Night-watcher. Dawn-walker.

Published works include: *Silex Scintillans* (1650), *Olor Iscanus* (1651), *Silex Scintillans II* (1655), *Thalia Rediviva* (1678).

Further reading: *Henry Vaughan* by Stevie Davies (1995).

Notes: 'High noon thus past, thy time decays.'

VAUGHAN Thomas (1621-1666). Speculative philosopher, poet, younger twin. Unlike his brother Henry, he remained at Jesus College, Oxford, for 10/12 years, latterly as Fellow. 1645: Rector of native parish, Llansantffraid. Fought (with brother) in Civil War. Ejected from his living as 'a common drunkard, a common swearer...a whoremaster'. London: study and practice of alchemy. Claims to have discovered the secret of 'extracting the oyle of Hacali' (alchemy's *prima materia*). Died at Albury, near Oxford: 'operating strong mercurie, some of which by chance getting up his nose marched him off.'

Publications: *Anima Magia Abscondita; or A Discourse on the Universall Spirit of Nature* (1650); *Aula Lucis, or The House of Light* (1652); preface to *The Fame & Confession of the Fraternity of R.C., Commonly, of the Rosy Cross* (1652).

Note (from *Oxford Companion to the Literature of Wales*): 'For him metaphysics and divinity went hand in hand and his search for the world's *prima materia* was a use of the language of physical alchemy to express the idea of the regeneration of Man: "matter", for him, was "the House of Light."'

WATKINS Alfred. Born Hereford, 1855. 'Local merchant, amateur archaeologist, inventor, photographer and naturalist, notorious in academic circles as the author of a heretical work, *The Old Straight Track*.' (John Michell)

Watkins' occupation as a brewer's rep allowed him to travel extensively, on horseback, through the Welsh Marches. His moment of revelation came, as John Michell recounts, at the age of 65. 'Riding across the hills near Bredwardine in his native county, he pulled up his horse to look out over the landscape

below. At that moment he became aware of a network of lines, standing out like glowing wires all over the surface of the country, intersecting at the sites of churches, old stones and other spots of traditional sanctity...Watkins privately maintained that he had perceived the existence of the ley system in a single flash.'

below. At that moment he became aware of a network of lines, standing out like glowing wires all over the surface of the country, intersecting at the sites of churches, old stones and other spots of traditional sanctity...Watkins privately maintained that he had perceived the existence of the ley system in a single flash.'

Michell's introduction to the 1970 reissue of *The Old Straight Track* (originally published in 1925) concludes: 'The clear, modest style...has reminded some of Watkins's fellow countrymen of... Parson Kilvert, for both invoked the same *genius terrae britannicae* from the red Herefordshire earth that inspired their mystic predecessors, Traherne and Henry Vaughan. There would be no poetry without heretics.'

WATKINS Vernon (1906-1967). Lyric poet, Neo-Platonist. Born Maesteg, Glamorgan. Moved on, with bank manager father, to Bridgend, Llanelli, Swansea. Educated: Repton School & Magdalene College, Cambridge (see *Lions and Shadows* by Christopher Isherwood).

Employed for many years as a clerk at Lloyd's Bank, St Helen's, Swansea. Initially a member of loose-knit, artistic/boho circle (meeting at Swansea's Kardomah Cafe) that included poet Dylan Thomas, composer Daniel Jones, painter Alfred Janes. Break in psyche, self-described as 'a revolution of sensibility'.

Served military police, RAF, during Second World War. Married Gwen Davies (an Enigma code-breaker) at St Bartholomew-the-Great, Smithfield. His best man, Dylan Thomas, failed to show.

The pure poet: years of work in the bungalow at Pennard, Gower; bus-commuting to Swansea. 'The defeat of time was integral, in his view, to the function of the poet...The idea of the replica and the moment which is all moments.' (*Oxford Companion to the Literature of Wales*)

A talk by Watkins in Oxford was major inspiration (in Yeatsian phase) for Philip Larkin.

Freed from his labours at the bank, Watkins died on the tennis court, while Professor of Poetry at the University of Washington, Seattle.

Published by Faber (under patronage of TS Eliot), books include: *Ballad of the Mari Llwyd* (1941), *The Lamp and the Veil* (1945), *The Lady and the Unicorn* (1948), *The Death Bell* (1954).

Further reading: *Portrait of a Friend* by Gwen Watkins (1983).

Notes: 'Vernon was always fascinated by the more dangerous path he might so easily have trodden...Dylan was his *alter ego*.' (Gwen Watkins). 'At first the Living repel the Dead, and finally the Dead break in and turn the Living out into the dark, but they are never brought together.' (Gwen Watkins).

WEST COUNTRY SUICIDES. See: *Open Verdict (An account of 25 mysterious deaths in the Defence Industry)* by Tony Collins. Sphere, 1990.

Quotes: 'Most of her answers were unintentionally curt. But clearly she felt that Vimal had not jumped willingly from Bristol's Clifton Suspension Bridge.'

'Peter was found dead in a cottage in the grounds of the Marconi factory at Frimley near Camberley, Surrey *(Norton note: 'cf. Death of Ignatius')* . "He took a wire off a lamp, stuck one side of the wire to the right molar tooth and the other side to the left molar tooth *(Norton note: 'cf. Death of Mr Ford')* and plugged himself in," said a detective... Police ruled out foul play. The cottage was out of bounds to all unauthorized personnel and the factory has twenty-four hour security measures.'

'A young computer expert at the Boscome Down air base led an amazing double life as a transvestite, an inquest heard. Bachelor Mark Wisner who worked on computer software for the Tornado warplane, had a secret fetish for photographing himself wearing women's clothing. But his quest for sexual stimulation ended in tragedy two weeks ago, when he suffocated after a sexual experiment went disastrously wrong. He was found dead at his Darrington home wearing high heeled women's boots, suspenders and a PVC top.'

'In the case of the 'lady in the lake', as it became known, the shortfall of forensic evidence was not only conspicuous, it was embarrassing...

...Physiotherapist Marjorie Arnold, out walking her Alsatian dog, saw the body of a woman lying near the edge of Taplow Lake, a popular sailing and fishing spot close to the homes of celebrities such as Terry Wogan, Michael Parkinson, Ernie Wise and Frank Bough. It was also 150 yards from a manned police checkpoint...Mrs Arnold stopped a motorist and together they pulled the body ashore. The dead woman seemed about 20-years-old...She had been gagged with a blue scarf, a noose was tied around her neck, her ankles were secured with a tow rope and her wrists were tied behind her back. She had been face down in eighteen inches of water for an indeterminate period...

Within a day of the body's discovery a high ranking police officer spoke of suicide. Six months later that view was officially confirmed. A pathologist employed by the Home Office declared that Shani had tried to strangle herself, gagged herself, bound her ankles, tied her hands behind her back and hopped in stiletto heels into the shallow water where she drowned.'

Further reading: anything by Stewart Home.